I0691322

The Bunny Hop

THE BUNNY HOP

Dara Lebrun

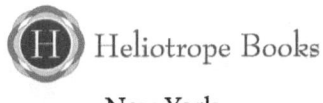 Heliotrope Books

New York

Copyright © 2014 Dara Lebrun

All rights reserved. No part of this book may be reproduced or transmitted in any form or by any means, electronic or mechanical, including photocopying, recording or by an information storage or retrieval system now known or here-toafter invented—except by a reviewer who may quote brief passages in a review to be printed in a magazine or newspaper—without permission in writing from the publisher: heliotropebooks@gmail.com

This is a work of fiction. Names, characters, places, and incidents either are products of the author's imagination, or are used fictitiously. Any resemblance to actual events or persons, living or dead, is coincidental.

Designed and Typeset by Heliotrope Books

Cover by Judy Tipton-Katzman and Naomi Rosenblatt with Dara Lebrun

For

P

life is short,
love is long

"Like a child from the womb, like a ghost from the tomb,
I arise and unbuild it again."

—*Percy Bysshe Shelley*

Part One

1

By the time I noticed him hovering at my door I had no idea how long he'd been there. "Your office is dim," he commented. "How can you see the keyboard?"

If I were differently disposed I might have told him I'd learned to touch-type in eighth grade, and that I enjoyed the cinema of a bright screen against darkness. Or I might have asked, "Do you need something?"

Instead, I continued to shade the logo design and hoped he'd go away.

He walked in and peered over my shoulder. And since he was senior to me—yes, this Beelzebub of a new hire was executive creative director, the position I should have been offered—I had to endure his scrutiny.

"That's the approved logo, isn't it?"

"Umm-hmmm."

"Or it was before you—what the hell are you doing to it, Molly?"

"Trying 3D," I explained, turning around to him. "Extruding."

("They'll hate you," Eleanor had warned, "when they see you can write copy and design the campaign." But they'd never hated me when they'd needed me.)

"Why 3D?" He sneered, as though I was misguided.

"Just playing with it."

I turned back to the screen.

"Have you nothing more fun to play with in your spare time?"

He circled my chair, his footfalls slow and deliberate. It was 6:50. I hoped that someone else was around, that he hadn't waited for us to be alone.

Then he parked his barely existent butt on the desk beside me and crossed his arms. Paunch gathered at his chin in a wattle and at his torso in a belly, leaving those incongruously stringy arms and legs. He tended to nod, like a bobble-head toy, always in the process of making a point and never getting to it.

"Molly Sarah Douglas," he pronounced into the after-hours silence. "Isn't it time some lucky fool slipped an engagement ring on your finger?"

Eleanor had warned that something like this would happen, but I never believed her. She'd reached her professional prime thirty years ago, when upholding her dignity in a man's domain had taken some doing. Things were surely different by AD 2000 in New York City. I glowered at Jack. If Larry and the other agency honchos weren't so delighted with him, I would have told him where to stick it and with what velocity.

"*Taste Takes Time*." I repeated his tagline, which our client, a manufacturer of luxury wristwatches, had vetoed in yesterday's meeting.

"*In a hurried world, give her time*," Jack rejoined. The client had found my tagline persuasive and romantic.

("Nice guys finish last, and smart girls don't finish," Eleanor had cautioned. I'd chalked that up to a second-wave feminist cliché, nothing that would play out for me.)

"So," continued Jack, with his disconcerting nods and raised brow, "he's giving you time?"

"In every sense."

Luckily I'd kept that dumb photo of Thomas and me around, though I'd broken our engagement half a year ago. I didn't want to broadcast to my colleagues that I was single. I got enough grief about it from my mother.

Jack's eye seemed to fall on the framed photo, suggesting that he'd researched my office beforehand. Certainly he must have found my middle name in some file. I doubted Larry even knew it.

"What's his name?" Jack asked with a smile.

"What's your wife's name?"

His smile grew snarky, and I remembered Eleanor's advice for such occasions: "Grab a Kotex in front of them and hightail it to the ladies room. They'll never bug you again."

So I saved my logo file, closed the application, and stood up.

"Please," he said, uncrossing his stringy arms, planting both hands behind him on the desk. "Don't let me stop you."

I opened the drawer where I kept personal supplies, seized a box of tampons, and chucked it regally into my purse. Then I trotted out of my office with no intention of returning until the next day.

The walk home was chilly without a coat. I rejoiced in getting out of Dodge but pondered who was the bigger moron—she who fled like a hunted hare, or he who remained staring at the mutating phosphors of her screen saver, slowly realizing that his prey had escaped?

"You tied his balls into Scout knots without trying," my neighbor Claudia insisted when I assailed her on the stairwell for an interpretation.

"No way. I showed him how easily intimidated I am."

"You showed him how you wouldn't stick around to be intimidated. And if you were really intimidated, you wouldn't have flashed your tampons at him."

I almost joined her burst of laughter, but still felt too frazzled.

Claudia's lips bore their inevitable cherry red lipstick, like a rubber shape slapped onto her face. To top it off, she had slicked and yanked her dark hair into a bun.

"How 'bout some hair with your grease, Claw?"

"Don't I look great?"

While not tall, she was imposing and fleshy—"voluptuous," in her own words. Part "Italian stallion," and part Cuban, Claudia spoke with tropical aggression, belting out words as though each deserved emphasis. And she chewed gum constantly—I'd wager, even in her sleep. The only time she didn't was with a Wild Turkey or mojito.

"You seeing Jordan tonight?" she asked me, chomping on her sugary stick.

"Not that I know of."

Claudia's question implied double-edged condemnation. She wouldn't approve of my seeing Jordan, nor would she approve of my forgoing him. Jordan was supposed to have been a one-night stand, but we'd evolved into a fling. Sometimes I wouldn't see him for days, and sometimes he'd ring my bell late at night and want the world.

"Then come with me, 'cause I'm gonna catch Bertie at the bar," she announced.

"Not."

"Oh, don't be so cynical, Molly. It will kill you."

But we both knew that Claudia's cynicism had killed it off with Bertie—the latest in her line of female lovers who could have been mistaken for a boy. Claudia had been married to an actual boy for three years. She awakened one day, proclaimed herself a lesbian, and proceeded to replay her marriage with various macho women. These liaisons ended as disastrously as the marriage to Rob, with yelling and threats, objects thrown, eyes blackened, and police appearances.

But Bertie, who was smarter than the others, didn't take the bait. She stepped aside once she sniffed it, saying to an incredulous Claudia: "Not for me."

I tried to dissuade Claudia from stalking because I knew Bertie had reached capacity. Claudia insisted, "She'll forgive me because she knows about my childhood." Of course we all knew about Claudia's childhood, or at least her version of it, which sounded sadly plausible.

"Bertie was fair to you," I reminded her. "Even good to you. Don't make a fool of yourself."

"You always take her side. Betrayer."

Eventually I caved because I had a reason to join Claudia at the bar where Bertie doubled as a DJ and bouncer. Though it was technically a girl's bar, a number of straight guys also hung around, and one of them had worked with Jack. This video editor and his girlfriend came in to stare at an absurdly beautiful blonde bartender called Eugenia. It was Thursday. Eugenia would be there, and so would Rick and Terry. It might behoove me to chat with Rick about the guy who was trying to sabotage my job.

2

"Thank God for crime!" Claudia exclaimed. "How else would I earn a living?"

Claudia's career, unlike mine, had spanned many industries. I'd stayed in advertising for fifteen years, after interning with Eleanor. Claudia had been everything from a high school guidance counselor to a dom in a fetish club, where her skill set included peeing on men's faces in fake toilets and whacking them with canoe paddles in basements and streamlined penthouses. She'd also worked in demolition, which was where she'd met Bertie—ripping down the same condemned building in Greenpoint, getting the same dust in her eyes, coughing up the same grime. As we took seats at the nearly empty bar, she revealed her latest ambition: "There's something you can do for me...I wanna work for Jordan."

"Doing what?" I asked. "Carrying his saxophone case to gigs, making sure he's paired his socks and they haven't disintegrated before he puts them on?"

"Finding customers," she said, under her breath.

"Oh," I answered. "You'll have to talk with him. I keep out of that."

"Well, are you cool with it?"

Jordan was my fling, not my boyfriend. He probably should have remained a one-night stand since he was much too young for me. His sideline income didn't thrill me, but I couldn't justify meddling. What else could a twenty-four-year-old tenor sax player do to make ends meet? And the weed was artisanal.

"We'll work out a commission rate," Claudia assured me. "You know I'm always reasonable."

"Always."

Neither Bertie, nor Rick or Terry were around that night. But Eugenia, the blonde bartender, swanned by through the flickering light of votive-style candles placed along the bar. In a simple black button-down shirt and jeans that hugged her lanky legs, she landed nonchalantly by us.

"What'll it be tonight, ladies?"

"You're paying," Claudia informed me. And then she asked Eugenia for a shot of Wild Turkey with a side of seltzer.

"Is there such a thing as a half-screwdriver?" I queried.

Eugenia pondered that for a second before stepping away.

She reappeared with Claudia's shot and seltzer, which she set out with a cocktail napkin. Then she rolled a highball glass gracefully down her arm and caught it. After placing it on the bar she about-faced and aimed jets of Stoli and orange juice into it, expertly filling half the glass behind her own back. It later occurred to me that Eugenia might have used the mirror by the bar to coordinate her feat.

She faced us again and, to complete the performance, clipped a long red straw in half with a Swiss Army knife, stuck an orange slice on the rim, and slid the drink over to me with a cocktail napkin and a wink.

"How much?" I asked.

"Eight," she said.

"That's too good," I protested.

She shook her head, smiling inscrutably before she wandered off.

Claudia leaned in to whisper, "Nice going. Eugenia's pretty aloof."

We clinked glasses, and Claudia downed most of her shot.

"Hey," she whispered again, ribbing me, "I wonder if she thinks you're my latest conquest."

I shuddered at the suggestion, while Claudia put her head on my shoulder and started cooing. The bartender's grin suggested that she took Claudia with the necessary grain of salt.

"Don't worry," Claudia assured me. "You're not my type, Molly. Too femme, and self-possessed. I look for hearts that break open."

Rick and Terry always called the place "Eugenia's," but it was actually The Bunny Hop. I never understood why, since none of its patrons—gritty older dykes, cross-dressing queens and trannies, the hunky young butches—were bunny-like in any sense. Even the classically feminine women were stylish and chic beyond a cottontail trace.

But a lacquered découpage of Playboy centerfolds adorned a beam beside the bar. And a clever medley of bunnies, painted iridescent white, silver, and gold, danced between pink triangles in a stencil over the black wall by the pool table.

Some girls were playing billiards, and a huddle of curmudgeons down the bar from us griped about their beer. Their hairstyles were like suburban housewives': shortly cropped, white, and stiff. But their baggy jeans and leather jackets suggested redneck adolescents.

"Are you sure this is Bass? It doesn't taste like Bass."

"Why not?" asked Eugenia, and her nagging patron suddenly had no words.

"The Bass is perfect," declared a tall man with a shaved head.

"Speak for yourself," snapped one of the curmudgeons.

"That's Arbie," Claudia whispered to me again, Wild Turkey tingeing her breath. "He was a Marine; now he's on SSI. Straight. But hangs out here all the time. Some women don't want him around, but Eugenia likes him 'cause she buys lotto tickets with him."

As I took that in, Bertie entered with a pack of pals in sweaters and lumber-man's jackets. Claudia stared into her seltzer as they horsed around, guffawed, and buttonholed one another. Bertie had probably noticed Claudia sitting with me but pretended she hadn't.

"Yo Blondie!" she called out, thumping big fists on the bar. "Eugenia! Get over here, you skinny fuck."

Eugenia glided down the bar toward them.

"Quit calling me names."

"Oh, eat shit."

"So I'll serve Lainey. She's never rude."

Bertie gave her the finger.

"Listen, asshole, we want five Blow Jobs."

"She's treatin'!" piped one of the other women.

"Says who—no way, I'm treatin'!"

I whispered to Claudia, "What's a Blow Job?"

"You should know better than anyone here."

Eugenia scattered five shot glasses on the bar like a Zen gardener tossing rocks. I tried to watch through the muddle of arms and bulky sweaters, but I couldn't see what the bartender was concocting.

Finally Claudia told me, "It's Baileys and Kahlúa with whipped cream. It's supposed to look like a guy's come—eugh! You can't touch it with your hands."

We watched as Bertie hollered, "No cheating, ladies!"

The five of them lined up together and linked arms. In one motion they bent over the bar, gripped the shot glasses in their mouths, and hurled backward so their "blow jobs" went down the hatch.

Now I was amused. "Five women on a blow job. There's a record." I couldn't wait to tell Jordan about it.

Claudia was less entertained. "That's how Bertie would rather spend her time than be with me," she whined. "She always had more fun with her friends."

"Well, maybe her friends don't humiliate her. You picked on her all the time, Claw. People don't like to be picked on."

"Thomas didn't mind when you picked on him."

"Maybe Thomas has a problem. Maybe that's why I didn't want to marry him."

The bar had suddenly grown busy, and Bertie and her friends dissolved into other customers. Claudia said something to me, but the music revved up, putting her on mute. Tipping my head to the beat, I took in the sparkling eyes, craned necks, spiked and moussed hair, the spectral hue of gender and color around me—hardcore tomboys in their cuffed jeans with key chains; the pretty girls with long, shimmery hair, looking like any women you'd see in Manhattan shops and restaurants; the drag queens in beehive wigs and feather boas.

Although sorry not to find Rick and Terry, I was already feeling better. Nothing would happen to my job. I'd overreacted to Jack's baiting. I sipped my lovely half-screwdriver, resolving not to work late again at the office. I could take projects home with me on disks.

"She's with *her*!" Claudia then screeched in my ear, tugging at my sleeve. "Look." I glanced at Bertie, whose arm was around the sultry woman with bangs and tapioca skin called Lainey. "The body isn't even cold."

"Claudia, the body's been in a morgue since Christmas."

And it was almost Saint Patrick's Day, with bright green streamers hanging from the ceiling and shamrocks pasted around the mirror by the bar.

"Talk to her," Claudia beseeched me. "She always liked you. I think she likes you better than me."

I was to act as Claudia's diplomat, to somehow remind Bertie of her redeeming traits. I intended nothing more, and I didn't think it was going to do a damn bit of good. But when I approached her, Bertie blustered about how grand it was to see me. Puffing on her usual rum-soaked cigar, she introduced Lainey, who looked a little like Lena Horne.

"Molly was the sweetener," Bertie explained as Lainey and I shook hands, "when Miss Thang went foul."

"Miss Thang?" asked Lainey.

"Walking out now…"

"What?" I was shocked to see Claudia elbowing her way toward the door. "But she told me to talk to you," I confessed.

"Sagittarius," Bertie muttered. "Unworkable. I tried. You know I tried. Some people hemorrhage when you do exactly what they ask. Go figure." Then she whispered, right in my ear, "And she's broke. Dirt broke, spinning out of control."

As I watched Claudia exit The Bunny Hop my eyes were drawn to Eugenia, juggling beer bottles behind the bar. She caught one in each hand and waved them before the delighted customers. Unaccountably she looked at me for a second.

Bertie was telling Lainey how she and Claudia met on the demolition job. "And those were the only walls we knocked down together. The rest of the time, she was building them up."

"*Mucho mistrust*," hummed Lainey.

"Muchos jalapeños you ate yesterday will burn your butt today. So where's what's-his-name?" Seeming eager to change the topic, Bertie twiddled her fingers at me as though playing a saxophone.

"Jordan's 'clubbing' on the west side."

"Is everything good?"

"It is." And I elaborated: "'Maybe you can't always get what you need, but if you don't try sometimes, you just might find…you get what you want.'"

"So…you're getting what you want?"

"Enough for now."

But what Jordan would become—beyond the antidote to years in a sensory deprivation tank with Thomas—I wasn't yet sure.

3

Perhaps what repelled men in Eleanor's era now had the reverse effect. Jack couldn't take his eyes off me the next day or stop bobbing his head, perhaps reminding me that he now knew where I kept tampons. His dopey, bobbing head almost made me carsick.

While I've been called "cute" and "pretty," I never considered myself a de facto turn-on. I have a pleasant face, whose centerpiece of sea-green eyes is a rare bequest from my mother. But I'm pale, a bit scrawny, and not busty—sexy only when someone knows me, and sometimes not even. I would not be a star or supporting actress but an extra. So Jack's woozy gaze perplexed me, as he seemed to barely notice Kendra, the curvy African American receptionist, or Jana, the Swedish account rep—who were both more the head-turning types.

Friday morning we were to present a PowerPoint proposal to Lustrella for their online catalog. Both executives were men, and since I'd spearheaded work on the site, Larry thought I might present it most effectively. Before the client arrived, Jack and I hooked the laptop into a slide projector.

"Here! Let's prop this on a couple of books so it centers on the screen. Oops... it's tilting. Here—have you got it, Molly? Are you okay, Molly?"

My team and I had been working on the presentation for weeks and I was nervous. Years in this racket not withstanding, client presentations put me on edge. But Jack's "oilier than thou" kid gloves threatened to hoist me over.

"We're aiming to distinguish Lustrella from other commercial paint sites that use virtual color chips," I explained to our client as I stood by the slide projector. "To that end, we've prepared the honeycomb template of hues that you approved last month. Of course, anyone who expects paint on a wall to look as luminous as colors on-screen may be disappointed, but they will have already purchased the paint."

I shifted to the next slide, a list of bulleted points outlining the advantages of this approach. Larry insisted that clients respond more to such abstractions than to our actual samples, though I put faith in the samples.

"In addition, I've designed a simple color-combining tool based on the work of Albers and Mondrian—not a model that requires sophisticated plug-ins to upload, but simple, flat color rectangles, easy enough for a child to use."

"Of course, *if* that child has grown up with a mouse and monitor," burbled Jack. Even Larry shot him an unappreciative glance, and Larry was quite the advocate of his newest hire.

"Nowadays kids do," I commented, "though my intention isn't to make this feature into a child's toy, but simply to encourage end-users to feel welcome and proficient. Studies show that consumers don't remain on a site whose interactivity frustrates them."

"We like this," said one of the executives. "I think we've found a good direction with bottom-line functionality for our customers."

Once the slide show concluded and online metrics were reviewed, a new launch calendar was charted. After that, Kendra relayed our guests' coats to them. As she led them to the door, Jack grabbed my shoulder to showcase his collegial humor in front of Larry.

"Quite the fireball, isn't she?"

"Molly's always spot on."

(Larry loved British idioms.)

"Hard to believe a catch like this is still single."

Jack didn't remove his hand from my shoulder but imperceptibly stroked my bra strap with his index finger.

"She's as discerning about men as she is about words and images," Larry eulogized, not seeing all there was to see. I sustained my most taxidermic smile as though I was posing in a family photograph. "Which is my nice way of saying, she's pretty fussy. But her time will come."

"In a hurried world…"

We all laughed at Jack's cleverness—or was it mine?

"…'Time is on our side,' if I might quote Mick Jagger," Jack said with a laugh.

"Actually the quote is, 'Time is on *my* side,'" I corrected him, wriggling away from his finger and hoping he would take the hint about my *years* with the agency, compared with his *weeks*. "And speaking of time, I'm overdue for lunch."

But I went into my office, closed the door, and collapsed into my Aeron chair, dizzy from the fumes of this latest exchange—and not hungry at all. Much the opposite, I felt queasy.

A clever hunter, Jack had covered his tracks. Now if I ever mentioned his tasteless visit when I was alone yesterday evening, Larry would say: "Oh, he was just kidding. Don't take it all so seriously, Molly."

As far as Larry was concerned, we heterosexuals were all generically attracted to each other anyway, and in a reproductive frenzy until our hormones ran dry and our mates started dropping off—unlike men, whose love for each other was more nuanced and erotic.

My shoulder still damp from Jack's unwelcome finger, I studied the photograph of Thomas and me that I kept on my desk. Alessi had taken it two years ago when we'd gone up to play tennis one afternoon on their clay courts. I was wearing a cap-sleeve tennis dress and Thomas had a pale yellow Lacoste polo shirt and white shorts. Our eyes strained against the sun, and we looked pretty boring.

I slipped out another photograph that I didn't always display, because it might have seemed like boasting.

"Damn!" I whispered to the crisp, younger version of Eleanor that I held between my thumb and forefinger. "I've got to speak to someone about this jerk, but not someone from the office. We can't have it backfire, right?"

I studied our faces for some clue as to how the conversation might sound were Eleanor still alive, as though I could wrest it from the cosmos.

The last time I'd seen her, age had shriveled Eleanor's cheeks into little prunes and slackened the flesh beneath her jaw and arms. We'd met at Balthazar for tea and pastries, and she'd told me: "Keep this under your hat, but I'm not long for this world." Beyond her usual arthritis, she felt afflicted by a new sense of burning nerves and exhaustion.

"Have you been tested?" I'd asked.

"What do they ever tell you? Even computers are more blunt. Darling, in the parlance of technology, I appear to have a 'permanent fatal error.'"

A month or two later, she died—not from sickness so much as carelessness. She had not taken her blood thinner. She probably hadn't remembered where she put it because she never knew where she put anything. That was why she had hired me, and my predecessors and successors.

When someone subtle and brilliant like Eleanor goes, I feel all the more maddened by youth with its cell phone drawl and silly fashions. I prefer older versions of everything, like old cars and buildings, and ancient forests. Cultural clichés have us "letting go of the past," and "moving on," implying that the future holds some great cache. But what is it without history?

I examined my own head tilted beside Eleanor's, my dark hair longer than now, falling past my shoulders; my guileless, open-mouthed smile from the days before the oyster of my world had begun to yield empty shells.

It was not even ten years ago.

4

We didn't meet each other's lips, only the warmth around them. A man who plays the horn knows about breath and air.

My silk kimono was open at the waist, my dark tresses all over the place as neck-length hair can be.

"Do you think this towel is sexy, or is it compulsive of me?"

"Very sexy."

"Why?" I breathed into his cheekbone.

Jordan giggled, probably embarrassed by his legacy of stains on my sheets. The more we tried this challenging position, the more scrambled our effort became. He was amazingly slender, like an electric bass guitar, a virtually boneless Filet of Boy.

"The towel makes me feel…we're at the beach. Fucking on the beach…"

"Or we're a sandcastle, and the tide has just come in."

He leaned back as I sank into him and threw the sheet over us.

"Swish," I whispered, whisking away the towel, and he laughed more.

"You're insane. But you smell awesome. There's a damn city under my arm."

"You're not obliged to smell as good as a woman," I reminded him, inhaling his musk and snuggling my head onto his chest with its scant patches of black hair.

We were supposed to meet Claudia so she and Jordan could discuss a professional collaboration. I'd promised to call her in the morning, but we didn't seem to be doing that. It was Saturday, lazy time, and while we'd been at it for three months, I still relished Jordan's perceptive touch after the numbness with my ex-fiancé, Thomas. I'm not one to dislike sex any more than chocolate, but Thomas' version of sex was like mildewed chocolate—even more frustrating because it was supposed to be a treat.

So I availed myself of Jordan's lips, running my fingers through his ringlets of black hair as his tongue dove down my throat. We shook like two maracas, our legs locking us into syncopation.

Then came banging on my front door, and a voice squawked: "Molly! Are you guys in there or what?"

I stroked Jordan's stubble as we slowly disengaged from each other's warm, slippery skin, my groin almost seizing. I wanted more of him and what we'd been doing. As if he knew, he grabbed my thigh and whispered, "To be continued."

5

"Thank God for crime; how else would I earn a living?"

Claudia was so like a performance that I could anticipate lines I'd heard before. She and I were both surprised when Jordan lunged at her, a finger on his lip.

"Don't say that so loud."

"I'm being general," Claudia defended herself.

He sat down again beside me. We were in a Greek diner, and I was buying everyone breakfast because neither Jordan nor Claudia had a sou that morning, and criminal incomes are unpredictable. Jordan was expecting payment on a delivery from last week, and Claudia had stopped wasting unemployment checks on telephone psychics telling her how Bertie now felt about her. In a fit of self-pro-motion, she appraised her contribution to Jordan's enterprise: "The lesbian market could be a *mecca*."

"I'm sure someone's covering it," he replied. "But look, if you can make it work…" He regarded her with shining brown eyes. I brushed a strand of dark hair over his forehead and behind his ear.

"Have you studied your competition?" Claudia grilled him like the grilled feta cheese on rye she was eating.

"You know, I'm an artist. This is my day job."

"Well, you don't want to be underbid."

"It's not like that." Jordan dropped his fork and spun his already shredded, greasy napkin in his hands. "I got only a few customers. I find them the best stuff I can—virgin buds—"

"Don't excite me." Claudia flicked her tongue at us.

Jordan cracked up and continued. "I retail it, like my parents always did, and we leave it at that. I'm not looking for a *market*; I sell to friends, you know?"

"His approach is select merchandise for select clients," I summarized.

"Making a little money, keeping yourself in smoke. But don't you want to ex-pand?" Claudia persisted. "Maybe I could help you fry bigger fish."

Jordan leaned in, lowering his voice as he always did when he discussed such matters in public. "If that means meeting guys from Colombia in hotel rooms and getting shot, fuck it. If it means getting busted by undercover narcs, fuck it. Call me small fry, but I'm not dealing weight. Just one or two more accounts—you know, friends, people you can trust."

"And if I score them and move renewals?"

Jordan nodded at Claudia with satisfaction. "Anything with friends is awe-some."

"Having sampled your goods, I know connoisseurs who will appreciate it."

"Not Bertie," I piped up. "We don't want to jeopardize Jordan with your melo-dramas, Claw."

"I wasn't even thinking of her. I do know other people. Besides, she smokes only cigars."

"Cigars?" Jordan turned to me and smiled again. His jaw practically shimmered with six-o'clock shadow. But his eyes were bright and clear, his skin smooth—the frost of middle age had not settled upon that brow.

Sensing my appreciation of him, Jordan slung his arm around my shoulder and turned back to Claudia, saying, "You don't look like a dyke."

"You don't look like a dealer."

Jordan shot a finger to his lips again. "I'm *not*. I'm a middleman. And don't talk so loud!" he repeated. "You never know who's hanging around."

"Nobody here cares what we're talking about," she insisted.

Claudia and I glanced at the unoccupied wobbly tables, a couple of elderly ladies in a booth by the window, a guy by himself in a stained parka at the counter doing crossword puzzles, and the few stray waitresses in white shirts and black skirts who seemed barely awake.

"Claudia," I said, "if you're going to work for him, do it his way. Remember—that was one of my caveats." The other was that I didn't want her selling to minors. I didn't want to hear about her hitting up the super's kids or students at the public school around the block.

"It's simple," Jordan continued, still barely above a whisper. "Don't say any word starting with D. Even on the phone. We call it inventory, supply, lettuce."

"You hear that?" I double-checked with Claudia.

"You'll get no trouble from me," she assured us. "Only results."

After lunch Claudia would head to the Gay and Lesbian Center for her weekly support group, then onto Corona, Queens to visit her mother and borrow money. Jordan was meeting a tall drummer with dreadlocks called Zikomo, or Z, to play at the Union Square subway station. And I had to let my housecleaner in.

As we left the diner, Jordan asked if I'd come to his gig later in Brooklyn.

"Maybe," I told him.

He yanked gently at my scarf.

"What does 'maybe' mean? Can I count on it?"

"If I don't poop out. Remember, I'm an old lady."

"Stop it, Chardonnay."

He called me Chardonnay because when we'd met, at a rave around Christmas, I'd introduced myself as "Chardonnay Shine," a color chip from Lustrella's catalog.

"Hey," I whispered, taking his hand, "do you have enough cash 'til pay day?"

"I'll score something in the subway and the tip jar tonight."

"The Union Square station? That's not even pocket lint."

I opened my wallet, slipped out two twenties and handed them to Jordan.

"Pay me back when your ship comes in."

Claudia and I watched him swagger down the street with his saxophone case, the frayed bottoms of his jeans dragging along damp sidewalks. On this March morning the tops of high buildings along First Avenue vanished like they'd been airbrushed into mist.

Claudia turned to me, swaying her hips.

"Sugar Mamacita, wowie!" she chirped.

"That wasn't sugar, that's a loan," I said sternly.

"Lucky boy."

We began walking to the corner, where Claudia would get on the subway and I would head home.

"That's what I need," she decided. "A girlfriend with a job. And a heart. Hope he appreciates you. He's pretty cute, but you know guys. I hope he doesn't take you for granted."

"He already does," I admitted. "And that's okay. He's a fling. I'm not building this to last."

"You may not be," said Claudia, "but I think he knows who butters his daily bread."

6

I almost wished that Helena, my housecleaner, was not coming. I craved solitude after a stressful week at the office with Jack, the night with Jordan, and the long morning with him and Claudia. Before Helena flounced through the door, in her same inexplicably cheerful mood, I listened to phone messages that I hadn't had time to check when Jordan was here. All week someone with an unfamiliar cell phone number had been calling and hanging up. I wondered whether Thomas was using a friend's number, though I doubted he'd be so clever.

But that afternoon I discovered it was Alessi's husband, "Hedge Fund Pete."

"Molly," he enunciated slowly and ominously over my answering machine. "It's Pete. Please call when you can. Things are not good."

A week ago Alessi had told me over the phone that their cells were mingling in a petri dish, and she was "taking it easy, just waiting." If the third in-vitro attempt failed, they would give up on having children.

I glanced at my watch. I could probably squeeze in this call before Helena arrived. Though I felt a certain dread at doing so, I pecked in his number.

"Hey! Thanks for getting back to me, Molly."

"Of course. What's up?"

"Well, not our hopes. The impediments are more serious than we thought."

"I'm so sorry."

I wandered into the bedroom as we spoke and sat on my unmade bed. As if to undermine this phone call, Jordan's condom peeked out between my crumpled sheets. Had it slipped off without our noticing, or had he just left it there?

"She's taking it very hard. Some days she doesn't even get out of bed."

"Shit."

I didn't know whether I was saying it on Alessi and Pete's behalf or my own. Though it seemed unsavory, I picked up the condom and examined it—thank God it was unbroken.

"I can't really talk now, I'm driving," Pete told me. "But could we maybe meet for lunch…You work in midtown, right?"

"Yes."

"Well, let me invite you. This is something I'd prefer we discuss in person. How does next Wednesday look for you?"

We set the plan for Wednesday. After hanging up, I tossed the condom across my room, missing the trashcan. I had to walk over, pick it up, and dump it in—discarding the rind, not the good memory. A second later I thought to wrap it in a tissue so Helena wouldn't see it when she emptied my trash.

In all likelihood, Jordan and I had dodged that bullet. I was expecting my period any second. But if by some chance I was pregnant, I considered whether I might offer Alessi my child. What else would I do with the love child of a guy thirteen years my junior who couldn't rub two quarters together? Maybe I would rise to the challenge of that irresistible anomaly, who might even demonstrate musical talent and would undoubtedly have dark, curly hair.

Maybe this accident would become my oblique entrée into parenthood.

Maybe that was how my child would happen.

7

We observed an unspoken code of ethics in the unisex bathrooms at the office. Men closed toilet seats after peeing, and women left no sign of our periods. The homey comfort of mosaic tiles, floor rugs, and piles of plush paper towels made for easy navigation of my period, which had sneaked up in the middle of the workday, quashing misbegotten hopes of pregnancy by storm and by Jordan.

But I felt confident that I had left the WC spotless as I surrendered it to Enrico, a junior designer just out of Larry's alma mater, the School of Visual Arts. Enrico was so flitty that I seemed to interact with his mannerisms more than anything—like sipping a cup of tea with too much lemon and sugar to catch its flavor. He was a hard worker, and had an uncommon knack for drawing with the mouse.

"You wanted to check out my comp," he recalled when he saw me at the bathroom door.

"That's right. Shall we meet in ten minutes?"

"We could," he replied with a classic drop of his wrist, "but my tummy's growling. Can we say after lunch?"

"Of course."

Then I was shocked by a familiar voice behind us.

"Is Molly Douglas here?" it asked intently.

There was Jordan, before Kendra's reception desk in his loose green pants, a striped T-shirt hanging below his black corduroy jacket, cheeks unshaven, his ringlets of dark hair splayed and ragged.

"Who's *that*?" drawled Enrico, looking back and forth between Jordan and me. I didn't answer but marched up to reception with my hand on my hip.

"You should be in school now," I scolded. Then I explained to Kendra, "Truant cousin."

She seemed relieved that I recognized him.

"Can we speak for a second, cuz?" he asked.

Before Enrico could make some excuse to be introduced, I pushed Jordan out to the elevator banks, past the column of glass bricks and the sliding mahogany panels with gold lettering that said Larry Applebaum + Partners.

"Nice office, Chardonnay Shine."

"What are you doing here?"

"I gotta ask you something, but I don't want anyone to hear."

One of the elevators opened with a buoyant *bing!* Jordan steered me into the cab just as Jack Ashlund and a print producer got out.

The elevator door shut and Jordan pushed the twenty-second floor.

"What are you doing here?" I repeated.

"Look…I hate to put you on the spot like this, but I couldn't get you by phone for two days." He regarded me like a plaintive and hungry cat.

"I've been hard to reach," I admitted. I'd been avoiding my mother's infernal calls about Easter plans as I still hadn't worked up the nerve to remind her that Thomas would not be joining us this year.

Jordan stared at me and swallowed; his sharp Adam's apple dipped.

"I need to borrow five hundred bucks. I need it today. I'll get it back to you the day after tomorrow, with ten percent interest."

"Are you crazy?"

"Like I said, I hate to do this. But we've got to front something..."

"Who's 'we'?"

"Me and Claudia."

I should have guessed she was behind this.

"She calls it her 'cadre of expatriate lesbians in Paris.' See, it's not like here..." He lowered his voice, although no one could hear us in the damn elevator. "Across the pond they get meth or blow, but they really want a good hit of Western Hemisphere weed. If this goes like I think, we'll be singing hallelujah."

"And if it doesn't?"

"You know I always get back what I borrow."

"Yeah, but we're talking twenty or thirty bucks for food. This is slightly more."

"You net, like, five hundred dollars a day here, don't you?"

"Not quite."

Jordan's large Picasso-black eyes solicited me. I knew that five hundred dollars was a huge amount for him. Still, I appreciated the plight of any executive whose artsy girlfriend showed up at his office stroking her tresses and asking for her next semester's tuition.

The elevator opened on the twenty-second floor. I pressed the button for six and the doors closed again.

"If you weren't a damn brilliant musician, I couldn't be bothered with this, I want you to know," I said as we began descending.

I had seen him play three times, the white boy in quartets with blacks and Latinos. These groups performed atonal improvisations that were too sophisticated to enjoy without being high. But Jordan also loved oldies and played them divinely in subway stations. He'd bought an elderly woman to tears with his simple rendition of "Something Stupid Like I Love You." She'd thrown him a flurry of bills before boarding the D train.

I was lucky if clients liked my concepts, if they'd sell a product I sometimes hadn't even tested.

I had to respect him.

"Thanks for the compliment," he replied. "Does that mean you'll do it?"

"There's one way I can be persuaded—if you sign a notarized statement that you'll owe me what you've borrowed. It's what Eleanor did when her sons borrowed money from her. I'll go to my office now and type it up. You can meet me at the bank where we get our direct deposit. I remember seeing a notary there."

"You're the best, Chardonnay. But listen, to protect yourself, write that you're helping me pay my rent, and that's what I'll owe you for, okay?"

"So if you're caught committing a federal crime it won't be traced to me."

"Something like that."

Or something stupid like *I love you*, or at least *I like you a lot*.

The elevator stopped on ten. A beefy man wearing a hairpiece and a poorly fitting suit boarded. I glanced from him to Jordan, calculating that if I lost five hundred dollars, it could be considered a tariff on sexual gratification.

I had my purse with me, from my trip to the girls' room. So I took out one of my business cards, scribbled the bank's address on the back, and put it in Jordan's hand.

"Listen—go now, before lunch, when it will get busy. It's two blocks from here. Try to snag the notary." I glanced at my watch; it was 11:40. "I'll meet you as soon as possible."

The elevator doors shut on him and the paunchy older man, and I slid back between the mahogany panels that said Larry Applebaum + Partners.

Kendra watched me emerge three minutes later in my jacket, carrying a folded piece of paper on which I had written our "contract."

"Lunch," I called blithely over my shoulder.

She was on the phone, and what I said barely registered.

8

The next day, Wednesday, I spotted Hedge Fund Pete in the office lobby, wearing a charcoal gray cashmere coat and holding a cell phone to his ear. His oversized Dolce and Gabbana sunglasses drew double-takes from my fellow employees, who were swathed in scarves and overcoats and carrying umbrellas.

Never rude, Pete ended his wireless chat as I scuttled to him across the travertine floor. "Pardon my shades, Molly," he said as we kissed briefly on the cheek. "Haven't slept in ages and I look like shit."

"I'm sure you don't."

The last time we'd seen each other was June, when Thomas and I had gone up to play tennis on Pete and Alessi's clay court and we'd all burbled with plans: Thomas and I discussing our wedding date, Pete and Alessi confident about their second in-vitro fertilization. We'd acted like people who would soon have families. Now Pete and I faced each other, several deflated dreams later.

"Did Allie mention what we're going to talk about?" he asked as we walked out the door and headed east, toward Lexington Avenue.

"Nope. She said that she'd speak with me too but wanted you to 'explain everything first.'"

Whatever "everything" was.

As we passed a loud construction site, our sentences shrank into abbreviations.

"She okay?"

"Not really."

"Meds again?"

"For now."

"Hi Molly!" someone called above the din, wanting to make an impression. There was Jack, on his way back to the office with a lunch bag.

I waved curtly and muttered "ugh" under my breath.

Pete took me to a pub on Third Avenue that served lobster bisque and shepherd's pie. Generally he preferred sushi, but for some reason men—my dates, colleagues, or my oldest friend's husband—associate the name *Molly* with pub food.

Once we were seated at a table with its inevitable vinyl red-and-white-check-ered cloth, Pete removed his sunglasses. Unfortunately, I knew what he meant by "looking like shit." His usually fresh, boyish eyes appeared bloodshot, and the cute baby fat had vanished from his cheeks. He looked uncharacteristically drawn, his brown hair starting to pale by his temples in its first frost of middle age.

As usual, he was well dressed. When Alessi had first met him, she told me, "He has more shoes than I do. And they're shiny, like caramel or flan." When they were younger, Pete and Alessi went to London, Paris, or Milan for a weekend to shop. Her father had initially wondered if Pete was gay and described him to the rest of us as *pédé*. But then again, Alessandra's father also thought my brother was gay. To this broad-shouldered, loud Italian father, any reserved man who didn't bet foolishly on the Super Bowl was "gay."

"Get whatever you'd like," Pete invited me when the waiter approached us.

"I'll have a Cobb salad."

"That's all?"

"It's fine."

Why did he care what I ate anyway?

Pete ordered a deluxe cheeseburger and then started talking.

"We've been telling the world that it's my low motility, which is part of it," he began. "But the real curve ball is that she's prone to miscarry—it's a combination of a weak cervix and scar tissue. She's got good eggs and we've always conceived, but she loses the fetus. She hasn't wanted people to know. She's…furious at her own body, at her past."

He didn't have to say more. I knew what it had taken for Alessandra, with a Roman Catholic upbringing, to have that abortion back in college.

"When I called you the other week she was shredding her tampons with a razor…now she's starting to pull out her hair." He sighed sharply. "Mother's Day will be worse than last year."

This news sat heavily on me as I listened, but it hardly surprised me. If Alessi were pregnant there would be drama, if she had a screaming toddler there would be drama, if she had a rebellious adolescent there would be drama. Now drama arose from not knowing if those other dramas would come to pass.

"Your brother is lucky," Pete continued. "He knows that he'll be a dad soon. There are men in this world who have not been able to put food on their family's plates—but they have families. That's something that, despite my recent earnings from the fund and everything else, I may never know."

"Pete," I pleaded, unable to keep hearing this. "What about adoption? Plenty of kids in this world would love parents like you and Alessi."

The waiter came by to pour us ice water, though suddenly I felt neither thirsty nor hungry.

"We're considering adoption," Pete told me. "Of course, it's no quick fix, with months of waiting lists and travels to strange places." He sighed again; I saw his chest rise and sink with it. "We've come so close to having our own. And we're going to try once more, but we need help."

Then he fell silent.

"What kind of help?"

"Look—this wasn't my idea. I told her it was a long shot. But you know how she gets…"

He put his face in his hand for a moment.

"*What's* a long shot?"

"Oh God, Molly. This will sound bizarre." Then he looked up and blurted: "Allie could have stitches in her cervix, but it still might not work. Her OB-GYN said that our best hope was to implant our fetus into another woman who could bring the child to term."

My jaw must have dropped onto the checkered tablecloth.

"Like I said, I told her we couldn't ask Molly to do this. She's got a job, and a busy life of her own…"

"I'm so sorry about what you're going through," I said, wringing the cloth napkin on my lap. "But…there's no way I would do that. What about Nicole or Gina?"

"Nicole…" Pete grimaced. "She and Allie aren't speaking. She feels you're more her sister than either of them. Her best childhood friend…"

"Pete, I can't do this. What would I tell Larry? 'Hey, I'm going to show up in the office pregnant for a couple of months. Not that I'm married, or anything.'"

The waiter planted our respective plates of food before us as though Pete and I were mannequins in a store window display that he didn't wish to topple.

"Besides, and more importantly," I found the nerve to say, "I want my own child. And I'm sorry, Mick Jagger, but time is no longer on my side."

"We would not ask this favor without doing one in return," Pete replied steadily, oblivious to his steaming cheeseburger and thick golden fries. "You would, of course, be our child's godmother. My dad really wants a grandkid. His grandkid. He's agreed to cut you in on the fund…We've done this kind of favor for friends before. That's the way we'd regard it—not as payment to a surrogate mother, which has never been cool in New York State, but as a big favor in return for a big favor."

This chat was trumping Jordan's visit to my office yesterday in its shock value.

"I don't have the cash for that kind of principle. You know that."

"We'd take care of it."

"You're going to give me two million dollars to have your kid?" I shrieked my words at him; then I covered my mouth.

"Here's how it will work," said Pete, a bit more confident now that he was discussing business. He leaned down, opened his briefcase and removed a manila folder that was, amazingly, labeled *Molly*. It seemed more interesting to him than his lunch.

"You may not know that the hedge fund takes a twenty percent profit as our fee. We're doing well right now. None of our investors were hurt in this latest hiccup—"

"Hiccup, Pete?" I snapped. My 401K had plummeted in early March.

"From our percent we'll give you the two million you need to start your own account. Meanwhile, we'll give you a credit card to cover your medical expenses, legal fees, and compensation for lost wages. This was how Allie suggested we do it."

I was too overwhelmed to speak, much less eat my Cobb salad.

Pete opened the folder. Across the table I saw columns of figures. The type was small, but the numbers were long. Some were highlighted with yellow marker.

"I can't exactly give you a prospectus—you know these funds aren't SEC-regulated, even though we've actually registered with them. But this will give you some idea of the returns you can expect. Here are some recent audits and N.A.V.s—a little due diligence."

He slid the folder to me, but I didn't touch it any more than I would have touched flypaper. Two years back I had heard about some hedge fund hemorrhaging nearly five billion dollars. Even though I knew that Pete tended to be conservative, numbers like these intrinsically made me giddy.

"Look it over. There's paperwork from in-house counsel on how we'd transfer funds to initiate your account. I've also included some articles about surrogate motherhood. There are aspects of it you should know before we discuss this plan further."

"Pete," I began, probing the egg in my Cobb salad with my knife, "this is an extraordinarily generous and...imaginative offer. But I've got a good salary, a healthy 401K, and you know...for all their disappointment that I'm not marrying Tom, my folks won't disinherit me."

I had never seen Pete so forlorn and uncomfortable.

"Maybe you should advertise," I went on, "Give this chance to a woman who really needs it. Let me point out, I'm no spring chickadee. For your fourth in-vitro, you should get someone in her twenties. It's possible I too could miscarry..."

"She knew you'd say no."

Pete suddenly burst out laughing.

"You're just so Protestant, Molly! Any hedonistic Catholic or Jewish girl we know would agree to this deal in a heartbeat."

"Then why are you asking me?"

I tried not to sound furious as I massacred the egg and then began squashing avocado slices with my knife.

"Well, we don't want a stranger, or someone who's financially desperate. We don't want anyone who might make trouble for us about keeping the child. Allie asked that you think it over for a while, and give us a final answer on May first."

"My answer won't change," I told him. "But if it makes Alessandra feel better now, we'll speak again on May first."

Pete licked his lips and sipped nervously from his water glass.

"May I be frank about something?"

I stopped destroying my food and looked squarely at him.

"I've survived so far—and you've been nothing if not frank."

"I'm not trying to push you. We're asking a lot, potentially. It's your life, and your choice. But I think…you could do so much more with yourself." He sipped his water again and blotted his lips with the cloth napkin. "You could be the next Eleanor if you wanted—the next mega-copywriter with a flair for visuals. Or you'd be the next artist with a flair for copy. That's why she had a soft spot for you. You don't need to slave away for someone else's profits. You could start your own agency, like she did. And you'd have the capital if you went with our plan."

I began speaking to that, but Pete held up his hand to stop me.

"Sometimes Allie and I think you've put yourself on hold, waiting for some perfect guy to come along—then you'll buy the apartment, or start your business. But you don't need to wait."

So the "marital-editorial we" had weighed in about me. I started forking down my salad. Pete still didn't touch his food.

"I'm too young to start my own stint," I said between forkfuls of lettuce, bacon, and pummeled egg. "I'm still learning the ropes. Eleanor was over fifty when she struck out on her own. I'm not seduced by these headaches—hustling for clients, paying other people's social security. I'd rather hitch my star to someone else's wagon than oil squeaky wheels.

"In short, Pete, I'm going to have to decline your offer, though I'm moved you both think so highly of me. Basically, I'm fine with things as they are. I'm not hankering after profits."

"Clearly not."

"I like my life. And I want more of it."

9

Jordan knew how to touch a woman.

Most guys—well intended, even eager to please—didn't understand that the jabs and jostles beloved to a puppy dog did not tend to translate for the pussy cat.

As we wound down, my fingertips grazed his brow and cascaded down his neck and shoulders before landing on the barely comfortable mattress. His place always smelled like earwax and apricots, a cloying scent produced by men under thirty who rarely did laundry. Sometimes it seemed aphrodisiac, and other times rank. The quality of life was higher in my apartment, but I stayed at his now and then for the novelty.

In the next room his two roommates, Dustin and Charlie, chatted boisterously over beer and TV. Only a soiled Mexican blanket nailed up in the doorway separated us from them. Thank goodness their television was loud with canned laughter and voiceovers, because Jordan and I needed privacy. My period was just ebbing, and I decided we could do without a condom. When our bare skin mingled for the first time, sex took off by itself, our bodies following along. He wasn't doing it, I wasn't doing it. I couldn't tell what came from him or belonged to me—a hallmark, that I've rarely enjoyed, of sublime fucking.

I tingled to my toes as sleep began to overtake me.

Earlier that night, Jordan had paid me, as promised, six hundred for the five I had loaned him last week. With my one-hundred-dollar profit, I invited him to a Spanish dinner of seafood paella with a bottle of smoky chardonnay.

We'd then cabbed over to the far reaches of Brooklyn to hear guys with lustrous dark hair and magnificent shoulders play Cuban music. Since we were near Jordan's apartment in Sunset Park, we landed there rather than at my place in Manhattan.

As I dozed off, the steam heat hissed and clanked through pipes louder than the conga drums onstage.

"Whew! It's sweltering…Mind if I open the window?" he asked.

I was too exhausted to reply.

"You falling asleep?" He sounded disappointed. But I'd been on overdrive all week. When I wasn't given assignments at work, I had plenty else to compose: "No, Alessi, I'm not mad at you. Just surprised. Yes, I will keep an open mind. I realize the fund has fewer than thirty investors, that this kind of offer doesn't come along every day"; "No, Mom, I haven't made up with Thomas. We don't see each other anymore. We're no longer engaged. He won't be joining us for Easter. Please understand that, and stop hinting and asking me…"

After all that effort, I longed for the sexy oblivion I had just enjoyed with Jordan. But he seemed restless, scrambling up from the mattress to push open a window, then bounding out of the room. Beneath his strident footfalls the wooden floorboards wobbled.

Either an hour or three minutes later, he asked if I wanted a hit of his joint.

"No," I breathed.

"You always fall asleep after sex…like a guy."

I rolled over, pulling the sheet to my chin. I noticed that my toes stuck out and bent my legs so they wouldn't.

"How many guys do you have sex with, Jordan?"

"None."

"So how do you know they fall asleep after sex?"

"It would be nice to talk sometimes after making love, don't you think?"

"If I never talked again, it would be too soon."

He had no idea how stressful my week had been. I was not going to tell him about the lunch with Pete. In fact, Pete and Alessi had asked that I not liberally discuss their offer because, as it happened, surrogate motherhood was not legally enforceable in New York State. Ongoing contentions raged over the idea of "baby-brokering" and "surrogacy for profit." That's why Pete had described it as a favor for a favor and asked that I keep everything quiet.

Anyway, I didn't want Jordan to know that I was turning down two million dollars—I wouldn't hear the end of it. I even wondered myself whether I was making a sage decision.

"Claudia's got a point." His inhale squeaked; then he coughed out his exhale.

"She says you and I are in two different relationships: I'm in love, you aren't."

At the mention of Claudia, my spine stiffened like a curtain rod. I slid up, propping my torso with my right arm.

"People my age don't fall in love anymore."

"That's a crock, Molly."

"Wait 'til you hit thirty-seven—you too will forget how to idealize."

"I'm not idealizing what just happened here on this crummy mattress. Am I?"

"Well…" I sighed. At times like this our age difference seemed a great divide. "You're talking about lust," I said. "And friendship. A combination more reliable than love. Still, you're a young American with Hollywood dreams, and I don't want to short-circuit them by talking anymore about this."

Mumbling crossly, Jordan extinguished the joint in his ashtray and shoved it away so that the ashes nearly spilled over.

"For another thing," I rambled on, now rather awake, "it's fine with me if you do business with Claudia. I'm glad she's found you a nest of expatriate Parisian lesbians hungry for weed from the Americas. But keep her out of our bedroom…"

"Well how am I supposed to feel when she tells me you're 'on the prowl'?"

"She's being a jerk. She has no girlfriend and no job. You two probably hang out all day together chitchatting, don't you?"

"You totally dodged—"

"Just saying she's full of shit."

"Really? You don't check out guys at the gym?"

So much for mentioning to Claudia that I once noticed a guy on the bench press.

"She's exaggerating, as usual. And if we don't stop talking about her, I am going to get dressed and go home, where I can have some peace…"

I drew my legs in, preparing to stand up. Jordan grabbed my arm.

"Can't I know where I stand?"

In the other room Dustin and Charlie giggled along with reruns of *The Honeymooners*. I would recognize Jackie Gleason's histrionics anywhere.

"Jordan." I sighed again. He was probably hoping for a different answer, but I had made it clear that we were dating, not mating—and that dating is underrated as an end in itself. Hadn't I had loaned him five hundred dollars, taken him out on the town and then made love without a condom?

He was getting spoiled.

"We had a great dinner and conversation tonight about John Coltrane and arpeggiments…"

"Arpeggios," he corrected me. I called them his "saxophone squiggles," and he explained how they blended different scales.

"You've brought wonderful things into my life. Can't we just enjoy this?"

I ran my finger along his scratchy chin and warm, humbling lips.

"Don't start thinking Claudia's thoughts," I continued, retracting my hand. "They haven't served her…"

"You don't get it," he lamented. "Before we met, every conversation I had was spinning my legs in water. With you, I touch ground. And nobody ever cared so much if I eat or starve—not even my family."

"But don't you want someone your age?"

He turned away, grumbling, "I am beyond insulted…"

When he looked back again, defiance glinted through his dark eyes. "You're making a huge deal about thirteen years," he charged.

I drew my legs back in. This was easy for the younger one to say.

"When I was born, Kennedy was president. When you were born, Gerald Ford was in office, right? That's a chunk of time," I pointed out. "You don't even remember the sixties. Besides, I had my period in 1975—in some other culture, I could frigging be your mom."

"Well we're not, and my mother is, like, frigging fifteen years older than you, and I can't stand girls my age. Stuck-up little ice queens who want me to spend money I don't have. And then they don't kiss me goodnight. They're not like you."

"I wasn't like me at that age either."

At twenty-four I was more conservative, shy, and prone to pointless infatuation. "And to tell you the truth, Jordan, being in love never brought out the best in me."

It had generally reduced me to a self-conscious, jealous wreck. Looking back, there was little pleasure in it, except that short-lived vertigo of anticipation—as it quaked beneath the guillotine blade.

"You're getting a better version of me now than the guys I fell in love with."

"Don't say another word about them, or anyone you flirt with at the gym, okay?"

"I never raised the topic," I reminded him, lying back down. Overheated and uncomfortable, I wished I was home and hated how his scratchy sheets felt practically like emery boards against my skin.

"I need you, Molly," he moaned hoarsely. "I'm like a cracked ceramic and you're the glue that's holding me together."

"Well, thanks. But I think music is your glue."

"Music is the glaze that makes me sparkle. But I'd be broken into pieces without you…You don't believe me, do you?"

"No," I said.

Actually I wondered whether he wasn't buttering me up to spring an even greater financial request on me.

Hesitantly I spread out beneath the merciless sheets again, annoyed that my feet stuck out and that the mattress was so thin and bumpy. Why were men averse to creature comforts? I had to hang curtains at Thomas' place and bring over bath towels and silverware.

"I don't want to share you with anyone," he said. "That's what I'm getting at."

Beset by discomforts, both physical and emotional, I rolled onto my back. His ceiling seemed far away. I assured him, "You're the only guy I'm dating now."

"But, does that mean…"

"I just ended my engagement last fall. Please. I can't start making promises."

But my words were overtaken by a sibilant blast of steam from Jordan's radiator.

10

The next morning I found myself in the shower with a flying water bug. Too shocked to scream, I stepped quickly out of the bathtub. As I shivered and dripped onto the tile floor, my heart pounding, Jordan banged on the door.

"'Ey Molly! Could you hurry up? Dustin's got to take a shit."

With a brittle towel wrapped around me, I unhooked the door so The Dust Ball, as I called Jordan's roommate, could stagger in, grabbing his butt and whimpering. I then gathered my nightgown and fled, vowing never to put myself in that position again.

"Hitchcock shower suffused with Hieronymus Bosch hell," I huffed as Jordan escorted me to the R train. "A *flying* water bug? Leave it to your apartment."

We giggled up Fourth Avenue to the subway, passing Laundromats and Pentecostal churches. In that first week of April, bright green buds had popped onto the bare tree branches, and morning breezes swept our cheeks. I suggested that we find a bodega for some coffee, because naturally there had been none at Jordan's.

"Can't wait to get back to civilization," I groaned as we exited the grocery shop, each with a hot Styrofoam cup of coffee in our hand. While Jordan had lovingly watched me procure them, I'd felt myself clench with impatience—though I realized he was normal, and that he was right. People who had great sex and argued intimately should appreciate each other the next morning. Yet I too was right, sensing that between our age difference and temperaments, we wouldn't last long and there was little point to getting more attached than we were. "Got to wash off the mildew," I commented, sipping the sweet coffee.

"Think of Elvis—*don't be cruel*," he bellowed as I ran downstairs at 53rd Street to catch my train.

At home I reveled in the cheerful, bright enamel of my bathtub, the aroma of fabric softener from velvety towels. After a hot shower devoid of flying critters, I cracked the windows open, grateful that my apartment faced the quiet alley. Sunlight the hue of lemonade sifted through my Irish lace curtains. I would have felt relaxed but for a tiny red light on my answering machine that twitched like an eye.

The calls were from Alessi. She had also been emailing me.

"What did we do wrong?" her phone message began. "Were you mad that I wanted you to speak to Pete first? I thought he'd explain it better because he knows the fund. But look, would you prefer cash as well as an account? All you have to do is ask. We'll do anything to make this work."

I didn't call her back, and maybe that's when everything began to feel peculiar.

Over the next week I began to detect new scents in my apartment, like glue or plastic, as though someone else had been there. Pens vanished from my desk, my fluffy bathroom towels seemed to have been yanked and not put back the way I would put them back. When I got home from work, a half glass of orange juice sat in my sink, and I hadn't drunk orange juice that morning. Or at least I didn't remember doing so.

Several explanations for this occurred to me:

1. I was not remembering what I did because I was distracted by Alessi's solicitations.
2. Claudia was using her set of my keys to sit in my chair, use my pens and towels, and drink my orange juice when I was not around.
3. I had poltergeists in the apartment, or:
3a. I was receiving mystical messages from ancestors who were restless for me to reincarnate them.

Or maybe it was just the Lilith-like, chaotic spirit of Eleanor shaking me up, urging me not to be so tidy and functional.

Jordan didn't even call to divert me. Usually he left chatty recaps of his day on my voice mail, or saxophone riffs from some old show tune. I could imagine Claudia advising him to "Hang back. Don't be so available. Make her come to you." One of Claudia's specialties was coaching men in the infallible lesbian tactics of seduction.

And gallingly enough, it worked. The silence that replaced Jordan made me miss him, just as the moon grows brighter when the sky darkens. I dreamed of his hands falling over my thighs like brook water. I longed for his lips and tongue to soothe my nipples when his teeth and stubble had set them on fire. I even felt affection for his jealous nagging.

But his absence hatched a counterclaim: if I were no longer capable of falling in love, not even with this adorable young swain—if too many wrong and stupid things had drained me for too many years—then why should I not help Pete and Alessandra have their child?

I had checkmated myself, holding out for a hypothetical love that would inspire marriage and parenthood. But when I'd told Jordan that "people my age don't fall in love anymore," I had not been lying.

As I dressed for work on Thursday morning, a week after the crazy lunch with Pete, I wondered whether a windfall of cash might renew my life. Or would it merely entrench me in Alessi's? I dreaded to think I would meet a man who defied the odds, and fall in love with him precisely when I was a pregnant surrogate mother. That would be my luck.

"You're my last hope," Alessi had implored when we finally spoke by phone.

"Why is everyone so all-or-nothing with me?" I retorted. "There are millions of women on this planet who could help you."

"Things always work when you do them, Molly. They always did."

She meant those motley aptitudes known by girlhood friends, like fifth-grade math homework, ice-skating, folding bedsheets at summer camp. Alessi and I had shared all that.

"I can't explain it to you," she went on. "But Pete and I already love this kid."

"Then line up other candidates to be your surrogate mother."

"It must be you," she insisted. "That's part of our love. And it's nonnegotiable."

11

"You look nice today, Molly," Enrico greeted me by the coffeemaker. I had slept poorly and was in desperate need of coffee by 10:30.

"It's the neckline," I told him.

Tension with Jack at the office had happily subsided. While I didn't trust his sudden neutrality, I had put on my favorite velour shirt and risked a low neckline.

"You should always show more skin. You have really nice skin."

I found my skin too pale and easily sunburned to rate as "nice."

"Do you like my earrings?"

As he tilted his head, sapphires flashed from his ear lobes.

"They're gorgeous. I like your brown highlights too," I said.

"You don't think I went too light?"

As I shook my head I sensed that the time might be provident for a life-altering dialogue with him. En route to work, I had decided that I might pose my question about helping Pete and Alessi to an outside party, someone with nothing at stake in the situation. But I would describe it as though it were someone else's dilemma, not mine.

"I just got the weirdest email from a friend," I began. "I'm not sure how to advise her. Do you know what a gestational carrier is?"

"A *what* carrier? You mean like a carrier of AIDS?"

But then Larry stomped over, prepared herbal tea and lemon for himself, and grumbled: "We have to talk, Molly."

"Do we?"

Behind his back Enrico struck a diva pose and batted his eyes.

Larry turned around and Enrico abruptly straightened up, smiling cryptically at me. So much for my conversation with a "remote confidant."

I followed Larry through the labyrinth of cubicles where account reps sat typing or murmuring dulcet words into phones. We ended up at his master suite with grand windows, caramelized bamboo floors, Turkish rugs, and fichus trees. He closed the door.

Then, without preamble, Larry slammed a pile of papers on his desk.

"How could you have okayed this?"

Behind wire-framed glasses, his brown eyes flared.

I bent over and looked for myself. Of course I would have recognized the colors and typefaces of this old corporate branding program for Scott & Talbot, an accounting firm.

"I didn't okay this. I didn't even see it."

"Molly," he said through tightened lips, "you signed off last week. That's why Jack sent it. Remember, we had to push this through for quick approval?"

"But I didn't sign off."

He rifled through papers, shaking his head. Then he produced a routing sheet with the initials "M.S.D." woven together in my instantly recognizable cursive. I gasped.

"You're sure it was for this pass?"

"Why would I waste my time if it wasn't? Do you have any idea how embarrassed I was?"

Flustered, I couldn't recall recent work for this firm, one of our highest paying accounts. I knew that we were going to create a new branding strategy for them, but I didn't think we'd passed the initial stage of notes and sketches. Maybe I really was losing it.

"I should have double-checked myself," he admitted, "but I've come to trust your eyes like my own. And sometimes I can't get to it all, you know. I can't get to it all. And I never thought you'd make such an egregious error—you, of all people. My right-hand woman..."

"I didn't think we'd gotten past the first sketches, Larry."

"Hello-o. That's what we were supposed to send them."

"But I haven't seen finals..."

"Jack said he gave them to you last Monday."

I shook my head no, and Larry scowled.

"I'm so sorry to say this..." he began—and I felt my guts spasm—"but people have seen you running around at lunch with strange men."

"What?"

"Look Molly, we know you're popular and scrumptious. But you've managed to keep your private life off the premises. Perhaps you've been...preoccupied lately? Regretting the breakup with Tom?"

Now that was a slap across my face. It took me a second to recover.

"I had lunch last week with Peter Foley," I finally said, remembering how Pete and I had passed Jack on our way to the pub. "My oldest friend's husband, the hedgie. You met them, years back—Pete and Alessandra."

"Well, Jack described him as an upscale gangster in a dark suit and sunglasses. And Kendra mentioned that some unkempt kid showed up in the office demanding to see you..."

"My sister-in-law's cousin," I said quickly. "Family skirmish. Kendra knew that."

Kendra constantly carried on personal phone conversations during work hours. She was hardly one to cast stones.

"Whatever these situations are, you've GOT to keep your focus here," Larry scolded me. "The thumbscrews are on, what with everyone learning the software in Windows. We must keep our edge, and you've been a big part of our edge. I appreciate how hard you work; I've told you many times. But I also know how rarely you take vacations. I'd rather see you take a little time off being the Rock of Gibraltar so you don't crack. Maybe...you know, maybe you need a good vacation, Molly..."

"I hate vacations," I retorted. "They disorient me. Can I make a copy of this routing sheet?"

I took the xeroxed copy back to my office, shut the door quietly, and slumped into my Aeron chair. I remained like that for ten minutes. If I were the kind of person who still cried, I might have wept. But I hadn't cried for years, even when I should have—like when I broke up with Thomas, or heard about Eleanor's death.

Something was catching up with me.

12

I worked for Jack six years ago. Not my favorite person. Tell your friend that he has a history of getting people fired, and he's especially weird with women. I know he's a recovered coke addict and that, for supposedly raucous behavior, he'd been canned in New York from one of the biggies—from J. Walter or McCann or somewhere. Which is why he makes the rounds at mid-sized agencies like hers.

Fascinated, I tilted the printed-out email from Rick's friend in the candlelight. I had to read it a third time.

He's had Tourette's syndrome since he was a kid and can't stop nodding his head. The coke probably made it worse.

"Knew it," I said, meaning all of it, including the coke addiction.

But Rick didn't ask for an explanation of what I "knew." He was watching Eugenia shake Bloody Marys and pour them, with a swoop of her arm, into glasses. She wore a T-shirt, suspenders, and pinstriped pants, her flyaway blonde hair bouncing to her shoulders. I watched her too for a second, reflecting that her hair had probably been white blonde when she was young and had mellowed now into a naturally golden honey. Rick seemed as riveted by her as I did by this email.

Schmoozing is his strong suit. JackASS, as we called him, can sell the proverbial snow to Eskimos but knows nothing about production or technique and has blown a budget or two. He depends on others to clue him in, or take the fall.

"I like your friend," I raved to Rick.

"Look at those suspenders and pinstripes. You gotta love her."

"I mean this friend."

I rattled the email printout before his besotted face. Since I'd last seen him, Rick began sporting a goatee that complemented his scalloped brown hair and beret. Not everyone can pull off a beret, but Rick looked particularly arty and "downtown" that evening in a brown leather jacket with a black scarf.

"Oh, Katie," he said. "She's good kid."

"I'd like to be in touch with her about this creep, Jack."

"She lives in California now, but maybe I can arrange it."

Meanwhile, Claudia slithered around the bar in search of a cigarette, migrating from group to group, as though she was doing the *grand aleman left*. She boasted a collection of pithy T-shirts that, to the sharp observer, betrayed the essence of her character. Tonight's slogan, emblazoned across her generous bust, read *Instant Idiot—Just Add Alcohol*.

I'd been in the strange position of enticing her out to The Bunny Hop to meet Rick and Terry with me, though I hadn't encountered much resistance. Desperate to pay her rent, Claudia had taken in a roommate last week—a roommate with a "voice coach" who did little other than practice eighties hit songs, like "I Will Survive," or "Total Eclipse of the Heart" in the living room each night. She was putting Claudia in the market to get out of her apartment as often as possible.

A Chesterfield now in hand, Claudia made a point of asking Eugenia for a light. The bartender complied dutifully.

"Is Bertie around?" Claudia asked before her inhale.

Eugenia shook her head no.

"So what's with her and Lainey?"

Eugenia shrugged and, before stepping away from us, the stunning blonde bartender winked at me. When I ignored her overture, she winked again, to make sure there was no mistaking it. Then other customers came in, and Eugenia was gone. I sat there feeling like I'd swallowed a peppercorn of pure flattery.

"Shakespeare said it best," Rick intoned into my ear. "'As she goes, all hearts do duty...Unto her beauty...' We're all individuals. But some people are also iconic."

"Are you iconic?" I asked him. "You seem to be."

"No," he said, in full voice now. "I'm an individual with a phone number, a passport, memories, and opinions. But I don't have archetypal presence."

He indicated Eugenia, bustling behind the bar, who seemed to know she was being discussed, like a cocky child.

Then Terry skipped in, crying, "Tomorrow's my birthday!"

"So how old *are* you, Honey—twenty-five?" asked Eugenia. "I'd serve you cake, but all I've got are pretzels and potato chips."

"Oh, don't worry. I'm totally stuffed anyway."

Eugenia snatched up a small bag of barbecue-flavored potato chips and doused them with rum. Then, using the lighter with which she'd lit Claudia's cigarette, she set the bag of chips on flambé. Rick and Terry applauded and laughed; now they were treated to that peppercorn of flattery. After the aqua ghost disappeared from its edges, Eugenia tossed the bag of chips to Terry, who caught it awkwardly, as if she was surprised she could.

"Have some," Rick coaxed her. "They're from Genie."

"But I've, like, totally blown my calorie count for the day. Totally."

"Terry thinks she's fat," Rick stated to Eugenia, who rolled her eyes.

"Just look at me if you want to feel better," Claudia interjected.

Terry was as far from fat as the Eiffel Tower is from Disney World. She was actually tall and well proportioned, with long brown hair and sweetly gaping lips.

She grabbed my shoulder. "Oh, darling, are you all right? I couldn't believe your messages today."

"She's being harassed on the job," declared Claudia.

"I wouldn't go that far…" I began.

"Go that far. Don't kid yourself," said Rick.

"Is that what you think?" I asked him.

"What you described is in any employee handbook," he assured me.

"But Jack hasn't made explicit threats or requests. It's all below the radar. I can't prove anything."

"He's creating a hostile work environment," Rick continued.

"It's meant to intimidate you," added Terry, her eyes wide.

I didn't want them to say this, because if it was true, there was nothing I could do about it. Larry was sold on Jack's virtues. In a company of fewer than fifty employees, there was no real H.R. department, only an office manager who ordered paper clips and oversaw our benefits. They even had outsourced payroll.

"So what am I now, a sitting duck? Oh, let's get me drunk!" I clapped my water glass on the bar.

"'O, let my keel burst! To the sea depart!' Rimbaud, *Drunken Boat*," Rick quoted. "I seem to be in a poetry mood tonight. Gene, please get something to soothe her nerves. She's had a rough day."

Eugenia looked like she already knew. Or she may have heard it in my voice as I entreated the others to explain my situation.

"Out of everyone in the office, why me?"

"He's threatened by you," hazarded Terry.

"But I have no power. I'm a subordinate."

"Read Katie's email again," Rick prompted me. "Look at what she says: He depends on other people to clue him in. We can surmise that this new kid on the block doesn't want any venerable insider catching him in that act."

"So he's scared I'll call his bluff?"

"That's my guess."

"How far-fetched. Anyway, if he were pleasant and garnered my good graces, I'd naturally clue him in."

"A guy like that never thinks you'd like him or be fair if he was normal to you," Rick explained. "He's got to screw you first. It's how he gets his kicks anyway. I know this type."

"So do I." Terry shuddered.

Rick pointed to her. "Rhode Island School of Design." Then he pointed to himself. "Cooper Union. Best art schools in the country, right? And neither of us has a staff job. We're lucky to keep freelancing. And it's not because we lack skills or talent. It's just that…"—he whipped out a pen and produced a masterful rendering on a cocktail napkin of a bullfrog swiping a fly with its long tongue—"bullfrogs eat dragonflies."

"What do you do for health insurance?" I asked them.

"She has family. I've got good luck."

I realized with a jolt that family and luck had served me better than they served most people. But I wouldn't replace medical insurance with either.

Not a moment too soon, Eugenia presented me with a frozen drink that looked like a landscape of pink and ginger snowballs with a tiny Japanese paper umbrella, slices of orange, and a cherry.

"Back home we call this a Daiquiri Euphoria." Her faint Southern lilt also evoked *back home*. "Chin up," she added, gazing at me with eyes so blue they seemed contagious.

"Oh wow!" swooned Terry. "I'm moving in. I want to live in it."

"Wow!" I repeated, oddly moved by this Daiquiri Euphoria.

Terry offered me some potato chips, which, along with the drink, became my dinner that night.

"What will you do about Jack?" asked Claudia, smoking her Chesterfield beside me now. She had been strangely quiet throughout our discussion about him.

"Well, I can't accuse him of forging my signature on the routing sheet—everyone would think I'm the whiner who resents that he was hired as my supervisor. So I'll tune out around him. I'll go so blank that he won't find me interesting, and hopefully he'll stop picking on me."

"I've tried that," said Rick. "I've tried blending in to a fault, but I always snap. That's the problem. They know you'll snap. Especially when you're a creative type."

"I won't snap," I said firmly. "I'll wait this out. It can't go on forever. If I don't believe that, I'm a fucked duck."

I sipped my strong daiquiri and started doodling on a napkin, like Rick had. I could see, from his sketches, that he drew excellently. So did Terry. They should have health insurance like other top-trained professionals.

I doodled a duck on its behind with legs stretched out and labeled it *Sitting Duck*. I drew another duck lying on its back with legs stretched straight up in the air and labeled it *Fucked Duck*.

Rick peeked over my shoulder and wrote with his pen *Ducked Fuck*.

"Illustrate that one. Hey, can a one-legged duck swim in a circle?"

But someone else had joined us—Eugenia, her eyes wide with delight at my ducks and Rick's bullfrog and dragonfly.

"Can I keep these?" she asked.

"Of course," said Rick.

"Please." I pushed mine over to her as though I wanted to be rid of it. "But don't ask me to draw a ducked fuck or a one-legged duck swimming in a circle."

Eugenia regarded me with endearing concern.

"You'll never win their game," she said, as though she was speaking in a code I should know. "Play your game."

I repeated, "'You'll never win their game. Play your game…'—that could be a tagline. It has the right rhythm. While I adore the sound of it, I have no idea what you mean. Who are 'they'?"

"Anyone who's playing you."

"How do I know what my game even is?"

Rick, Terry, and Claudia watched Eugenia lean over and tickle my ear with her whisper: "You've already won."

13

But I could point to nothing I'd won lately.

In its own trite and mild way, my life was going to seed. That much was clear the next day at work, when co-workers fell radio silent as I walked by. The camaraderie at The Bunny Hop remained behind its Easter-decorated door. Away from Daiquiri Euphorias was a world eager to chastise and isolate me for unnamed offenses.

Not helping matters, Mom insisted that I'd prioritized my career to the expense of everything else…and I was beginning to agree with her. By contrast, my younger brother was already married, with a first child on the way. As we'd grown up, my mother had carped on him for not doing as well in school as I had, about his escapade with wonder drugs in tenth grade, about the conferences with his teachers and the principal—while I had graduated with honors. But now the tables had turned, and all eyes would be on me at Easter.

"Who are you expecting to meet, at your age?" Mom had interrogated me when I'd told her it was over with Thomas.

"I don't know," I'd said.

"Well, I don't either."

I avoided phone calls with her because I didn't care to be reminded that "most decent men your age are married," and "having children won't get easier with time." She was completely accurate, but there was nothing I could do about it.

That's why I'd stuck with Thomas doggedly for three years, as we stick with a prize parking space even as it becomes inconvenient. My youthful passions had burned up in their own fire while others had paled like stars in a parallel galaxy— and I was getting too old for all this. I was not a star, destined to contract and burn for centuries in an ultraviolet nebula. I was a finite and organic being who would reproduce now or never.

And I liked the prospect of children, of walking in the woods with them or reading them bedtime stories. Everyone claimed I'd be a great mother. Yet I'd wondered how great I'd be at anything in an anemic marriage. I wasn't fool enough to believe in endlessly romantic love, but most people seemed to find intimacies more nurturing than my compromise with Thomas.

Perhaps, I thought as I walked home from a grueling day of innuendo at the office, Eugenia had "already won." She didn't have to plumb the miserly depths of biological time clocks, or try to find men who weren't dysfunctional. She was gorgeous and ensconced in a community that revered her. She had a clear role—the hot-ticket lesbian who all the girls were probably dying to date. She could speak for herself, not me.

By the time I reached my street, I had managed to plunge myself into a low mood and was heartened to find Jordan on my stoop.

"Waiting for Claudia?" I asked tersely.

He shook his head and pointed at me.

"Flatterer."

I squeezed his bent knee, which protruded through tattered blue jeans.

And that was it. He'd come upstairs, his saxophone case over his shoulder. I wouldn't ask him why he hadn't called for days, and he didn't ask why I hadn't.

As we pattered up the staircase with its threadbare carpeting, we heard Claudia's roommate belting out "Total Eclipse of the Heart" from behind their door.

"Not one note on pitch," Jordan whispered as I unlocked my door, and we fell, laughing and breathless from the climb, into each other's arms.

"I dig your cannabis cologne," I whispered, my lips sliding over his scratchy cheek as he wafted me across the floor to my bedroom, for a total eclipse of the legs and mind that I needed after that turd of a day.

"Where did you learn to touch women?" I asked as we lay together and twilight darkened my bedroom walls.

"I don't know."

"Yes you do."

"Maybe."

"You, Mr. It Would Be Nice to Talk After Making Love?" I mocked him, and he laughed nervously.

"An older woman," he finally confided. "Like, older than you are now."

"And how old were you?"

"Sixteen?" He asked as though he wasn't sure.

"How did you meet her?"

"She was a friend of my mother's." He laughed again. "It was inappropriate. We were pushing things."

"Was she beautiful?" I asked.

"No," he said. "Just hot. And patient. Not at all as pretty as you. She gave me my horn, you know. The 1952 Conn 'Lady Face.'"

"That was lavish."

"It had been her dad's."

He didn't say more. I offered him rose tea and lay around in my kimono as he played Cole Porter into the night.

At one point we wandered to the window and looked out at blossoming leaves in a glow from my kitchen lamp, passing a joint between us. I felt close to him, but not like husband and wife. Not even like a boyfriend and girlfriend, and yet not a mother and son. There was no description for whatever we were.

14

The next morning Jack, Larry, and Jana, the account rep for Scott & Talbot, stood waiting by my office like See No Evil, Hear No Evil, and Speak No Evil.

Jack's face was shiny enough to seem lacquered and Jana's nose was so upturned you could look up her nostrils and see her brains—or something.

"Molly," Larry began impatiently. "About the approvals for Scott & Talbot. While I've communicated with Angus Scott, we thought you might write something as well."

"Since this was your oversight," Jack reminded me.

"So embarrassing," Jana emphasized.

Maybe they'd pin me to the wall and hurl knives?

Bolstered by a night of Jordan's erection grazing my butt and seeping between my legs, by the euphoria of sweet ginger daiquiris from the night before, I said, "Larry, I told you that I hadn't approved this pass."

I noticed Jack trying to catch his eye surreptitiously.

"There's no email trail on this," I continued.

"I emailed you several times," said Jack with his inescapable nod, and Larry—so eager to believe him—nodded in tandem.

But I had gone through the entire month's emails the day before, and no one had written about the new branding program for Scott & Talbot. The only emails from Jack were general, addressed to the entire department. There was nothing about that account.

"You wrote to me?" I asked Jack. "Show me where."

"Well,"—he sniggered, as if this should be obvious—"I don't keep all my emails…"

"Well, I do. Larry knows I do." I looked at the man who might have evidenced loyalty to me, after years of building a business together.

"We're splitting hairs," said Larry.

"And I'm splitting," I said, pushing my way past them and into my office with a moderate slam of the door.

They could say what they would. They could fire me, subject me to a life without a salary or health insurance. I would not cave, and I would not play their game.

And I would not have references, I realized, with Eleanor dead and Larry now dead set against me. It would not be easy to find another job.

I studied the xeroxed routing sheet. Maybe I was preoccupied and doing things I didn't remember. More likely, someone had forged my signature reasonably well.

But I noticed a new email from Alessi, which she had apparently also sent to my home. Her subject line was *Final Offer*.

We'll cut a check from Pete's office $500,000.00 tomorrow if you'r ready to mov forard, was all she had written, with several glaring typos. For all I knew she had accidentally added another zero. She must have dashed it off in a tailspin, on the verge of despair.

I felt no better.

Maybe it was time to pool our resources.

Alessi and Pete would be good for their part. Pete did everything by the book and had no record of fraud or tax evasion. And he kept emphasizing to me, "This isn't just an investment opportunity, like a mutual fund for wealthy people. We're really hedging so our investors don't lose their assets." He worked with a brilliant research analyst named Huang, whom I'd met several times. Huang knew the markets inside-out and helped Pete model every trade mathematically.

But my fear of job loss seemed a paltry reason to bear their child. And who would I be, running to Pete to rescue me with his hedgie money as he had rescued Alessi? While I was glad that she'd married him, I privately considered Alessi weak and puerile, unable to pull her weight. Would I become that way too?

Nevertheless I stood up, ready to bolt back to Larry's office to say I was not only splitting but quitting.

I sat back down as another voice directed me: "Call Alessi first."

Then another: "Don't you dare. This is all a ruse anyway. You're giving Jack and Alessi just what they each want. What do *you* want?"

I didn't know. Someone else, someone more removed, might know better than

I. Someone else would have to prompt me, like a Magic 8 Ball. And because I didn't trust anyone at the office, I decided to solicit Terry's advice—not Enrico's.

I reflected with fondness that Terry was not a close enough friend to bid for my uterus. She listened to my woes and offered candid feedback. She had overcome anorexia and might cast light upon the emotional murk of hormonal changes brought on by pregnancy.

I turned back to my desk and instant messaged her: *I am in scalding hot water because of JackASS.*

Bummer! she wrote back. *What happened?*

Let's just say my days here aren't numbered. But my weeks are.

Meet us at Eugenia's tonight and we'll talk, Terry wrote back again.

Must we always go to Eugenia's? It's a gathering place for people who perform the same sexual act, like meeting at a bar if you wear the same shoe size, or like the same pizza toppings. And we're the odd ones out.

You're funny! Personally, I like feeling ogled without the attrition of slimy guys. Besides, we always bring Eugenia Win for Life tickets on Thursdays.

I supposed that settled it.

Maybe I'll see you later, I typed back and got offline, thinking that for all I knew, I had won for life.

The problem was, it was no longer my life.

15

Tonight, bartender, I'll have roulette on the rocks.

If I was not going to approach this decision with my usual circumspection, weighing pros against cons or altruism against capital gains, if I called instead upon shapes of geese in flight or tea leaves in china cups, I must do what the Delphic Oracle said. Otherwise there was no point in my seeking Terry's guidance at The Bunny Hop. Otherwise I could think it through myself and make a damn decision.

But every time I tried even listing pros and cons, I checkmated myself. I needed someone else's input, someone with no horses in the race.

Too restless for buses or subways, I trudged three miles downtown from my office, pooped by the time I crossed Houston Street. I didn't want to say yes to Alessi; I didn't want to say no to her.

Let someone else say it.

Let Life say it.

Let Terry tell me what to do.

I pushed open the glass door with a colorful Easter bunny taped to it. Inside, a crowd had clustered around the bar and of course Rick and Terry were among them.

At the center, Bertie and Eugenia locked hands in an arm wrestle. Each sat on a stool with an elbow planted on the bar. Considering that Bertie was much heftier than Eugenia, their gridlock surprised me. But Eugenia was taller, and her scrunched eyes exuded willpower.

Beneath her panama hat, Lainey of the lovely tapioca skin smiled wryly and waved to me. Terry took me aside and whispered, as though they were all characters we'd been following on a reality TV show: "Bertie called Eugenia a 'trailer camp tramp' and said she could slam-dunk her in an arm wrestle. Eugenia said she was sick of the insults."

I should have rooted for Bertie, since I knew her better. But I could not support the provocateur today. My heart sank as Bertie began to prevail, wrestling Eugenia's trembling arm toward the bar.

But Eugenia pushed back, refusing defeat.

"She's really strong," I said to Terry.

"She was a ranked tennis player in Louisiana," Terry told me. "She played pro tournaments and was just shy of a doubles match with Chris Evert."

Eugenia revived her arm to its three-quarter standing. When Bertie stood up for leverage, that tall guy Arbie with the shaved head shouted: "Fault!"

Some women chorused in with him: "Yeah, hey, no standing, Bertie."

"Fuck it!" Bertie yanked her hand out of Eugenia's.

"Tie!" cried someone.

"NOT!" Bertie cried back. "I was winning!"

She skulked off somewhere with Lainey, grousing and gesticulating.

Meanwhile Eugenia drifted back behind the bar, bypassing the outstretched arms of admirers. Arbie cupped his hands and bellowed: "Advantage: Eugenia!"

Terry explained, "He comes in every day, with an egg sandwich on a roll and the *Daily News*. His name is Arbie or something. He was a Marine and he's not gay. But since he plays lotto with Eugenia, he can hang here, even though some customers don't like him." I remembered that Claudia had painted him with similar strokes.

The jukebox kicked on while rowdy girls at the bar slapped hands and high-fived Eugenia. She turned her cheek demurely for their kisses—even her vanity exuded a brightness in which they basked.

"She would have made a good tennis star," I observed.

"Oh, totally," said Terry. "Too bad about her back injuries."

"What injuries?"

"Herniated discs, I think. Something like that. You'd never guess because she's so poised."

If anyone, I then realized, Eugenia could tell me something I didn't know. That's why Terry was devoted to her—Terry didn't know it either. Eugenia had advised me not to "play their game." I could mine her depths to clarify what on earth that meant, in this world of game-playing. Men confessed to their local bartenders as to a priest and in that sacerdotal way, I could share my plight with her.

"Let's get a drink," I suggested, eyeing empty stools at the opposite end of the bar from the revelers.

"So the hull's hit, but the ship isn't listing?" Rick asked as we sat down.

"I don't know what kind of 1990s bubble I've been floating in," I told them. "To think I could remain secure forever. Who's ever so lucky on a job?"

"What happened today?" asked Terry.

My gut burned when I recalled them all standing by my office and deciding I'd screwed up, blaming me and derailing me with no evidence.

"You know, I've never been in trouble, and I'm no good at it." I shut my eyes in the dizziness of implications for a moment. "I'm actually thin-skinned."

"You could get another staff job," Rick suggested logically. "Have you worked in television? I hear CNN is looking for people."

I ceded his point without enthusiasm. Certainly I could show persuasive samples to a new cast of characters in print, new media, or TV. But I was getting old in advertising years. There was no guarantee that another job would be better than what I had. It might even be worse.

Still high from her victory, Eugenia ambled our way down the bar. Her stylishly tousled hair and flushed cheeks were dramatically offset by a black Harley-Davidson tank top adorned with its landing eagle.

"Stella Artois on tap."

She glided the glass and a napkin to Rick.

"Diet chocolate martini for the lady."

I didn't dare ask Terry what was in that.

"What can I get you, cutie?"

Eugenia smiled warmly at me.

"How about two minutes of your time and a gin martini?"

She went off to perform her martini rumba, and when she returned, I pardoned myself from a rather stunned Rick and Terry.

"What's up?" Eugenia asked, pouring my martini smoothly into a glass with a toothpick-speared olive.

Propping myself upon one knee on the barstool, my other foot on the floor, I said: "I work in marketing. Would you be willing to answer a short survey we're developing for a client in legal advocacy?"

She asked, in a tone that was neither friendly nor unfriendly, "Why do you want my opinion?"

My heart shot into my throat. I couldn't believe I was doing this.

"We need a random sampling. I've gotten a lot of responses from New Yorkers and northeasterners…"

"I'm not typical of where I'm from," she said. "I'm kind of…barely on speaking terms with it."

"Doesn't matter. We need some regional variety."

"All right."

She stepped back from me, crammed a cigarette between her lips with a smoker's frown, and flicked a lighter over it. I opened my leather bag and pretended to look through it.

"I'm sure I have a copy of the survey…Thought I did…"

"Be right back."

She placed her cigarette on the rim of a glass ashtray and pushed it away from me, clearly used to accommodating nonsmokers and always able to identify us. Then she headed down the bar to refresh people's drinks and light their cigarettes.

Rick appeared to ask me, "What are you doing?"

"I'll tell you after I do it."

Of course I had no intention of telling him and Terry much at all.

He backed off as I rummaged in my bag for a spiral notebook and ripped out a page.

Then I wrote: *Date* and *City of Birth*, and *Religious Background*. I listed several annual incomes. My hand quaking slightly, I drew two little boxes and wrote *yes* next to one and *no* beside the other.

Whichever box Eugenia checked would cast our lots—Pete and Alessi's, their potential child's, and mine.

I handed it to Eugenia with my pen when she returned.

"I couldn't find the survey, but I remember it perfectly. We don't even need your name. Just a couple of demographics, and one yes/no question."

"Don't go spreading this stuff around, okay?" She glanced over the questions.

"It's confidential on our end too," I reassured her. "And I appreciate it."

After filling in the demographics, she handed the paper back to me. As I sampled my martini, I read through long, slanted writing that she was born in Monroe, Louisiana, would be thirty-six in August, and described herself as "Southern Baptist gone pagan." For annual income she had written *Duh!* beside *Under $100,000.*

"Okay," I said, placing the paper on the bar between us and leaning in as though to confess. Sensing the significance of this matter, she lowered her head to mine.

"Here's the yes/no question: would you bear the child of a wealthy, infertile couple if they gave you a hedge fund account worth two million dollars?"

"Say *what*?" She laughed, reached for her cigarette, and took a drag. A loose tuft of blonde hair trickled down her forehead and over her cheek.

I repeated the question, strangely pleased to watch her beautiful features flinch under the stress of my quandary.

"I'd do almost anything for a couple of million bucks," she said finally. "But I can't wrap my head around all that. You know, my kid brother was hit up for donor sperm last year—seems there's a shortage in our blond-and-blue-eyed pool."

I leaned in more since she was soft-spoken, like a muted clarinet, and still had that faint regional accent. The jukebox and shouting around us nearly swallowed her words. "He didn't do it, though he needed the cash. Figured he wasn't just giving his sperm…he'd be giving his kids to total strangers."

"No genetics or sex involved in this equation," I clarified. "Just the old turkey baster: their egg, their sperm, your uterus—gestational surrogacy."

"Got it," she said with a nod. "They want *their* kid so bad they'll pay the stork two whole Texas digits."

"The hedge fund account could net you a couple of hundred grand a year in profit, after taxes and commissions."

"For how many years?"

"As long as you want."

"And it's liquid?"

"There's a lock-up arrangement…Ask it to flow and it flows."

"Hot damn!" Cigarette in her mouth, she continued speaking. "'Course I'd do it." She grabbed the pen. "That's a no-brainer."

But I stopped her before she could check my little *yes* box.

"Is it really?" I defied her. "Let's explore this for a minute, Eugenia. It may not be your child, but it is your time, your energy, your body…"

She removed her cigarette and exhaled before speaking.

"Well, babe, working this bar is my time, my energy, my body…and where's my big reward?"

More hair fell over her eyes, softer and less brash than dyed blonde hair. This was the real deal; I could tell by the downy roots at her temples. She looked like she'd been dipped in sunlight, and some of it had stuck to her brows and eyelashes.

Enjoying my attention, she raked a bit more hair with her long fingers. Blondes look seductive with hair in their faces like that. We brunettes can't pull it off—we just look like mental patients.

"Suppose this rich couple completely invaded your privacy?"

"Privacy?"

"Let's say they drove you crazy, micromanaged what you ate…"

"Most people drive me crazy. How many clouds have a gold lining?"

I felt sudden tenderness for Alessi, my recklessly generous friend.

"Yo, Gene!" someone roared from down the bar.

"Blondie, we need some change…"

"Privacy," she muttered again, before whisking off to those customers.

"How's it going?" Rick ventured over to ask.

"We're getting somewhere," I replied obliquely, swigging my martini and looking away from him. When Eugenia returned, he politely stepped off again.

"Strange survey question, if you don't mind my saying," she commented. "Who wouldn't go for a deal like that?"

"Most women we've asked say no."

Eugenia parked a hand on her lean hip and asked, "Why?"

"Well," I told her, "religious women claim this procedure intervenes with God's will. And they believe the gift of life should be free, or at least not for profit…"

"You know anyone with AIDS or cancer? Ask them how free the gift of life is."

"Our client opposes religious groups. That's why she's advocating for surrogate motherhood in New York State. But beyond religious objections, most secular women just say they'd feel used."

"Used?" Eugenia threw her head back for a moment. "Pardon me—getting a couple of million for nine months? Women's work finally paying off and we shoot ourselves in the toe." Then she leaned in and whispered, "You can bet that if guys gave birth, this wouldn't be a survey question. It would be a black market."

She drew back and looked almost severe, as if to hint that I should use my head. But that was exactly what I didn't want to do.

"Personally," she went on, "I don't want to be bartending when I'm fifty years old. I wouldn't do it tomorrow, if I had a choice."

She lifted the pen, and again I stopped her.

"What would you do with all that money?"

Her eyes turned especially blue, even in the low light.

"Sweet Jesus. What would I NOT do?"

"Seriously..."

"Well, I wouldn't blow it up my nose, if that's what you're thinking. If I got in on hedge fund money...you know...can you imagine the difference even a few good people could make?"

I hadn't been imagining that.

"You're tempted by the cash," I persisted. "Everyone is, abstractly. But few people can actually handle having it."

"Let that be my problem. Okay, I'll tell you exactly what I'd do. First, I'd pamper myself after I had the baby. I'd go to the spa, get massages. I'd help my friends out of debt, buy a bigger house for my kid brother and his family..." She shut her eyes for a second as if she was riding in a convertible with a breeze on her face. "If I made a serious profit after a couple of years," she continued, opening those bright blue eyes again, "I guess I'd buy land in Hawaii or some south sea island like Bora Bora. I'd start a surfing and coconut-harvesting utopia. But before anything..."— she held up her cigarette—"I'd quit this nasty habit."

"You should anyway."

"No motivation here, with everyone else's smoke."

It was disconcerting that someone of such feminine beauty held her cigarette like a guy, without a trace of daintiness. It was also disconcerting that a former pro tennis player smoked cigarettes.

"Have you ever been pregnant?"

She shook her head.

"Did you ever want a child?"

She balked as though I'd asked her if she ever wanted to drive across frozen tundra.

I narrowed my eyes at her. "Would you really subject your streamlined abs to the ravages of pregnancy, even for that kind of cash?"

A smile lifted her lips again as I hit the vanity nerve. She was the kind of person who smiled as much with her eyes and her cheekbones as with her lips.

"My mom had six of us," she said. "Last photo I saw, she's still a string bean."

"Suppose you had twins. That happens with these inseminations."

"Then I'd ask for twice the payment."

She flipped her head and dragged on her cigarette again, apparently entertained.

"So you'd go through all these exams and hormone shots and morning sickness and varicose veins."

Still smiling, she squashed her cigarette in the ashtray. Then she picked up my pen and checked the *yes* box.

"Couple of ultrasounds won't kill me. Set me up with this deal."

"I wish I could."

She brushed my arm gently with her index finger. "You can."

After that, a chubby woman with cat-eyed glasses and a couple of older women with short hair settled at the bar, and Eugenia scurried off to them.

I folded the survey form into my bag and sneaked behind the pool table for a moment to myself. The air was light. I remembered an embroidered silk jacket I had seen last fall in the Fifth Avenue windows of Bergdorf's, an unjustifiable indulgence. But now I could have that, or any number of wardrobe delicacies, without sacrifice. The next time Jordan asked for a loan of five hundred dollars, I could blink it out of my eye.

And there would be a next time. In fact, I could keep a stable of strapping young gigolos if I wanted. I could pay off their student loans, feed them, and outfit them in the latest overpriced ripped jeans. Anything was possible.

I slipped out my cell phone, eager to tell Alessi that I was on board with her.

But when I made my announcement, my old friend said nothing.

"Hello? Are you there?" I asked.

"Where are you, with all that noise?"

"At a bar with friends."

"Great, Molly! So…will you still love us tomorrow?"

"What?"

I put my free hand into my other ear so I could hear the cell phone better.

"Is this just your mad mood of the moment? I know how you are. Are you going to treat me and Pete like you treat your boyfriends, here today and gone tomorrow?"

"How could you say that?"

"Easily. Look, call me tomorrow morning if you feel the same way."

She was going to drive me crazy, but Eugenia was right: a downpour is worth it when the cloud is lined with gold. As the old song went, "make sure your umbrella is upside-down." My whole life would be upside-down.

When I returned to the bar, Terry linked her arm into mine.

"You broke the record," she whispered. "No one talks to Eugenia for more than three sentences at a time. She must like you. Let her know you're not gay."

Finishing my martini, I surged into a grand, dizzying mood. My thoughts were far from the bar and whatever Terry was saying. As for Larry and Jack, they could think what they wanted about me. It was no longer important.

"Hey, would you teach me some 3D programs if I hired you?" I asked Terry excitedly.

"Sure. That would be fun."

As Terry and I carried on like two silly teenagers, I sensed Eugenia's disdain from behind the bar. The conversation that had uplifted me seemed to have saddened her. Meanwhile, Rick fanned her Win for Life tickets out on the bar.

She glanced at them and then over to me, like an animal about to be shorn of its fur. Somehow she knew I was skipping off with her dream.

PART TWO

16

"I can look my life in the eye again," Pete confided the next day at his office. Outside the long window behind him stretched a panorama of New York harbor, the sun-glazed bay studded with ferries and barges. Further in the distance Lady Liberty cut her familiar silhouette against the horizon.

"I'm not feeling shabby myself."

And why should I, with an initial fifty grand in case I got axed from my job? The rest would go into my account with Goldenrain Asset Management.

"There aren't even thirty investors, you know," Pete reminded me. "One is pulling out to buy mortgages—a class I avoid. I'll set up an account in your name next week. Meanwhile, let's get you a cashier's check for the fifty."

We were moving inexorably fast. But I thought of Eugenia last night crowing, "Sweet Jesus…if I got in on hedge fund money…"

And I beamed at Pete.

"Molly, when we spoke two weeks ago, you didn't want to do this. Now you're the poster child of enthusiasm. What changed your mind?"

"A conversation last night in a bar."

"So Alessi told me. With anyone we know?"

"Total stranger."

"Perfect. Who?"

"A bartender who's about our age. I phrased it all to her as a marketing survey question. She made a good case for earning two million dollars in nine months doing something benign."

Pete shot me a "tried to tell you" look.

"This person has no stake in it. She doesn't know me from Eve."

"Alessi says you can keep a secret like no one's business. That's another reason we wanted to work with you. See…" He sank back into his leather chair. Then he leaned forward. We were both jittery, like astronauts losing gravity. "Here's the drill. In the months ahead, we'll be more frank with each other than friends usually are."

"Okay…"

"Most of our colleagues and, for that matter, our competitors, are aboveboard. But a couple of them would love to get ahold of some scandal and blow us out of the water. Not that we're household names. I don't think we'd make tabloid headlines. But within the wealth management community…"

"I hear you. There's a river rat at my office trying to smear me, which is why I'll be canned."

It was time for a hedge fund account, a back door "fuck you" fund.

Pete went on, "Surrogate mothers aren't supposed to be New York State residents. People do it here, but there's…ambivalence, as we've discussed. We'll have to get around that. So we appreciate your tact."

"You can count on it."

He seemed heartened.

"I'll get you a credit card for your medical, travel, and legal expenses, so we can separate costs associated with the procedure. You know that we'll do it at an assisted fertility center in Oregon. That's where we've gone before."

I didn't know but nodded.

"It's the best in the country. By the way, I'm sorry for how she spoke to you last night…" he murmured in a familial tone.

"Please don't worry."

"No. I worry. I can't tell you how bad things have been. We're going to deal with it in therapy. You'll be coming with us."

"I—*excuse me*?"

"We've been working with this agency. Even though they didn't match us with our surrogate mother, of course, they suggest that we all get counseling with a trained social worker."

"Since when?"

"Since now."

"Don't you remember the fiasco psychoanalysis Eleanor forced down my throat with the deaf-mute quack? You know I hate all that."

"I used to hate it too," said Pete. "But I probably owe my marriage and future family to it."

Apparently clouds with gold linings would not prove lightweight.

"You know, Pete," I began, "we should write out an informal agreement about what to expect before the attorneys draw up our papers. This way, we won't be springing things on each other."

"Good idea," he agreed. "We're friends, but we're also..."

"Family now. And we're partners. You're handing me a lot of money today. If you like, we can even get our statement notarized."

And the word *notarized* made me wonder if I had an alibi for Larry.

17

Rummaging through my drawers at home later, I slammed my fingers against every silly thing from my passport to a pair of sunglasses; I could not have felt more flustered had I been at Eleanor's twelve years ago in a whirlpool of cancelled checks, unread magazines, and dog biscuits. No doubt that my own piles were tidier than hers had been, the corners squared off and not avalanching all over the room. But they made equally little sense.

I too faced a mixture of stuff I wanted to keep, in a cloying way, like a well-designed direct-mail piece; a dazzling postcard from a friend in Madagascar; a folded issue of *Advertising Age* with a survey that suggested single women were happier, on the whole, than married women—and scrap paper I should have tossed long ago, like membership to a video rental that had closed; a colored Post-it with someone's email address; and a scribbled shopping list of Perrier, toilet paper, butter, toothpaste, and Ajax. I flung it across the room, howling at a decibel that I seldom achieved, "Dammit!"

Why was I so upset; why did I care that I was finding every dumb paper but the notarized agreement that Jordan and I had signed the other week? I was planning to leave the job. Why was it important to vindicate myself in Larry's eyes?

I simply had to see if my hunch had merit. Had I been at the bank lending Jordan five hundred bucks when my initials were recorded on that routing sheet? As it happened, I would need credibility if I wished to start a business, and Larry had been my longest employer.

But it was more than that. Larry Applebaum and I had spent hours together, not only business hours but evenings and weekends. That's what it had taken, as we built up our clientele. And actually, I had not minded. What was I missing on Saturday afternoons—a flurry of bridal or baby showers? I preferred designing a campaign or editing copy to sitting in some chain restaurant, sipping dank wine as present after present was divested of its identical wrapping paper because the bride or mother-to-be had registered at a department store and knew exactly what she was getting anyway.

Larry used to thank me profusely for my overtime, but he was exempting me from occasions more wearing than the job.

"When people at these showers ask me what am I doing or who am I doing, I'm really bored by my answers. You'd think I'd like talking about myself," I had told him once.

"Not in those circumstances," Larry agreed. "It's like filling out government forms."

"Or even worse—it's like lip-syncing your own life."

"Odd that you think so," he commented. "Thought I hated these occasions since I'm unwelcome. But you're straight, you're an insider."

"Not really. There are subdivisions of the straight world too. The unmarried among us are never insiders after a certain age."

When Larry had hired me, we'd both been dating. Sometimes for fun we accorded our dates celebrity nicknames, more aptly with his "Jude Law" and "Matt Dillon" than my "Ted Kennedy" (a typical frat boy with arrested development) or "Al Pacino" (who must have worked for the CIA and mysteriously vanished to a country I could never pronounce on the Caspian Sea).

Larry and I had shaken hands on "never wanting to be the kind of people that settle down with someone and talk about laundry and car insurance."

Then one evening four years ago, when we were working overtime on an annual report, he'd gasped. "Molly, don't kill me. I actually met someone I'm dying to settle down with and talk about laundry and car insurance."

I had been excited for Larry when he described Steve—no movie star moniker, just Steve—Larry's blond, WASPy counterpart. I knew about Steve through all their phases of courtship: jumping in with zesty infatuation; Larry describing "unprecedented bonding and empathy, even beyond sex"; Steve pulling back because Larry was "too high-strung and intense"; Larry begging me for "WASPy advice on not being intense"; me pleading "Celtic and not strictly WASPy" enough and too temperamental for my own good; Larry complementing my control of it and eliciting tips that I doubted were useful; Steve finally moving in with Larry, and the rest "being history."

They had the prescience to buy a "fabulous" historical brownstone in Carroll Gardens with a yard, just before the city's real estate values spiked. For three years now they had lived there with a dog called Buffy and two Siamese cats. I had visited a number of times with Thomas.

The cold, impatient way Larry had spoken to me yesterday afternoon didn't reflect our years of collegial friendship.

Furiously I unbuckled my leather bag and turned it over. Onto the floor spilled the usual suspects: keys, wallet, checkbook, lipstick, hairbrush, Tampax, a snifter of perfume, small bar of deodorant, dental floss, an old Altoids tin filled with condoms.

Then came the spiral notebook and the folded paper from it with Eugenia's "survey." For a moment I unfolded it and glanced again at her long, slanted handwriting. *Monroe, Louisiana. August 15, 1964, Southern Baptist gone pagan.* One day, I resolved, I would show up like Santa Claus at the Bunny Hop with a round-trip ticket for her to Maui or Bora Bora. It was the least I could do.

The next morning at the office I found my notarized agreement with Jordan, and the bank withdrawal slip for five hundred dollars, in my desk drawer. It proved that I had indeed been out of the office when the routing sheet was "signed off by me."

It was a while, though, before I was able to bring this evidence to Larry's attention. He was away for a couple of days, in Philly schmoozing a hopeful new client.
Meanwhile, I'd taken several afternoons and one long lunch to be draped in sweet
little Alice-blue gowns so my orifices could be probed and smeared. As a finale,
my uterus was pumped with water so the ultrasound could detect any abnormali-
ties—and I was proclaimed sterling.

I had also insisted upon a neuropsychological evaluation, telling Alessi and
Pete that I'd been "forgetful lately." They thought I was silly, but I didn't want to be
their surrogate mother if my memory was impaired.

Obliging my idiosyncrasies as I obliged hers, Alessi found a psychologist who
performed evaluations for dementia and "age-related memory decline." Dr. Halpern, who looked like a rabbi without a yarmulke in a herringbone tweed jacket,
told me that I was the youngest patient in his years of practice to have requested
this evaluation.

"And frankly, on the basis of our clinical interview, your IQ scores, Wechsler
scales, and your memory-complaint questionnaire," he told me, "I don't understand why you're here. Misplacing pens or not remembering a glass of orange
juice in your sink are hardly impediments to cognitive performance. There's no
indication that you have any problem."

"But I'm doing things and not remembering them *the same day.*"

His office smelled like an oily scalp, or like a beard. He must have had the
same Danish Modern couch since the 1970s, its pillows filled with pebbly, decom-
posed foam.

"Short-term memory is volatile by its nature. This is true for everyone."

I bit my lip. He didn't grasp the significance of that glass of orange juice. I
didn't even want to mention that strange odor of glue and tiny shavings of colored
plastic I'd noticed in my rug.

"In the presence of distractions, short-term memory starts to decay," he continued.

"But that's tragic," I protested. "Life is full of distractions."

Once Larry got back to town, I thumped on his door with my notarized agreement and xeroxed routing sheet in tow—ready to prove my innocence and indict someone else. The door was partly opened, and he was on the phone. I caught agitated fragments of conversation like "…all being relegated to administrative functions now…straying from Gropius, Breuer, and the Bauhaus. The industry's been broadsided by Microsoft."

I peeked in and beckoned to him.

"Is it important, Molly?"

"I think so."

"I'll call you back," he said to whomever he'd been speaking with.

I strutted across the caramelized bamboo floor and presented my 'exhibits.'

Larry stared from the routing sheet to the notary's stamp. He ran his finger along the embossed seal, concluding: "Even *you* can't fake this in Photoshop."

Then I showed him my bank teller's withdrawal slip.

"Who's Jordan Radfar?" he finally asked.

"One of the so-called strange men I was observed with on a lunch break the other week."

"He must be cute if you were lending him five hundred bucks."

"Cute and broke."

At this Larry looked up and peered intently at me through his glasses.

"I got it all back," I added. "The point is, there's no way I could have routed the job out the door at 11:54 and been at the bank at 11:53."

"No disagreement, Molly."

"Besides, I don't write fours that 'box step' way." I pointed to the four in *11:54* on the routing sheet. "I always made 'sailboat fours' ever since I was a kid. Do you still have my job application? I had fours in my phone number."

"Look, I believe you," Larry ceded. "I'd be an idiot if I didn't. It's all here, with a notary stamp and seal." He solemnly handed the papers back to me. "Anyway, you're not behaving like a culprit, but like a beleaguered victim. Now the question is, of course…if you didn't erroneously route this job, who did? And why in hell did he or she sign your initials?"

I knew perfectly well but shrugged as if I was stumped.

"Someone underwent considerable effort to pull off this forgery."

"Bet they traced my signature on the lighting table."

"Who around here would be…devious like that? I screen everyone so carefully before I make a job offer. I get references and cross-references. We've never had a problem before, and we sure don't need one now. Has anyone been giving you grief? Do you have a sense of who this could be? We've got to find out and get 'em out of here."

"It's not me and it's not you," I said. "I wouldn't rule out anyone else."

"But why would an account rep sabotage us? It must be someone who covets your position. One of the new designers? Gee, do you think it's Casey?"

"Who knows?

"Maybe she wants your job. What motive other than jealousy could there be?"

If Larry couldn't see for himself, I didn't want to be the messenger who risked getting shot. I still hadn't quite recovered from his telling me last week that I "might need a vacation."

An hour later I got an email from him, which apparently was sent to everyone in the office. *From now on*, Larry wrote, *all jobs must be signed off by either me or Molly Douglas. Anyone, including senior management, who authorizes an outgoing folder without my signature or Molly's will be terminated immediately.*

My cheeks warmed. I raised fisted arms—my team had just scored a run. I could imagine the shade of Jack Ashlund's skin as he read this one. I could imagine his head stopped midway in its bobbing.

"Yessss!" I hissed under my breath.

I even sent Terry an IM. I didn't want to appeal to her only when I was down.

Today is V-JackASS day.

Was he whacked?

No. But the tables have turned. My name has been cleared.

So you can stay on your job, can't you?

If I were second in command now, I certainly should.

18

By the time I got home I was miserable.

Alessi and Pete saw from my test results that I was a first-rate candidate for surrogate motherhood, with no scar tissue, no tipped uterus, no fibroids, no ovarian cysts. My blood was clear of HIV, hepatitis, and venereal disease. My progesterone level was dandy. Dr. Halpern had emailed them that my brain function was not only typical, "but sharper than normal. Her IQ is in the top two percentile. Why is she worried about her memory? Tell her to relax."

The problem was neither my physical condition, nor my circumstances. I was the picture of health and security, with cash flow, fifty grand stashed in an interest-bearing CD, and a hedge fund account for two million dollars. I had a sizzling sex life and had just neutralized a slimy supervisor.

My problem was indecision, or inability to live by the decisions I had delegated to someone else. Alessi had it right—would I still love them tomorrow?

I trudged upstairs and stopped, my heart heavy with buyer's remorse. Why on earth had I agreed to blow myself up with Pete and Alessi's gametes and live in seclusion to perform this secret deed for a decadent amount of money that a stranger named Eugenia had ideas about spending?

Mentally, I flagellated myself for being susceptible to a barroom flirt. Would she really lie back with open legs in a sweet little Alice-blue gown while a male gynecologist routed around her private parts, she of the philanthropic dreams to start utopias in the South Seas? Would she really tolerate psychodrama at a social worker's with Pete and Alessi?

As I passed Claudia's door, her roommate, Lauren, was belting out into the evening that she would survive, she would survive!

It was, of course, inexcusable that I blame Eugenia for anything. She had even asked, "Why do you want my opinion?"

Why did I?

Finally upstairs, I turned my key in the lock, opened my apartment door, and screamed. The oak table flickered with candlelight and a vase of orchids, almost like a hallucination until…

"Surprise!" called a couple of voices.

Claudia stepped forward in gray pleated trousers, a T-shirt that said *Mojosexual* and pink ribbon in her black hair.

Strung across my living room was a huge banner with *We Love You, Molly!* scrawled in magic marker.

Had she found out about this sweetheart deal? Had Eugenia spilled the beans?

A guy in a double-breasted suit stood by her side, grinning.

"Oh my God!"

I walked, trancelike, over to Jordan, stroked his shaved cheeks and coiffed hair, and inhaled cologne. If my brain was distressed, my senses were intoxicated.

"We scored today, thanks to her." Jordan pointed to Claudia. "It's even more of a go-go-go than we thought, with the girls in Paris."

"They laid out for Western Hemisphere cannabis."

Jordan and Claudia slapped each other's hands in jubilation.

"If we keep this up I can even dump the old songbird by summer," Claudia cried. "She is driving me fucking insane in my own home."

"She's even driving me insane as I pass by on my way upstairs," I confessed.

Then my doorbell rang—short, swift, nasal.

"Now who's *that*?"

"A delivery from the Thai place. We know you well," said Claudia. "A meal that will never touch the kitchen. Molly's favorite kind."

She buzzed the delivery boy in, took the large paper bag of food from him, and tipped generously. I was still too stunned to speak as she pried plastic lids off rounded tin foil platters, gurgling, "Scrumptious, fuckable food that *we* can afford now!"

Jordan gallantly pulled a chair out from the table for me.

"Jordan as gentleman," I remarked over my shoulder. "I'll have to acclimate."

"Drug money," he commented.

"It's an exciting new direction for him," added Claudia, licking her finger of papaya sauce and repeating, "Yummy, fuckable food."

"It was time for a change in my style," he volunteered. "My grandmother will like it."

What would they think of him in my office now? No more an "unkempt kid," Jordan had become an arm-trophy boyfriend. I couldn't take my eyes off him as he sat smiling awkwardly.

"What's wrong?" he asked.

"Nothing. She *likes* how I buffed you up," Claudia insisted. "Right? She's in shock that I've done such a sweet job. But a lesbian knows what women want."

Indeed, more women would want him now that Jordan was no longer my gem in the raw. I couldn't let that on.

"We all know about 'fag hags,'" I began. "Well… Jordan's becoming…a dyke tyke."

They laughed and kept repeating, "We love you, Molly!"

"What is this 'we love you Molly' business?"

"Well, we do. You help us when we're down."

"You introduced us," Claudia pointed out.

"You treat us to incredible meals," Jordan added.

"We don't want you to feel unappreciated."

"So this is Molly Appreciation Night."

"We want to give you something back, for once."

"I'm…thank you." I looked back and forth between them. "This is very touching."

I treasure my privacy but that night was grateful not to be condemned to a lifeless apartment.

"So what can I serve you?" asked Claudia. "Crispy Basil Duck Spring Roll to start? Pad Thai? Garlic Prawns? Coconut Red Curry with Bamboo Shoots and Shrimp?"

"A little of everything, please."

Claudia ladled the steaming delicacies onto my plate and Jordan got up to pour me mineral water with a twist of lime.

"Talk about service—this is like having a husband and wife at once."

"We'll perform different tasks," Claudia established. "He'll do sex and live music. I'll cover fine dining and flower arrangement."

Yes, I thought, and I will foot the bill. This was, after all, some version of Alessi's scheme. She too now had a husband and wife.

"This beats a mail-order bride," I commented. "Looks like I've got the Value Pack."

"Well you *can* think of marrying Jordan," Claudia declared, "now that he's presentable and earning money—even if he's not earning in a presentable way."

"At least I could meet your family at Easter," he said as he sat down again, after pouring me a glass of water.

"I don't even want to see my family on Easter. Why would you?"

"It would help our relationship."

So that's what this fanfare was about—their latest strategy of hooking me. I was almost relieved because the lovey-dovey routine was becoming stressful.

"You can't let it rest, can you?"

I reached out again and stroked his silky cheek.

"Molly, this guy adores you. You keep saying you want to have a kid. Well, he's extending your biological clock."

"How do you get that?" I asked Claudia.

"Add your ages together and divide them by two. That will be your median age, as parents."

"You've hired quite the publicist here," I said to him.

But I realized that Claudia actually had a point.

I shouldn't blow this chance, at my age—especially now that I was being groomed to spend a year bearing someone else's child.

19

Pete and Alessi's attorney, Harry, was still hammering out our surrogacy agreement, raking over imponderables, such as any of us dying during the pregnancy—and the extent to which I might breastfeed the baby. Once the agreement was drafted it would be sent to my attorney for redlining. We would probably not sign off for another few weeks.

I had time to back out of the agreement and topple Alessi's apple cart as I had toppled Thomas' less than a year ago. Everyone had plans for me, and I had disappointments for everyone.

But Saturday, when I went up to visit them, I saw that opting out was not remotely possible. Alessi even outlined my pregnancy diet: No exotic spices, trans fats or refined carbs. Saturated fats, whole grains, fruits, and vegetables would become my new staples. My intake of alcohol and coffee would have to be rationed and, by the way, Alessi didn't think I should be having sex just now. She was no fool. What with Murphy's Law, she feared that I would get pregnant and derail the whole plan.

Pete was more benevolent. "If Molly's content and well," he claimed, "everything will work out."

Before Alessi could accuse him of oversimplification, Pete reminded her that I'd be using birth control pills. I had been apprised but had forgotten, in my general excitement, that Alessi and I would synchronize our menstrual cycles by taking the pill together for a month or two before the grand insemination. That way, her eggs would land in the right place (my body) at the right time (her cycle).

We'd be given twin prescriptions, like our matching fifth-grade friendship bracelets. I had never resorted to the pill before and wasn't looking forward to it.

"I don't want to get fat and moody. I'm moody enough."

"It's only for a couple of months," Alessi reminded me. "And the day you get fat, Molly, is the day I stick to a budget."

That got more than a chortle out of Pete. They sat across from me on their burgundy chaise, her left hand with its sparkling diamond on his knee. It was always strange to see Pete in jeans and a V-neck sweater because I pictured him perennially in customized British or Italian suits. Wood snapped in the hearth, mingling its fragrance with the braised beef casserole that Alessi had in the oven. She had just brewed us a pot of orange spice tea and was serving it with a tangy aperitif called Limoncello from the Amalfi coast.

It was good to see her up and about again—even as I was being torqued into some abridged version. Gracious, attentive hosts, Pete and Alessi were again the charming couple who'd inspired envy among our peers since the day he suddenly flew her to Aruba on a private jet and proposed to her on his knees in the sand.

"So what's his name?"

I reached for the glass of orange spice tea, brought it to my lips, and sent it away again—too hot to drink.

"Can we get a name here for this guy you've been porking?" Alessi persisted.

"No."

"He's that unimportant? Then why are you having sex with him and risking our plan?"

"What kind of a question is that?"

I laughed uneasily at my old friend. Every day since the surprise Thai food "Molly Fest," I'd come home from work to find Jordan stretched out on my sofa, either fast asleep with a Coltrane CD playing or getting high as he watched a loud game show.

I would accuse him of wallowing, living presumably on the advance from his Parisian customers and donations from me. He'd call me a "bourgeois skin horse."

"Well," I would reply, "something pays for your dinner, doesn't it?"

Inevitably, when night fell and took our pants down with it, all was forgiven.

"You sure work fast," Alessi goaded me now. "Didn't you and Thomas just break up last summer?"

I leaned back on the Windsor rocker and folded my arms.

"Hey, uh, 'A'—" Pete stroked her arm. "Think we can ease up on Molly?"

This reference bore the significance of something discussed in therapy. Pete and Alessi met each week with a couples' counselor as well as with the social worker whom I would also soon have the pleasure of visiting. As my life became a bonanza of hormones, theirs was quickly becoming a bonanza of therapy.

Was any child worth all this?

Then I felt him for the first time, like a star in the afternoon sky. I didn't yet know him as Andy, but I sensed a twinkle of the child I was helping into human existence.

The Buddhists claim there are four ways to be born—from a womb, from an egg, from warmth, or from a miracle. In-vitro included all of these, reshuffling the egg into womb via warmth and allowing for the miracle.

That was how Andy had been drawn to Earth and turned away, ejaculated by his dad and suctioned from his mother's follicles, mated in a petri dish, and implanted back in her womb, only to be declined several times by the border police between human life and the Great Unseen.

"You'll have to tell your boyfriend something," Alessi was saying to me. Yes, I would. Jordan was presenting problems for her. But June and the insemination still seemed a long way off. We hadn't yet gotten through Easter. One more season remained for my taking, before the terms changed.

And it was the succulent transition between Lent and summer that embroidered branches with blossom and stretched daylight into the evening skies. In June I would surrender my autonomy just when light began its own surrender. This year, much would disappear.

"Or are you planning to just disappear?" she continued.

"I can't 'just disappear.' I'm not a nomadic twenty-one-year-old."

In our college days both Alessi and I had left baffled young men awaiting us at La Gare du Nord in Paris, or the ferry to Block Island.

"We know that you'll need to tell the important people in your life something, when the time comes for you to…overhaul your usual existence," Pete said. "Here's the story we came up with."

I reached for my tea again, which was less scalding, and took a sip.

"You know how I told you, when we cut that check for fifty grand, that I'd make it look like you two are going into business and that I'm your investor?"

"You said we'd make an S Corp, or an LLC."

"Exactly."

"So the story begins," said Alessi, pouring herself more Limoncello from her crested glass decanter. "You've been nervous on the job. You've told most people about that, right? Your boyfriend must know."

"He does."

But of course, that was all changing. Larry had once again become my ardent fan, prancing daily into my office to analyze his spreadsheet of employees that was annotated with suspicious actions or remarks. Jack was still managing to fool him.

"So you're bummed about your job," Pete continued. "And she's blue because of the IVFs. You two hang out together and Alessi offers you a chance to go into business with her. I agree to invest in it."

"What kind of business?" I asked.

"I've got something in mind," she said, "that has to do with interior design."

Alessi had decorated her entire home with finesse and ingenuity, combining eighteenth-century American antiques with streamlined high-tech gadgetry. She had even painted every room herself, declaring it better exercise than a week at the gym.

"The idea is," she explained enthusiastically, "we'll drive around the Poconos and those less-than-chic counties across the river, like Orange or Sullivan, and buy historical houses that are in disrepair—you know, handyman specials. Dad's guys can help us fix them up. We'll do some basic decoration and then turn them over for a profit."

I nodded, cradling a warm porcelain teacup in the palm of my hand.

"We could go to estate auctions and country antique stores, you know, keep ourselves busy instead of waiting around for this baby to pop out."

If I went through with it there would be a stretch of time, between early winter and late March, when I might live with Pete and Alessi to avoid appearing in public with my engorged belly. A real estate and home decor venture would surely occupy us and perhaps even be fun and profitable—so long as I was living like a renegade.

"The story line will go that since you were spending so much time with me and we're in business together, you had volunteered to be my surrogate mother."

"Oh, I did?"

"But at first we didn't go for it," said Pete. "We told you that we decided to adopt. Still, you convinced us to try surrogacy at least once."

I wasn't sure I liked this.

"We said we're hesitant, since New York State discourages surrogate parenting agreements. How did Harry phrase it again?"

"Void, unenforceable, and against public policy."

"But," Alessi continued, "to rephrase Balzac, there's no crime without a great fortune. So we agreed that we'd pay only for your surrogacy expenses and give it a try. Any other big money you've got will come from our business venture and investments together. That's what we've told Harry, for the record."

"We also told him you live in Connecticut."

"Well, I used to. It's where we went to high school."

"Exactly. We've already got you a p.o. box in Greenwich."

"The explanation pretty much holds up," I had to admit. "So long as I don't go into detail with people about how much money I'll have."

"Which you don't want to do anyway," Pete advised.

One person in the world might do a double-take, and that was Eugenia. She might recall the undoctored version of our plan from my survey question.

"Watch what you tell people," Pete suggested. "Now that you're entering the multimillionaire ghetto, you too could be blackmailed. It's not just us."

Eugenia didn't strike me as the nosy or blackmailing type. Still, I planned to keep my distance.

20

But it appeared that our conversation had stuck in Eugenia's craw. At work on Monday morning, Terry wrote, *Guess who asked after you at the Bunny Hop?*

I imagined that Eugenia spoke to a million people at the bar, and I wondered why she was asking about me.

What did she say?

Wants to know if you're coming in again. She has a question. I offered to email it to you, but she wouldn't say it. Aren't you intrigued?

No, I wrote back, and quickly changed the subject. *Tell me what you think. My oldest friend wants me to go into business, flipping houses in the Poconos. Her dad manages contractors, so we'd have handymen at prime rates.*

I wouldn't leave your day job, now that you don't have to… could you do it on the side?

That's what I'm thinking.

Damn! That girl in the next cubicle brought in her toasted bagel again. Wish I didn't have to smell it.

Burned?

No, smells great and I can't stop thinking about it. But I'm cutting out carbs. They turn to sugar in our bodies.

You can take a little sugar, I wanted to write.

Of course we who came of age in the aftermath of Twiggy felt obese if our limbs seemed the slightest bit rounded or convex. But I knew more was going on with Terry. *You could have a bagel every day and it wouldn't matter,* I wrote after a while.

She didn't reply.

But in came an email from JackASS—who had changed his tune with me, as though I had opened the door on him peeing and he wanted to forget that I existed. When we passed in the corridor he looked away briskly and walked on. If I suggested something at a meeting, he chorused a quick assent. Gone were the unwelcome comments about my being single and "such a catch." Gone were any remnants of gratuitous intimidation, his slowly bobbing head, and roving marble eyes.

In this email Jack was trying to schedule a meeting at 4:30 on Friday with some designers and me.

Are you out of your mind? I wrote back to him, brazenly cc-ing the others.

That's Good Friday. You may not have a life, but the rest of us do.

Yes you're right Molly. We will resume next week, he replied, also cc-ing the others.

I reread his meek email several times, pleased with my whip cracking. Where had good manners ever gotten me? Almost fired from a job, almost married to Thomas.

A minute later, someone appeared by my partly opened door, cooing: "Knock-knock."

There was Enrico, his highlighted hair in a scruffy ponytail, his sapphire earrings glittering.

"Come in."

I swiveled around in my chair to face him.

"Can I tell you…I am so glad you put Jack in his place. You are my best friend."

Enrico leaned over and embraced me, briefly patting my back.

"In fact, I was wondering if I could leave after lunch on Friday?"

Half the staff planned to take Friday off, and many of us would be out next week. Technically, I was not supposed to grant anyone permission to take such liberties, even though I supervised Enrico and the other junior designers. We all reported to Jack, at least in theory, while ultimately Larry approved everyone's time off.

But I hadn't sought Jack's permission to leave for my medical appointments. I had just written Larry a note that I would be out at those times.

"It's fine," I told Enrico. "But please let Larry know that you've spoken to me."

Now I would see where my boss stood. If Larry reprimanded me for stepping out of line, then I could count on more surprise reversals from him.

But if he said "a-okay," then I really had become his second in command.

And where, I wondered, would that leave Jack?

21

"You got a bitch at home," Claudia observed. Jordan hung around my apartment like a sedated housewife, sleeping until noon, getting high, watching TV, playing music, and making half-assed attempts to shop and clean. But I felt flattered by his dependence on me and, as spring ripened, randy and glad enough to see him after work. These would be my last weeks of privacy before I went to the fertility center in Oregon. And he still represented an escape from Pete and Alessi—albeit an increasingly abstract one, as I started the birth control regimen.

When I got home from work that Monday evening, before Easter Friday, the building exuded music—Lauren's hearty rounds of "I Will Survive" as I climbed the stairs, and, sure enough, Jordan's squiggling, squealing arpeggios as I nudged the key into my lock.

I walked over and stroked his shoulder. He put down his instrument and turned his head up to me, his dark eyes topsy-turvy. I pattered my fingers down his chin, past his sharp Adam's apple to the tip of his chest hairs.

"So," he said, after we had nibbled each other's lips. "I'm writing a Charles Ives-type polytonal duet for sax. It's called 'Making Love to Molly.'"

"You're crazy."

"Wanna hear the tenor part?"

I tossed my bag on the sofa and skipped to the refrigerator—not that I'd find much. But sometimes a hit of flavor from restaurant leftovers helped me wind down after a long day at Larry Applebaum's.

"You're coming to my gig tonight, right?" he called.

"Yeah. Jordan—what's this?"

"I made tuna sandwiches for us and got some pickles and chips. Hey, let's eat. First set is at nine, but I gotta go early for tech check."

He popped up behind me at the fridge to retrieve the two sandwiches he'd left on a plate, under a canopy of Saran Wrap. As he carried them and a carton of orange juice to the table, I went to the bathroom to wash my hands. On a shelf across from the sink sat the plastic dispenser of my new birth control pills. I slid them into the medicine chest behind a bottle of peroxide.

When I returned to the table Jordan was stuffing a paper towel into his collar. I sat across from him, hoping he hadn't noticed the birth control pill dispenser in the john.

"You'll meet my sister tonight, Chardonnay. She's off this week for Easter break."

Jordan's younger sister, Robin, studied art history at Bard College, up in Annandale-on-Hudson. Now and then he'd get calls from her.

"She's staying with her friend Liz, who'll be at the show too."

I bit into my tuna sandwich and nearly keeled over sideways. Jordan chomped away, wiping his mouth and talking. But I sat there with a lump of slime lodged in my throat, suddenly in the same bind I had suffered as a child once our cook had gone back to Argentina and my mother had taken over at the stove. The only way I could swallow what Mom cooked was by squirting ketchup or tartar sauce over it.

I began to gag, but Jordan didn't notice. He was telling me about the players in this band—those I knew, those I didn't, who would be on which instrument, and how eager Robin was to meet me.

I pardoned myself by raising my index finger, then walked into the kitchen, grabbed a paper towel and soundlessly spit into it. Through years of practice, I had mastered the art of the soundless spit. As a kid I hadn't understood that food was meant to taste good until I visited Alessi's when I was eight or nine. I didn't know that people erupted into expressions of "Ummmm," and "This is delicious," and thanked the cook. That had not been our family dinner table.

Then I noticed, beside the ripped bag of Lay's potato chips on my kitchen counter, two empty tins of cat food—tuna flavored cat food! I didn't know whether to crack up or throw up.

My phone rang and the machine answered with its usual abridged ditty: "At the tone…"

"Molly, are you there? Sorry to bug you…"

This seemed to be a night for siblings. It was Matt, my brother, so I darted across the living room to answer, gesturing frantically to Jordan as he took a hearty bite of his sandwich.

"Hey," I said into the receiver.

"You're home. What's up?"

"Not much. How are you and Tamara?"

"Good. Everything's good. But brace yourself—Mom got a face lift last week…"

"She didn't need one."

"I had no power of attorney to stop her. And she's been on my back about you and Thomas. Like, why isn't he coming to the Easter brunch, aren't you still getting married, when will you make up your minds, yadda yadda…"

"She doesn't get it, does she?"

Across the room, Jordan looked interested, and not in the least bit effected by eating cat food. He'd added quite a dollop of mayonnaise—maybe that did the trick for him.

"I wondered if there's anything you prefer that I tell her," my brother offered.

"Thanks for asking, Matt. Say that you have the impression Thomas and I haven't been in touch for months."

Jordan crunched contentedly on some chips.

"That's what I've been implying, but well, you know, Mom wants a whole libretto…"

"Sorry you're being put through this."

"No biggie," my brother demurred. "Just wanted to give you a heads-up. Listen, we're doing the amnio tomorrow."

"Oh, I'm sure that will work out."

Jordan waved his arms at me and arose from the table, wiping his mouth with the back of his hand.

"If it's Matthew," he called, "invite him to my gig tonight, Molly…"

I put my finger to my lip. Jordan rose from the table and walked over to me, repeating, "Invite them tonight."

"Who's that?" my brother asked.

"Nothing," I said with annoyance. "No one."

Before I could control myself, I nudged Jordan's hip with the phone, accidentally hanging up on my brother.

"Dammit!" I cried to him. "Can you give me a moment of privacy?"

Jordan stared at me, the whites of his eyes growing around his dark irises.

"Why did you hit me?"

"I barely touched you."

"And you called me 'no one,' didn't you?"

"Stop being pushy," I barked at him.

"Stop pushing me away."

"Thanks for the cat food sandwich."

He squinted skeptically.

"Catfish?"

"No such luck. Cat food. As in pet food," I snapped.

"*What*?"

The phone rang, and caller ID flashed: *Douglas, M & T.*

"Hi," I said breathlessly to my brother. "Sorry I got cut off."

Robin was easy to find in the crowd that was lined up outside the club to pay a ten-dollar cover charge. Her long, dark hair was parted in the middle; she wore a navy blue zippered sweatshirt, low-rise bellbottoms, and high-top sneakers. The giveaway that she was Jordan's sister was the shape of her big, black Picasso eyes, which unfortunately didn't work as well on her narrow face as they did on his more sculpted one. She also had an arching nose that Jordan had been spared. So far as I had seen from photographs, he was the pick of their litter. Beautiful people are often the family fluke, or else they hail from a comely bouquet of look-alikes.

"I'm his sister," Robin was explaining to the pale, thin girl in a black turtleneck at the door. "He said he comped me."

"Can I see some ID?"

Robin fumbled in her back pocket, opened a shabby wallet, and was promptly rubber-stamped on her knuckles.

Meanwhile, other friends of Jordan's, like his roommates Dustin and Charlie, were shaking quarters, dimes, and wadded-up dollar bills from every recess of their pockets.

"Didn't he comp us too?"

"Only one comp per player," explained the pale, sullen girl.

"Can I barter a service to get in?" Dustin asked her. "I give great massages—I studied shiatsu and reflexology."

"I'll read your tarot cards!" called someone else.

I elbowed my way through them and handed the girl a hundred-dollar bill.

"Could you hold on a second, please?" she asked me.

As she went inside to verify that my offering was not counterfeit, I overheard someone say, "Molly's getting us in! Maybe she'll buy drinks too."

I caught eyes with Robin, who stood by the door. Her expression was not friendly.

The sullen girl in her black turtleneck popped back, nodded at me, and rubber-stamped my knuckles with the club's round indicia.

"I want to let in nine other people too," I told her.

"Which nine?"

"Before I answer, do I qualify for a senior discount? I'm over thirty-five."

The girl didn't smile. Perhaps she was too near my age herself.

We gathered around cabaret-style tables, only one of my nine guests acknowledging the treat. A squat blonde with blotchy skin and a silver stud in her nose chimed, "Think yaouwww" in the nasal way that many kids spoke.

I never understood how our country had spawned a generation that couldn't pronounce vowels. After all, we—their role models—did a decent job of it. In old films the elocution of American girls was lovely as cherry blossoms, each word landing with the tart, precise cadence of Grace Kelly or at least that "Somewhere Over the Rainbow" sincerity of Judy Garland. Now our girls hawked and squawked everything out their noses. To top it off, this generation famously ended every sentence, whether or not it was a question, in an interrogative tone and said everything too quickly anyway. If such trends continued, I wondered if I would understand American English when I became a senior citizen.

"I'm Liz?" continued the squat blonde.

"Molly."

"Oaaow! You're, like, with Jordan?"

I nodded, feeling silly.

"I had, like, such a crush on him? Like, in high school? Don't worry; I'm, like, so spoken for now?"

She was corralling Robin and me around one of the small tables with a candle and ashtray upon it. Robin nodded a cool hello, but we did not shake hands.

"Glad to meet you," I said. "I've heard a lot about you."

Dustin hurriedly pulled up a chair beside me and asked, "Hey, is Claudia coming?"

"Sorry," I told him. "This is her Lesbian Ballroom Dancing night."

Claudia was taking classes and attending lectures, now that her discretionary income permitted it. She was tired of meeting women at bars or fetish clubs, she claimed, and hoped to expand her dating horizons. More than anything, she wanted to "leave Bertie in the gravel and push on."

"I want to ask her out," Dustin continued. "Whaddaya think?"

Dustin would have been handsome if he combed his shaggy brown hair and didn't have "a ring at the end of his nose, his nose," like Edward Lear's Piggy-wig. He also had a penchant for orange plaid anything—pants, bathrobes, jackets—and was known to wear women's vintage bathing caps in the rain.

"You can always ask," I told him. "But she's pretty set on girls."

"Jordan said she was married to some tough for years. I don't get that. How do you pull a switcheroo in midstream? I never got the AC-DC thing…"

"AC-DC?"

"You know," he said with an intrigued smile, "swinging both ways."

"She says she's gay."

I always figured that being gay was like being left-handed: a certain percentage of people found it more natural, despite culture's discouragement. But Claudia did strike me as more ambidextrous, or AC-DC, than she would admit.

"She is super hot," Dustin raved on. "A gender unto herself. We would understand each other, you know, like you and Jordan do."

Robin raised her finger to her lips and hissed an angry "shhhh!" at us.

Stage lights went on, and a solemn voice over the microphone announced: "The Blake Jones Quintet."

At the drums sat Zikomo with a Taj Mahal of Rasta hair falling to his shoulders in shimmering layers, his eyes bright against warm, raspberry black skin. Despite being riveting, Z was also Jordan's only friend without that "meal ticket look" in his eye. Whenever we met he would take my hand demurely and say, "How are you, Molly?"

Blake, by contrast, had never grunted a word to me from behind his thick glasses and tangled hair, though he nodded appreciatively when I graced the tip jar.

Tonight, as ever, the band delivered on its commitment to "noncommercial, unsmooth, anti-fusion for the serious listener." They began on an Armstrong and Ellington-like keel, with woodwinds playing off brass. As they progressed, the pace grew more frenzied, Jordan's sax sounding like it had a frog in its throat as it violated the meter of the stringed bass. Z's percussion arose like mist over it all.

At one point Jordan and Blake took each other on in a woodwinds cockfight; their improvised duet-duel drew spontaneous applause from the audience. Of course, Robin was the first to stand up, and all of us joined her. Some guy behind us took to shouting, "Dexie! Dexie!" I was impressed with how Jordan had artfully sublimated his anger at me from earlier in the evening. He was pissed that I hadn't invited Matthew and Tamara, to join us—and mortified that I'd been right about the cat food.

Throughout the set, Liz took cell phone calls as if she was operating an escort service. For fun, I counted how many times she inserted the word *like* into one sentence.

"Hello-o! Ow, hiii! We're, like, at Jordan's gig? Yah, it's like really awesome?"

Her routine passed muster with Robin, but any time Dustin and I whispered two syllables, Robin would lacerate us with a fierce "shhhhh!"

Between sets I discovered that Robin did not suffer from pinched, flattened vowels or meaningless interrogatives. She spoke to the others around her with the doleful declaratives of a young intellectual, bandying words like *syllogism* and *necromancy* as she burrowed her brow with the duty of thinking.

She avoided me until Liz wandered off on a cell phone call and Dustin left to buy cigarettes. At first I didn't realize that she was addressing me, then I mistook her charge for a compliment.

"You've gentrified my brother," she was saying.

"Actually, our friend Claudia did the makeover."

"I know the whole story. Claudia did it so you'd be nicer to him. My brother is now a kept man."

"Is that how he describes himself—'gentrified?' and 'kept?'"

"He doesn't need to. It's obvious to everyone."

"News to me."

"My brother is a luminary in the underground jazz world," Robin eulogized. "Didn't you hear him tonight?"

"Do a haircut and shave change that?"

"Hey, does deforestation change the land? Anyway, it doesn't matter. He says you're still a bitch to him."

I finished my gin and tonic in a swift gulp and placed my glass on the little table.

"Who's the bitch now?"

She looked surprised.

"Maybe he's a fool for you, but I hear through your smooth talk," she sneered.

"And what do you hear?"

"I know you don't love him." She leaned in as though to spit at me. "Even you know that you don't love him. You're just keeping him around until you dump him, and you probably have that day circled on your calendar."

I stood up, my heart pounding, and grabbed my jacket from the back of the chair. Liz returned, her cell phone sounding off again with the merry jingle of a Bach cantata.

"Hello-o? Heyyyy! Where are you? Come on, like, catch the second set."

"I'm out of here," I told Robin, who looked somewhat pleased. "If Jordan asks why, you can explain. I know it's a long shot, but try telling the truth."

I turned and walked out.

"Hey, where you goin'?" Dustin bumped into me at the door.

"Home. Not feeling great."

"How come?"

"I forgot to have dinner tonight."

"You've got the Drinking on an Empty Stomach Blues. Wow. Not a bad song."

"Write it," I challenged him. "Try serenading Claudia. I'm sure it will be a hit."

22

I chain-locked my door. Jordan could have all the keys to my apartment in the world, but now he couldn't get in.

Still shaking, I poured a glass of filtered water and sat for half an hour, cooling down. I wondered if he would come by later. Maybe he'd go clubbing with the boys in the band, or with Robin, Liz, and Liz's cell phone.

A gray sweatshirt hung on the chair where he'd been practicing. His stand and sheet music were also there. Who ever said he could move in? Maybe the more pertinent question was: who didn't?

I folded the stand and sheet music, wrapped his sweatshirt around them and slid all of it into a corner of my living room.

Then I took out a piece of paper and began writing.

Jordan,

We can't keep collapsing into each other's worlds. Tonight I learned, in a way I will not soon forget, that this is not producing good results.

Why don't you call me when you feel ready, and we'll go out and talk in neutral territory, not your place or mine? I think, and I hope, that we can still have a relationship—but not the one we've been having.

Thanks for respecting my wishes,

Molly

I reread what I had written to make sure that I believed in it, folded it inside an envelope, scribbled Jordan's name on it, taped the envelope to the door, and chain-locked myself in again. Whether or not he would appear was a toss-up, but I wanted to feel prepared.

Around two I awakened to pounding, kicking, rattling.

"I can't believe you fucking locked me out."

I rolled over in my bed.

"What happened?" he cried. "Why don't you talk to me? Why did you leave my best gig?"

I almost got up to speak to him through the closed door, but then I remembered that he could have called earlier in the evening, or the next day, as I'd asked. He didn't need to wake up half the building.

I curled a pillow over my head. If he had the nerve to badmouth me to his sister, let him suffer the consequences like a man.

Finally he departed with a last slam. He must have hurled his entire body against the door.

The next morning I found my letter ripped into pieces and strewn over the doormat like white rose petals.

As I picked them up I missed Thomas.

We'd been together for three years, nearly gotten married, and then I ended it putatively over nothing. For all that, he never raised his voice or spoke ill of me to other people.

Jordan disappeared for a while and I wondered if "it was over," and, if so, whether "it was just as well." I had not gotten there yet. In a pathetic way I craved his touch and missed chatting and laughing with him. But I knew that he wouldn't father my child; I breathed in that flawed hope like the stink of a latrine, expecting it but still choking on the Fate that would eventually leave me childless and alone.

I changed my bed sheets, vacuumed, and dumped out a mound of unsightly papers. And I scheduled an appointment with a twenty-four-hour locksmith to change the cylinders in my Medco lock. Unfortunately, the fool showed up an hour late, tinkered with my lock, and decided he needed another plate for the wooden doorjamb, which was warping slightly.

"Theees old buildeeeng!" he kept saying, in broken English. He was from Serbia or Slovakia or some such place, and had a mouthful of gold teeth and smelled like gasoline. He promised to come again the next evening, but I had to cancel because I was working late with Larry. Meanwhile, I scheduled an appointment with a local place for the Wednesday after Easter, which left me at risk, for several days, that Jordan would appear unbidden.

Thursday evening before Good Friday, I got home around 7:00 to strains of Benny Goodman and His Orchestra wafting from my apartment with a heady scent more evocative of Bob Marley. Unlocking the door, I began to get high on my own apartment.

I first noticed his leg on the stool, big foot in a sneaker. Jordan had slouched on the sofa, his white shirt half-unbuttoned and half-untucked from his jeans. The television was on mute. Several CDs lay spilled on the floor beside him. I had always asked him to put them back in their cases so they didn't get dusty or scrambled. A bottle of Chivas was cracked open, and an empty glass stood by the CDs. *There stands the glass.*

"Why don't you just pour whiskey on my music collection?"

He stared as though he wasn't seeing me.

I threw down my bag, snatched the remote from him, and killed the TV.

"Jordan," I began, "many great epochs have fallen into decline. Just ask your studious sister what happened to the High Renaissance style, or the Roman Empire. And so our relationship has succumbed—early in the game, I'd say."

He continued to gape like he wasn't quite sure what he was seeing or hearing.

Then I noticed my "Memory Box" beside him on the sofa. In this round millinery box I stashed everything from family photographs to my second-grade report card, my first crayon drawings, Mom and Dad's wedding announcement from *The Baltimore Sun*, which was so yellowed that I had laminated it. Jordan picked that up now and studied it.

"*Ross Douglas to wed Glynnis O'Meara*...Quelle deb! She fucking looks like

Jackie Onassis."

"Mothers of a certain vintage…I'll be sure to pass on the compliment. She lives for them."

"And when she asks you who said it, are you going to say, 'Nothing. No one?'" He imitated my words from the other night in a high, snobbish voice. Then he laughed. "Ross and Glynnis. They sound like a single-malt scotch."

They unfortunately did. I couldn't remember his parents' names, but they sounded like Europeans who'd met in a pottery commune in upstate New York in the late sixties. I had seen one photograph of them in oversized jeans and sweaters, their long, dark hair blowin' in the wind. Even though my mother could not cook for her life, she was tidy and elegant and smelled like floral perfume, while my father smelled like cologne and menthol. That was something I appreciated about my parents, in an animal way. Jordan's parents didn't look aromatic, though there was a raw appeal to them.

"Who said you could look through all this, anyway?"

As I gathered a smattering of glossy black-and-white photographs beside him on the sofa and placed them back into the box, Jordan pointed to a photo of Alessi and me on our way to a volleyball match. We were fifteen.

"Who's that?"

"A friend."

"Pretty," he crooned. "Great legs."

"She married rich, like I should have—and maybe still can," I retorted as Benny Goodman and His Orchestra launched into "Don't Be That Way."

My eye fell upon a shot of Mom in plaid Bermuda shorts and a polo shirt and me in a striped sun suit. She knelt beside her open-mouthed, chatty toddler, regarding me with pride and affection. At least I had proof that it had once been the case.

I reached into the crack between pillows to make sure nothing had slipped in.

"Jingle Bell Jingle Bell Jingle Bell Rock!" Jordan belted, in time with Goodman's staccato horns.

He'd found our inane holiday cards, the kind with studio pictures of the offspring. I looked over his shoulder to one of Matthew and me posing in a sleigh that was piled high with wrapped presents and set against a painted winter wonderland. *Merry Christmas from the Douglas Family* read the ribbon-like script.

I was about four, with my dimpled Shirley Temple–smile and black curls. Poor Matthew, at two, wore oversized glasses to correct his congenital esotropia, or crossed eyes. I remember how Mom and Dad had taken him to specialists and were even considering surgery. But the glasses helped, and he was fine by the time he turned four.

Once, I had held his pudgy hand as we stepped into the kiddie pool at some state park, where other kids had laughed meanly and splashed his glasses. He started to wail and I took it upon myself to shove one of those kids backward into the shallow water and make her cry—which had only made Matthew bawl louder. My mother had been off with other adults, and I'd realized that I was in charge. Later that evening I had been scolded for "fighting with kids at the pool," but I knew that I'd been chivalrous.

"Now there's a babe. What a babe!"

Jordan put down the old Christmas cards and grabbed a color print of Matt and Tamara on their wedding day.

No one would guess that my brother had been born with an inward-turned eye. As a groom he looked affable and boyish, his brown hair cropped short, his head tilting sweetly toward Tamara's. My sister-in-law glowed with golden skin, thick dark hair, and black eyes that popped out of her face, like the women painted on Attic vases. In the photo she smiled at Matthew with understated sensuality.

"Is she hot, or what? Check out those sweet little lips. But I gotta say—your brother looks kinda dorky. Nice, but dorky."

I grabbed the picture from Jordan, put it with the other loose ones into the box, and covered it with the lid.

"Get out of here."

Jordan blinked at me, so I repeated myself, louder.

"I said, get out of here!"

"Molly, Jeez, chill."

He held out his arms as though he was conducting a séance. I could not tell if he was really far-gone or only pretending.

I shoved his leg off the footstool.

"Move."

"Baby, I didn't mean any harm."

"No one calls my brother 'dorky.'"

"I was kidding."

"Well, it's a knee-slapping riot. Besides, I asked you to call me like a civilized person so we could meet on neutral turf and talk. I didn't invite you to pry though my photos, ruin my CDs, and drink my booze."

He sat upright.

"You're breaking up with me?"

"I wanted to talk. Didn't you read my note before you tore it up?"

"How 'this is not producing good results,' like some glib marketing shit?"

"Well, what should I say: 'Fuck off, Turd-face, this situation sucks'?"

"That would have been better."

"Tell me how that would have gone down."

"Can't we talk right now?"

"Not after you insulted my brother."

"Chardonnay..." he groaned, teetering to his feet and reaching for my hand, which I flicked behind me. "I don't get why all this happened."

"Ask your sister."

"She had some honest words with you."

"Honesty, to quote Jane Austen, is an 'overrated virtue.' If you haven't noticed, civilization has produced remedies to it, like manners and hygiene..."

When Jordan waved me away and sat down again, I heard myself lose control. "Will you just get out of here already? How many times do I have to—"

"Go easy!" he shrieked, standing up again.

"And don't come in again without my permission!"

"Okay, okay!"

"Are you just saying that, or will you respect what I'm asking you?"

"Of course!"

As I steered him to the door, I normalized my tone and asked like a concerned hostess, "Did you have a jacket or something?'

He shook his head.

I opened the door and watched him falter down the staircase, lurching against the painted wooden banister. Halfway down he froze for a couple of seconds, turned around, and looked back at me in agony, his brows creased, his large, dark eyes piercing the distance between us in a Marlon Brando-On-the-Waterfront-type way. He looked more adorable than ever, and he knew it.

"That Benny Goodman tune is called 'After You've Gone.' Weird…"

"It is…"

"You are breaking up with me, aren't you?"

"Call me," I reiterated. "We'll talk."

But he stopped by Claudia's door one flight down, knocked softly on it, and was admitted.

"Damn!" I seethed.

I didn't want him in the building, but there was nothing I could do.

As I went about my business, I could feel him downstairs, telling Claudia everything we'd said. I could feel her pity for him, and even Lauren's pity for him. I could see Claudia making him a cup of tea, and saying: "Don't cry." Oddly, Claudia didn't like to see people cry. Whether or not she'd had any hand in the tears, she tended to feel culpable.

By 9:30 I was fit to be tied. I had to get out, away from Jordan's energy, which I could still feel like a jellyfish sting. I packed my nightgown and an outfit for work the next day into a carry-on bag and tossed my cell phone onto the sofa, where the Memory Box remained. I slammed my front door, hoping they'd hear it, and clambered downstairs.

For once, Claudia's apartment was silent. Lauren was neither singing nor practicing her scales. I stood for a moment, my ear to the door. Faintly, I descried the exaggerated din of television voices, but I felt everyone's awareness that I was standing there. So I scurried down to the street and bolted outside and down the stoop, swinging my bag. A gust of night air welcomed me as I gazed up at the cornices of buildings that deckled a Maxfield Parrish sky, not looking back to check whether anyone was watching me from Claudia's window.

At Third Avenue I hailed a cab heading uptown. Slamming myself into the backseat and tamping down the button lock, I remembered the film version of *Breakfast at Tiffany's* and all the checkered cabs. When we came to New York as children to visit our grandparents, Matthew and I sat on the little gray jump seats beside our suitcases.

"The Pierre Hotel, please," I told the driver now. And uptown we sped.

Once I found myself in the marble-floored lobby with its trompe l'oeil brick wall, I asked for a Single Parkview room at the reception desk. This would be my home tonight. In the tradition of Dorothy Parker and Eloise, I would seek salvation in a distinctive New York hotel. But the woman seated behind the laptop insisted that no Parkview rooms were available since I didn't have a reservation.

Pete and Alessi had advised me to show fangs in such circumstances.

"I didn't like it at first," Alessandra had said, "but people won't believe you've got money unless you act this way. It's really counterintuitive."

So I put one hand on my hip, slammed my credit card on the mahogany desk, and demanded: "A room that overlooks the park, please." Sure enough, her diligent search yielded a Twin Parkview on the 9th floor.

Inside the room I turned on only lamps, none of those drab overhead lights. Then I managed to raise the blinds and draw all drapery from the windows. Across Central Park, stardust shafts of buildings glittered in the dark. For a long time I stood barefoot on the plush carpet, just looking.

23

In this first year of the new millennium, Passover and Easter overlapped conveniently for our Judeo-Christian family. Fritz and Zipporah Szabó, Tamara's parents, were in town from Palm Springs, as our parents were from northern Connecticut. The vaunted Sunday brunch was finally here, and Thomas was not with me.

Passover had actually begun on Thursday. We were all invited to a Seder at Tamara's cousin's, but my parents and I had pardoned ourselves. The Seder plate with its bitter herbs and sacrificial lamb had moved me last year. But my father dozed off several times during the interminable *Haggadah* reading, and Mom had to pinch his arm and poke him in the ribs. He awoke with a start each time. I'd noticed more playfulness in Mom than usual.

Now when I arrived at my brother's, Zipporah, whose name in Hebrew means "little bird," squeezed me into a jovial hug. A slight woman with hair dyed the color of cherry soda, she had out-danced everyone at Matthew and Tamara's wedding, spinning my father around like a revolving door.

She hailed from Borough Park, Brooklyn, but had met Fritz Szabó, her Hungarian-born husband, in Israel. Fritz lifted my hand to kiss it and called me "Molly Picone," as he always did, referencing some Yiddish movie star. "But where is the boyfriend?" he demanded, with a twinkle in his eye. "Where is your Thomas?"

The chatter as my brother took their coats happily overrode that topic. Zipporah came laden with a bag of eggs, matzo, and fresh Nova lox, announcing: "I'll make *matzo brei!*"

"But Mommy, everything's all prepared," protested Tamara. "We have egg salad and herring."

"So, we'll have *matzo brei* too."

"We don't need any more food."

"What we don't eat you can save."

Their bickering wound its way into the kitchen as Mom and Dad arrived in their London Fog trench coats. Dad held Mom's coat as she slipped out of it, as though they were both unveiling their spoils. Mom and I exchanged a perfunctory, floral-perfumed embrace, an almost apologetic hello. I then leaned up to plant a filial kiss on Dad's cheek.

Mom handed a plastic container to Matthew.

"The sauerkraut I promised."

I whispered to my brother, "Remind me to avoid it."

Matthew shot me a pained look. Even though she'd picked on him incessantly in childhood, he was strangely protective of my mother, and I had crossed his threshold of sarcasm.

Formal greetings were then exchanged between the two sets of parents. Dad and Fritz shook hands. Zipporah, fixing an apron around her waist, surveyed us about whether or not we'd ever tasted *matzo brei*. I actually had, at Larry's once, but I didn't mention it.

"Come on!" she beckoned to Mom and me. "I'll show you my recipe."

"But Ma," pleaded Tamara again, "The kitchen is all clean now."

"I'll clean it again. After all, this is a special occasion. Don't you remember how you loved Grandma's *matzo brei*? Now I'll be Grandma, so I'd better start practicing. Or actually, Glynnis—you can be Grandma. I'll be Bubbah."

"Fine," said my mother.

I had to constrain myself from saying, "Really, Mom? You don't want to be 'Bubbah?' Really?"

When I pardoned myself to use the bathroom, Mom followed, seemingly on a mission to trail me.

"You can go first if you need to," I offered.

"No, dear. I was just going to refresh my makeup before lunch. So what do you think? I've got my chin back."

"You look great," I said. "But you didn't need the nip and tuck."

"I was losing my jaw line."

"You weren't."

"You haven't seen me since Christmas. I was starting to get that awful waggle of flesh beneath my chin—it just appeared one day."

"A new star you didn't want in your galaxy."

"So unbecoming on women, you know," she continued. "I'm not even six-ty-five. It had to go."

"Doesn't it aggravate you that satellites have scoured the far reaches of our solar system, but no topical cream prevents jowls?" I asked.

"Well, it must aggravate you, since you comment so explicitly."

I stepped into the bathroom to pee. Mom had become obsessed with her appearance since Matt and Tamara had informed her that she'd be a grandma. After years of her pressure on me to marry and have children, she now cowered at the implications.

"Your brother's gaining weight," she remarked as I exited the bathroom, leaving the mirror for her primping.

"I don't think so."

"You always defend him."

"Okay, it's heft, not fat. A common side effect of marriage," I rattled off. "According to a recent consumer survey, married men are twenty percent more likely to be obese than single men..."

Then she grabbed my arm.

"What on earth went on with Thomas? I don't mean to pry—maybe I've been too much of—"

"We're just not compatible," I interrupted her, hoping for a split second that this synopsis would suffice.

"What does 'just not compatible' mean?"

She gripped me and stared, like a marveling child and an aging woman at once.

"I was exercising damage control."

"Excuse me?"

"He was a drip, Mother."

She recoiled.

"What a nasty thing to say about a good-hearted man."

Of course if I had said that he sucked in bed, I would have been giving him too much credit.

"He loved you."

"He was depressive."

She loosened her grip on my arm and clucked disapprovingly.

"That's just men. Wouldn't you say I'm more cheerful than Daddy?"

So is the hitching post down the road.

"Men must be cared for," she went on. "They're not right without us. Even when they're clever and capable, they need someone to shore them up."

"I don't think all men need a cheerleader."

"Well, I'd beware of men who seem too full of beans, but you do tend to work with homosexuals, don't you?"

"I've never dated them," I said pointedly. "Anyway, Alessi's husband isn't depressive. She's the one who gets into gloomy moods, and he tries to snap her out of them."

"Well, your friend Alessandra…" Mom raised her carefully shaped eyebrows. Her eyes, the same hazel green as mine, darted as she inspected me.

"What about her?"

"She's always been, shall we say…"

"Shall we say *what*?"

"She's always been one to do things her own way."

"Whose way should she do things?" I protested. She had a husband who was easy on the eyes with brains in his head and money in the bank. That was more than most of us.

We both became aware that Fritz was orating about something; we could hear him from two rooms away. "And *he's* not exactly a deadbeat," I pointed out.

"He's not American."

"Oh, okay, got it. American men are depressive—foreigners can be a one-man Punch and Judy show—I'll keep that in mind."

I started back to the dining room when Mom asked me, "Who is your new cleaning woman?"

"I don't have one. Just Helena."

"Well, I tried to reach you and this Spanish woman answered your phone. Actually, her son answered. Julio. What did she say her name was? Grecia or something?"

Claudia's mother's name was Grecia, and Claudia could fake a Spanish accent perfectly. And she came from Corona, Queens, which Paul Simon had immortalized in "Me and Julio Down by the Schoolyard." I stopped walking.

"When did you call me?" I asked Mom.

"Last Saturday."

I had been up at Alessi's, drinking spice tea and Limoncello as we plotted our face-save story. Jordan knew I was away.

"Helena—you know, my regular housecleaner—is out of the country for vacation," I quickly told my mother. "I guess the agency sent over this other person. I wasn't there. I just left cash."

"Well I didn't like this boy answering your phone. It seemed odd."

"Thanks for telling me. Hopefully Helena will be back this week."

Mom went into the bathroom, and I stared out the window. Nine stories below on Broadway, pink-and-white cherry blossoms cascaded buoyantly over the islands between traffic, and taillights glowed like a stream of red balloons.

After this tidbit from Mom, I congratulated myself for not confiding in Jordan and for playing my life close to the vest. To shake disturbing premonitions about what the hell he and Claudia had been doing in my place without me, I wandered into the kitchen to watch the showdown.

"Listen," Zipporah advised Tamara as she stirred crumbled matzo and cream into a bowl, "don't let those maternity shops on Madison Avenue lure you into spending on a *schmata* what you'd spend on a gold necklace. You wear the *schmata* seven times in your life. If I were you, I'd go to Bolton's, buy some cheap, large-sized shirts and dresses..."

Tamara's belly jutted through her blouse like a cushion was tucked into it. Absently she spread her hands over the tender spot. Soon I too would bear such protrusion. Mom would probably think I was "putting on weight" and lecture me on sensible dieting.

"Bolton's has closed, Mommy," Tamara was saying.

"What do you mean, closed?"

"I don't think the chain exists anymore."

"Nonsense, darling. I saw it on Twenty-third Street yesterday. I was thinking, we'll meet on Tuesday, I'll buy you some all-purpose shirts and jumpers..."

Tamara sighed, and I glanced at her with empathy.

"Can I help with anything?" I asked.

"I guess you could take out hors d'oeuvres."

In the living room Fritz was urging my brother to vie for partnership in his firm. My brother felt that he wasn't ready, that he had to prove himself as an associate. From what I overheard as I helped serve appetizers, Fritz claimed that "aggression demonstrates an interest in something" and that Matthew shouldn't falter. Before he retired, Fritz had been a successful life insurance salesman and knew every tip for wielding aggression.

Dad paced around, running his index finger along paperweights and ashtrays. The more boisterous Fritz grew, the more my own father clammed up. Sometimes I wished I could shake Dad so the unsaid words would tumble out of him. He was incredibly smart. But, of course, why should he bother to speak since his wife did such an exhaustive job for both of them?

I bumped into Matt on my way from the kitchen as I brought out a plate of olives and another with cheese and crackers.

"Never a dull moment with the Szabós," I whispered.

"Voltage," my brother whispered back. "You might say the old man cuts to the chase."

But we hadn't seen anything.

Brunch was served on heirloom china that my parents had given Matt and Tamara on their wedding. A heap of *matzo brie* steamed from the large central platter, and smaller plates of egg salad, white fish salad, herring, Nova lox, Scottish salmon, and bagels were circulated. I was faint with hunger and helped myself liberally to everything except Mother's dismal, gray sauerkraut.

Before we started eating, my brother suddenly struck his glass with his fork, as if to propose a toast: "Everyone. We have some news."

The room grew quiet.

"We went through with the amnio and—we're having a daughter."

Gooseflesh climbed over my arm and settled in my heart. But none of us could say anything. Tamara's golden cheeks and dark eyes glowed across the table. She and Matt held hands.

"A normal, healthy little girl, they told us," she said with a catch in her voice.

"Oh," said Zipporah with a sigh, "God bless."

For Fritz and Zipporah, as for my parents, this girl would be their first grandchild. Tamara's two older sisters were worse pariahs than I. Nurit, the eldest, was dating a Lebanese guy who rarely let her out of his sight. Beautiful Dahlia, the middle sister, had hooked up with a Jewish man—but he was married. I must have seemed dauntingly normal to them, with Thomas by my side at the wedding. My breakup with Thomas was more acceptable than their relationships. All in all, Matt and Tamara's new family member was a coup for our generation.

I noticed Dad removing his glasses to dab his eyes with a napkin. I had never seen him do anything like that.

"We've got a name picked out," Tamara continued.

"At first we were going to keep it secret," said Matt.

"But then we figured, since we all know she's a girl, why shouldn't you know her name? She's Mira, for Grandma Miriam."

"And my family," said Mom, an O'Meara by birth.

"Exactly. And she'll have Molly's and my initial too," added Matt.

But the mention of me at that moment—unmarried, nonreproductive me—was abrasive.

"Ah," said Fritz decidedly. "Molly should have her own child. Like Nurit and Dahlia."

"Who says they won't?" asked Tamara.

Again, no one could reply, not even the garrulous Szabós. My parents glanced at each other; Mom put her arm on Dad's shoulder.

"Molly must marry first," declared Fritz, appearing to stumble exultantly on the obvious. Tamara dropped her fork.

"Such a pretty girl," lamented Zipporah, shaking her head at me as though my appearance were wasted since no man was licensed to it.

"Please leave Molly alone," Tamara scolded her parents. "No guy is going to make her more beautiful or intelligent than she already is."

I said, to my own surprise, "Most of them subtract from me."

But Zipporah just shook her head and insisted, "You haven't met the right one."

"Too many young men," charged Fritz, cutting into his herring, "have taken to *schnorring*. They make a lifestyle of *schnorring*."

"By snoring you mean they've become lazy?" asked Mom.

"It's a Yiddish expression, Glynn," Dad prompted her. "It means freeloading."

Suddenly Fritz pointed across the table at me with his fork and bellowed to me: "What you need is someone who will provide. Then you can enjoy life a little, not work so hard."

"There is a Yiddish saying." Zipporah interrupted her husband. "'Love is nice, but bread is nicer.'"

"Well, wait a minute there," Mom blustered at her. "Thomas had a respectable job. He wasn't taking advantage of Molly."

"He earned half her salary," Fritz proclaimed.

"Fritz, he worked in insurance..."

"He worked in compliance, not sales. The guy couldn't sell whiskers to a cat. Molly needs a bigger player, she needs a mensch," Fritz decided.

"Well I, for one, will miss Thomas in the family," Mom countered. "It seems to me a loss. Ambition is well and good, but Thomas was loving and trustworthy. That's most important."

My father nodded sympathetically. Both my parents seemed to be mourning my engagement to Thomas more than I was.

"I don't understand these bums," Fritz went on, trying to catch Dad's eye. "How can a man think he will attract a woman if he can't support her? Men demand much of women; they must return something. If a man cannot provide, a woman loses interest, all interest, including sexual."

"Daddy!" Tamara stormed at him. "Enough!"

I was seized with a nervous urge to giggle and bit the inside of my mouth to suppress it. It didn't help that the Szabós were politely sweeping Mom's disgusting sauerkraut under their lettuce leaves. Poor Matt obliged himself to eat some by swathing it in lox with horseradish.

"One last thing." Fritz held up his index finger. "Molly, we know a young man you might find interesting. Israeli, but he lives here, in New York. Oh, and he's reform. Of course he prefers dating Jewish women, but he's been known to....play in different fields."

"Well healed," chimed Zipporah with a wink at Mom.

I wanted to scream at everyone: *That's the last thing that matters now!* I need a rich man like the sub-Sahara needs a sandbox.

"He is the son of Zipporah's second cousin. Nice-looking fellow, about forty. Has an import business. Would you like that we give Ari your phone number?"

"Sure," I said flippantly, through my stifled giggles. "Why not?"

Fritz nodded with satisfaction and continued to fork down his herring.

Zipporah smiled and said, "You never know..."

But my parents exchanged a more resigned glance, with faint amusement—even if it was gallows humor.

They knew.

24

The phone startled me awake, and then Tamara's soft appeal came over the machine: "Will you ever forgive me for not handling my parents better yesterday? I'm so sorry and embarrassed...I hope they didn't ruin your brunch. I really gave it to them after you left. Maybe now you know why one of my sisters is catatonic and the other is a Prozac junkie. Please call us. Matt and I would love to see you. Maybe we could rent a movie or just do something fun."

I jumped out of bed and threw the covers over my pillow. Quite the pack we were, Tamara's outcast sisters and I. Just what will little Mira make of her aunts? I never had to contend with such characters—although when I thought of it, Aunt Eileen had gotten her license revoked by driving into a picket fence, and Aunt Bridget, whom I resembled, had supposedly seduced a priest. But even such picaresque scandals were staged behind the respectable curtain of marriage.

As I prepared coffee the phone rang again, and it was Alessi. After Mom's smear of her yesterday, my immaculate pregnancy loomed as an act of defiance, an excuse to take time out for myself, and to live with luxury and panache.

"Okay," Alessi began, "we were going to meet the social worker tomorrow for our first three-way huddle. Well, I was wondering if we could postpone so Pete and I can see her alone. We've got a kink to tackle."

"Not a problem. Can you tell me what's up?"

Alessi reminded me that, in the event of their death, she wanted me to become the child's custodian. With apprehension, I'd agreed to this formality. I figured that if they both tragically expired—and if I had a kid of my own, by then—then my kid would have a sibling. And if I didn't have a kid, then I would have a kid. Whatever the case, this seemed the least I could do for Pete and Alessandra.

Still, Pete preferred that his parents be named custodian. She felt her own parents were getting short shrift, and she wanted to discuss that with the social worker. Alessi admitted that her father had earned the short shrift with his tasteless invectives about how "your fag husband can't get you pregnant, so you're hiring little Molly."

Years ago, when I had known Alessi in grade school, Dominic called me "Little Molly." To such people I would be eternally ten years old. He had always been warm and paternal, the kind of man who liked females considerably more than other males—and Alessandra ranked among his favorite females.

"I know my father can be a jackass, especially to poor Pete," she was saying. "He lays our whole failure to conceive on Pete, because of course I never told him about—my scar tissue. I don't blame Pete for being put off, but we can't let that dictate our choice of the kid's parent in an emergency. Your age is more appropriate. He was saying, well, his folks are a couple—but by the time this might come to pass, I told him, hey, one of them could be gone, and Molly could be married."

"Most unlikely," I assured her. "I have the opposite of the Midas touch with men. Every guy I touch turns to poop."

"Do I detect trouble in paradise? What's going on with Mystery Man?"

"That is, in fact, a mystery to me."

And I intended to get to the bottom of it.

I told Kendra that I had an appointment in the afternoon, even though I would not be going to the social worker's office. I planned to go home and see whether "Grecia" and "Julio" were indeed in my apartment, before the cylinders would be changed, and just what they were doing.

It felt eerie to be home on a weekday afternoon. I tiptoed upstairs, past Lauren's "Killing Me Softly," which erupted theatrically from Claudia's apartment. Formerly "The Songbird," Claudia now called her "Bugs Bunny," since Lauren had two prominent front teeth. She tended to wear thermal underwear tops, bellowing pink sweatpants, and white running sneakers that looked fatter than sausage heroes.

"*And there he was, this young boy.*" Lauren stopped, cleared her throat, and began again, in another curdled key: "*And there he was, this young boy.*" Then she began again. I could imagine Claudia climbing walls and gouging her fingernails into plaster. "*And there he was, this young boy…*"

I stopped at my own door and listened. I couldn't hear anything but slid my key quietly into the lock nonetheless, a thief entering her own home.

And there he was, that young boy, seated cross-legged upon the Persian rug on my living room floor—sweeping golden green dust ball-like buds into plastic bags all over my coffee table.

Claudia, who was sitting across from him, jotting on a yellow legal pad, noticed me first with an "Oh shit!"

I marched in and slammed my purse and coat down on the sofa. Beside Claudia lay an industrial saw and an open packet of blades. To my astonishment there was also a box of dildos in different colors, like gumdrops.

Claudia quickly covered it, and Jordan jumped up and ran over to me. Claudia began packing the plastic Baggies and a small scale into a cardboard shoebox, then collected her saw, blades, and the box of sex toys into a knapsack. A huge cerulean blue dildo sat on my coffee table beside an open jar of blue paint.

"What the—"

I disengaged from Jordan, who was whining manipulative appeasements into my ear, grabbed the obscene rubber thing, which was still damp, ran across the room, and hurled it out the window.

Claudia and Jordan gasped in horror.

"I'll get it," she announced.

But before she could scramble out my door, I ran over to grab her fleshy arm with my sticky, blue-paint-smeared hand.

"Keys."

She rooted around in her pocket, pulled them out, and deposited them into my other palm.

"I'll explain later, Molly. It's my fault. Don't be mad at Jordan."

"Get Buddha!" he groaned, standing up as she exited and slammed the door.

"It's not what you think," he began, once we were alone.

"Got any more clichés up your sleeve, Skippy?"

"Well, um—I mean, we only—"

He glanced at me like a puppy who knew he'd peed off the newspaper. But those shiny black eyes held no sway. Everything magical about Jordan had become common.

"We weren't using the sex toy."

"*Buddha*?"

"Fuck, I hope she finds it."

"I don't," I said sharply.

"Cut us some slack, Molly. That nine-to-five shit doesn't want us, but we need to live. Can't our ingenuity count for something?"

"If I may ask, what *were* you doing with—"

"Claudia's sending the dildos to some chick in Paris with love letters, like they're gifts for her. You can't imagine a customs officer handling that. Claudia's brilliant idea. We used her friend's Sawzall to open up 'Buddha' and make a sampler pack—you know, indoor-grown, outdoor-grown, sativa, indica—then we glued it back together and the glue even looked like those fake blood vessels on the fake dicks. We're gonna make millions with this."

If I weren't livid I would have burst out laughing.

Sensing a break in my indignation, and knowing my capacity to find humor at bizarre moments, he minced over in a last-ditch effort to embrace.

But I pushed him away with more force.

"I would have rather come upon you having some kinky affair with her than using my apartment as headquarters for your cottage industry."

"Thanks."

"Oh Jordan, fuck you. I could have been implicated."

Of course, packaging dope dildos from a Manhattan apartment might be more benign than laundering hedge fund profit in a state that didn't recognize paid surrogate motherhood. That was precisely why their intrusion unnerved me.

"We met here just a couple of times in an emergency. Lauren's always down at her place, singing—Dustin and Charlie are at mine—and you know, Molly, New York City cops don't randomly check apartments for weed. They wouldn't have the time— "

"I don't care," I interrupted.

"They're more likely to get a cut of profits," he went on. "Guys pushed nickel and dime bags on the street five years ago."

"You put me at risk. From Day One, I wanted no part of your business."

"No one I've worked with has ever gotten caught."

"I also asked you not to come here anymore without permission. Remember? You kept saying, 'Okay, okay.' You and your sister can call me a bitch, but actually I've been a colossal wimp—if not a fool—and you've taken every opportunity to compromise me."

He hung his head. I wasn't sure how much of that was for show and how much was genuine remorse.

"I just wanted you to call me," I continued. "Why didn't you?"

"I've given up on talking with you," he mumbled, his head still down.

"I'm not so unreasonable."

"That's the problem." He lifted his face, twisted with an emotion I couldn't place. "You're too reasonable. You live in your brain. I live in my gut."

Faintly, I could hear Lauren trill that line about strumming with his fingers from downstairs, over and over. I wished she would quit stopping halfway through a phrase and just sing, even if it sucked.

"I know the kinds of things we say when we talk," Jordan continued. "There was no use. You wouldn't tell me the truth anyway."

Now his words rang like lines from a painfully amateur play. But when he scampered out of the living room and came back with my birth control pills, I must have sunk inches into my Persian rug.

"What you don't get," he told me, "is that I'm always a step ahead of you. I know about these, Chardonnay."

"Then you know I need them for a medical reason," I said quickly.

"Yeah, *right.*"

He tossed the dispenser in the air and caught it.

"Give that to me."

"Maybe I'll spray them around the room, like Johnny Appleseed."

"Give it to me now, or I'll give your name to the feds."

He handed it over, spastic with belligerence, almost missing my blue hand.

"Have your way. Fuck him in peace."

"I'm not fucking anyone—including you."

"Guess we can agree that's best."

There was his first assent to our parting. Though I'd known it was coming I felt sick as a mountain climber when the rocks start to fall.

"If you respected me, you would have been straight about him," Jordan went on, watching for my response.

"There is no 'him,'" I said crossly. "I wish there was."

"You don't even lie well. You are so not worth this—I so should have gotten out when I found out about him a couple of weeks ago. But I was already in too deep."

"There is no other person," I repeated.

"Bullshit doesn't help. You and Claudia both. She tried to tell me it was a fucking lesbian, but I know you too well. You're busted—you can't even put this on Claudia."

"What in fuck are you talking about?"

"A couple of weeks ago, Claudia, Dustin, and I were in the Brooklyn Botanic Garden, getting high and looking at the blossoms by the lily pool," he recounted. "We ran into some friend of Claudia's, another cute girl—you wonder why the hell she's gay. Anyway, she hung with us for a while, and I overheard her ask Claudia, 'So, what's with Molly and John?'"

"John?"

"Don't pretend you don't know. Just stop it."

Actually, I wished I knew some guy named John, and that he was handsome, mature, and protective, and would accompany me to doctors' offices and clinics, and care for me as my belly grew.

"The bartender," Jordan enunciated, his face getting red.

I was mystified for a moment and then slowly said, "You mean Gene?"

"Gene, John, Joe Schmoe—the guy who won't use a condom, like I do."

"Just calm down." I clasped the plastic pill dispenser tighter in my hand.

"Claudia wasn't even at the bar, but this girl saw you having a long heart-to-heart with John."

There was, of course, a cause-effect relationship between my fateful chat with Eugenia and the birth control prescription. Yet Jordan's intuition was stained with wine, pot, and too many daytime soap operas. I also sensed that he was trying to incriminate me so I could be guilty of something to equal his betrayal.

But I did register a distinctly emerging danger. Jordan wouldn't have thought of "Buddha" and peddling his wares in France. He had been selling plastic Baggies to only a couple of friends when I'd introduced him to Claudia. She was pushing him into another league of pushing. God knows what assholes she had blown his way in that wicked world.

The last thing I wanted was for Claudia to ask Eugenia snoopy questions about me. Any mind that could construe a sex toy into a marijuana sampler would stop at nothing. I suddenly realized why built-like-a-brick-shithouse and Marine-cut Bertie avoided her so trenchantly. Bertie was terrified. Claudia had become a wild card, and her need for money off the books was making her wilder. There was no telling where she might go if she caught even the faintest whiff of my arrangement with Pete and Alessi.

Though it might humiliate me, I had to make it look to Claudia like I'd been flirting with Eugenia and not discussing anything of consequence. If people were asking her about Eugenia and me, it was only a matter of time before Claudia would investigate for herself.

"Okay, Jordan, I'll come clean about something," I said. "I got ripped one night and flirted with the bartender. But I was so stressed I would have flirted with a barstool. It meant nothing."

"Yeah, well, we saw you run out the door with a suitcase the other night, and you looked chirpy, like you were going to meet the man. And then there was that time you said you were visiting your friends in Westchester and you never came home. I waited for you that night."

"I didn't tell you I'd be home or expect you to wait for me."

"Molly, isn't it time we come clean about a lot of shit?"

Suddenly his cell phone grumbled from the coffee table like a starved belly. He leaned over, answered it, and said under his breath to me, "Claudia." For a while he listened to her, then he frowned and tossed me the phone, mumbling, "She can't find Buddha. Where'd you throw the thing?"

As I spoke to Claudia he strolled to the window, planting his hands on the sill. His T-shirt hiked up slightly, revealing a tender band of skin I used to stroke and the elastic crumples of his boxer shorts.

"Did you pitch to the right or the left?" Claudia asked me, over the cell phone. I put my pill dispenser aside, grabbed at the air, and swung my arm.

"Maybe the right…"

Looking at my blue-stained hand, I realized my life was becoming a farce that made Aunt Bridget's seduction of the priest seem like a sweet old Bing Crosby movie, and Aunt Eileen's drunk driving like a low-budget British comedy.

"All right, so let's find the super of that building," Claudia was saying. "I'll tell him I had a Viagra moment. Ya know? Wanna come down and help me?"

"I'll send Jordan."

I snapped off his phone and walked over to him. Out the window, on the flag-stone four stories below, Claudia shrugged up at us with a goofy expression and blew a pink bubble of gum.

"So…is this, like, hit the road, Jack?" he asked without looking at me.

"Let's not prolong anything."

"Will I even see you again?"

"I'm sure you will when you come and go from Claudia's."

"You never took me seriously."

"You don't take yourself seriously."

"I take myself way seriously. And if I gotta stuff plastic dicks with weed to pay some bills—worse shit has happened, Molly."

He turned from the window and shuffled toward the door, nearly tripping over his feet since he barely lifted them.

"Wait a sec," I said.

He looked back, almost hopeful for a moment. But all I did was recover his gray sweatshirt and music stand from the corner where I had stashed them.

"Want a bag for all this?"

I packed his booty into a black Barney's bag, padding it with the sweatshirt so the music stand didn't pierce the paper, thinking that this was my last motherly gesture for him. Ever.

25

By May, wind had stirred blossoms into greenery, sweeping stray petals over sidewalks and bunching them in gutters. White leaves turned beige, but the pink remained bright as confetti underfoot. I watched a little girl in Stuyvesant Park scoop some into her hands and let them skitter off in a breeze.

The cylinders in my lock were changed, and I became the proud owner of a new set of keys. At work I readjusted the photograph of Thomas and me by my computer, determined not to broadcast that I was alone.

Jordan's wake found me not only restless but also snappish and horny. Birth control pills and an initial progesterone shot from the clinic proved no antidote. I even began to wonder, *Was it so bad that he used my apartment for a Bonnie and Clyde operation without telling me?* and *Isn't getting laid worth tolerating his sister's catfights now and then? Or eating his cat food?* But such excuses were like jigsaw puzzle pieces with the right color and pattern in the wrong shapes.

The sun had set on Jordan and me.

I daydreamed that Tamara, who worked in book publishing, might introduce me to an editorial intern, or that Pete might find a financial analyst in training. But who was I kidding? What cool young guy would want a woman who was thirty-seven and bearing someone else's kid? At that rate I might as well be with Jordan, who knew my quirks and foibles. Back to Square One, yet I didn't call him and he didn't call me.

One night, I logged onto porn sites for the first time in my life, planning to hit those cussed chat rooms and create a fake name like "JadedJill" or "PussyLava," and try techno sex. But the glossy throng of bodies in dumb poses on-screen were anything but savory: men's penises looking more like shiny slugs than any I had seen in the soft light of a bedroom, and women's genitalia evoking squashed road kill or a strange species of bat. I hoped we didn't really look like that. I quit those sites and entered Robert Mapplethorpe's name into the search engine. His graceful nudes and interesting faces restored my appetite for the human species.

The next day Pete emailed that Goldenrain was on the upswing, out-hedging its own bets, and "welcome." Alessi's title read *Breast-feeding still open question*; I didn't want to read that one just yet.

Then I heard from Rick.

Bad news. Terry's got the blues. Hope to be seein' ya tonight at Eugenia's.

I wasn't eager to be noticed in the Bunny Hop again. Nevertheless, I appreciated how Rick and Terry had spent time dissecting Jack and my job. I also wondered what had occasioned Terry's blues. I felt that I should show up and support them.

But when I got to the bar, which was no longer adorned with glittering paper eggs and Easter bunnies, I didn't see Rick or Terry at all. It was 6:35, and Rick had written that I could catch them "between six and seven."

"Annoying," I muttered, flitting by booths and the pool table, then back to scan the bar seats.

Eugenia was where I'd left her, as though she hadn't budged for weeks. Today she wore a white tank top with a small black apron over her jeans. Too bad Mapplethorpe had not lived to photograph this statuesque subject as she leaned against the cash register blowing smoke rings shaped like horseshoes. Nothing so common as a birthmark or freckle besmirched her custard-smooth skin, to say the least for a scab or pimple.

Do but mark, her forehead's smoother
Than words that soothe her...

"They left," she was saying. "Your buddies left."

Propping her cigarette on a glass ashtray, she reached over to produce a sheet of lined paper that was taped closed with a small Band-Aid. On the front it said *To: Molly via Bar-gram*. Rick had sketched a rather wonderful silhouette of Eugenia as a stamp.

Terry feels terrible, it said inside. *We'll see you another time. Enjoy the scenery. It enjoys you.*

I asked Eugenia, "So what's the skinny on our anorexic friend?"

She shut her eyes at my dumb pun but smiled when she opened them again.

"Terry will be all right. Nothing disastrous. You should talk to her."

"I plan to."

"Say, uh," Eugenia came closer to me, leaned forward on the bar, and lowered her voice. "You know that weird survey question you popped a while back? Who wrote it?"

"My boss."

"Does your boss know what they *really* pay you to have other women's babies?"

"Probably."

"Do you know?"

I shook my head no.

"Well your boss' quote is far-fetched. The other week I went online with friends who are paying back student loans. We looked into it, and they'd do better behind a bar, so I'm teaching them to mix drinks. Where do you think your boss got those numbers?"

"From the client. And I can't tell you who that is."

"'Course not."

She leaned in closer, the inescapable blonde hair falling over her face. Aside from ambient cigarette smoke, she exuded a faint aroma of tea rose and cinnamon.

"If the fees were anywhere near your example, it'd be a great way to fill your coffer without hurting anyone or getting mixed up in nasty stuff. Mind you, my friends might still go for the ten or twenty grand to start paying off school." She tossed her head again and confessed surprisingly, "Can't believe I've been hangin' with these kids lately. Friends with 'em, dating 'em, like Over-the-Hill Hilda."

"You too, huh? How young?" I asked.

"Oh, twenty-two, twenty-three—like they say, I've got socks older than that. Early twenties is my limit. I wouldn't touch teenagers, or straight girls of any age."

Just as Pete divested himself of "certain asset classes," I had to assume.

"How 'bout you?" Eugenia asked, her hair still falling flirtatiously in her face.

"My latest was twenty-four."

"You catch 'em like a falling star."

"Well, my star crashed and burned," I said, still pissed to think of Jordan.

"They're kids. You can't get too involved."

"Beware the sexy young lover who sneaks up on you."

"No one sneaks up on me." She leaned in again and said, "The older we get, the more of them there are anyway."

I pulled back from her. Kids probably seduced her all the time. For me, Jordan had been exceptional.

"The older we get, the less likely that they'll take interest in us," I pointed out.

Then someone tapped me twice on the shoulder, and I turned to see Claudia in a T-shirt that said *In Dog Beers, I've Had Only One.*

"Sorry to break up the pillow talk, ladies," she began. Glancing around, I noticed that the few girls at the bar had been watching Eugenia and me with interest. It was mostly a feminine crowd that day in blouses and cardigans with long, permed hair.

"Did you and Jordan ever find Buddha?" I asked Claudia.

"Yeah—in the yard next door with broken glass and dog shit. That deal is on, but speaking of dogs, I got a bone to pick with you."

"You mean a lock to pick, don't you?"

"You could have talked to us, Molly."

"What would I have said? What part of 'I don't want criminals in my apartment when I'm not home' don't you understand?"

Eugenia walked off snickering. The girls at the bar watched her, not us.

"But you never said anything!" Claudia snapped, more fiercely once we had no audience. "You always seemed happy to see us. You knew he was there every day, like it was his home—he was your bitch, your wife."

"My mistake and I admit it." I appreciated Eugenia's point about not getting too involved. "But I didn't know the extent of your unauthorized visits…"

"Oh, you knew we were there!" Claudia shouted, garnering attention from the girls down the bar again. "We left orange juice glasses in the sink and messed up your dish towels, as kind of a sign."

"Why didn't you try smoke signals?"

"My point is, you didn't seem to care. We left these traces, and you never said shit to him or me, so we figured…"

"Figured *what*?"

"Just can't stop heckling people, can you?" snarled another voice behind me.

I looked around and there was Bertie, breaking two months of silence with Claudia. Lainey stood at a strategic distance around the bar's curve with her Panama hat tipped over her face. Claudia's eyes widened, and she chomped manically on her gum.

"To what do I owe this privilege?" she demanded of Bertie.

"Compassion for Molly," said Bertie. "She was probably being her kind, helpful self and you're rubbing her nose in it."

"I'll rub your nose in Vaseline."

"You can dish it out, but you can't fake it."

"Me? I've been woman enough to talk, unlike certain cowards…"

They lit into each other like Jordan and I had two weeks ago, their voices loud with spite. Eugenia sidled back down the bar to us.

"Hey, Bertie, can't you carry on somewhere else? People come here to get away from their misery. They don't want yours."

"Fuck you too, you beer-swilling honky-tonk!"

Eugenia looked from Bertie to Claudia.

"Just keep it down," she repeated. "Got a problem understanding that?"

"I got a problem understandin' yo' hillbilly English," Bertie scoffed.

"You know, Bertie, your insults are all reruns. You haven't found one new stupid thing to tell me in years," Eugenia retorted.

Claudia laughed and applauded while Bertie snapped at Eugenia: "Then try these for size—Femme Tomboy. Failed athlete."

Eugenia blinked for a moment, somewhere between peeved and burned. She flipped her head, and Bertie begrudgingly followed her down the bar.

"Eighty-six her," Claudia called after them. "You can do it, Eugenia!" Then she eagerly asked me, "So what's goin' on with you two?"

I wanted to scream: "Nothing! I've spent ten minutes with Eugenia in my life." But here was my grand opportunity to decoy the conversation about surrogate motherhood and convince Claudia that Eugenia and I had been flirting.

I smiled foolishly. "Can't talk about it."

(In Claudia-ese that meant, press me like grapes at the vineyard.)

"You swore you'd never want a woman."

"But she's not a woman, she's a goddess."

"You got it bad." Impressed, Claudia snapped a purple gum bubble that produced a sour scent. "That's why you came here, right?"

I didn't let on that I'd expected to see Rick and Terry.

"Please don't tell anyone," I begged Claudia. "I feel so vulnerable."

(In Claudia-ese that meant, scream it to the world.)

"Jordan didn't even believe me."

"Oh, Claudia. How could you be so insensitive as to mention it to him?"

Though I feigned distress, I hoped she would tell Jordan that Eugenia was a woman and that my relationship with her was social, that I hadn't been seeing some guy behind his back—just in case he believed his own claim.

"So, you just cruising her, or you gonna sweep her off her feet?"

"I'm not in her league. And besides I wouldn't know what to do."

"With her you'd learn fast."

"A moot point. She doesn't date straight girls."

"True, but..." Claudia dropped her voice a register and mouthed, "I don't think she knows you're straight. She asked me, and I dodged."

A puss of purple issued from her lips with a quick snap.

"Can I buy you a drink?"

"You want an excuse to talk to her, don't you?"

"No—I'm just tired of looking at your gum."

Claudia shook her head deviously. "So transparent, Molly."

"Listen, I'm just relishing the latency. It's refreshing to idealize someone, and I know men too well to idealize them anymore. With a woman, I have no history of betrayal or disappointment. It's a clean slate. And I can't help it." I swooned and recited a line that could make Larry's next campaign. "Every time I see her, it's love at first sight."

Taken aback, Claudia snapped a smaller, paler purple bubble.

"Her beauty is too sweet," she said. "I get cavities just lookin' at her. Bertie's a balanced meal."

"Bertie's a *guy*."

"You so don't get it."

"I so don't."

"Hey, Molly!" Bertie suddenly called from down the bar. "Come 'ere a second, will ya?"

"She's gonna blame it all on me and try to get me eighty-sixed," Claudia surmised. "Just watch. But I won't give her the satisfaction. I'm outta here."

Claudia gave my shoulder a brief shove and whispered in my ear: "Tip from a veteran: you stare too much at Blondie."

When I got down the bar, Eugenia eyed me like she knew exactly what Claudia and I had been saying, though she couldn't possibly have heard.

I intentionally looked at Bertie, not at her.

"Was Claudia pestering you?" Bertie asked. "Even before I came over?"

"Well, if she didn't bug me here she'd bug me at home, so it doesn't matter."

"But she *was* bothering you..." Bertie turned to Eugenia with unexpected deference. "See? She's a troublemaker. Don't let her in here."

"I'm not solving your domestic problems, Bertie. You haven't been nice enough to me." Eugenia then slipped back behind the bar because a new pack of customers had arrived and the place was filling up for the night.

Bertie steered me to a booth where Lainey met up with us.

"Bad-mouthing Eugenia again?" Lainey asked Bertie as we took our seats. "You are so jealous—I swear, she gets to you more than Claudia."

"Claudia makes a fool of herself, but Eugenia makes a fool of you," I added, unable to help myself.

"That pinup from Podonk? Can we put something to rest, girls?"

Settling onto the cushioned booth seat beside Lainey and across from me, Bertie slid a small, rum-soaked cigar from her vest pocket and handed Lainey one. She offered one to me as well, and I declined with a shake of my head. Then she continued. "I am so not jealous of Eugenia Drury. Maybe she doesn't literally come from a trailer park..."

"Hardly," said Lainey. "More like disowned by a conservative Southern family."

Bertie lit both of their cigars, and I surprisingly didn't mind the sharp whiff.

"I know Eugenia like few people do," Bertie bragged, exhaling and sinking back against the cushioned seat. "Certainly not those shameless chicks who wait down the street after her shift at two in the a.m. I know that she changes three hundred and sixty degrees when she's not behind a bar, like a brilliant actor getting offstage and into mousy little street clothes.

"Here's the truth—Eugenia's an illusion. She has no personality. The bar talks for her. After hours, believe me, she's a social retard, a crumpled cocktail napkin."

"Maybe she's exhausted after a night's work," argued Lainey.

"It's weirder than that. She mopes around and stares into space; her eyes lose expression…"

"She's probably still depressed about that girlfriend."

"The Latina poet who dicked her over two years back, or is it three now? You might say it's time to bury that one." Bertie drew on her cigar, then turned to Lainey. "Dyke dramas. I'm willing to bet twenty bucks that if you went out for coffee with her you'd be bored silly, and you couldn't make Mona Lisa laugh."

"Bet thirty I'd have a grand ole time and enjoy her sardonic wit and insights."

"You'd say anything to win your own bet. Let's find a more objective party…"

Both of them puffed on their cigars and looked me over.

"*Fifty* bucks," declared Bertie. "Molly won't get through it."

"Fifty," agreed Lainey, "Molly will have a blast get more than a smile from Mona Lisa."

They shook on it.

At the bar Eugenia came my way with a flip of her fair head. I wished I wasn't participating in this little sham, though it contributed to the impression that I was flirting with her and not talking secret hedge fund schemes. It would explain any number of mysteries and draw lines in the sand that I needed.

I would also learn whether Eugenia had made my decision for Alessi—or if the bar had done so.

"You want anything?" she asked me.

"Two Stolis and a Corona Light?"

"No more marketing surveys?"

"As a matter of fact, here's one: may I invite you for coffee to thank you for participating in mine?"

She looked back with mild surprise, and, it seemed, disappointment.

"It's not a date," I said emphatically. "Just a plan. A way for me to thank you."

"You don't owe me anything."

"I kind of do. People get paid to be in focus groups—I'd like to do something."

Turning away to prepare our drinks, she murmured, "I'll think about it."

"It's okay," I said quickly. "Never mind."

I felt relieved to tell Lainey and Bertie back at the booth, "The bet's off—not happening, and that's just fine."

But when Eugenia came with our drinks, Bertie accosted her.

"Wassa matter, you community college dropout? My friend Molly's not good enough for you? Not pretty enough, not smart enough?"

"I didn't say that."

"*'I'll think about it!'* What kind of arrogant horse shit is that?"

Face boiling, I stared down at the Formica table with gray helix patterns upon it that looked like egg drop soup. Eugenia slid my Stoli on the rocks directly in front of me.

"Molly and I have a plan Sunday, right?"

"Sunday's fine," I said.

"I didn't mean to put you off." Suddenly a finger was under my chin, and Eugenia gently tilted my jaw upward so I would look at her. "Sorry if you felt I did."

Her sapphire eyes burned with pride.

I was ready to give this a fair trial—but if Eugenia could throw so much emotion into one glance, I doubted that Bertie would win the bet.

26

My first words to Elizabeth J. Muldoon, DSW, when she stuck her head into the waiting room and we established that I was Molly were, "I'm famished! Would you mind if I eat my lunch here?"

Her first words to me were, "Go right ahead. By the way, Peter and Alexandra can't make it today."

I wanted to say "Alessandra," but followed Dr. Betsy, as Alessi called her, into a windowless room with honeydew green walls and upholstered chairs that were various shades of straw. I noticed diplomas on the wall and the classical reclining couch. How much psychoanalysis was a DSW expected to perform? I knew only that I didn't want a nanosecond of it.

In one corner sat a small fountain made of slate slabs. But instead of helping me relax into an unruffled and yogic peace, the gurgling water made think that a toilet was broken.

Dr. Betsy closed the door as I fell, light-headed with hunger, into an armchair. I plopped my bag from Au Bon Pain on the end table beside me, spreading a napkin over my skirted lap. The soup had burned my hand when I'd ladled it into the little container at Au Bon Pain; I'd been jiggling, spilling and bumping into the wrong things all day. When I caught my reflection in windows I looked like a bleached photograph of myself, the kind I want to crush.

Ravenous from the blustery morning, I dunked my seven-grain bread into the corn chowder and devoured the whole slice in two minutes.

"Please pardon me," I begged the social worker. "All I had today was coffee—I know, these on-the-fly eating habits will have to change. So, where are the Foleys?"

"Something came up for them."

Wiping my hands on another napkin from the bag, I inspected Dr. Betsy. She was probably seven or eight years older than I, wearing a gray twill-weave pants suit with a baby blue cotton blouse. Her shortly cropped chestnut hair thinned slightly at the crown of her head, but she had teased and sprayed it as though this was no concern. She had large dark blue eyes with scantly applied mascara and widely spaced eyebrows upon a wide forehead. Glancing around the room at her various diplomas and certificates, I noticed photographs of children who were obviously hers, with the same wide brow.

"In a way, Molly, I'm glad that we have the chance to speak alone. I've known Peter and Alexa—excuse me, Alessandra—for half a year. I'd like to have some sense of where you're at before we start our work together."

"Where I'm at about what?"

Having finished the bread, I went for the remainder of my soup with a plastic spoon.

She sat back and sighed, one leg draped over the other, her feet in loafers and panty hose. For a while she was quiet, and the room filled with my slurping and the oh-so-peacefully gurgling fountain. But I was too hungry to care. Since Pete and Alessi weren't with us, I regretted spending my lunch break there. Of course, thanks to them, I could quit my job if I wished. I didn't need to wake up in the morning and be anywhere, or tell any supervisor that I was going to lunch.

Yet income from the job still seemed valuable, landing in my account with the comforting sanctity of direct deposit. I also felt addicted to the workday rhythm even as I resented it. Besides, no matter how often Pete reassured me that we couldn't end up like Long-Term Capital Management ("Over-leveraged, over speculative!" he declared) I didn't trust the funds-built-on-funds world.

At least I knew how my job ran.

"I want you to hear something," Dr. Betsy finally said. I told her that she was welcome to disclose it. "I had tried, rather hard, to discourage them from hiring you. Nothing personal against you. But generally a surrogate mom is married and the mother of at least one child."

"Actually, I agree with you. What made you relent?"

She had barely any lips, but her smile made up for it in dimples.

"It wasn't my decision, of course."

That was a polite way of saying: "You know Alessi."

"It's a lot to ask of you," she continued. "Pregnancy can bring up all sorts of emotions."

"It already has."

"I know the story, by the way, about their financial offer. I can understand why you've agreed to do it."

So one more person was in on our secret.

"Ultimately, I didn't make the decision because I was hard-pressed for money," I explained. "I kind of pulled a straw."

"What do you mean?"

"I didn't feel equipped to make such a decision—to give a child life or not. It seemed beyond the scope of logical thinking. So I let life say it for me."

Betsy looked confused.

"What you'll find out about me," I continued, "if Peter and Alessandra haven't already warned you, is that I am a ridiculously stable person with a ridiculously unstable life. I have no excuse for it either. I didn't have a tragic childhood, like my friend Claudia from Corona, whose father beat her with a belt buckle to her bare skin while her mom ignored it. My parents have always been"—I shrugged—"reliable. Not violent or hysterical. Opinionated, at worst. My mother can't cook for her life, my father doesn't tend to talk, but—they're pretty normal."

"How is your life unstable?" she asked.

"I'm in control of everything, except what really matters. Like two weeks ago, for example, I broke up with my boyfriend—or my boy toy, or my 'bed partner,' or whatever we call such a person these days. My second breakup in a year. I seem to be racking them up at record rates. Did Alessandra mention Thomas to you?"

"Why don't you tell me about Thomas?"

"Well, Thomas and Jordan were my version of Sacred and Profane Love. Thomas was marriage material to the point that, two months into the game, I felt we had been married for fifteen years. Alessi nicknamed him Tom the Nice Guy because he was so upstanding. Not a mean bone in his body—but not a bone, either, if you probed hard enough. Which I developed the bad habit of doing.

"Jordan, on the other hand, is a hot, irrepressible twenty-four-year-old jazz musician who fancies himself the next John Coltrane. You know, there's always a scruffy young guy in Washington Square Park or the Haight playing melancholy saxophone with an instrument case open for donations. That's Jordan.

"You might say that I like variety, though they're both losers—maybe Jordan's too young and talented to call it yet. I don't know. Alessandra thinks I attract losers."

"And what do you think?"

Somehow Dr. Betsy tricked me into a corner, and I didn't appreciate her prompting me, with psychotherapeutic conceit: "Are all men losers, Molly?"

"Well of course not," I said condescendingly to her. "My father isn't. My brother isn't. My boss isn't—most men I know aren't. Only the ones I date. And don't ask me why, because I have absolutely no insight. Best guess is it's a coincidence. Or maybe lovely romantic things just don't happen to me."

"What sort of lovely romantic things just don't happen to you?"

"Oh, for example, the way my brother and sister-in-law met."

I scraped the bottom of my soup container for every last taste of bacon and sweet cream, then thought of the Chicken Tarragon sandwich on Rosemary Foccacia still in the bag. When Dr. Betsy said nothing more, I recited the heart-warming family tale as I eagerly unwrapped my sandwich.

"My brother was flagging a cab one torrentially rainy Saturday night—when, of course, everyone in Manhattan flags a cab. But low and behold, one stopped for Matthew, who didn't have an umbrella and was soaked. He was about to get in when he noticed a couple of distressed girls with umbrellas at the curb and, being a gentleman, offered them his cab.

"He told them he was so drenched that it didn't matter if he got more wet, but they still had a chance to stay dry. Wanting to reward his decency, Tamara insisted that he join them in their cab and that they drop him off. Before he got out, she gave him her phone number. Now that's a way to meet someone—not on the Internet or through some dopey setup. Just when you're not looking for it, but it finds you."

"Certainly that's desirable. But it doesn't always happen."

"Having worked in advertising, I'm not one to trick fate with a dating profile. I'm already out of fate's good graces. And I would have surrendered everything for blissful sex, if Jordan hadn't…" but I didn't want to divulge exactly what he'd done. He deserved my anger and silence, not my betrayal. "If he hadn't pushed me to the breaking point, we wouldn't have broken. Why do people push things to the breaking point? You're a social worker. Perhaps you have some theories about that."

"Every case is different," said Betsy.

I took a huge bite of the Chicken Tarragon sandwich, suspecting that if she were Jewish or German she would have theories. Being an Irish Scot myself, I could get away with snobbery against my own.

"Personally," I said, once I resurfaced from the sandwich, "I believe that affluence and advanced medical care permit us the luxury of thinking too much about relationships. And if you think too much about anything, you'll bore it into the ground. Jordan worried himself nuts about what was going on with us, and so did Thomas, as a matter of fact. It's like picking a scab with hopes that it will heal."

She smiled uncertainly, a morass of dimples.

"So you've kept your men wondering."

"The opposite. I've been clear to the point of frustrating them. They don't want anything but compliments and reassurance."

I ducked into the sandwich again and extracted another chunk of it.

"But here's the strange thing," I went on, after I'd finished chewing and swallowing. "If I hadn't loaned Jordan five hundred dollars last month, I wouldn't have been able to prove to my boss that I was out of the office when the slime bag who was sexually harassing me faked my signature on a routing sheet. But pardon me, I digress again."

"Let's get back to pulling the straw. Please tell me what you mean by that."

"I didn't literally pull a straw or toss a coin. I asked a woman I barely know if she would be a surrogate mother in exchange for a hedge fund account, and I decided in advance that I would do whatever she said. This, of course, was when my job hung in the balance.

"I was at my wit's end—scared of losing the job and disappointing my oldest friend, Alessi, or getting shanghaied into this crazy arrangement and feeling stuck.

But now I'm completely glad to be doing it. Thank God I asked Eugenia, the tall, blonde tennis-player-extraordinaire-gone-bartender in a lesbian club downtown, and not Terry, the anorexic straight girl with a crush on her. Eugenia said she'd do it."

Betsy looked blindsided and said, "That's the strangest reason to be a surrogate mother that I've ever heard."

"Sorry it wasn't something wholesome, like desperately needing money, or finding pregnancy euphoric."

"Let me ask you a frank question," she hazarded. "You seem to have a number of friendly associations. But do you feel that you'll have an emotional support system during your pregnancy?"

"Probably not, but I don't need one. I've always taken the best care of myself."

I suppressed a belch and put my hand to my lips.

Betsy looked unconvinced and reminded me annoyingly of my mother. I wished that Pete and Alessi were there too. Why had they not come? Why had Terry and Rick not shown up at the Bunny Hop yesterday? I was sick of being left in the lurch by couples.

"The most I can do for you is to help you establish an emotional support system," Betsy continued. "Because you will need one."

"Well, I've got Pete and Alessi."

"You'll need other people too."

"No one else really knows about it yet. Are you aware of the weird legal status of surrogate mothers in New York State?"

"Of course I am. That was another reason I tried to discourage them from hiring you."

"Yeah, me too. I guess we both failed. Whatever Lola wants, Lola gets, right?"

I smiled at Betsy. No dimples this time; she played poker-faced. Pete and Alessi were her clients. I could see she was trying her best to serve them and not having the easiest time with me.

Back at my office I called Alessi immediately.

"Thanks for standing me up at the shrink's. And by the way, couldn't you have found someone more innovative, who wouldn't spout every cliché about emotional support?"

"Don't underestimate her. Sometimes Pete and I find she's more on the ball than the PhD we see for couple's counseling."

"She didn't like me..."

"No surprise. She can't stand us."

Suddenly Alessi called out into the background: "Sweetie! Molly doesn't think Dr. Betsy likes her."

I could hear Pete laughing and replying, though I couldn't make out what he said. Alessi came back to the receiver.

"He said Dr. Betsy thinks he's a big swinging Wall Street dick with a crazy wife. Our shrinks shouldn't like us too much or they won't have the gumption to help us."

"Why is Pete home today?"

"We had a final meeting with Harry to draft the paragraph about you being our kid's custodian if we croak. When you approve it, we'll set up a meeting to sign the silly thing already. Maybe we can do it Monday."

"Send it to me and my attorney—Hey, 'A,' can I ask you something private?" I looked over my shoulder to make sure that my office door was closed. "Have the birth control pills made you really horny?"

"Are you kidding? After that last miscarriage, both Pete and I are on sabbatical from sex. You're probably sizzling because you know you'll give birth."

"Let's hope I do."

"Are you back in the saddle with Mystery Man?"

"No way. It would be great to get laid, but these days I don't even need to..." I then lowered my voice to a whisper. "Not to sound like a sleazy paperback, but even a breeze on my neck will do the trick. And forget running downstairs to catch a subway. Absolute exhilaration."

"Sounds fun."

"Too extreme."

Suddenly I realized that someone was knocking softly at my door.

"Someone's here, Alessi. Gotta run."

"Em, Molly! Knock, knock! Knock, knock!" he chanted.

That could be only Enrico.

"Come in," I called as I replaced the phone into its cradle.

Enrico appeared at my door, his hair pulled back into a ponytail and his rhinestone earrings glinting.

"Can we speak for a moment?" he asked.

"Of course."

With his textbook droopy wrist he drew my door shut. I pulled over a spare chair for him and noticed, for the first time, his trim thighs and concisely curved butt as he sat down.

"Oh, is that your boyfriend?" he asked, pointing to the photograph of Thomas and me by my monitor, smiling stiffly in our tennis outfits.

"I hope not."

"I know," he continued with a delighted grin. "You like that boy with black hair who showed up here last month, don't you?"

Yes, the one who wanted five hundred dollars to transform my living room into a narcotics export center behind my back. Taking a breath and exhaling forcefully, I asked, "What can I do for you today, Enrico?"

"Well, I'm having a problem, and I'm not sure you can even help me. But my boyfriend advised me to speak with you, since you are my supervisor. And you're the only one around here, frankly, who knows what she's doing."

"What kind of problem?"

"This is so hard for me to say—I never thought this would happen in a gay-owned business. I never thought I'd say that I'm being sexually harassed."

"By a man?"

Enrico nodded. I felt suddenly ill from having wolfed down my food at Dr. Betsy's and wondered if Enrico was about to tell me that Larry had hit on him. I had sensed peculiar tension between them. Already, I felt awful for Steve.

"What's going on?"

Enrico's eyes slid toward my door and back again to me. Then he leaned in and confided, "Jack isn't propositioning me. But he's saying really sick stuff."

I tried to keep poker-faced, as Dr. Betsy had with me. While I was tempted to take Enrico under my wing and assure him that I felt his pain, I wondered whether this might be Jack's ultimate plant.

"I feel so cheap!" Enrico sputtered. "You won't believe what he says. Like once, he was watching me draw with the mouse, and he asked why I didn't use a Wacom tablet. I told him, I had learned on the mouse and gotten used to it."

"You draw well with the mouse," I said.

"Well, thanks. But anyway, then Jack tells me: 'I can see you've made the best of being born with the wrong equipment.'"

As my jaw opened, Enrico swiped my arm briefly with his fingertips.

"And listen to this. When we were comping up those labels for the Blue Orchid Tea House he asks me, shouldn't the type go above the logo? I told him it looked better to me underneath, and he said, 'Well, you're a bottom, aren't you?'"

"Have you kept a record of all this?"

"Not until last night, when I was telling Bruno. He typed it into his laptop."

"Good. We should pursue this legally, since we don't really have H.R."

"Could we?"

He implored with long-lashed brown eyes.

"Under federal law, this isn't supposed to happen. Harassment is illegal in any workplace. We'll have to prove it happened in order to make a case—or even a threat."

"But he says the nasty stuff when we're totally alone, with no witnesses."

"I can't go into detail now. But there have been other complaints about Jack," I whispered. "We may be able to prove a pattern."

"Oh my God! I am so glad I talked to you. I don't want to leave this job. I can't, really—Bruno's hours were just cut back. But working under these conditions…"

Enrico scowled.

And I realized that we might have to do something radical.

27

With its rusticated tiles and fresh lilies, the ladies room at La Café Idealisme seemed like a cottage in Southern France. To clinch the pastoral impression, someone had painted a vine of ivy along the three white toilet stalls. I was not on a toilet seat myself but a velvet settee, hoping for cell phone reception.

"Bertie?" I whispered into my phone. After all, Eugenia could come in at any minute with her own claim to pee or wash her hands. This was not like dining with a man, where the ladies room served as a reprieve from wilted conversations.

"How're you holding up?" Bertie asked.

"Well, it's great to talk with someone who actually *says* something. You're right about her going mute away from the bar."

"She dissolves like a sugar cube."

"I'm in the girls' room because I couldn't take it."

"Maybe I'll spend Lainey's fifty bucks on leather boots."

"The jury isn't in, and the night is young," I reminded her. "But so far, you're winning the bet."

I was disappointed in both Eugenia and myself. We were like caricatures—I the manic anchorwoman prying news out of her, the town recluse. I'd managed to learn that she danced upon the bar only on New Year's Eve, that she didn't put much alcohol in the drinks of notoriously low tippers. But aside from these random revelations, she answered my questions with a shrug and didn't ask any of her own. Altogether, she seemed dour and remote, hardly the charmer I knew from The Bunny Hop.

I had taken her to La Café Idealisme rather than "out for coffee," as Bertie and Lainey suggested, because guys who asked me "out for coffee" seemed chintzy. I understood that dating gets costly for guys, but since I had invited a woman out, I decided to pursue it as an exercise in how I would like to be treated—meaning, taken somewhere memorable with no sense that my host was pursuing agendas in excess of my delightful company over dinner. But Eugenia seemed appalled when I met her at the entrance to La Café Idealisme.

"A little fancy, isn't this?" she protested.

I had to shove her inside, where the decor worked its magic: Cézanne's apples and pears set against the gray crock and folded afghan; Matisse's goldfish in a tank; Braque's pipe and Picasso's guitar mounted in the Cubist section. An accordionist, the likes of which Édith Piaf rhapsodized in throaty trills over the speakers, lingered in his red and yellow harlequin-patterned costume.

When we were seated in the Matisse section, Eugenia glanced apprehensively at the potted palms and orange trees but said nothing. And so began my crusade to engage her in conversation when it was clear that she resented being there. Maybe she'd guessed that Bertie and Lainey put me up to everything, and saw my invitation as the ruse it was.

"Now you know I'm not jealous of her," Bertie declared over the phone. "Why should a woman with top IQ and interactive skills be jealous of one with neither? The dumb hick just happens to be pretty enough to turn everyone's heads until you talk to her and see that no one's home. Sorry I stuck you in that position."

"Sorry I took you up on it," I said.

After we hung up I consulted the mirror over the ceramic sink with its mermaid-shaped faucets of tinted glass. My reflection stared back boldly in her black silk blouse. I had vetoed the Nicole Miller print and gone pitch-black, with a silver necklace and amber centerpiece.

"Thank God I'm not a homo," I said to myself, whipping out a comb from my purse. "No wonder these women drink themselves silly. And no wonder guys bungle everything on dates when we're regally quiet and undecipherable as the Cyrillic alphabet." I was raising my voice, and it felt good. "Who in hell can blame them? It's nerve-racking."

Then, from one of the white stalls with ivy painted so expertly upon it, a long, low fart emerged—tentatively at first, then gathering confidence. Whoever had been sitting there for the last five minutes, listening to my conversation with Bertie and my soliloquy before the mirror, knew more about me at that moment than anyone else.

When I returned to our table, Eugenia's blue eyes followed me as though to make sure I was back.

"Everything okay?" she asked.

"Long bathroom line," I reported.

"Funny, since there aren't many customers on Sunday night."

Insolently, she glanced around the candlelit room and then at me.

"If you're that observant," I said sternly to her, "then why are you sitting here not saying a word?"

"What should I be saying?"

I wanted to smack her but restrained myself. I was going to be exemplary that night.

"Okay, for starters—what would you like for dinner?"

When the waiter came by, I insisted upon sparkling water, snidely adding, "Sparkling as my companion's wit." She smiled back with equal disdain.

We ordered escargot and frisée salad for appetizers. She chose duck breast in a wine marinade, and I opted for *Poulet au Riz Basquaise*. Neither of us was remotely won over by the wild dove and *Pigeons à la Béarnaise*, or saddle of hare. Such gamey offerings were one thing in the rambles of eighteenth-century France but a different matter in Manhattan at the dawn of a new millennium.

I was still undecided about wine. With her duck and my chicken, we could do either red or white, and we should aim for something dry and certainly not sweet. I hated super-sweet wine and would rather drink Coke. I glanced at the wine list, and my eye fell upon a bottle of Pauillac for one hundred and eighty-five dollars. That should get a rise out of her.

"Would you please tell us about this bottle?" I asked our garçon.

"I can, mademoiselle, but maybe I shall fetch our sommelier?"

He indicated another guy in a red and yellow harlequin-patterned costume.

"I'd like to hear it from you," I said, flirtatiously cocking my head at the garçon.

"Well now, 1982 was a particularly good year in this, eh, terrain. It is a thick and silky wine; it has structure, it has depth. You will very much enjoy."

I was about to order it when Eugenia asked the garçon for a moment alone with me.

"Molly, do you have any idea of the markup on a bottle like that?" she scolded. "It's not in the single digits."

"I don't care," I said. "I like the atmosphere here, don't you? If that's what I'm paying for, it's better than paying for root canal or a parking ticket."

"Look, I'd be happy with this Côtes du Rhône, or that Pinot Noir."

Both bottles she pointed to were listed in the forty-dollar range. I wished she wouldn't fret over my expenses, but I always did that with men who took me out—I never allowed them to impress me. No wonder I wound up with losers, and no wonder she didn't want to date them at all.

"Oh, let's go for the Pauillac. It sounds delightful."

"If you have cash like that lying around and gathering dust," she chided me, "why don't you sponsor a little girl in Thailand or Nepal? Save her from a life of sex slavery. Or, God knows, help a kid here; we're not immune from trafficking. Isn't that more important than a pricy bottle of wine?"

"Without a doubt," I agreed—more than shocked.

But she'd come out of hiding. This was the person who had guided my decision to be Alessandra's surrogate mother. She was not a smoke-and-mirrors specter at the Bunny Hop bar. The balance of the bet tipped into Lainey's favor.

"Okay," I told Eugenia. "I will sponsor two girls—somewhere. One in your name and one in mine. I promise you that. But you,"—I pointed to her—"please let me get the Pauillac."

Her eyes appeared to blaze through their own reserve, and she broke into the first grin of the night. "You drive a hard bargain."

As it happened, she adored the wine once she tasted the trickle our waiter provided for her to sample. At her nod, he directed the snakelike tongue of red wine into each of our glasses, entreating us to enjoy "the long finish."

I raised my glass, and she raised hers.

"Eugenia," I began, deciding to go rococo with flattery, "in a world that, as H.L. Mencken put it, has 'a libido for the ugly,' where architecture is becoming bland and utilitarian, where car design, fashion, and furniture are pointedly clumsy, where art and music are often sloppy, if not embarrassing, there is one last reserve: a beautiful face, especially a beautiful woman's face. The world, despite its love of shoddiness, still cannot resist that. Eugenia,"—I smiled at her, my voice faltering—"you are incredibly beautiful, charismatic, and mysterious. I toast you."

I clinked her glass. She barely moved.

"I can't speak like you do," she finally said. "And I won't try. But—likewise."

She wound her arm around mine, I wound mine around hers, and we sipped from our own glasses. From overhead speakers, Jacques Brel crooned his smooth, cynical ballads, and the accordionist echoed the tune as he meandered around potted palms and orange trees.

Dinner was so sumptuous that I didn't want it to end, like sunset on a mountain lake. Eugenia and I traded tastes from each other's plates and paced ourselves so as not to trundle through it too quickly.

"I dread when the past tense will kick in about this meal," I told her as I forked up the delectable remains of my rice and chicken. "Here's my disclaimer—I can take people out for dinners like this, but I can't cook them."

"Well, seein' as you call this is a *plan*, not a *date*, I'd wonder what kind of red carpet you roll out on a date."

"You really want to know?"

"I can come up with some educated guesses."

Our garçon then brought over a small chalkboard of dessert offerings. We would top the evening with flan on fire since that was one of Eugenia's own specialties. I reminded her of how she had flambéed Terry's bag of barbecued chips.

"So where did you learn your bartending acrobatics?" I asked as the garçon cleared our china plates, silver, and crystal goblets, and the busboy crumbed our cloth. "Juggling beer bottles and pouring drinks behind your own back?"

"This Haitian guy called Mango worked with me at my aunt Carlene's inn. I stayed there a couple of summers. They make the best crawfish bisque on the Gulf Coast."

I took the occasion to drill her on the difference between Creole and Cajun cooking, and could she recommend any Gulf food place in the city?

"Nothing to literally write home about," she said. "No one here knows how to make gumbo or jambalaya worth my nickel. Even blackened fish is too greasy."

"Then you should open a place," I said. "You've got the following."

"Almost did once." She eyed me warily. "Did you know that?"

"No. But do tell."

"It's not a nice story. You don't want to get me started."

But after the flambé streaked our table and we poked forks into the custard and brought it to our lips, she disclosed her tale over decaf espresso. Something about that Pauillac had relaxed her—or maybe she was just getting used to me.

"In a nutshell," she began, "two partners and I were going to open a bar with Gulf Coast soup and finger food. Figured we'd get some live music—blues singers, jazz, zydeco, Cajun. It was my idea. We thought Hell's Kitchen would be a perfect pre-theatre spot for people who get peckish but didn't want a huge dinner.

"I researched price points around there and made a business plan. My partners loved the concept and felt it would fly. We were calling the place 'Eugenia's.' We got the DBA and opened an account in my name, because I was the US citizen in that trio. This filthy rich Venezuelan guy was going to back us. But then he and my other so-called partner figured that fifty percent profit was better than thirty-three. Just as we were incorporating Eugenia's, they took another DBA behind my back and opened up—check this out—Aunt Carlene's Cajun Kingdom. They even copped my aunt Carlene."

"So where is this place? Can I show up with whipped cream and toilet paper?"

"It didn't last six weeks. They didn't know what they were doing." Eugenia removed a pack of Camels from the leather jacket that was draped over her seat. "With restaurants, you've got to talk to people. They were conceited..." She crammed a cigarette between her lips and muttered, "South Americans, like I said. Neither of them was legal here. Look, I don't want to go on about this."

She lit her cigarette with a swift flick, and I sipped my espresso.

"So," she said on her exhale, "if that happened to you, would you have ratted it to the INS?"

"I would have been tempted."

"I couldn't bring myself." Eugenia drew on her cigarette again, facing away from me. I thought she might clam up, but after her exhale the words came.

"She was my girlfriend. We lived together for four years. I was supposed to marry our Venezuelan backer and get him a green card. We'd be married for two years, and he agreed that we'd file for divorce. But then she, my ex, hinted that 'he expects to have marital relations with you,' and I was like—'Excuse me? That's not part of the deal.'

"In her opinion I was naïve. She came from such a different place, a dirt-poor family in Colombia. She's back there now because she got deported, just after their restaurant tanked. Can't come back here for ten years. They caught her at customs with a fake driver's license. Funny—some people can't say enough shit about this country, but they're always the first to get a fake driver's license or passport. 'Gringo,' she called me."

When Eugenia finished her cigarette, she snuffed it, saying, "Hope I didn't stink up this table. You don't smoke, do you?"

"No. Never started."

"It's a revolting habit. I'd quit, but after that crap went down I started up again."

"You must have been insanely angry," I commented, finishing my espresso.

"I had to take lessons in how to be that angry—started kickboxing classes." She leaned back in her seat and gazed at the ceiling. "If anyone wonders why I stick to flings with twenty-two-year-olds…well, I don't swim anywhere with undertow these days."

28

"Couldn't you open Eugenia's with your aunt from the Gulf Coast?"

I shoved my hands into the pockets of my suede jacket as we started up Sixth Avenue, she at a fast clip with her long legs in tight, faded jeans, and I just about keeping up.

"Oh hell. My aunt and uncle wanna retire. Last thing they need is a business in New York City. That dream is dead in the water." She aimed a mock rifle south, toward Canal Street and shot: *kablam!* "Its ghost is dead in the water, not even bleedin' anymore. Why are we talking about it?"

"Cajun finger food with live music is a great idea."

"Who needs another great idea?"

"Put it out in the world and see."

Suddenly she slipped her arm over my back and her hand fell on my arm. To politely discourage her, I took my hand out of my pocket, moving my arm. But her long fingers found mine and interlocked with them.

"Please forgive me, Molly. I can pour it on a little thick."

We seemed to slow down, our heels scuffing on the sidewalk.

Part of me thought, almost audibly: this is uncomfortable. I'm not gay. Another part of me realized that an enthralling person had taken my hand.

"I don't live far from here," she said. "Can I invite you up for tea and a glass of port? My roommate and I just got a bottle of Taylor Fladgate—and you can meet his cats."

"What a nice invitation. But I actually must get home."

She said nothing. Clearly, people didn't decline her invitations.

"I have to sign legal papers in Greenwich, Connecticut, tomorrow, believe it or not," I went on. "And make a morning train."

Of course Pete and Alessi were sending a car for me. But I didn't want Eugenia to know that. At the corner we stopped walking, and I gracefully removed my hand from hers as though I was extracting it from a nearly closed door.

"I should head east here. Well, this has been lovely. I'm so glad you joined me."

She stared back, bemused. I wasn't sure whether to give her a hug, a peck on the cheek, or just a little wave good-bye.

But with the grace of an Olympic diver, she swooped me into an embrace and guided my lips to hers. Her full, amazing mouth bloomed against mine with the skilled hint of a tongue as her finger grazed my cheek. I had never been kissed so expressively. There are "I love you" kisses, "I love life" kisses, "I love kissing" kisses—but this was all in one.

To heighten its potency, I had not been touched by anyone since Jordan and was beyond ready to be. Brazenly, I plastered myself against her firm, lanky frame, which was actually taller than his, wrapping a leg around hers, hoping to telegraph: "Okay, daredevil. Try me."

She took me up on the challenge, offering her leg generously and reaching under my jacket, her warm hands trickling over my blouse; I lost no time in lunging my own hands beneath her sweater, around her smooth back to her surprisingly bony spine, our lips and tongues still infusing each other with just enough Pauillac and flan to offset the night air.

"Your kiss has a long finish," I stammered at last.

"My kiss? Can we share ownership?"

She was no weakling. She had, after all, tied with Bertie in an arm wrestle and almost played doubles with Chris Evert. As she walked me backward to a chain-linked fence, I felt like a mighty anaconda was winding between our legs.

"Take me upstairs," I suggested.

"Didn't you have to get home?"

Then I reached over and did something Jordan had once so marvelously done to me on the street—I wedged my flat palm against her crotch. Caught off guard, she grabbed my wrist and held my hand over my head, pinning me against the fence.

"Fickle," she said, breathing into my ear. "Aren't you?"

By this time I was ready to burst in seven directions on the street like an open hydrant. And then my alluring companion did the worst thing imaginable: she dropped my hand, pulled away from me, and started brooding. No man would do that if we'd come to so much of a boil.

"Christ, Eugenia, stop *thinking*," I begged.

She looked back at me, flipped the pack of Camels out of her leather jacket, and popped one between her lips. She kept it there without lighting up and muttered with it in her mouth.

"You make me think. You said you had to get home, and I'm being bad."

"Forget what I said. I was shy and scared…"

"Well, you'll be shy and scared twelve times before we make it upstairs."

She removed the cigarette and held it in her hand, pointing at me with it. "I know your kind, cutie. You need time to figure out what you want. I should be a decent dinner guest and help you into a cab. Know what I'm saying?"

"I guess you're right," I admitted reluctantly, my heart chopping through my ribcage. She was more right than she realized. "But I don't want to leave you."

She looked back sweetly. "It will make our next meeting better."

My mouth dropped open as she tossed the unlit cigarette into the street and bounded to the curb, waving her arm at an oncoming taxi, whistling through her fingers. So, this is what guys mean by "blue balls." I staggered to her and the cab like a cripple, amazed that I was actually missing the reliably boorish behavior of men at such moments.

"Hey, look," she whispered, her hand on my arm, her breath warm along my hair. "Come by the bar tomorrow around midnight. It's Monday. I can close early, and I'll take *you* somewhere nice."

"Midnight? I'll be dead."

"Nap in the afternoon," she advised, opening the cab door. "Siesta. Works wonders even for me."

"But I—I work during business hours."

"Thought you were signing papers in Greenwich. I'm sure you can find a good hammock."

As I plopped onto the seat and she gently shut the door on me, I realized my pants were soaking as though I had peed in them. Eugenia handed the driver money, then reappeared at the half-opened window with blonde hair dangling in her eyes. For a moment she remained, gazing and idyllic as an angel.

"Molly," she prompted in a raspy whisper. "Buckle your seatbelt and tell him where you're going. I'll see you tomorrow."

29

We popped our first bottle of Dom Perignon at Harry's law office, after all papers were signed and last questions resolved. Then Pete took us to brunch at a seafood place along the Sound for more champagne, crabmeat, and oysters that were just becoming seasonal. Barely anyone was there on a Monday, but we kept that surprised young waitress busy. And Alessi rewarded her with a tip beyond the cost of the meal.

"I always wanted someone to do that," she mentioned as we trotted out to the parking lot. "Waiting tables can be thankless. I remember it well."

I wondered if anyone had ever left Eugenia that kind of tip, and how she would handle it. As Alessi and I drove to Stamford, I swirled that daydream like a snifter of brandy.

We'd said good-bye to Pete, whose driver would bring him back to the city office, and set out in the Jaguar for an afternoon of decadent clothes shopping. Beginning in Stamford and working our way to White Plains, we would hit everything from Nordstrom to Neiman Marcus—a far cry from my shopping ritual with Mom in those New England outlet stores. My mother was always so thrilled by bargains and had developed a vulture's eye for them.

"But someone's gotta buy retail," Alessi insisted, behind the wheel and her sunglasses. The car roof was down, and a brisk, sunny wind whipped through our hair. "You'll develop the appetite for it. As with any appetite, don't sate yourself. Only buy things you'll live in—pure silk, cashmere, leather. Go hog wild on that."

Generally I regard fashion trends as contests as to how obscenely much people will spend to look obscenely hideous. But a line of strapless evening gowns at Neiman Marcus caught my eye when I imagined them on Eugenia—particularly the midnight-blue satin or the silky black mesh that I pinched between my fingers.

"Mournful," Alessi commented, coming up behind me. "You don't want to look like someone out of *Angela's Ashes.*"

"A bit beyond their price range. I was thinking of this for a gorgeous blonde friend."

A gorgeous blonde friend I had kissed last night, the way I'd kissed men.

"Listen," said Alessi. "When you get your first nut of cash, you think about who else to spend it on. You want to buy gifts for everyone you know."

"I hope I'll always feel that way."

But I was also actually thinking of how many children might be saved from sex trafficking for the cost of these dresses.

By nightfall, Alessandra and I sat together in her sauna. She spoke of an herb she'd learned about called trillium that would "soften my cervix" if I began ingesting it weeks before labor.

"I want the birth to be as painless as possible for you," she said, splashing a bucket of cold water over herself. "God, knows, you've been great about everything, Molly. More than a friend."

"Yes," I murmured, "everyone's redeemer as I fall from grace myself."

Alessi eyed me inquisitively as I shifted around on the cedar bench. In fact, I was thinking not so much about herbs and labor but about being with a nude woman and feeling completely not aroused. If anything, my assessment of Alessi's body wasn't charitable. I noticed, for example, that she slumped, that her posture was getting bad. But her face, in the steam, was slick and rosy, her eyes expressive and alert.

"If you do Lamaze and take this herb, there's no way you'll need a C-Section. And I'll get you ointment to eliminate stretch marks."

She was my friend. We had sat together naked in saunas and changed clothes in department store dressing rooms and gym lockers for decades. Still, even after last night's episode with Eugenia, Alessi could not have seemed less sexy to me if she was an eggplant.

"I've been talking to a girl in my support group about prenatal yoga."

"Why does everyone need support groups these days?" I groaned, remembering the session with Dr. Betsy. "Don't we have character anymore? Can't we manage our lives without someone holding our hand?"

And what would Eugenia, who had held my hand last night, think if she knew that I was sitting naked in a sauna with another woman now? If I were gay, wouldn't I be turned on with any reasonably desirable nude woman? Wasn't I that way with men?

But I wasn't. Most men didn't attract me. Most people didn't—men or women. The ones I found desirable were few and far between, and that's why they drove me crazy. I knew better than to see Eugenia later on. It wouldn't do a thing for either of us. Just as I had needed to exit my building to avoid Jordan the night he had gone to Claudia's after our spat, I now needed to escape the entire island of Manhattan to avoid her.

"Look, you're exceptionally stable," said my old friend, smearing her face with a costly Australian mudpack she'd ordered from some website, carefully excluding her eyes and lips. "But you know the song—*we all need somebody to lean on.*"

I wiped my forehead as sweat tickled it, my hair damp and clammy.

"I may need physical help after a point."

"You can live up here. Or we'll hire someone for you."

Alessi then popped on a stiff, woolen elf-type cap. She handed me one, saying that it would keep my head from overheating, but I refused. If ever I had the choice of being uncomfortable or looking like a geek, I would suffer nobly.

"You'll be glad to know," I told her, "that I'm declaring myself a Dating-Free Zone until after the birth."

She nodded happily at that, explaining that the hormone-balancing properties in this facial mud from Australia were derived from wild yams. Her face now amply coated with it, she appeared ready for a role in Kabuki theater with her crazy hat, or at least some misbegotten porn shoot.

And for a moment I almost felt Eugenia tap me on the shoulder, as if to say: "Where the hell are you?"

30

The next morning Kendra didn't even look at me as I breezed by her desk after 10:30. Once in my office, I shut the door and booted up my computer to a torrent of emails from Enrico—his accounts of Jack's harassment. Promptly, I made a folder of them on my zip drive, so it wouldn't show up on the intraoffice network.

After that, I wrote to see how Terry was doing but never got a reply.

"Demon mail" bulletins reported that no emails had reached her.

If you don't mind my asking, I finally emailed Rick, *what did you mean last week by "Terry feels terrible?" Everything okay?*

She has uterine fibroids. No malignancy. She may remove them because of her anorexia and BDD.

I've heard of AC-DC and ADD. What's BDD?

Body Dysmorphic Disorder. She's so obsessed with her weight that she can't function. She's not at work."

Wish I didn't have to be.

I wrote that but didn't mean it. I was glad enough to be somewhere familiar, even when Larry barged through my door with a pile of manila folders and cases of disks. They all flew from his arms to the floor as he stumbled over the threshold. After scouting around to reorder the zip disks and CDs on my spare chair, he took a seat on my file cabinet, just as JackASS had done two long months ago. Larry now clasped the bundle of folders and manila envelopes on his lap, announcing, "We gotta talk, kid."

I sat with my legs crossed, one shoe hanging off my foot in defiance. I'd heard this "we gotta talk" line from him before.

"We've had a little shake-up here. I had to let Enrico go yesterday."

"Why?"

"Because *he* forged your signature on the routing sheet last month. I always knew it must be one of the young designers, remember?"

I put a hand to my open mouth.

"Good thing Jack got it out of him. But Mike Haft left too, 'in solidarity.' I don't know, maybe something was going on with those two."

"Enrico lives with his boyfriend…"

Larry smirked.

"He's a provocative boy. But you wouldn't understand that. What do women know about raw sex?"

"More than you think."

I flashed upon Eugenia's blonde hair dangling over her face, her breath along my ear as she pinned me against that chain-linked fence Sunday night.

"Oh, Molly, you believe those lover boys of yours are fireworks on wheels, but you have no idea how men tame themselves to be with the gentle sex. It's the difference between fresh and canned vegetables…"

"There's a lot YOU don't get, Larry!" I nearly screamed, my hand now down from my mouth. "For starters, you fired the wrong person."

"I didn't! You missed a nasty little scene here yesterday. And where, may I ask, have you been disappearing to with all these sick days? Seems like you're out every other day, Molly Malone. What's the deal?"

"I'm seeing a shrink."

"Thought you hated shrinks."

"They come in handy sometimes."

"But how the hell often do you go to a shrink? At my worst, I went twice a week…"

"I have uterine fibroids!" I exclaimed. "I may need surgery."

"Why were you out all day yesterday? Shrink appointments are fifty minutes and not one second more, don't I know? And how many scans and ultrasounds do you need?"

Then my cell phone rang its plain little jingle, no musical frills. I saw from the caller ID that it was Bertie, and I snapped the phone off.

"Ah. You're having an affair." We both looked at my phone. "That's the only explanation for this rash of disappearances."

"Since when is a woman sidetracked by anything so raw as passion?"

Larry grinned sheepishly from behind his wire-framed glasses. This was the problem; I adored Larry even when I wanted to pull his ears off.

"Not to be suffocating, but I need you now, girlfriend. You can't flake out on me." He slammed the manila folders onto my desk. "We're down two designers now. You'll take on both of their workloads, until we hire a new one. Today you'll go through Mike's and Enrico's electronic files. I may need you to work overtime—and I want you to interview these junior candidates before Jack and I do."

There were days I would have relished such insider privileges. But today I felt weary just imagining the tasks, and the fallout for poor Enrico.

31

"You got rave reviews from Blondie," Bertie had told my voice mail. "Call me for details. And for God's sake tell us who won the bet. Lainey and I are on tenterhooks."

I called Bertie during my coffee break, out of surprise as much as curiosity.

"So?" she barked at me.

"You lost."

After a full beat of silence, she said, "Wow. What the hell happened?" in a single breath.

"I don't know. You tell me. What was this rave review? I made an ass of myself, and I will not see 'Blondie' again."

There was no reason for me to go to The Bunny Hop now that Terry was out of commission. I would sponsor two girls in countries known for sex trafficking, as I had promised Eugenia over dinner. I would do that. Then I would send her a card with information about her sponsorship, once Alessi and I were out West for the grand insemination. That was the plan.

"I asked if she had a good time with you," Bertie told me. "She said yes."

"And the rave review?"

"That *is* a rave review from her! Usually she tells everyone how bored she was or how her date's perfume reeked. For her to just blush and say yes, she enjoyed herself, means you struck gold. She was giving everyone chocolates last night at the bar, and she even took a hit of my cigar, which usually makes her sick. I overheard her tell someone you were coming by. Did you?"

"Of course not."

"Well, what went on with you two?"

"A kiss good night that bucked me for its bang, Bertie. I'm so ashamed. I can't face her. I must keep away."

"Look, before you get all melodramatic—you're in a position people covet."

"Too bad it's wasted on me."

"She'll grill me about you. Shit, Molly. We didn't plan for this."

"Tell her I had to leave town suddenly on business. I will have to, next month. I'll send her a card."

I didn't mention to Bertie that before I fell asleep at night, Eugenia's remarkable face appeared beneath my eyelids as though I'd been anointed by the likes of Puck. I would wriggle under my sheets and box my pillow, thinking, "What in hell am I supposed to do with you? I'm already going to be pregnant without being a mother. Must I fall in love with a woman when I'm not gay? How twisted beyond recognition can one person be?"

Toward the end of the week, I was horrified when *Bunny Hop, The* popped onto my caller ID one evening. How, I wondered, pacing frantically around my living room as the phone rang, had she gotten my number? But Bertie's baritone blasted over the machine.

"Ya there, Molly?"

Still shaking, I picked up the phone and asked, "What's going on?"

"I'm at the bar with some friends. Hey, we wondered if you'd like to join us Saturday night for Mexican food. Eugenia's taking the night off from work. You around?"

"Is she standing there?" I asked.

"Yup."

"Will you be there too?"

"Both Lainey and me, yeah."

"What do you think I should do? You know my situation."

"Oh, join the fun."

Maybe a group occasion would provide the most honorable way to integrate with Eugenia, rather than vanishing with a postcard addendum from Oregon. I had agreed to go to Pete and Alessi's on Saturday but would be spending quite a lot of time there in the upcoming months. I could change the plan.

"Okay," I agreed gingerly.

"Great." Bertie sounded relieved.

"Call me when she's not standing beside you, all right?"

"Sure," said Bertie.

But by the time Saturday night rolled around, I had not heard from her. And when I got to the Mexican restaurant where we were all supposed to meet, I saw festoons of colored lights and shiny murals of coconut trees but no one I recognized. I walked out again and around the block, under boughs now full with leaves, past a flower stand where lilacs smelled fresher than the air. I wondered whether, against my better judgment, I had imagined the whole phone call from Bertie. I laughed cynically at myself for having tossed the birth control pills in my purse in case I didn't end up at home later.

When I walked back into the restaurant, Eugenia spun around. She had been sitting at the bar and probably saw me enter in the mirror. Her wavy hair spilled down to her shoulders, outstanding against a black shirt and a man's dinner jacket.

She nodded me over and I stood beside her, my heartbeat so startling that I could barely see what I was doing.

"Bertie and Lainey cancelled on us," was all she said.

I probably looked petrified and began bumbling like a giant hiccup.

"That bad, huh?" she asked. The blue of her eyes seemed to playfully deepen.

"What do you mean?"

"You were planning to disappear."

A woman apparently knows these things about another woman.

"Well, I was going to send you—a card."

She reached for a Camel, paused, slid it back into the pack, and looked back at me with dismay. "Care to sit down?"

I took a seat beside hers as a corny Mexican tune with harp and concertina tinkled on the jukebox. "*Fulanita, Fulanita, ay-ay-ay!*" sang the doleful voices.

"When you're bitten by a snake," Eugenia said, "the venom leaves your body slowly. But I could have spared you that depressing-ass story about being cheated in business by my ex…"

"Please don't spend another second blaming yourself."

She had no sense of the wicked web spun around her.

"I was a jerk the other night," she insisted.

"No," I corrected her. "I was a jerk."

"Taking me out to a five-star dinner when you hardly know me. Disgraceful."

She laughed like she was genuinely tickled, her features more delicate and chiseled than I remembered them. She seemed to emit a sharp light when I leaned closer to her, like sun reflecting on a windshield and almost obscuring itself.

"Guess I've been out with so many kids lately that I'm out of practice with ladies my age."

I was going to say, "I have no previous experience whatsoever with ladies" but didn't want to own up just then. It would have burdened the night, and I wanted this glow, this excitement, to last longer. For months I would be suspended in formaldehyde in Alessi's attic. I wanted life to be memorable while it could be.

"Now I've ambushed you again," Eugenia observed, her words almost lost against the mariachi chorus, the merry concertina belying those minor chords.

"I'm glad you did," I whispered, dying to touch her.

"I won't do it a third time," she said, to herself as much as to me.

"You won't have to. Let's defrost that sadness from your smile, can we?"

I brushed a finger over her cheek with a shaking hand. People at the bar watched us and I didn't care. Saturday night was still mine. "But we're new for each other, and I must beg a little patience from you."

The sarcasm left Eugenia's expression.

"That sounds fair," she ceded. "Now that you mention it, I could use a little patience myself."

32

I gazed, the next morning, into the misty eyes of an orange tabby cat that seemed as curious about me as I did about him. Another cat lay over my head on the pillow, a tortoise shell with white fur on her neck like a feather boa.

I was lying on Eugenia's bed, without her but with her roommate's cats. I had been introduced to them last night when she scooped them out of the room, reminding them that she loved them but needed privacy sometimes.

A royal-blue robe was draped over a chair by the bed with my clothes folded upon it. That was helpful, since my clothes—so far as I recalled—had been gleefully tossed around. A towel and a toothbrush, still in its package, had also been left for me.

The room was spare but tidy, its window covered by a Japanese paper shade that admitted a filmy blush from outside. Before it hung a spider plant with starry shoots and an overflowing pot of Swedish ivy. The pale yellow walls were ornamented with a colorful, torn kite and a vintage calendar with a hula dancer.

If the existential word for Thomas' apartment was *empty*, and for Jordan's was *chaos*, this room expressed *impermanence*. Its theme was being somewhere else, moving. A mountain bike stood in the corner with a stash of helmets, several tennis rackets, jars of yellow balls, and reasonably neat piles of clothing that I recognized —not without a flurry of sentiment—from the bar, like her long faded jeans and black Harley tank top.

I put on the blue robe and noticed, as I moved, that I wasn't tender in the usual places after awakening with a man. Instead, I felt like a giant butterfly had rapped its wings over my skin. And hadn't I been a quick study, so adept that she couldn't guess this was my first time with a woman? But like a confused little moth myself, I fluttered around her room now, eager to learn more about the sylph who'd filled my night with passion, weaving her long, graceful body around mine, tying us into knots and bows.

"Don't you ever sleep?" I had whispered affectionately.

"Not when there are better options."

As a grace note, I wasn't even expected to reciprocate. She was having her period and had worn a pair of red silk boxer shorts that she forbade me to tamper with. So I had been spared the challenge of mastering that learning curve on the spot.

I scrutinized her bookshelf, the murder mysteries and lesbian erotica, classic American novels of the Hemingway, Steinbeck, and Carson McCullers variety, a pinch of feminism from Emma Goldman to Camille Paglia. The poetry books were mostly Spanish—Borges, Lorca, Neruda—inspired probably by the Colombian ex-girlfriend who'd tried to swindle her Cajun café.

Then I explored her tennis rackets, tracing their round heads with my finger. Some had wooden braces over them, others didn't. When I was in high school I'd pined after the athletic boys, especially when they were charming. Something about Eugenia's lanky arms and legs reminded me of those adolescent athletes. When had I become enamored of couch potatoes like Thomas and Jordan?

The bedroom door squeaked open and she appeared, light on her feet as a cat. She wore cut-offs that accentuated her long, trim legs, a white tank top and a maroon bowling shirt with the name *Gene* embroidered in yellow. Her cheeks were flushed from a morning walk.

"Got us strawberries and croissants," she announced cheerfully.

That was another first. No one had ever brought me breakfast.

"Thanks. I haven't even made it to the shower."

"Hope it wasn't 'cause Clay was hogging it. I told him not to."

"No, I'm just lazy," I explained.

I walked over to her, and we folded effortlessly into each other's arms, where we had spent the whole night.

"Sweet of you to leave me the robe," I managed to say.

She stepped back slightly, looked me over, and asked, "How are you?"

I nodded nervously.

"Really good. Too good."

"Me too," she acknowledged. "We've got to be careful."

33

Once alone in the bathroom, I popped my birth control pills: the first thing we do after sex with another woman—particularly to increase our chances of getting pregnant… with someone else's child.

Beneath the sink the orange tabby cat rooted around a litter box. Now I remembered this was "Errol," since her auburn head spots were shaped like Errol Flynn's scalloped hair. The kitty was "kinda butch," in Eugenia's words. Around dawn and through a dream I'd heard her whisper, "How'd you get back here, Errol? Thought I'd eighty-sixed you."

Once she completed her business in the cedar chips, Errol was up for grabs. So I picked her up and just looked into her opaque, guileless eyes, which were the yellow green of martini olives. We had a friend in common.

Hair still wet from my shower and feet in socks, I pattered into the kitchen, where Eugenia's roommate, Clay—a tall, slim dancer with long eyes that looked as though someone had stretched them back, and a sculpted mound of dark hair— sat with another handsome gay guy and Eugenia, around a vintage Formica table. I took a red vinyl seat across from her. Clay was saying that the entire kitchen, with its tin ceiling, gas stove, and bracketed floral curtains, had been duplicated from a 1956 *McCalls* magazine ad. Clay and Eugenia sublet from a woman who lived in the New Jersey Pine Barrens and owned an antique shop that specialized in forties and fifties memorabilia. Half of her collection seemed to be there.

Eugenia passed me a bowl of strawberries and a sky-blue Fiestaware plate with an almond croissant.

"Can I pour you some coffee?" she asked.

It was exceptional—Chicory New Orleans–style roast with steamed milk.

"Whenever I'm down there I stock up. Have you ever been?" she asked me.

"No, but I've always wanted to see the French Quarter."

"Come with me next time." She invited me with that flip of the head and flaxen strand of hair in her face.

"That's where your mom's from, right?" Clay asked as he stirred the steamed milk in his own cup.

"A little west of the city, White Lake."

Then she and Clay and the other guy began chatting about Mother's Day; yes, it was Mother's Day. I half-listened, interjecting a witty remark now and then. But something crazy was going on, which I didn't want to think about. I couldn't look at Eugenia, and I couldn't stop. I wanted to be alone with her, to talk more, to not share her even with these two. It seemed a shrill decibel of possessiveness, and unlike me.

As if she sensed something, she asked me if I'd like to take a walk after we finished breakfast. She was slated to meet friends at a grass tennis court in New Jersey and play doubles, but she had time to stroll across town with me.

"Do you play?" she asked as we started down the steep staircase from her apartment.

"Not well," I confessed.

"Let's hit balls sometime."

I had always been the "events planner" with my boyfriends, the one who suggested ideas and trips and made all the arrangements. So I enjoyed her describing where we might go to play tennis, as she tamped her pack of Camels against her palm and selected one. Wary of overstepping, I nevertheless grabbed it out of her beautiful mouth before she could light up. She stopped walking down the stairs and raised her brow at me. I stopped too.

"Do you really need this?" I asked.

At first she didn't answer but studied me with surprise. Then she said, "Actually, I don't."

She plucked it from my fingers, replaced it in her pack, and said nothing further as we walked into the bright morning.

"Can I ask you something?" I began. Before she consented, I launched into, "Why were you so silent that night at Café Idealisme?"

"Silent? I was talking your ear off."

"I mean at first. Before we ordered the wine?"

She smiled mischievously. "Bertie sets booby-trapped dates for me with, you know, born-again Jehovah's Witnesses, or kinky straight girls. She just hoped I'd feel stupid with you. But I loved your way with words, so the joke's on her."

"It's good that you see it like that," I began. "I'm a little embarrassed…"

"Oh, you had no idea what was going on. She's been doing this for years."

"How many Jehovah's Witnesses have you dated?"

"I never take her up on it."

"Why does she do it then?"

"People fuck with your reality to get to your head. Know what I mean? Gives me a pain in the chittlins."

"Chittlins?" I asked.

"Chitterlings, Yankee."

Her hand found mine. She squeezed it as we continued walking toward my neighborhood and agreed to play tennis next Sunday.

"I'll come by The Bunny Hop," I offered, eager to see her before then.

"Well, I'm there every night except Sunday and Wednesday. Always a pleasure to see you, babe, but don't feel obliged. If I didn't work there I wouldn't want to hang around those insane girls."

"It's fun for me."

"Listen," she added. "Never take my moods at the bar personally. Please. Sometimes I'm sick of it and I get so grumpy. Especially with people I want to see, because then I'm tempted to relax."

"And it's your workplace."

"Thanks for getting that."

"Chitterlings?" I repeated. "Chittlins?"

"Yankee." She laughed again. It was a sweet laugh, light as gingerbread. "You have no idea, do you?"

"Could you clue me in?"

As we walked across Third Avenue, we began to swing our arms.

I arrived home to an unexpected saxophone serenade on my voice mail. Listening to Jordan's riffs, I filled in the lyrics that I'd heard Ella Fitzgerald sing:

I'm so so sorry, so so sorry...

I thought it would be one of his exclusively musical messages. But Jordan cleared his throat on my microchip and began: "Coltrane always said, 'We're here to grow into the best good that can come of us, and in my case, that will come out of the horn.'

"Molly! I don't expect you to call back, or to ever forgive me. Some things can't be forgiven, and there aren't two sides to every story. I just want you to know how sorry I am—not just for breaking your trust, but being jerk enough to defend doing it. Sometimes I walk down the street and just, like, die." He cleared his throat again. "I've broken my own heart. You didn't break anything. Even if we never meet again, let me share the musical diary of a man who's broken his own heart."

Then the monotone robot voice said: 'Sat-urr-day, nine thirt-y p.m.' I had been sharing nachos and sangria with Eugenia at the Mexican restaurant when he'd called.

34

Pete appeared in his usual tailored suit with a cheerful blue shirt and silk tie and shook Dr. Betsy's hand as though he'd entered a board meeting, with a formal "How are you today?" Alessi wore jeans and a striped cotton shirt, as though she'd been out gardening or strolling through Greenwich Village and buying bongs, slutty underpants, and jars of chutney. She sank into an armchair, glanced at me, and piped out, "Hail, hail, the gang's all here!"

Then silence overtook us, undermined by only the chugging air conditioner and the steady trickle of Betsy's little fountain of sanity.

"How is everyone today?" our social worker ventured in the saccharine, professional voice she had used with me the first time we'd met.

"Fine." Pete sounded pleasantly distant, or as Alessi often phrased it, "preoccupied with volume trading." He wasn't really with us.

"Alexandra?"

"Alessandra. You've seen me worse."

Then she and Betsy turned to me.

"Good thing I have a sense of humor," I squeaked out.

"So now, your paperwork is all complete?"

"About a week ago," Pete confirmed.

"That must be a relief," said Dr. Betsy.

"A victory over the whims of natural selection," Alessi cried.

"Was Molly named the child's custodian?"

Yes, and Alessi added that it made sense, since I was also to be his or her godmother.

"What did you decide about breastfeeding?"

How dare she ask that? All I could see was Eugenia's berry-like nipple dancing before my eyes. I put my head in my hand and began giggling—which set Alessi off.

"What's funny about this?" asked Dr. Betsy ingenuously, which made us howl and slap our knees. From the corner of my eye I saw Pete glance at his watch.

"I'm—I'm trying to imagine what my mother would think if she knew what my week was *really* like!" I sputtered.

Alessi grabbed my hand, and we both shook with refreshingly senseless laughter. I felt glad to be bonding with her rather than with Pete, since he often protected me in our three-way dealings. While I appreciated his empathy, I didn't feel that I should be more bonded to him than I was to my friend.

"You've got to know Molly's mom," Alessandra explained, wiping her teary eyes. "You had to be there.'"

"Well let's come back here, shall we?" commanded Dr. Betsy.

Alessi and I burst into a final binge of hilarity.

"We left the wording open," Pete broke in. "We said something like, 'at the Intended Parents' and Surrogate's discretion.'"

"We'll wing it," Alessi added, her laughter subsiding, "based on how we all feel. If Molly is up to it, she can breastfeed the baby at first and do the pumping thing after a while. You know, we'll just see."

"I don't recommend that you 'wing it' or 'just see,' Alexandra," said Betsy.

"Well, we don't know how we'll feel."

"I suggest that you make a plan, even if you end up changing it. Considering the tension I see in this room now, I wouldn't be surprised if some confusion develops over Molly's role with the baby."

Truthfully, the child was far from my mind—abstract as a retirement fund.

"Well, I'm not putting Tubes on My Boobs," Alessi declared. She added, in an aside to me: "It's this fake breastfeeding system for women who can't accept that they needed to adopt, or to hire a surrogate."

"It's not fake to them," Betsy argued. "It's a real way for them to bond with their baby."

"Oh come on, Dr. Betsy. It's elaborate deception—not the bond I want with *my* child."

"I'm out of this loop," I reminded them.

Dr. Betsy explained that a device was available for women who were not naturally breastfeeding or needed to supplement their milk. The lactation aid included a bottle with a long thin tube that was placed next to the mother's nipple so the baby could actually latch to the nipple while the tube was surreptitiously slipped into its mouth.

"Those moms want to compensate for feeling deficient," Alessi continued. "I dived into that and grieved about it for months. I'm over it now. It's fine with me if Molly feeds the child directly from her body—the body that the child will have lived in, and that will have naturally produced milk."

"You wouldn't feel upset to see Molly bond like that with your baby?" Dr. Betsy asked.

"For heaven's sake, the kid will have me in his face for years. Why shouldn't he bond with his godmother too? We have this cultural bias that Uber-Mom should dispense all nurturance. But really, there have always been wet nurses, midwives, nannies—to say the least for dads, and brothers and sisters."

"With assisted fertility," I volunteered, "it takes a village not only to raise a child, but to have one."

Dr. Betsy looked me over disapprovingly. She'd gotten a haircut that made her nose look longer, and I noticed foundation cream flaking over a rash on her cheek. It occurred to me that not only did she lack imagination, but that she seemed to have no sense of humor.

"How do you feel about feeding the baby?" she asked me.

"I'm prepared to do it."

Who was I to disqualify a new experience?

"And if it takes another two months out of your life?"

"We'll manage…"

Betsy shuffled in her seat and sighed.

"Another life is at stake here, an infant who can't live at the mercy of what the adults around him happen to feel about feeding him."

Alessi and I exchanged a loaded glance. Had we been overly flippant without realizing it? Or did we simply trust our ability to manage this part of our plan when it became relevant?

"I recommend that Molly and Alexandra meet with a lactation counselor after the insemination and set up a tentative calendar. Maybe Molly can feed for the child's first two weeks, for instance, and then start pumping milk once she resumes…"

"This is sounding like an arbitrated contract," Pete commented with a chuckle. "And by the way, Betsy, my wife's name is Alessandra, not Alexandra."

Giggly again, Alessi raised her fist, chanting, "Molly can pump!"

Now it was Dr. Betsy's turn to sink her head into her hands and shake her head—and she didn't laugh.

35

Eugenia had asked me in bed, "Did you think this would happen?"

I had shaken my head no.

"I wasn't sure either," she'd told me.

What had made her unsure? Had she picked up on my distance from the gay world when I sat in The Bunny Hop that night with Claudia and my half screwdriver? Or could she tell I'd been intrigued by her, even before I'd known?

I pondered all that as I headed out to see her at the bar Tuesday evening. If I had a chance at the noisy bar, I might say, "I had an incredible time with you Saturday, and I consider you the ultimate girl crush. But I'm straight, and I date men."

Or of course, I could tie a rusty anchor to an air balloon.

I ended up at the florists, in pursuit of the perfect long-stem rose. At the back of the promisingly fragrant store, lodged in a glass case like beer bottles, a selection of roses displayed their wiles. Bountiful white ones globbed together like snowfall—but white seemed chaste for this occasion. Red was strident, almost bitter, and pink seemed girly and dilute. So I picked pale champagne edged with orange, a rose with the glow of an antique lampshade. The vendor wrapped it with a cut of fresh fern in green tissue.

It would be the only rose I would give a woman.

Then I darted into a Puerto Rican grocery store, knowing how Eugenia liked those Win for Life lotto cards, but also knowing they offered false hope and promises. Still, I decided to humor her with one.

By the time I arrived at the bar, I was more jittery than I expected to be and couldn't understand myself. Soon I'd be out West in a fertility clinic getting hit up by a turkey baster, and that would be my life for the next year. Why was I a furious bundle of nerves, nearly unable to walk over to Eugenia?

Behind the bar, in a black tank top flanked with gray suspenders, she looked like something out of *Key Largo*, or another forties gangster film—like the tall, tough hero and the sexy blonde heroine at once. She juggled two beer bottles, caught one in each hand, and delivered them to a customer who appeared to be a plump fellow with a mustache.

Then I remembered Terry and Rick laughing—"not politically correct laughter," they had apologized—about "the gal with the mustache drinking beer through a straw. *The prettiest girl I ever saw...*" Rick had hummed.

When Eugenia noticed me walking toward her, she brightened and cried, "Hey!"

We embraced, she leaning forward over the bar, my arm sliding over her suspenders and soft shirt. Her pronounced shoulder blades reminded me of her amazing body. I held the rose and fern in my other hand, and our cheeks pressed together.

When we drew apart, I handed her the flower.

She took it with a modest smile, unwrapping the green tissue paper. I climbed into a bar seat; she filled a vase with water from the sink, and slid it between us on the bar. As she placed the rose and fern in the vase, they found their balance.

She lowered her face to the petals and inhaled, then passed it to me like she was passing hors d'oeuvres. Billiard balls crackled behind us, and the jukebox blasted Sinéad O'Connor and then a robust Johnny Cash tune.

"Let me get you something, babe. I should warn you that the wine here is better for saving money than for drinking."

"Wrathful grapes."

I threw my head back, and she leaned over to say in my ear, "How 'bout a blood orange Daiquiri Euphoria to match the rose? Or a chocolate kamikaze?" Her nuzzle at my earlobe piqued me in a happy way. "Julep with mint from the banks of the bayous..."

"Ey, Gene Baby!"

We stopped caressing each other and stared into three scowling faces, one with a mustache. The other two looked haggard, if not aggressively devoid of make-up, with sacks beneath their eyes and their hair matted. My mother wouldn't be down with their droopy chins; no nip and tuck here.

"We want a drink, not *coitis interruptus*," scolded the one with the mustache—definitely a woman, who had a high, whiny voice.

With pluck, Eugenia stared back at her.

"I just served you, Nicki. You gulp that beer so fast you'll be more fit for heart-burn than *coitis interruptus*."

"No. She wants one."

Nicki pointed to one of her friends.

"Well, wait your turn now. I'm serving someone else here."

"*¿Tu Habla Ingles?*" Nicki asked me bluntly.

"None of her girlfriends speak English," commented the one who presumably wanted a drink. "That's not Eugenia's style."

"Migda spoke better English than I do," Eugenia objected. "She spoke five languages. I bet Molly speaks ten."

"Migda could charm birds out of the trees. Have you found yourself a new charmer or a new snake?"

"Pay them no mind," Eugenia advised me under her breath. "So—what'll you have?"

"Make me a daiquiri," I told her. "That way you can turn up the blender so loud that I won't hear their drivel."

Then I slapped the Win for Life card from my jacket onto the bar.

Taken aback, she whispered, "You're a pisser."

36

On Friday evening I stopped in my downstairs tracks, halfway from the ground floor. Claudia was sorting through envelopes on the table by our mailbox-es, her hair pulled up at the crown of her head, revealing dark froth of curls that bubbled up her pale neck. This was the first time we'd run into each other since our tussle at The Bunny Hop that produced my first date with Eugenia. Claudia stopped fidgeting with mail and looked into the row of metal mailboxes as though she knew the footfalls were mine.

"I'm dating Dustin," she announced, still not facing me.

"I'm dating Eugenia."

She turned around as I completed my descent.

With an air of newfound respect, she held the wrought iron door open for me as I bounded onto the stoop. She followed, but there was nothing we could say to each other now. If I taunted her about her alleged "moratorium on penises" she could quip about my alleged addiction to them, how I "never could fathom what happened in sex without them." If she reminded me that I thought sleeping with a woman would be "dull, and beside the point," I could remind her that she had dismissed all men as slimy hairballs. In short, we were checkmated by too many moronic, drunken arguments with each other.

"Are you having a good time?" I asked, as we started walking.

"Dustin is so-o-o sweet," she said, closing her eyes and chomping on her gum. "Not pushy. Not a jerk. A breath of fresh air in the sewage fumes of dating."

("On good behavior," I translated to myself. "Motivated.")

"And your moratorium?" I inquired.

"Oh it's still in effect. He's gotta earn every centimeter."

I felt sure that Dustin would find creative ways to meet that challenge.

"Well, you don't want to deprive yourself of what men do best," I advised her. "Not that it's as indispensable as the world would have us think."

She flapped around like a matador's cape and stared at me with her overdone mascara. "You didn't score a night with *her* yet, did you?"

With her Queens accent, Claudia pronounced the female pronoun as *ha*—ha, ha, ha. I simply grinned.

"No fucking kidding!"

I kept grinning.

Claudia grabbed my arm, almost pinching me. "That's like getting an audience with the Dalai Lama. Eugenia is notoriously aloof."

"Not with me."

"She probably loves that you're not all over her. She had to win you. Don't ever let her think she has or she'll dump you like a pile of laundry."

Claudia dropped my arm and continued walking down the street.

"She wouldn't hurt me gratuitously," I said.

"She has a reputation for being callous."

"Look, if women throw themselves mindlessly at her it doesn't surprise me if they end up with rapped knuckles."

Claudia kept walking briskly.

"You must be seeing a bit of Bertie."

"As a matter of fact, I played pool with her last night."

It had been my second visit to The Bunny Hop that week, and the orange rose still glowed in its vase at the bar. Eugenia kept it there, she told me, because Clay's cats would eat it at home.

There had been more of a crowd than on Tuesday night, a virtual arcade of tattooed arms and necks, hair dyed all the primary—and for that matter, second-ary—colors, like chartreuse, pink, and orange. The bartender was too busy to hang around with me. So I ended up at the pool table with Bertie, Lainey, and their friends. Once Eugenia swung by and shot a round on her way to the supply room. Of course she knocked three striped balls down the pockets, leaving Bertie, who was playing solids, hollering the usual blue streak at her.

Before taking off, Eugenia had grabbed my waist from behind, edged her fingers down my back. I froze and thawed at once.

"I owe you," I whispered. "Big time."

"No one's keeping score."

That's when we decided where and when to convene on Sunday. She had to watch a Yankee game on TV with friends in Brooklyn later, but we'd meet in the park for the morning round of tennis we'd spoken about.

I confessed to Claudia, "Even if it doesn't last—because how can I go into my forties with a consuming girl crush?—it's a revelation."

"Well yeah," said Claudia. "Sex with another woman rocks the stratosphere. You only have such amazing sex with guys if they're your soul mate. Hey, did she do you with a dildo?"

"No," I boasted. "We don't need one. We've got plenty going on without disembodied dickies."

I dismissed the sex toy blithely as Alessi had dismissed the lactation aid.

"It'll never last, so don't worry about your forties," said Claudia, in her know-it-all tone. "You need polarity. You're both too femme."

Just as I felt faintly fond of her, Claudia pissed me off.

"I think we've shot those played-out roles to the wind."

"Don't count on it," she sneered.

37

Springy on her toes, Eugenia whacked the yellow tennis ball through the air. When I was lucky I managed a return—once, maybe twice—before she burned me with a hard spin. She won every rally, though we weren't playing across the net, we were just hitting against a wall. All the courts were taken on Sunday morning in this park by the East River, so we grabbed a handball court. Around us balls puckered as they bounced on the asphalt and then slammed into the walls.

I felt like a dweeb in my cap-sleeve tennis dress, the same one I had worn in that photo with Thomas. Meanwhile, Eugenia was smarter-than-stylish in her faded cutoffs so short that her front pockets peeked out beneath the fringe, a white tank top, and headband. The more I watched her instead of the ball, the more my game degenerated.

At one point I just stood back, my right arm drooping like spaghetti and my racquet head grazing my ankle, to let her prevail. Even people who didn't know us stopped in their tracks to watch her expert ground strokes.

"C'mon!" she called to me with flushed cheeks. "What happened to you, kid?"

"There's no point. You're creaming me!"

She seemed elated.

"At least I can do one thing better than Molly."

"Oh, you can do a lot better than I can."

The longer we played, the fewer balls I hit to any avail. I mauled one at the wall with my measly excuse for a two-handed backhand, and to my surprise she didn't retrieve it. The ball just hobbled back past me. I turned around and saw her hunched over, face down.

"You okay?" I called.

She shook her head no.

I ran over and she straightened slowly, grabbing my hand. I slid my other arm around her taut, thin waist and walked her unsteadily to a bench.

"What's going on?" I asked.

"My leg's numb…It'll pass," she mumbled. "It'll pass."

I went to collect her racquet, the balls, and our canvas bags.

"Can I get you some water?" I asked when I got back to the bench. We had already gone through the bottles we'd taken along.

"That would be great."

More than water, she needed a moment of privacy. I could see her blue eyes looking outward and in at the same time, and I remembered that Terry had mentioned herniated disks.

So I ran to the footbridge over the FDR Drive, hoping to search nearby streets for a store that sold bottled water. A run-down supermarket was nested in the housing project that flanked the FDR. I don't know which kind of supermarkets disturbed me more—those in rough neighborhoods like this, with dim lights and yellowing meat, or those in wealthy suburbs chock full of suspiciously bright colors.

But I entered with a mission, not in my usual supermarket funk. And when I found my grail—a small, cold bottle of Evian—I scurried back to the river park with it.

She seemed better when I returned and invited me to take the first swig.

"Your form is good," she said. "All you need is practice. I should practice too. We can never practice enough."

"But *can* you—is it okay for you?"

She shook her right leg.

"This bullshit is from my hours at the bar without good support. Just a pain that comes and goes."

"Pain in the chitterlings?" I asked.

"More like pinched nerves. I'll need back surgery one of these days." We started toward the footbridge, and she seemed to have recovered. "So, did you send your mom flowers last week?" she asked, probably hoping to clear the conversation of her ailment.

"I called her."

"That was it?"

Eugenia tapped my butt playfully with her racquet. As we walked over the footbridge, I explained that I'd made my fuss in late April for Mom's birthday, when I sent her scarves and costly perfume.

"Knowing you, I'm sure it's plenty costly," Eugenia teased as we descended into the Lower East Side.

"Did you send flowers?" I asked her.

"Oh, my mom gets a jungle every year from all six of us."

"You have four brothers. So you must have a sister too."

We passed streets of dusty orange housing projects with tinkling ice cream vendors and Puerto Rican families heading to the river with picnic bags and radios. Men clucked and whistled at us as they passed. Eugenia didn't seem to care.

"Tessa's blind," she was saying. "Always lived at home. They'd never have her institutionalized. So my dad helps her get flowers on Mother's Day."

"Does she look like you?"

"She's six years older, with darker hair. But people guess that we're sisters."

"And she's beautiful, and she's never seen herself, or seen you?"

"Tessa can see shadows. She knows when someone's in the room or when she's alone. She could see fairly well until she was six or so. Just before I was born."

"What happened?"

"Well, she'd been a premie—came out a month early. For her punctuality, she was rewarded with lights in the hospital that killed her vision. My folks never forgave themselves. Dad changed his whole career and became a biomedical instructional engineer—you look shocked," she said, and swung her racket in the air. "You probably didn't think my folks were professionals, the way Bertie talks about me."

"Oh no..." I began.

"'*Southern redneck hick*,'" Eugenia imitated Bertie. "You know, Bertie's never been south of Staten Island. She has some misconceptions." Eugenia swung her racket again, as though serving a ball. "Mom's a pediatric nurse—pretty much retired now. I'm First Generation 'Trailer Trash' here. You can imagine how that pleases them."

"I can indeed."

"You can? Your folks must be proud as hell of you."

I shook my head. "I should be married with two kids by now."

"Oh, well I should be a neurosurgeon's wife, with a pool and a yard."

"Do they know that you don't want to be? I mean, unless the neurosurgeon was female."

"They know what they want to know," she said briskly. "They've been told everything, but they prefer their version."

"Which is—?"

"They know me better than I know me."

"So how would they describe you?"

"Not 'thinking rationally.' Brainwashed by media and confused people."

"And how would you describe you?"

"More direct than most people can take, including them."

I hoped to segue this topic into my background, which I badly wanted to address. It was time for me to be more direct than I'd been with her. But before I could conjure an opening sentence about never having felt emotionally and sensually drawn to a woman before, Eugenia was shepherding me onto a crosstown bus, and we were fumbling for MetroCards and talking about something else entirely. She never asked me to her place, and I never agreed to go—I just followed like a puppy.

As we climbed the steep stairs to her apartment, she mentioned that Clay was in Fire Island for the weekend; the AC had been left on for the cats, and "Check it out, I'm not getting winded on the fourth flight. Guess why?"

"Don't know," I said.

"I had only two cigarettes all day yesterday. You're inspiring me."

"Me?"

Eugenia unlocked her door, and we both welcomed the temperature drop and relief from humidity.

"Hey kids!" she called to the cats, whipping her headband off. "You want anything cold to drink, babe?" she asked me. "We've got water, iced coffee, or beer…"

"Water's fine."

"That's what I mean."

She disappeared into the kitchen as I sank onto the black deco sofa with teak arms that curled over like fiddleheads. Although its vintage was earlier than the fifties décor in the room, it still worked with the parchment lampshades, the wooden window blinds.

"Ice?" she called.

"Please."

"If I were alone," she continued, now back in the living room, "I'd have a cold beer, or a gin on the rocks or something. But you don't need booze or cigarettes. You're not twitchy."

She handed me a glass of ice water and knocked back her own, settling beside me on the sofa.

"Which isn't to say you're a teetotaler—most of whom're just drunks-not-drinking, which you probably know. You seem to enjoy a glass of good wine or two, but you don't overdo it."

"You're saying that I'm not addicted to substances. Which doesn't mean I'm not wound tightly—'cause trust me, I am."

She looked me over, weighing whether that might be so, her smile getting frisky, her eyes large and sweet. I felt desire rise. We were going to kiss. We were going to do more than kiss. I caught my own breath.

"Actually—I should warn you—I'm a mess," I told her.

Now our bare legs touched, and my groin was starting to tremble. But I had sworn to myself that I would not be amorous with her unless I told her that I was "straight but not narrow," and that I was being primed to bear someone else's child.

"I'm a mess too," she replied. "All sweaty and tacky, and I can't stand myself. Let's take a shower."

She got up, placing her empty glass on the sailors' trunk that served as their coffee table, throwing off her tank top and wriggling out of her sports bra. Standing there in nothing but cutoffs, she basked in her magnetism for a moment before prancing to the bathroom. I remained on the sofa as I untied my sneakers and bunched my damp, stinky socks into them.

"Oh my God! You gotta see this! Errol has taken over the sink." She whooped with laughter. "Come in here!"

But I arose slowly and shuffled to the bathroom, where shower water already hissed and her cutoffs hung from a hook on the door. Errol had curled herself into the cavity of the sink, one paw folded neatly over the other.

"The water's magnificent!" Eugenia called from behind the shower curtain.

But I stood watching the sink mirror steam over, glancing down into Errol's yellow-green eyes, the color of martini olives.

"Getting a little modest there, Molly?" Eugenia asked after a while. "You were hardly modest last weekend."

She popped her smiling face between the curtains, her hair darkened by water and flat on her head, blue eyes sparkling and cheeks ruddy. I had to look away.

"I'm sunburned unevenly," I mumbled, "like a poorly grilled flounder."

"Oh come on!" She said that like a real southerner—"come awn."

I dragged my feet to the tub and stood there, wondering what Alfred Hitchcock would think of my getting into the shower with an innocent blonde.

"Gene," I began, "before anything more happens with us, I want you to know that I—well, actually this will sound ridiculous, but actually, I'm straight. Or let's say, until I started getting to know you—"

A jet of water shot into my face, and all over my stupid tennis dress. I shrieked with laughter as she continued to aim the showerhead at me.

"Get in here already!"

38

It was the first time I saw her nude, because last week she had worn those red silk boxer shorts. Now I beheld her full glory of long, muscular legs, curved thighs and prominent hipbones, a small gold navel ring, and rounded breasts with just enough heft, a bit more than my own. My first dazzled thought was, how dare she have such a damn perfect body? My second thought was, why would someone who looked like that take any interest in scrawny, knock-kneed me?

What came out of my mouth was: "So, can I, uh—borrow your legs?"

"Waddaya plan to do with them?"

"You know, you're bad…"

"Actually," she said, holding the showerhead at her hip, "I'm good. If a bad girl is what you're after, I'll let you down."

"It's even bad that you said that."

She aimed the showerhead at me again and I howled. Then she propped it back in its cradle so she could take my face in both of her hands and kiss me, her warm lips scooping over mine as sudsy rivulets glided our torsos against each other's, emphasizing every slippery twist and turn.

"I," I began again, when her lips briefly left mine, but the words dissolved into sheer panting: "I, I, I…"

"Shampoo?" she whispered.

I leaned my head back, closed my eyes, and let her strong fingers massage and rinse my scalp. Like a soap bubble, an image came of my grandma Peg toweling off my hair at the beach when I was a child.

When the water stopped, Eugenia stepped out of the tub and threw a towel over her shoulders and another over mine. We stood for a long time on the bathroom floor as she leaned over me, patting me dry. Errol had left the sink. The mirror gradually cleared and we could see our heads together, her fair hair falling upon my dark head. I was thinking about how Jordan and I would look more like the Bobbsey Twins, with both of our dark hair—even though he was, of course, the opposite sex.

Eugenia rocked me in her arms, whispering, "Hot" at our mirrored image.

"I can't do this!" I cried, tossing off the towel and running from her. But to where? My clothes were drenched on the floor by the tub. Eugenia overtook me in the corridor and seemed to almost fling me into her room and upon her bed, like a cat toy.

"I can't be here!" I giggled, scrambling upon the cool comforter.

"Why?" she asked, seeming nervous. "Are you with someone?"

"Not at all. It's just, I'm not—" I had every intention of saying, "I'm not gay." What came out was: "I'm not beautiful."

She looked into my face, blinking her blue eyes.

"I don't deserve you," I went on. A finger landed on my lips.

"Don't talk like that. Who said you're not beautiful?"

I whimpered strangely, falling backward against pillows as she leaned upon me, her breasts crushing tenderly against mine. With one hand she yanked the covers down so I could climb beneath them with her.

We melted against each other. I yielded to her, opening my legs, my skin, my mind, my mouth, crying out, greedy for as much pleasure and attention as this generous being could offer me.

When she draped herself across the ruffled bed, her skin soft and fragrant like baker's dough, I became the kneading hands, the rolling pin. She exerted an almost gravitational force, pulling my face down her torso to linger at her gold navel ring. I exhaled over her loins, remembering how a man had done that to me, and how nice it had felt.

Then Eugenia threw her head back and dropped one of her long legs open. This was too sexy—and suddenly I was paralyzed.

I stopped everything, looked at the sunlight from the window pearling her face like the brush strokes of Pierre Bonnard, her profile soft against the headrest. On the street outside, a bus wheezed passed. I bit my lip, scarcely breathing. Something seemed gnarled in my eardrum—which I could only describe as an ethereal "instant message."

Just what do you think you're doing?

It was Grandma Peg.

What are you doing, Molly? What in hell are you doing?

I leaned forward and licked Eugenia's golden thighs, ran my teeth over them, bit and sucked them up into my mouth. She gasped, like a runner out of breath. But what would I do next?

Good question, Grandmother.

A strange fling from my youth popped into mind. Florence, Italy. His name was Angelo, and the dark room had smelled like stale nicotine. I was lying down, as Eugenia was now. The cherub-lipped boy had plinked his tiny kisses down my legs, which at first felt grand. But they never advanced, and I had ached for more to happen. Sex with an angel was frustrating—and now I understood where that poor angel feared to tread.

So I stopped devouring Eugenia's thighs and held my hand just over her triangle of fleecy hair, barely touching her as she eased back onto the bed.

Molly! The message came again from my deceased grandmother, rather hoarse and like a growl. *Haven't you carried on with enough unseemly boys?*

Yes, I had been a klutz the first few times I had touched them, as though I was madly defeathering chickens. I should have been more skilled with anatomy I knew, but familiarity provided no solace as I pioneered two fingers into Eugenia's soft, slick folds of skin…which, shockingly, didn't feel like my own; the whole labyrinth in fact confounded me. Of course I recognized her deep, spongy cavern, my mouth dry, my heartbeat deranged. It was one thing to have her, with her boyish confidence, do that to me. But for me to return the favor…

If you insist on going forward, then do a superlative job.

I had never been a rude child, never one to say anything like "shut up!" to my parents or my grandparents. But I wished Grandma Peg would give me some peace.

I let my face fall upon Eugenia and burrow over her loins. I inhaled a spicy aftermath of horse-chestnut shower gel, and moist warmth. She seemed excited by my breath on her, my finger inside her.

An hour later, we lay side-by-side, hand in hand, her right leg curled over my left, both of us still except for our breathing. Among its welter of veins, the ceiling plaster above us was chipped in the shape of a toy duck. I followed its curved head and beak, the tipped wing jutting from its backside.

"What's with us, Molly?"

I looked away from the toy duck and into her face, which was swept with glinting strands of blonde hair. I reached for them but decided I liked them in her face.

"What's with us?" she repeated, almost too quietly to hear.

I had no reply.

"I didn't think I had this in me anymore," she said. "Wasn't looking for it."

"Me neither."

"Well…" She propped herself up on her right arm, with the darling look of a kitten awakening from a nap. "What does it mean?"

I too had been wondering. I hoped my facial expression was friendly and not dumb—because I couldn't find words. Then my stomach churned and squeaked, and I rolled over, groaning with shame.

"Okay," she said. "It means time for lunch." Eugenia stroked my shoulder, and I felt the mattress shift with her weight as she stood up. "It means—shit, it's after three. We're hungry."

I watched her lanky figure walk across the room and acquire a pair of black panties, long jeans, and a clean tank top.

"Gene, my silly tennis dress is soaking on your bathroom floor. Can I borrow some clothes?"

She tossed me a sports bra from her dresser, followed by a tank top the color of green tea ice cream.

"Keep 'em—they shrank in the wash."

Then she opened her accordion-folded closet door, found a tan duffel bag from which she grabbed a pair of Levis and held them up for inspection. "These will be wide on you, but you can borrow one of my belts. The length will be perfect." As she tossed them to me I wondered whose they had been.

"Take any belt you like. They're hangin' over here. I'll meet you in the kitchen and we'll cook up some lunch."

"Remember, I don't cook. But I can set the table and wash dishes."

She stood by the arched doorway, one hand in her back pocket.

"You can cook fine."

I shook my head emphatically, holding the sheets around me with sudden self-consciousness.

"For your own good, don't put me to the test. I'll poison us."

"You know, you're so damn smart, but when you talk like this…" She said something I didn't hear as she exited the room. The bathroom door shut, and she blew her nose with a curt honk. How consoling that even she, of statuesque bearing, emitted embarrassing sounds.

Alone in the room, I thought to leave her a note that would answer the question she'd posed in bed. *What's with us?* I found a pen on her table and noticed a pile of napkins with drawings on them—my own drawings of the Fucked Duck and Rick's of the dragonfly and bullfrog. I tore a clean corner from one napkin and scrawled, *Every time I see you it's love at first sight.* And I folded it deep into a pocket of her leather jacket, where she kept her packs of Camels.

I found her on the window ledge in the kitchen, her elbow propped upon the long leg she had drawn up into an isosceles triangle. With a cigarette in hand and head tipped pensively, she seemed less of a tingling Bonnard and more of a solid Edward Hopper blonde, striated by rays of afternoon light.

When I came in she fanned the smoke and snuffed her butt into an ashtray.

"Sorry for the arsenic and cyanide. Okay, so we've got cilantro soup in the fridge I made yesterday. I'll cook wild rice, and we'll sautée some vegetables. You cut 'em and I'll make a sauce."

"I'm just warning you that when I cut vegetables I mutilate them."

She opened her fridge, which held a dizzying array of Tupperware, cans, and bottles. From the vegetable bin she produced two green peppers and then handed me a plastic cutting board.

"Last time I cut peppers I made a mess, with little white seeds everywhere."

"I'll show you how not to do that."

She stroked my back as she walked around me. A lock of hair had worked its way magically over her right eye and cheek. It always seemed to do that.

"I can't see myself trying something new with a knife," I told her.

"First cut off the stem, here at the top. Most of the seeds come off with it."

"If you do it, they will."

"Just try, babe."

"Could I have a beer? I need one now."

"Of course."

She took out two Heinekens from the fridge and juggled them for a moment before setting them down on the counter and opening one for me with her fingers.

I sipped the sharp, cool froth from the bottle, hoping she would forget about teaching me to cut peppers.

But she pointed to the specimen on the cutting board. I sliced off the top, and seeds did come out.

"Go for the bottom. Okay, great! Now, a vertical slice here. Not so terrible, eh? Just run the knife along the inside to scrape off remaining seeds and ribs."

"How biblical—seeds and ribs."

"And here's a bell pepper to julienne to your heart's desire."

It seemed disorienting to eat something I had helped cook, which was actually quite tasty, and the perfect finish to a morning of sports and an afternoon of passion. I asked her, "Is this the kind of thing you would have served if you'd opened your own bar with Cajun snacks?"

But she was sneaking Errol soup from an extra spoon and didn't answer.

"I have a lot—there's a lot I want to say," I hazarded as we walked along Bedford Street, passing Chumley's, where I had once eaten a memorable, delicious hamburger with a less memorable, drunken frat boy.

I was not sure Eugenia had heard me until she replied after crossing Carmine Street, "I'm not the kind of person who needs to talk about everything."

"Neither am I. But if I don't give you some background, things won't make sense. Maybe I could take you to dinner next week?"

We had just reached the station at Houston and Varick Streets, where we stopped walking. I leaned my tennis racquet against the railing.

"I appreciate the invitation, but babe..." My heart took a quick, hot tumble. Maybe she would turn me down. "As far as taking me to dinner, you outdid yourself two weeks back. No kidding. You think anyone's ever taken me to such an extravagant meal? Or let's put it this way, at least one that was really tasty? And not to mince words, but I know you earn more than I do. Still no reason for you to do all the treating. I'm happy to split costs with you."

It seemed that I was making a gracious offer, albeit, perhaps to offset my guilt about having deceived her this long about being straight—or whatever I was now—or maybe because I didn't feel nearly as incredible as she and wanted to make up for that.

"I've always been the big spender," she went on. "I supported Migda when we lived out in Brooklyn. Figured she didn't have working papers here, since she just did odd translation jobs. Made sense for me to carry the weight, right?"

She rolled her eyes slightly. "Not. The disparity might start with cash, but it leaks into everything. When she betrayed me, my friends said I was spoiling her rotten. I asked them, well, why didn't you say something? And they told me I always made excuses for her and that I never would have listened. They were probably right."

I became aware of a saline, almost bloody taste in my mouth.

"Just my way of saying I don't want us to get off on the wrong foot. Not that I ever thought I'd be telling someone else, don't be so open-fisted..."

I swallowed whatever tasted salty and metallic.

"Okay, so—no more of my little tricks?" I pleaded.

"Sorry."

"How about your little tricks?"

"But don't you like my little tricks?"

"Look," I said. "Without either of our little tricks, we wouldn't be standing here. We wouldn't have had this—wonderful day."

"Little tricks are one thing. Taking advantage of someone's kind nature is another."

She was far from the "callous" person to whom Claudia had alluded. No friend or boyfriend had ever hammered this out with me. A tear, of all things, nipped the corner of my eye. I blinked it out, staring down at my tennis shoes so she wouldn't see. Still, her hand settled on my wrist.

"I could stay with you and talk for a while," she offered. "Everyone would understand if I'm a little late."

For a moment, I considered this invitation. But I feared I would dissolve; the salty taste I recognized was tears too long unshed. It wouldn't be right to unleash them now. Yet, had I taken her up on the offer, I might have spared us both some radical confusion.

"It's okay," I told her. "Go watch the Yankee game with your friends."

"Are you sure? You seem upset. If you don't mind my saying."

She'd probably noticed the tear creeping down my cheek.

"Things have been nuts," I began. "At work someone got sexually harassed and fired—and I have to go out West in June for a—big assignment."

"How long will you be there?"

"A week or two."

She looked relieved and assured me, "That's nothing. I'll miss you, though."

Then the sidewalk quaked as a chariot from the underworld approached the station beneath us.

"Don't miss your train!" I felt almost desperate to be done with this.

"Wanna take my number?" she asked, rooting for her phone.

"Run. You'll wait forever for the next train on a Sunday."

"Come by the bar this week and we'll make a dinner plan, okay?"

"Sure."

As we reached to hug each other good-bye, I realized that we might never again speak so warmly, and with such good faith. I filled my arms with her sinewy back and ribs as if for the last time.

"Have fun," I said hoarsely.

Then Persephone took leave, sprinting downstairs as the train screeched into the station. In that second before it stopped and the doors opened, she would glide through the turnstile and gallop, with her long legs, into an air-conditioned car.

Suddenly, I began running down the steps to catch up with her. She was right. We must speak now.

But I heard the canned announcement: "Stand clear of the closing doors, please." And then the tuneless chimes as the train doors shut and the lord of the underworld wrenched her away.

39

Thank goodness the next day was Monday, and I had something definite to do—my job. The alarm clock squalled, ripping me from dreams. Gravity sucked my feet into slippers and I puttered to the kitchen in my bathrobe to make coffee, not Eugenia's wonderful chicory blend but my own normal blah New York City apartment coffee.

In the shower I could hardly bear to soap parts of myself, like my breasts or belly, which reminded me of what happened yesterday. My body was a new place, mine and no longer mine. Soon a fetus would share it with me.

By the time I got to work it was clear that I was having postpartum depression before I'd even gotten pregnant. The familiar, slightly annoying sight of Larry made me want to embrace him and bawl. I told him that I could stay late to make up for all the time I had recently taken off, and he said that was music to his ears.

So I stayed until eight in the evening, plowing through folders, finishing comps that Enrico had started. Maybe Eugenia was right; I didn't drink to excess or smoke cigarettes. But she didn't know how I relied on the daily grind as a palliative.

When I got home one phone message blinked for me, from a number I didn't recognize. I played it with unfounded hope—since we hadn't exchanged numbers—that Eugenia was checking to see how I was. But it was Jordan's daily saxophone jingle, "I'll Never Smile Again."

The next morning, Tuesday, Dr. Betsy cancelled our usual lunch session because she had a cold, and she asked if Pete, Alessi, and I might meet with her on Friday instead. That was okay with all of us. I stayed at work late again Tuesday evening, planning to go straight to The Bunny Hop afterward to make my dinner plan with Eugenia.

Around seven, Larry danced into my office in mint-green corduroy pants, a silk shirt, and thick gold lamé belt that he alone could get away with.

"I've got my Molly back!" he sang in a trembling falsetto. "Is there some kind of sheet music like that? There should be."

I was tracing one of Enrico's sketches on my monitor, thinking about how skillfully he had drawn using the mouse. Larry looked over my shoulder, the ginger limey scent of his Calvin Klein cologne infusing the room.

"You fired him unfairly, you know," I said. "You had no proof that he forged my signature."

"Jack told me he did."

"Well, how does Jack know? Did he catch Enrico red-handed? Why didn't he tell you the day it happened?"

"I think he got it out of Enrico weeks later."

"Did you hear Enrico confess?"

"No, but I trust Jack's account."

"I wouldn't," I said, saving the file with a swift double tap on my keyboard. Larry stood back a bit, and I swiveled around to face him. "You were attracted to Enrico, weren't you?"

"What kind of an allegation is that?"

"Look, just be careful. You wouldn't have fired a woman that way."

"I'd fire anyone who forges another employee's signature. We have enough to contend with these days."

"That's what I mean. You don't need litigation."

"We've never been sued," was all he said, and that was all I too would say—for now. "So how much longer are you sticking around?" he asked, glancing at his wristwatch. "I'm good for another half hour."

This felt like old times, with just us two in the office late, deciding how long we'd overwork.

"That sounds good."

"Do you want to go out for a bite after that?"

"Can't. Gotta be somewhere." I would see Eugenia within the hour. And I needed to. "Hey Lar," I added, "did you ever sleep with straight guys?"

He was clearly taken off guard by my effrontery—and so was I.

"Is this Salacious Question Day in Mollyland or something?"

I began to pardon him from answering, but Larry interrupted me, now enjoying the interrogation. "When I was young and stupid, I enjoyed that sort of thing. You know, it was a conquest. It's no secret that many straight people adore gay sex. And why shouldn't they? You're with a partner who actually knows the machinery. Hello."

There had been a moment with Eugenia on Sunday—my moment. "Don't stop," she'd whispered. "You're not finished yet..."

How had she known better than I?

"Well," I asked Larry, "what is 'gay,' if straight people also like it?"

"It's the fantasy, the predominant images inside a person's head," he reflected. "The suggestion that most floats your boat makes you either straight or gay."

As I drifted downtown on the Second Avenue bus to The Bunny Hop, I didn't find myself fantasizing about either women or men. Most people I saw barely caught my eye. My thoughts centered around Eugenia, who seemed to defy gender or, with her long bones and streamlined curves, to exemplify the best of both.

When I got to the bar and opened the tinted glass door, I felt almost lightheaded. But Persephone was still the hostage of Hades, and someone else had taken her place.

This other bartender had a nonchalant face and short, boyish hair with earrings clamped along her lobe. She was not someone who would have moved the needle of my sexual preference a millimeter; if she had been on duty that evening in March I would have come to this bar with Claudia, never met Rick or Terry (because they wouldn't be here either), never returned, and probably would not be

Alessi's surrogate, in a Jimmy Stewart-*It's a Wonderful Life* sort of way.

"Can I get you anything?"

The voice fell upon me like damp plaster, its tone lacking the tapestry of Eugenia's lilt.

"Actually—could you get me Eugenia?"

The woman eyed me disapprovingly.

"Eugenia isn't feeling well. I'm subbing for her tonight."

"Oh. Do you know what's wrong with her?"

"She didn't say."

"Could I leave her a note?"

"Look, she'll be in again Thursday or Friday. I'm Laurie, by the way."

"Molly," I said. "Nice to meet you."

As we shook hands Laurie's expression changed from disdain to wonder.

"You're Molly? Well *you* can write her a note. Here, I'll get you some paper." Laurie scampered down the bar, now very obedient. I took in the usual metallic scent of beer and cigarettes, a driving baseline from the jukebox—without the charms of Persephone to soften them.

"She may have thrown out her back or something," Laurie said, with an air of confidentiality, when she returned with a sheet of paper and a pen. "She sounded kind of down."

I thanked Laurie for the paper and pen. She assured me she would leave my note in a place that Eugenia would find it. Eugenia must have spoken highly of me since I was getting such royal treatment.

Sorry to hear you're not feeling well, I wrote. *I'll swing by again this weekend. Feel better. I miss you.*

As I looked up Laurie placed a Keir with a twist of lemon beside me, saying "Happy Tuesday!" with an apologetic smile.

The next morning my phone rang before I left for work. Ari Schwartzben, the "well-healed Israeli" that Tamara's parents were trying to foist on me, was calling again to make a date. I had never returned his first call and really didn't want to meet him. But I divined that my silence was interesting him more than anything, so I agreed to see him Friday evening. I figured I should do something, at least, that could get back to my family with impunity.

Sunday I reserved for Eugenia, and I'd go to the bar on Saturday night and make the plan. It was time to tell her about the "marketing survey" she had answered, about Alessi and surrogate motherhood, and Madame Tussaud's Wax Museum of Dysfunctional Boyfriends. Then she could decide, once she had the low-down, what she wanted with AC-DC me. Maybe—even though it would kill me—she would opt for being friends or acquaintances. Maybe that would be most fair.

I barely slept that night, tossing around like leaves in a gust of wind. I relived moments with her; there had already been marvelous ones. Then I imagined new scenes and conversations as I yearned for her, resented her, had explicit fantasies about her, wished I could simply call her up and ask her how she was doing. But though we had traversed bold terrains of intimacy, we had not managed to exchange phone numbers. She had offered, but her subway train was coming and I'd pushed her away. I could have gotten her number from Bertie—but then again, she could have gotten mine.

Thursday morning I propelled myself to the office with habitual force, grinding my way through morning crowds on the subway, diligently dodging bodies so I might claim a metal pole or handle to steady myself as the train bolted its way beneath Lexington Avenue. But at the 28th Street station, something familiar crept through my sleepy ears, something that had run in my veins like blood: a hoarse saxophone across the tunnel playing "Something Stupid Like I Love You."

The train doors opened and closed and opened again, and a conductor's grumpy voice bade us, "Clear the doors! Move into the car."

I tried to look out the window to the station across the tracks, but an express train zooming up to Grand Central blocked my view. Through its windows people flitted past like images on a shuffling deck of cards.

Finally the doors to my train closed with a triumphant *ding-dong*. As we grunted to a start, a recorded voice informed us cheerfully: "This is a Bronx-bound Six train. The next stop is 33rd Street."

All the way to the next stop I deliberated. I could surprise Jordan and thank him for the music he left every day on my voice mail. That was all I wanted to do.

When the train doors opened again, I found myself disembarking and taking the downtown Six back to 28th Street. When I got off that train, sure enough, the sardine-like grays and blacks of office suits gave way to brighter colors of Jordan and Z against the tile wall with their instruments. In a rugby shirt and ripped jeans, Z hovered behind his snare; Jordan wore loose camouflage pants and a yellow T-shirt. He pivoted his torso with the horn upon it to the left and right, then up and down as though he was doing knee bends, his eyes shut and his cheeks filled with air.

I stood there, alternating my weight onto each foot. That talented boy with wild, curly dark hair had been my squeeze.

Most of their audience boarded the train I had left, some peeling dollar bills from their wallets, others sprinkling dimes and pennies like fairy dust into the open saxophone case between the two buskers. New people poured downstairs from the street. A few stopped to listen to the duet while others walked by, grabbing their phones or reading papers.

Z noticed me first, with a smile and a dip of the head as he tapped the rhythm: one, two; one, two, three, four. "*If You Take the A Train…*"

He nodded in time, glancing at Jordan, whose eyes were still shut, whose knees bent as he keeled left and right with that 1952 Conn saxophone around his neck—how limber!

Another local train stormed into the station, depositing people and acquiring others from the platform. An express roared downtown on the middle track. When Z and Jordan finished the Ellington tune, I began clapping, my fellow office-bound New Yorkers joining the applause.

Once Jordan's lips left the mouthpiece, I noticed that a peach fuzz mustache now lined his Cupid's bow and a spot of hair dabbed his chin. I wasn't sure if he'd noticed me, but Z came over with a hug.

"So good to see you, Molly."

"Great to see you too."

Then Jordan stepped over, his large brown eyes steady and guarded, his instrument still around his neck.

"Hey, Chardonnay."

"Amazing that you're up at this hour," I remarked.

"A man must earn his keep."

Jordan leaned in and kissed me on the cheek, releasing a musky scent that made me remember being naked with him in all sorts of positions.

"You going to work?" he asked.

"Well, I was."

"Want to get some breakfast with us?" Z invited me.

The last time I had sat down and eaten was Sunday afternoon in Eugenia's kitchen when we had cooked together. Since then I had been stuffing chips, pretzels, or cold chicken wings into my mouth indiscriminately as I worked or paced around my apartment. I realized that I felt faint.

The boys collapsed and zipped their instruments into cases with remarkable economy. "You look a little skinny," Z commented as we climbed back into daylight from the underworld. "Hope you're taking care of yourself."

"I've been doing a lot of overtime at the office this week."

"That's normal for her," Jordan interjected.

"Are you implying that I'm tightly wound?"

"Maybe," he said, glancing sideways at me.

We decided to take our bagels from a deli into the park at 23rd Street and Fifth Avenue, across from the Flatiron Building. It was nine fifteen. I could hang out with the boys in this limpid morning sunlight for an hour, I decided. I had worked past seven for the last three nights. Larry could spare me.

We squeezed in together, since bench space in this park was hard to land at that prime hour. As we unwrapped toasted bagels from our tin foil and began breakfast, Jordan and Z explained they were playing in the subway stations and streets together.

"We're kind of refugees from the Blake Jones Quintet."

"You don't play with Blake anymore?" I asked.

"Well we do," said Jordan. "But he never hesitates to replace us when it suits him."

"There's no commitment," Z affirmed.

"And we get a lot of mileage from just one horn and percussion. It's a challenge, to work without a chording instrument—you know, keyboards or guitar."

"Well, sometimes a bass player joins us. We keep it open, you know. We keep the energy moving."

They called their new band Black and White—not only a pun on their respective races, but a reference to music notation and to Ellington's *Black and Tan Fantasy*. Jordan told me that they now had a regular gig on Wednesday night in a tavern out in Brooklyn. It didn't pay well, but it had already "landed them a wedding."

"That's great," I said.

"Well, you always encouraged me to do more music and less of that other stint, you know, my 'sales job.' You were right. This is the direction I want to go."

"We're saving our pennies for an ad in *Time Out*," Z mentioned. "We want to do weddings, kid's parties, corporate events. You know, the kind of stuff Blake would never deign to consider."

"How does Blake make ends meet?"

"Nobody really knows. But he seems never to go without. God Bless the Band Leader Whose Got His Own."

We all laughed a little and, as I finished my bagel, I wondered where Eugenia was at this moment. I hoped she felt better. She told me that she usually woke up early, around seven thirty, even if she had gone to bed at three in the morning. She skated on Rollerblades, swam at the gym, or did kickboxing class in the morning. After lunch she took "a long afternoon siesta" before work at night.

What would happen if she Rollerbladed by us now, in this park? She would be startled to see me. And she would like Z but probably would not take so kindly to Jordan—not at all.

"I'd better get to the office," I said, crumpling my napkin and tin foil.

"So soon? You just got here."

He was still Jordan, despite his ghost of a new mustache. And I was, apparently, still the same Molly, a bit too flattered by his wanting me around.

"I have to work."

"Stay just a little while. It's been so long since we've hung out."

"Okay. Ten more minutes. Then I've got to skidaddle."

"Want a ride to work?" Z asked. "I've got my wheels over on Broadway and 27th."

"Sure. That's very nice."

As it turned out, there were more than wheels on Broadway and 27th; there was a stash of Acapulco Gold that would "blow my mind" deep in the glove compartment, rolled into the kind of collapsible tube artists used for oil paints.

Jordan and Z fit their instruments into the trunk and removed stacks of CDs from the backseat so I could sit down. As I climbed into the car, I felt like Pinocchio—betraying Gepetto, going off with the gang of boys rather than to school, not listening to Jiminy Cricket. But unlike Pinocchio, I had no strings. In fact, I was the anti-Pinocchio, held by gravity but by no worldly duties like marriage or parenthood, even pets. The Pied Piper could lure me anywhere and it just wouldn't matter.

Z enjoyed the second-hand wafts while Jordan and I passed the joint between us. We made our way slowly up Sixth Avenue, delayed by ungainly trucks and Con Edison digging up parts of the street.

Once the boys started goofing around up front, I sat back and worried. My pending conversation with Eugenia did not augur well. I imagined sitting across from her at a table, telling her that I had co-opted her opinion to set my course of becoming a surrogate mother. And I would tell her that I'd never been with a woman before, that she had initiated me on yet another unanticipated track. By the time I confessed everything, she would slam some bills on the table, stand up, and say, "Sorry, I gotta leave." I could imagine her doing that so clearly that it was beginning to upset me already.

Of course, she might find everything hilarious, or simply surprising.

Maybe she would catch my eyes warmly, as she sometimes did, and say: "You know, I really like you. Maybe there's a way we can work this out." But most likely, I reflected as Jordan passed me the dwindling joint and I drew its pungent fume down my throat, she would get quiet and moody. Because that's how she was.

Meanwhile, he called me every day and played music.

Anyway, how could I explain her to the people I knew? They would say silly things like, "Do you think you're really gay?" How could I tell them: "No—I have better sex with men than many women who are married to them. This has nothing to do with 'gay.' I'm just in love." Terribly few people would get that. And as for my folks, the one pronouncement that would go over like more of a lead balloon than "Mom and Dad, this is Jordan" would surely be "Mom and Dad, this is Eugenia."

"Last week we got high on this shit and went into lamp stores on the Bowery and looked at all the Waterford crystal chandeliers," Jordan recounted with great enthusiasm.

"Cool," I said. "Let's go there right now."

"You wanna?"

"Yeah! Turn around and let's head downtown. Traffic looked better that way."

"What about work, Molly?" asked Z gently.

"I'll come in late. I'm all caught up, and nothing important is going on."

"You need my phone?" he asked.

It might be helpful if Larry didn't recognize the number.

"Larry, something has come up," I told his voice mail. "I won't be in today. I'll make it up tomorrow and over the weekend if you need me. Promise. Thanks for understanding."

With a click of the "Off" button there were no more rules.

I was free, I was rich, I was raw.

40

The blue of her eyes was impossible to catch as it played in dappled window light, but in such warm, opal water I could swirl. A faux deco dancer, throwing back her long arms, was carved in the swimmy blue glass.

"Come on," Jordan nudged me. "Let's go in."

Z had left us at Bowery, where Kenmare turned into Delancey Street. This was the second lighting store we had visited, and it was darker and quieter than the first. We entered reverently, hand in hand, as if we were entering a Tuscan church with votive candles or an opium den trailed with fantastic baubles, a rainforest of prisms, a Rimbaud poem, a mystical scene from *The Magic Flute*, where the prince and princess become initiated. Points of color darted at me like deep-water fish, flashing their secret codes, making me giggle. Beneath a cape of crystal we marveled at emerald, purple, ruby red, amber sparkles in their breathless flux.

"What did you have in mind?" the young Asian woman asked.

Wasn't it possible to look and not have anything in mind?

"We just bought this apartment and we want something special for the dining area—you know, something to distinguish it from the living room," I said.

People in New York probably came in with that request all the time.

How large did we want to go?

"Jordan, didn't you measure the ceiling?"

"Something like this one here."

We stopped at a five-arm Waterford Etoile with sixteen sockets, she told us, and so I started to hum "Sixteen Candles." Jordan joined me with a doo-wop style harmony and she pulled a chord to illuminate the chandelier.

"So beautiful." I interrupted our song. "Too beautiful to live with every day."

"How much does it weigh?" asked Jordan. "Hey, it could be heavier than you."

He poked my arm.

The young saleswoman took out a calculator and multiplied the ninety-six pieces times an obscure, virtually Kabalistic percentage, and came out with some forty-five pounds—lighter than I was but heavier than the baby I would carry.

"How can we affix it to our ceiling if we don't have a cap beam?"

"Yeah," Jordan piped in. "We don't want it falling on anyone's head, you know."

The girl fetched a clamp that came with it and, she claimed, would hold it to any ceiling. But I was seeing Pompeian plaster dust, a fallen empire of contraband color.

"I'm still not convinced it won't take the ceiling down with it."

"Do you want a mini?" she asked us. "They start at eighteen inches."

Outside the store I lingered again with the blue glass deco figure in the window. It grew into a wave and broke over me. Dad used to tell us at the shore to "never fight a wave, because the wave will always win." The day before yesterday I had gone to The Bunny Hop and Laurie had been there instead of Eugenia. She hadn't been there. Maybe she didn't want to see me.

But last Sunday we started something that was not going to end.

"Wow," I said aloud as that became clear to me. And I put my open hand up to the window.

When we began strolling south, toward Broome Street, Jordan burst out laughing. He stopped on the street, bending over and pointing at me with the hand that wasn't holding his saxophone case.

"You are so fucking funny when you're high."

He mimicked me saying, "Wow," at the window, and I remembered what I didn't like about him.

"How's your bratty sister?" I asked as we walked on.

"She graduated from Bard last week. I think she's got some job serving apple cider and cappuccino at a café up there."

"I'm sure she does. I'm also sure she has some self-important crush on her art history professor, who's already forgotten her."

"How's your dorky brother?"

"Shit. I owe him a phone call."

I felt so lousy that I stopped on the street. Why did I keep forgetting to call Matthew and Tamara? Jordan paused awkwardly too, like someone about to be photographed. I became aware that I was looking at him.

"What?" he asked defensively.

"It's strange to be talking to you again," I said.

"I know. It's like we've met in some future reincarnated life, and we're fitting the pieces back in place."

Something would have to be put back in place or reincarnated, something to save me from the waves I couldn't fight.

Without Your Love…

He multiplied into a chandelier with saxophone-shaped arms, spinning around the small hotel room.

"Get over here!" I commanded.

He shook his head, cheeks filling with air and his vintage horn screaming with heartburn.

The joint warmed my fingers. I crushed it in an ashtray on the bedside table, stood up, walked over to him and leaned against the saxophone. He stopped playing, slipping the mouthpiece from his lips as he had in the subway three hours ago.

We stood dramatically still, like two life-sized marble sculptures Bernini could have carved. Then I began kissing him, scraping my fingers through his hair, grabbing small bunches of it and yanking them gently from his scalp, pushing his lips to receive mine. He said he needed to take the sax off his neck, and demanded, "What are we doing?"

What we had done was check into the Congee Hotel somewhere off Bowery, so we could both pee. We could have gone to a diner, but neither of us felt hungry. And we were curious about this barren hotel with no lobby, where we had to walk upstairs to an unadorned waiting room that smelled dank, like Chinese herbs and licorice, and wait a full-bladdered forever for the woman to tell me how much a room cost and swipe my credit card. Once we had landed the room and its toilet, we decided we might just as well light up the butt from Jordan's case.

Usually he was taut as a broom handle, so the little boy penis wagging between his legs surprised me when I unzipped his pants.

My first instinct was to slicken my hands with saliva, as I had with Thomas many times, and attempt to resurrect him. But something told me to refrain. So I pushed him down upon the king-sized bed that just about swallowed the room and made me feel far away, like we were in Hong Kong or Shanghai. We had not removed all our clothes, and that was consoling because we needed boundaries— and besides, I had been too spectacularly naked with someone else too recently.

So I stroked his chest through his yellow T-shirt. But he grabbed my hand away and sat up.

"I don't like myself now, Molly. You shouldn't like me either."

"Why don't you like yourself?" I asked, wondering if he found me less attractive.

"Because I was an idiot. We both know that."

"It seems you've done some thinking. You're a different person from the one who was an idiot." And if anyone was an idiot at that moment, it wasn't him.

"If we got together again," he warned, "other shit would happen."

"We're not getting back together."

"Then why the fuck are we here?"

"Because I want you. Just right now. We're both high—"

He looked moved but uncertain.

"You know," I went on, "I was mad at you for being such an idiot because I really treasured some things about being with you."

"I know you did," he said.

"We had good times too."

"And I know that you weren't cheating on me, by the way. I just wanted attention. I got jealous when you went out and saw people without me—I knew you weren't banging a bartender."

"Jordan, I have a strange question." I curled my hand on the bare patch of thigh where I'd began to roll down his pants. His skin was dry and scaly, not custardy smooth like Eugenia's. "How many women have you slept with?"

"Fucked, or just messed around with?'

"Actually made love."

"Oh, I don't know. Maybe you're the fifth."

"Sweet that you can still count them. Well, can you tell me—are all women the same basic shape—inside?"

Jordan squinted at me as though I had squirted lemon in his eye and he mouthed, "*WHAT?*"

"I'm not talking about the hole. I'm talking about the donut."

Outside in the corridor a man squawked something in rapid Mandarin as he stomped by our room.

"You know what I mean," I continued. "I'm not talking about the window—I'm talking about the drapery."

"You ask the fucking weirdest questions."

He didn't think to ask me why I was asking strange questions, but I could see that he was getting aroused. I stroked his thigh, jigging my own leg, which was still clad in linen pants, upon it.

"Well—yes or no? Tell me."

He laughed uncomfortably.

"Like pasta," I continued to prompt him. "You know, some pasta is seashells, some is like butterflies, some like wagon wheels—are women that way?"

Swelling toward erection, there remained some misgiving in him—as Shakespeare phrased it in an early sonnet—that "uncertain glory of an April day." But I didn't touch him. I slowly licked his soft, chunky lips, enjoying his mustache and dab of beard as I pressed myself against him. Then I drew back.

"God, I've missed you!" he cried in a scratchy voice that sounded almost girlish. Then he admitted, "I've been so lonely."

"Don't say that now."

He cooed something back in a baby voice, stroking my cheek and lips with his finger. Then he kissed me, his tongue hot and eloquent, his full hand on my face. This was Jordan as I remembered him in surrender, undoing my pants, nuzzling his head on my naked belly as I had on Eugenia's. I wondered if I too exerted a gravitational pull.

"Am I like a bow tie?" I whispered.

"You're a beautiful sea shell."

"What kind? Like a clamshell? A conch?"

"No. A sweet little cowrie."

My pants were now down to my knees.

"Did it surprise you, the first time you touched a new woman?"

"Yes it did."

41

That night—for a change—I barely slept. I lay awake, wondering what a hormone looked like. I could conjure the pinpoint roundness of atoms and molecules, the cell with its nucleus, the DNA helix. But even though I was being injected with hormones, I wouldn't recognize a biochemical if it fell on me like a raindrop.

When I dragged myself into the office the next morning with hair wet and straggly after a long shower, Larry was at the front desk chatting with Kendra.

He clucked disapprovingly at me.

"Nice of you to drop by today."

"Look," I pleaded as he began walking back to his office. "I stayed all evening on Monday, Tuesday, and Wednesday. I've never asked for overtime."

"And I appreciate it," he snapped. "But Molly, I need you to be more predictable. You're driving me crazy."

"Imagine how crazy I'm driving myself."

He indicated his office with his index finger, and I followed him inside. He shut the door behind him, and we both sat on the leather sofa by the fichus tree. Morning light trailed innocently through the window, the warm, pale light that had followed me to the park yesterday from Eugenia's room on Sunday, the light that had dissolved her into Bonnard-like brush strokes on her bed.

But all I could think, rather fiercely, was that she was ruining my life, spinning me in directions that no longer felt like myself.

"What's going on?" Larry asked.

I dispensed a surprisingly desperate sigh.

"Please bear with me. I seem to be going through a midlife thing."

"*Thing*? That's vague. You mean a midlife *crisis*?"

But there was too much sex and money involved for a crisis.

"Maybe more like a midlife disorder." Everything that used to be a problem or a crisis was, after all, now a "disorder."

"Can you talk about it?"

"Wish I could."

Kendra's voice, paging Larry, shot through our conversation.

"Larry, pick up line two. It's Angus Scott."

"Your old friend and countryman. I'd better get this." Angus Scott had been good-natured about our botched mailing, and we had redeemed ourselves with a design approach that he and his partner adored. Happily, I'd initiated the strategy. Jack had originally tried to veto it and was put in his place by Angus' partner.

As Larry spoke to Angus I planned what I would say. But instead of coming back to the sofa after the call ended, Larry opened a drawer in his old oak file cabinet and fished out a folded sheet of onion-skin typewriter paper. I sat patiently on the couch, suddenly seeing myself on Jordan's lap in the hotel yesterday, both of our pants snagged around our calves as we heaved and moaned like banshees.

Larry read aloud: "For all of her excitable imagination, Molly never fails to roll up her sleeves and get the job done. She is vital, reliable, and honest. Over the last years I cannot say that she has once disappointed me. Therefore I recommend her for your staff without reservation, as I know she will not disappoint you."

He carefully slid the paper back into the file, not having to tell me that Eleanor had written those words years ago, before he'd hired me.

As he returned to the sofa, I asked him, in as much as I was able to squeeze my words out, "Are you disappointed in me now?"

To my relief he whispered no.

"Just worried, sweetheart."

Maybe I needed someone to worry about me.

"I promise I'll stop being so erratic. Here's the drill—I'll need to take off some time for a medical procedure in about a month. But I will come in every workday before then. Once a week I see my shrink at lunch. That's the only time I'll take off."

"Do you need the fibroid surgery?" he asked sympathetically.

"Not exactly. But my condition is female-related."

"Are you okay? I mean, is something more wrong than you're letting on?"

Larry stared at me so hard I could see his ancestors overtake his face—hard-working Russian merchants and babushkas with apprehensive brown eyes and gnarled foreheads.

I had no answer for him. But I began to wonder if I really could join Enrico in a lawsuit against Larry, or even encourage that to happen.

42

Elizabeth J. Muldoon had earned her DSW at Columbia University, and her MSW at Fordham. I scanned the diplomas hanging on her honeydew-green walls as she and I awaited Alessi, who was stuck in traffic. Pete had been waylaid by a meeting about the Fed hiking interest rates, and he was not going to make it at all to the social worker's.

I didn't tend to vent my private concerns to close friends, much less a stranger with no sense of humor, like Elizabeth J. Muldoon, MSW DSW. But so much burbled up in me that I spewed forth almost kinesthetically, rumbling in my chair as I recounted Larry's confrontation that morning, the surprise assignations with my girlfriend—and my boyfriend—over the last week, and the pending plan with Ari Schwartzben that evening. I needed someone to talk to, even if it was Dr. Betsy (or, as Alessi sometimes called her, "Dr. Fucking Betsy").

But her face grew pink as a strawberry milkshake with every detail I divulged, and I saw that I had made a mistake.

"I didn't contact Jordan," I explained impatiently—why hadn't she understood this? "I ran into him on the subway."

"Which meant, of course, that you had to sleep with him."

"Of course."

"How do you think Eugenia would feel if she knew about that?"

"She probably wouldn't like it. But I don't know how strongly she wouldn't like it. We don't know each other well yet."

"How would you feel if she slept with a former lover this week?"

I tried to imagine that, but even the suggestion was unbearable. From its corner of the room Betsy's fountain recycled its dribbling water upon the slate slabs, and I wished Alessi would show up so we could talk about babies and lactation aids instead of this uncomfortable topic, that I, of course, had initiated. A peek at my wristwatch told me I'd been there for fifteen minutes.

"How would you feel if she'd done what you did, Molly?"

Betsy posed the question in a conversational tone, as though she genuinely wondered what I might feel. But I wanted to scream, "Stop trying to vilify me!" and sat for a while picking at a cuticle.

"You know," I finally said, "it's like a young girl who sleeps with a worldly man her first time. There's an implicit imbalance: he's had many women, but she's been only with him."

"So you don't think that what you've done may hurt Eugenia, because she's been with so many women?"

"Look, I have no intention of throwing my rendezvous with Jordan in her face. Actually—in some ironic way it might benefit my relationship with her. To tell you the truth, I was getting a bit fanatical. I could be convinced that her *internal organs* are beautiful—you know, her lungs, her intestines—any part of her. That's a little over the top, isn't it?"

"It sounds like you're in love with her."

"Falling." Let's not get ahead of ourselves.

"And so he'll catch you."

That was the most poetic thing I'd heard from Betsy.

"Well," I said after a while. "It's about time Jordan does something for me. Look—I care for him, too, but it's different. He's a kid. A cute kid. I enjoy him so much more now that I have an actual adult in my life."

My appetite for Jordan was like a craving for bread pudding, while Eugenia was more crème brûlée with brandied figs.

"I feel morally superior to Jordan," I confessed. "I seem to have had an ennobling effect on him. At best, I could inspire him, Pygmalion-like. Jordan is my moderate risk relationship, to use Pete's terms. Eugenia's my high risk. I can only drink her perfection."

"So you have diversified your dates."

"According to Pete, hedge funds that go belly-up aren't really hedging, they're just taking reckless and poorly leveraged risks."

Betsy sat back in her chair and folded her arms.

"You're hedging bets on your heart now?"

"I'm trying not to be stupid. I can't turn my life upside-down for one person."

"Why not?"

This was actually a good question.

"What am I going to do? Cut my hair like a sailor, get a tattoo, and never flirt with men again? That just isn't me. And if I tried to be with Eugenia as I am, I'd probably be called a 'lipstick lesbian' or AC-DC by all her friends. Everything you do in that community seems so scrutinized—every rip in your pants, every strand of your hair. Meanwhile, if you're straight you can just be a normal old person. Your love life isn't this niche market."

Betsy said nothing, so I continued. I had been thinking a lot about this.

"I don't even like the word *lesbian*. I hear it as *less-being*. Why is it the only sexual preference described by geography? Could you imagine if straight men were known at Cypriots and straight women as, pardon the pun, Cretans?"

Of course Dr. Betsy did not laugh. She could be counted on to not laugh. She looked increasingly distressed as I raised this legitimate point.

"Imagine if I told people, 'Well, I was once a Cretan, but now I'm a Lesbian. Moved from Crete to Lesbos; Sappho welcomed my change of zip code with open arms.'"

"So does all this mean you're not going to pursue Eugenia?"

"I fully intend to go to the bar tomorrow night and follow up on the plan for Sunday. I want her to know what's going on so she can make a clear decision about me. I mean, I am kind of dreading—"

"You'll tell her everything?"

I nodded. "Yes."

"Did you tell Jordan about her?"

"He asked me if I'd been with any man since him, and I told him that I hadn't."

I might have been imagining Dr. Betsy's condemnation. "Well, I hadn't!" I barked at her.

"You were intimate with someone else," she said calmly. "Does that not count, because she's a woman?"

"I didn't want to get into it with him. It's too new for me to know how to explain."

Then Betsy's phone rang, and she pardoned herself to answer it. We both knew it was Alessi, and I had a sinking sense we would not be seeing her today.

"I figured you might do that. Very well, let's aim for Tuesday then," Betsy said to the phone, confirming my disappointment. I wished badly that Alessi would bluster through the door, blabbing about traffic and parking. It would have been a joy to see my oldest friend at this moment.

"Maybe it's better that she not hear all this," Betsy finally said to me. "Because Molly, on the basis of what you've told me, I can't recommend that you go through with the pregnancy just now."

I grasped both armrests of my chair, sinking what existed of my fingernails into them.

"It's not your decision," I protested. "Alessi, Pete, and I have an agreement. We intend to go through with it, and you can't stop us."

"That's certainly true. But as the social worker for this case, I'm concerned about your ability to fulfill your obligation."

I was still digging my fingers into the arms of my wing chair and ready to spit.

"You may not be ready to take on this responsibility right now. Maybe you need another six months to work out your own needs for intimate partnership. Your recent behavior is your way of saying that to yourself, to me, and to the Foleys. I think we should speak about this together. Of course I wouldn't do so without your permission."

I curled my fingers, hearing them scratch the fabric on the armrests. The stupid fountain gurgled in its corner. I slid my feet in closer and sat up straight.

"Recent behavior?" I cried. "What are you talking about? I've fallen in love with Eugenia, and I feel close to Jordan. These are people I have spent time with. I'm not meeting strangers in public restrooms, like my boss Larry did in his gay heyday. Give me a break."

"I'm not saying you're wrong, or bad, Molly. I'm suggesting that you're not ready to be a surrogate mother."

"Would you be saying the same thing if I had two boyfriends—if Eugenia was Eugene?"

Betsy looked at me as though I hadn't spoken. So I repeated the question.

"If I was in love with one man, but also close with another, would you be telling me that I'm 'not ready' to be a surrogate mother?"

"Probably," she said. "I don't think you understand how demanding pregnancy can be, emotionally and physically."

"Women in all sorts of circumstances bear children. We're not namby-pamby."

I glanced around at her certificates, macramé wall hangings and photographs of children with her widely spaced eyes. There were no photos of herself, her husband, her parents; once people started having kids, they didn't tend to display pictures of adults.

Then it hit me that while those were clearly Betsy's offspring in the photographs, she had not given birth in the traditional way. She wore a number of rings but no diamond. Maybe she had used IVF or surrogates, and that's why she fancied herself the doyenne of assisted fertility.

"And in this twisted, malicious world," I continued, "I'm not married and I'm seeing two other unmarried people, who are both consenting adults—why am I not fit to be a surrogate mother? Who am I abusing or deceiving?"

"My goodness, Molly! You're deceiving both of them."

"But I'm *not*. I haven't agreed to marriage or fidelity. I'm really just getting to know each of them."

Betsy looked somewhere between staggered and sarcastic.

"Let's be honest about something," I leveled with her. "You haven't liked the sound of me from the get-go. I don't fit your surrogate mother profile. But you're overlooking the most important factor, which is my stamina..."

Now she shut her eyes with strain.

"But let's just suppose one of these respectable surrogate mothers of yours finds out, during her pregnancy, that her dear husband is having an affair, or losing his job. Or they learn that their own child is autistic. How stable is her life then?"

Dr. Betsy opened her eyes again, as though she had never thought of such odds.

"Unless a woman knows how to rely on herself, she's not stable. She's just in a temporarily stable circumstance. I know that. I'm used to taking care of myself. I don't depend on anyone."

"Scottish Woman, Tough as Nails," said the social worker. "That's how they described my grandmother."

"I'm sure with good reason."

"Would you—would you be willing to try something with me now, Molly? I'm afraid that what I'm doing here isn't really helping."

She was probably going to ask me to stop being a brat, but she was treading. And if she wanted to see tough nails, I could show them.

"Would you sit back, shut your eyes, and take ten deep breaths?"

"I hate deep breaths and drinking water. I do not aspire to be a 'relaxed person.'"

"Very well then, don't breathe. Are you willing to sit back and shut your eyes?"

"No!" I snapped. "I don't take time off my job to shut my eyes and breathe."

"Okay, just please sit back. Do you realize you are so stiff that you're practically standing up now?"

Reluctantly, I obliged her and leaned back—heaving a long, ironic sigh. There I sat, my eyes closed, aware that I was involuntarily shaking. My awareness made me shake even more. I was falling apart, and this professional, for all her pomp and platitudes, knew it.

"What are you feeling?"

Her local accent seemed more pronounced now that I wasn't looking at her. She had probably grown up in the Bronx or Long Island, and for a while I distracted myself thinking about that.

"What are you feeling?" she repeated.

"Upset," I said.

"Sink into the upset. What's there?"

Somehow, I knew what she meant by "sinking into" it. I was infiltrating a damp canvas tent in a forest. Inside the tent a fire burned in a pit of stones.

"What's there?" the voice came again.

"Terror."

Neither of us said anything for a while, but I heard myself sigh again and felt myself shake, my face trying to find some kind of muscular poise. I must have looked grotesque.

"Talk about the terror."

I grunted, casting around for some way to see it. Finally I alighted upon the one word: *loss*. It hung in the room like a strange shadow. It could have been *moss*, for the tendrils it was growing. I went on: "Losing everything I know—my body, my life, my job—their baby—the love of my family. The chance to ever be normal…" My voice then caught upon a sob. Betsy probably sensed that I was about to say "Eugenia."

"Of course I'll never lose Jordan," I said with the sniffly kind of laugh that comes with tears. "You don't lose people who need you—can't shake them if you want to…"

I opened my eyes as Betsy's cool hand placed a tissue into mine.

"We've got to stop now," Betsy said. "You did great work today, Molly. If we can do a little more I think we'll be okay."

43

The Bunny Hop was filled with surprises, like colored balloons and groups of gay men. Maybe it was some kind of a special night, a mixer. My heart melted like fruit in the sun when, through crowds at the bar, I caught sight of her Led Zeppelin T-shirt and blonde hair spilling from under a straw fedora.

I tried to elbow my way up front. She couldn't see me with eyes hidden by the hat's small brim as she churned out cocktails that a chubby woman with cat-eyed glasses distributed. Fedora tipped over her face and cigarette dangling from her lips, Eugenia barely acknowledged the hooting and caterwauling, including one maddening queen who kept screaming, "Calamity Gene!"

I knew only that I adored her, was delighted to see her again, and could toss everything else to the wind.

People passed by, tipping me this way and that as though I was a docked canoe. I had spent the day preening for this appearance at an East Village salon with Edwardian décor, getting my hair trimmed and blow-dried. While I had purchased a lace-up leather teddy, I didn't end up wearing it—I felt too ludicrous. And if I didn't recognize myself, Eugenia couldn't be expected to do better. I ended up in a burgundy velvet blouse I had owned for years.

When she raised her head to hand drinks to the woman with cat-eyed glasses, her blue eyes tore through my heart. As she swiftly turned the other way I learned that the Led Zeppelin T-shirt was from a 1971 tour. She still was not aware of me; there were too many people who were louder and wider, waving their arms, leaning on the bar, yelling and leering.

But as I stood there I realized that fate had come full circle. She had urged me to accept money from Pete and Alessandra, and I would share it with her. Somehow—I was not sure exactly how—I would get her out of there. She needed to get out.

I could feel my face flushing, my lips curling upward, my eyes softening, my fingers trickling a wave to her as she finally saw me. Something of the magic broke over her face too. She nodded; the cigarette in her lips did not deter a charming smile. But it became a remote and hapless expression with nothing behind it. I apprehended, with a certain horror, that I had become extraneous to her. At that moment I felt unwelcome—one more person for her to attend, one more relationship to steward.

I allowed a swathe of guys demanding Rolling Rocks to overtake me and haggle it out with the woman in cat-eyed glasses—who, I later learned from Bertie, owned The Bunny Hop.

I didn't want to order a drink and make Eugenia work any harder than she already was. As I pulled back from the bar I became aware of the loud, angry voices to my left.

"He doesn't belong here!" the Calamity Gene queen was shouting. "He's a fucking Marine!"

A group of men in sequined shirts and gowns surrounded Arbie, who was sitting with his *Daily News* and beer like a cornered stag.

"You don't run this place, Lola," the woman in cat-eyed glasses interjected.

A groan arose from the crowd of men wearing everything from wigs to wampum.

"Look, I'll leave," said Arbie, standing up. But the woman with cat-eyed glasses leaned over the bar and spoke to him. From where she stood, Eugenia glanced at the ruckus but continued mixing martinis and Tom Collinses.

"I mean, he can sit anywhere!" Lola continued his shrill lament. "I can't do that! He can go to any old diner! Why does he have to be here?"

Words were exchanged so quickly I couldn't catch them against the din of voices, the driving techno bass. Something about how he was handy to have around as a bodyguard, when Eugenia closed up the place alone at three in the morning.

"Oh, she's stronger than that old fart!" Lola was hollering. "Eugenia is stronger than a herd of elephants."

I decided I would leave and come back in a couple of hours. Hopefully, the noise and the action would have subsided enough for me to make a quick plan to meet her next week for dinner. We couldn't go out tomorrow night—I wouldn't allow her. After a night like this she must rest. I waved good-bye to her like a swimmer waves to shore, and she flung me a surprised, slightly irritated glance.

As I walked into the night I tried to regain the elation I'd felt initially at the bar. But instead, I felt convinced that she didn't want to see me. We hadn't been in touch for five agonizing days, and all she could cough up was this frail grin and dismissive nod.

Come on, Molly, I thought, correctively. She had back problems and was up to her elbows in alligators. *Remember, she asked you never to take her mood on the job personally? Remember that? And you agreed, didn't you?*

So I convinced myself not to go home filled with self-pity but to kill time and give The Bunny Hop a second chance later.

On Orchard Street the sportswear and ladies apparel shops had passed their business primes for the day. But for new pubs on Ludlow Street the night was young. Finally I wound up at a cool bookstore on Allen Street that featured its own fair-trade-approved vegan café along with scads of intriguing books.

But when I returned to The Bunny Hop around eleven thirty, the crowds and the cigarette smoke had gotten even thicker, and the music raged. I shoved my way in as though it were a subway car on a weekday—the one difference being that now people opted to stand in a filthy, noisy crowd for the fun of it.

I headed to the DJ stand, hoping I might find Bertie. Sure enough, she beckoned me over through her little window, and I climbed into her insulated quarters to escape the mayhem.

"Four more motherless hours," she grumbled, tinkering with her digital sound box.

"Thought you still did vinyl," I commented.

Bertie shook her head, her lips pressed in concentration. Her shirt and pants were fashionably wrinkled, as if she'd slept in them. From her unbuttoned collar her neck made a smooth ascent to her face, barely interrupted by a chin, like a young seal's. She glistened with perspiration.

"So, I never did get clear on what happened to you and Lainey that night at the Mexican restaurant. You were supposed to chaperone me."

"It's my job to mess with you, Molly," she said with a lopsided smile, continuing to work the dials on her digital audio player. "You wouldn't have wanted us to derail you from going home with Bonnie Gene."

"I'm afraid Bonnie Gene will derail me. Or just drop me." I stood near Bertie so we could hear each other.

"Why would she drop you? Last I heard she's, like, way in your camp."

"Will she be so enthusiastic when she learns that she's my first woman?"

"She may not like *that*. She's a bit of a purist. How did she put it? 'I don't want to be anyone's defining moment.'"

"It's a little late for that."

"The irony is that all these straight girls who meet her act like they're Saint Francis receiving the stigmata."

Bertie rolled her eyes and waved her hands around like she was doing the Hokey Pokey.

"All these straight women?" I repeated her words with distress, trying to get as much out of her as I could.

"None of 'em ever got as far with her as you, Molly."

"They were probably more forthright."

"Now me, I would've taken them up on it. You should have seen me when I was corporate. I did the whole secretarial pool."

"Will she drop me if I tell her the truth?" I repeated. "Will she consider me an AC-DC case, like Claudia?"

Bertie was still fiddling around with her audio settings.

After a while she said, "I can't read her mind, Molly, but that's not the sense I get. You shoulda seen how pissed off she was when you didn't show up here the night after your first date. She thought I meddled. And you know, she's not mean-spirited, but she's got a temper. So I offered to make it up to her by getting you over to that Mexican place."

Then Bertie looked over at the bar and sighed. "Poor girl hasn't had a second to breathe in hours. I wonder what happens when she has to pee."

I too looked out from the rectangle that had been carved unevenly into the plywood that separated the DJ stand from the room.

"Why are so many guys here?"

"Yesterday was a drug bust over at Dagger's, the hot spot in Brooklyn for cruising queens. And, it's The Bunny Hop's fourth anniversary. Actually, that was Thursday. But the party's tonight. Which is why I'm here, mixin' everyone's favs."

"She looks sad tonight," I interrupted, facing Bertie again.

"Well, it's her second crazy night in a row and her fourth year doing the same old shit—and the summer season is just beginning."

Bertie stopped setting up her tracks and stood back, wiping moist hands on her thighs.

"You know how she juggles beer bottles? Well, she actually dropped one yesterday. Broke it." Bertie shook her head. "Not a good sign. She's never done that before. I think she's in a weird mood."

"So it's not just me imagining things."

"People have been talking all week. She was out sick for a couple of days, no one knows why. We hope she's not having a sciatica attack. She's had herniated disks—that's why she couldn't play professional tennis. You know the whole story, right?"

Before I could answer, Bertie shook her head again. "You can't say she's had an easy time exactly. I'm prone to jealousy of her looks, and all the attention she gets..."

"You said you weren't jealous of her," I reminded Bertie, but she didn't seem to hear me.

"There's a reserve of untapped despair. A girl like that, from a small southern city, came to New York with ambitions."

"Why doesn't she get another job if she's frustrated here?"

"Doing what? She hates working for straight people. Everyone loves her here. Gail and Toby took one look at her and it was, like, 'Any shift is yours, sweetie.' But you know, we're at the age where you start to wonder if this is going to be the rest of your life."

"It won't be the rest of her life," I interrupted Bertie decisively.

Bertie squinted at me. "You're in it deep, Molly—aren't you?"

"I don't know."

"I don't think Eugenia knows. She made some offhand comment to me—please don't tell her, okay?"

"What?" I begged Bertie.

"I can't remember exactly, but it was something like how you're intelligent enough to get bored with her eventually."

I shook my head with exasperation.

"How could she think I'd be—" I could barely even get the word out, "*bored?*"

I remembered her pitching in bed like a wild fish on a hook; no wonder men loved seeing a woman come. I wanted to see it again and again, to touch her in different ways. I wanted to see photographs of her childhood and learn the names of her parents and her brothers.

"You know how people are about themselves."

"Bertie!" someone called out. Below the DJ stand was the chubby woman in cat-eyed glasses, Gail. "You ready to roll?"

"Yeahh-up!"

"We'll turn off the jukebox."

Once the music stopped, Bertie spoke into a microphone: "And here's a little treat for you fine folks who've come to celebrate our fourth anniversary on the Lower East Side!"

Everyone applauded and whooped when a big-band recording of The Bunny Hop itself came on.

Immediately people started lining up, everyone holding the hips of the person in front of him, which was no problem for the boys. The conga line got long rather fast, everyone tapping his right foot, left foot, hopping forward, then back, jumbling into each other, creeping onward as the track morphed into a lusty salsa version of the dance.

"Can you believe this?" Bertie squealed. "Man, it's goin' over well."

Then a crowd of girls with biking helmets pushed their way in, like a jetty of water against the current.

"Oh shit!" Bertie put her hand to her mouth.

"What?"

"You don't want to know."

"I do."

"You don't!"

My heart was pounding quicker than HOP, HOP, HOP.

"Tell me."

"This Brazilian chick hasn't been around for months—like, since Christmas." Bertie stood in front of me so I couldn't see the bar from the slight elevation of the DJ stand. I tried to get around her, but she blocked me. "Don't look!" Bertie even covered my eyes with her hands, groaning: "Oh shit. Oh Eugenia!" under her breath.

"What is going on?"

"If you like her, don't look."

Mercilessly, I shook my face away from Bertie's hands and shoved her aside.

A slinky girl with thick black hair had climbed onto Eugenia's back and Span-dex-covered legs were wrapped around Eugenia's waist. Everyone watching them cheered and clapped to the beat: HOP, HOP, HOP. The girl had taken off Eugenia's straw fedora and was waving it. Eugenia craned her head back, and the girl, who had high cheekbones and a killer smile, planted a brief kiss on her mouth.

Then, as if I hadn't seen enough, a man at the bar reached out and grabbed the girl's arm. I could have sworn it was Enrico.

I felt like someone had socked me in the guts so hard that I was going to vomit my esophagus.

"I'm gone."

"Wait!" Bertie grabbed my arm. "Molly, don't—"

But there was no waiting, no Molly, no don't.

44

Wending my way west, I nearly got mauled by cars and bicycles. I could hardly see where I was going, as though my head was wrapped in cellophane.

And the moon was a ghostly galleon, tossed upon cloudy seas.

Or crowded streets, snarled with kids yapping in their stupid, nasal voices, on cell phones and not on cell phones, sometimes so thick with them that I could hardly move. At one point in pedestrian gridlock, a guy mumbled, "Sorry," and I realized that his little dog was peeing on my shoe. Thank goodness I had not been wearing barefoot sandals.

On the next street a young woman lay between the gutter and the sidewalk, as another propped her head up and made her drink Evian water.

This was not the "I'm going to spend ten thousand dollars on laparoscopic egg retrieval" crowd and this was not the surrogate gestational motherhood crowd. At most it was the "I'm unmarried and have discovered bisexuality" crowd, but I didn't belong on those student-happy streets; I didn't belong in The Bunny Hop any more than poor Arbie did; in fact, I didn't even belong in my own family.

And I didn't belong in the raunchy bar where I stopped for a shot of grappa. But there is nothing like grappa to untwist the brain from its socket.

The bartender wore glasses and thick sideburns like guys had in the seventies. He moved slowly, without grace or method or anything like Eugenia. But that would be my life now, ratcheted down several notches of charm. My thoughts almost ran like the blurb on back of a young adult novel: *Who was I to imagine I could have held the attention of someone like her? What had I been thinking? If she were a handsome blond male bartender favored by female patrons acting like they'd received the stigmata from Saint Francis, would I have fallen so foolishly?*

Then the more pointed, sleuthing voice: but why had she gone out of her way to hijack me on a date in that Mexican restaurant; why did Bertie think, even tonight, that she was "way in my camp"?

Claudia's words came to me: "She had to win you."

Now I was yesterday's adventure.

"I'll have another."

I held up my glass, and eventually the half-hearted bartender with his dopey sideburns like long dog's ears came my way and replaced it. I slugged it, mourning that first half screwdriver Eugenia had served me. Damn. I would miss her forever—when I left town to get inseminated, when my belly rose like baker's yeast set into a rounded loaf. I would miss her when I was a doddering old lady in a wheelchair who couldn't stand the smell of myself.

I dipped my head again once I had the bartender's attention. He seemed surprised that I wanted another shot so quickly. I flicked a fifty out of my wallet and onto the bar. This would be my last week of booze before June, when I promised Alessi that I wouldn't consume alcohol, coffee, or red meat, when the business of impregnation would be fast and furious upon us.

But now, what I had was more grappa.

What's with us? I didn't think I had this in me anymore.

As much as I wanted reasons now to resent her, I knew Eugenia didn't say such things offhandedly.

I held up the empty glass and twinkled it like a star, trying to catch the bartender's eye. But he was watching a baseball game that roared on television. Still, his place was calm compared with The Bunny Hop.

"May I buy this round?"

A tall preppie guy with straight brown hair and a V-neck sweater stood beside me. He was probably Jordan's age.

"No thanks. I'd better get on home."

I was starting to shake, as I had in Dr. Betsy's office yesterday afternoon. If I was to cohort in this sorry state with anyone in that age group, I might as well find the young man who already knew me.

So I meandered to The Back Porch, where Jordan might be skulking on a Saturday night. He didn't seem to be there, but I came upon Z chatting up a small crowd.

"Hey there, Molly Girl. Hey—you don't look so hot…"

Three grappas under my belt and Z found me a bench by the window.

"Where's Jordan?" I mumbled, head in my hands.

"He has a gig tonight in Williamsburg with Blake, matter of fact."

"Can we call him?"

I looked up slowly, trying not to nauseate myself. As though producing a rosary or some item of religious totem, Z solemnly handed me his phone.

"It's Molly," I muttered to Jordan's voice mail. "Come over tonight. I don't care how late." I paused for half a minute before saying, "I need you. I really need you."

I put the phone in my lap and faced the loud, blurring room around me—my world, as it would be without Eugenia.

Z made me drink a lot of water. I have only a vague recollection of getting home, of Z and a friend of his patiently shuttling me to some dilapidated car that was parked near Lafayette Street and hoisting me upstairs to my apartment. On Claudia's floor we didn't, for once, hear Lauren's scales or sour singing.

When we got to my door I thanked them profusely and then kicked my shoes off, remembering that a little dog had peed on one. The pee now looked like dried caramel sauce.

"You sure you gonna be okay? Do you want us to stay with you?" Z's cinnamon-brown eyes radiated concern.

"Thanks—I don't want to crimp your Saturday-night style. Jordan will come soon."

After they left I turned on my shower and walked into it, fully clothed. I wanted to wash the memory of tonight out of the very fabric I was wearing—and I didn't want to touch a nude female body, even if it was my own. It made me remember her.

Once I had soaked myself and all my clothing, I climbed out of the tub and stooped over for a while, rocking back and forth. Water drooled onto the floor before me in a puddle, hairy with velvet strands from my shirt. Gradually I pulled everything off, like I was peeling off heavy layers of skin. I remembered my wet tennis dress on Eugenia's bathroom floor. Now it would be her memento of my "defining moment."

I dried off, trying not to remember how she had dried me after the shower we had taken together. Then I threw on one of Thomas' old blue BVD T-shirts just as the buzzer rang. Thank God I had not alienated Jordan by talking about her. Thank God I had not listened to Dr. Betsy.

Jordan's hair smelled sooty as I embraced him.

"It's good to see you," I whispered.

"Z was real worried about you." Jordan stood back with his instrument case, acting like I frightened him. "He drove to Brooklyn to tell me to get over here."

"That was sweet."

"What the hell's goin' on?"

"I drank too much grappa. Come in."

Jordan walked inside as I shut the door.

"Want some weed?" he asked nervously.

"Play," I said. "That's all I want. Music and companionship." I was maxed out on sex, not interested in drugs. I flapped my arm around. "Enchant the morning."

"Requests?"

Clearly relieved, Jordan settled on my sofa and opened his saxophone case.

"Blues."

"Sure the neighbors won't mind?"

I was so quiet most of the time that I had earned some grace from them. And if the woodwind blatted through their dreams they might recall that jazz had been played in this apartment before.

I lay back on the sofa, my feet touching Jordan's thigh.

His medley of sad love songs sounded almost like violin: "Blue Moon"; "Some Other Spring"; "In My Solitude"; "Tenderly"; and of course, "Something Stupid Like I Love You."

He played until his lip hurt and he began to snore between phrases. The sky turned dove gray and birds chorused in the alley, and my eyes dropped shut too.

We awoke to my ringing telephone. My first instinct was to panic that I had overslept and Larry was calling to scream at me. Then I remembered it was Sunday, and I wondered who would be so inconsiderate as to call me at noon. I assumed the culprit was my mother.

But caller ID told me that this call was placed by *Schenk, Roberta*. I grabbed the receiver and snapped Bertie off.

Jordan curled back into his fetal position, and I ran to the bathroom to pee and pop my birth control pill. The phone started ringing again, my voice robot got it, and Bertie's robust baritone filled my apartment.

"Hey Molly, you there? Hello? Look—about last night. I gotta clear something up—"

I dashed over and threw the phone across the room, ripping the cord from the wall jack.

Jordan sat up with a start, blinking his eyes.

"Who is *he*, Molly?"

"That was Claudia's ex—Bertie."

"You're full of shit. Why would you kill your phone over Bertie?"

"She's bugging me. Come here and check out the caller ID."

Jordan heaved himself up from the sofa, and we retrieved the caller ID device, which still said *Schenk, Roberta*.

"She sounds like a fucking guy."

We smiled at each other.

"You know, something I think about, as a musician?" he began. "There are, what, three billion people in this world?"

"More like six billion."

"Okay, six billion. And everyone has a different voice. How many different fucking voices can there be?"

I started to laugh. The more I looked at him, the harder I laughed. God bless him for helping me laugh.

From my purse I heard my cell phone ring. Too bad, Bertie.

"Jordan," I gasped through my laughter, "I'm going to have a child."

He shook his head. "No way."

"Don't worry, it isn't your child. Not to sound like a bad Polish joke—but it's not even mine."

PART THREE

45

"What do you know about Jack that you haven't told me?"

Larry's new haircut made his head seem pruned. Chin out, one leg folded over the other and hand on the doorknob for balance, he posed expectantly.

"What would you like to know about Jack?" I asked.

"Don't be smart. I need an answer."

"He's a dick."

"Could you possibly be more specific? We may be in trouble."

Larry pushed away from the door and strutted over to me, the lemony ginger scent of his cologne trailing him into my office. I was suddenly furious. If he'd been sober about Jack a couple of months ago my own life might not have swerved into detours.

"Would you have believed me if I told you the truth? You know how you get— you'd defend a raccoon in a trash can."

"I'm a dick," said Larry. "But Jack's a liability."

"What sunrise produced these rays of light?"

"Two pending law suits—one initiated by Enrico de Souza that you tried to warn me about, and I trounced on you. And another from a vendor, I won't say who."

"No surprise."

"Well I can't afford to hire attorneys and, for heaven's sake, go to trial! I get sick just thinking about it. All that waste of cash and I mean, damn, Jesus—sexual harassment of a gay man in *my* workplace?"

"Then fire Jack," I said evenly, "and offer Enrico back his job. He'll have no case against you."

Larry stared at me with embarrassed relief.

"He might not even take it back," I continued. "I'm sure his memories of this place are hardly pleasant. What happened with the vendor?"

"Jack pulled a job midstream and gave it to someone he knows."

Concluding that it was one of our offset printers, I grimaced.

"Pay the piper, Larry. Cough up their kill fee, and let them know that Jack is out of the picture. But show no mercy. Let him go—effective immediately. Like, this afternoon."

"I've been too stressed to think lately. Funny. Steve never liked Jack."

"Good for him."

"He thought Jack forged your signature."

"So do I."

Larry began pacing around my small office.

"Jack might have felt it was in his interest to knock out a creative director, given what I'd told him about my apprehensions—oh, why was I so trusting? Well, good thing I've got someone around here with a head where it belongs, on her shoulders."

"At least 'til the end of the year."

Larry stopped pacing and held up both hands, palms to the ceiling, looking vexed.

"Meaning what now?"

"I may be moving on around December, and I want to give you plenty of notice."

His mouth opened partially, like a small rodent's.

"No," he whispered. And then he said more decisively, "You can't do that to me. You just can't. You have no idea what's going on. This business with Jack is the tip of the iceberg."

"Then what's the *Titanic*?"

He went over to the door that was resting on its jamb and shut it fully.

"Listen, do you realize that we've lost thirty percent of our business this year? Steve says I should throw in the towel before we go into the red."

"And dry yourself with what?"

"Well, he thinks we should buy investment properties in Florida, while we still have cash to play with. I'm not sure. I'm just not sure about any of this. All I know is that I can't go on losing accounts to people who think they can hire their own support staff to design print ads, or get a couple of geeks in Brooklyn to host their websites. But from our clients' point of view, that certainly cuts costs, doesn't it? I mean, Molly, our pricing is no longer competitive. But how the hell else am I going to fork over these Madison Avenue rents?"

"Then why not go with Steve's plan?"

"I can't give up my life's work—besides, real estate is slippery, and my mother invested in me, you know, my own mother gave me money for Applebaum and Partners before she died. I can't give this up. I love the work. But I haven't been at the top of my game for a while—that's why you're sticking with me. I lose you and it's a sign from God that I'm sunk."

"Let's not get dramatic," I said, loving to hear how much I was needed, in view of how expendable I felt to Eugenia. I almost played with Larry's vulnerability in a mean way. "Well, pal, you may just have to forge on without me."

"Not possible. I mean have you got another gig lined up? Oh God!" he groaned before I even answered.

"Not exactly. There might be a way we can work out an arrangement. But I've got a caveat or two."

"What's that *Oliver Twist* song: 'I'll Do Anything'?"

"How about making me a partner? You're Larry Applebaum and Partners— but who *are* the partners? I've never understood why people say 'and Partners' or 'and Associates' when they don't have them. Maybe you need a real partner."

He popped his eyes and grinned, considering my offer. He hadn't expected it, and neither had I.

"We would have to sit down and talk. More than once."

"I'm game, so long as we can build in a three-month maternity leave next winter."

Larry stared at me, his mouth opening again. Then he emitted grunts of shock.

"I'm not pregnant. Yet."

"Now Molly, I know how women your age get. I went through it ten years ago with my sister. But I urge you not to do anything hasty or imprudent."

"It's not what you think."

"Sperm bank?"

"On that trajectory, but the details will have to wait. My brother doesn't even know yet."

Matt and Tamara would hear everything before I left town, before my regimen of progesterone shots began. I hoped I would recognize myself after that. And I would give them the unabridged version, not the vague summary I'd given Jordan. My brother and sister-in-law would know about Goldenrain Assets. They were the only ones who would know.

Larry lowered his butt onto the top of my filing cabinet and stared at the door to my office for a while.

"So now all your sick days make sense," he said. "I'm glad there was no trouble going on. I was starting to worry."

"I know. And I appreciate that."

"But listen. You'd better retain a horde of nannies if you want to be my partner and raise a kid on your own."

46

In June the rains came. My period came on the third. And a Gypsy family came to live in the storefront downstairs.

It was tough to keep track of who was who in this sprawl of hefty women with mermaid hair, diapered children, and listless men. But the hub of that juggernaut—whom I privately dubbed "Mama Cass," since she looked like the old rock diva—sat outside the store on a garden chair, a sparkly tiara in her hair, sunning herself with an aluminum reflector and crying: "*Get* your readings, *get* your readings!" like a hotdog vendor at Yankee Stadium. Sometimes I walked around the block so as not to pass her directly on my way to the stoop.

I repaired the phone that I'd thrown across the room, and Bertie's calls came. I never answered them and cut off her messages. Calls from Ari Schwartzben also came. After a completely cardboard date, he seemed eager to meet again and answer some questions I'd asked him about the Messiah. I figured I wouldn't be likely to date another Israeli businessman and should take the opportunity to learn.

Then on Sunday afternoon, Matthew and Tamara came. It was pouring heavily as the day they met, so they showed up with big, drippy umbrellas that we left open by my front door. I served them triple-crème brie cheese, olives, Triscuits, and tea. When I finished telling them about the surrogacy agreement, my brother sat across from me with the expression that crossed his face before he got motion sickness.

I had first seen it when I was four years old, sitting up front with Dad in the T-bird, with a seatbelt buckle that seemed as large as a lobster clamped over my belly. At the time, there were no special car seats for kids—and somehow we survived without them. Behind me, Matthew, about two, sat on Mom's lap, her fingers locked snugly around his little chest. To her left sat some female relative, her cousin or sister.

As much as the lobster-clamp seatbelt permitted, I twisted around on the bucket seat. When I saw my brother's head—green and groggy, ready to tumble off his neck—I hollered, "*Eugh!* Matthew's gonna THROW UP!"

"Sit down!" Mom commanded. She even reached forward to try and pin me to the seat.

"But Matthew's gonna THROW UP!"

To this day, I remember how earnestly I wanted to give Mom that information. And I remember her steady, impassive expression when she said to me, "No he's not."

Of course, she couldn't see his face, which had only gotten greener, when she leaned forward to discipline me. Dad slowed down and put on the blinker, gliding into the right-hand lane. I was thrilled that I had affected something so important.

"Ross, what are you doing?" Mom asked him impatiently.

"I think Molly's right," Dad said, looking straight ahead. I realize now that he probably saw Matthew in the rearview mirror.

Before Mom could argue, Matthew gagged out a lumpy, liver-colored mess that made the cousin or sister beside her scream. Cackling triumphantly, I held my nose.

I never remembered getting out of the car, how we cleaned it up, or even where we were going. I just knew that it was late summer. After that, whenever we drove anywhere Mom brought shopping bags of extra towels along and started Matthew on Dramamine.

"Yes, that's his carsick look," Tamara agreed.

"Some things don't change." But Matthew was not lighthearted after my confession.

"Can you get out of this?" he asked me.

"No. I've signed on the dotted line."

Matt sighed and Tamara looked at her feet. My lace curtain breathed faintly in the wind that brushed through trees in the alley. The rain that had ebbed to a drizzle was going to start up again.

My brother implored, "Why didn't you speak to us when we could have made a difference?"

"I didn't want to trouble you—you have enough on your plate."

"That's not who we are."

Clasping his hand, Tamara nodded in accord.

"You can always come to us," she added.

"Parenthood doesn't mean we're so precious that our loved ones should hesitate to ask for our help."

Matthew looked so sickly I had half a mind to spread a towel beside him. The last time I had done that, I thought ironically, had been when Jordan and I were having sex on the sofa and I was afraid his come would stick to the upholstery forever.

"Do you have any idea what you've gotten yourself into?"

"Of course."

"I mean, do you know that pregnant women are susceptible to hypothyroidism, gestational diabetes, migraines, and all sorts of other stuff?"

"Women have babies all the time," I said firmly. "The vast majority survive, and live well."

"And if you don't?" demanded my brother.

"You'll be heir to a lot of money. That's part of the reason we're talking."

"Alessi always has dominated you! She's so manipulative and self-centered—"

"She didn't dominate me, Matt. I held out on Alessandra for a couple of weeks, until I discussed this arrangement with an entirely detached party."

"Does that mean you're in therapy?" Tamara ventured.

This was a tricky question. I had avoided Dr. Betsy on the Tuesday that followed my miserable Saturday night at The Bunny Hop, saying I had a tight work deadline. That was the only session I had missed, and Pete too had been unable to attend. On their own, Alessi and Dr. Betsy had gotten into a vicious fight about breastfeeding and the lactation aid. It was now unclear whether or not we would be continuing with Betsy.

I answered Tamara that Pete, Alessi, and I saw a social worker together. "But at the time I made this decision I was not in any kind of counseling. I sought out a complete stranger—a bartender, actually. I described the situation to her and decided that I would do whatever she said she would do."

"Why?" asked Tamara, blinking hard with surprise, as though her eyelids were stuck.

Matt scooped up Triscuit after Triscuit and shoved them into his mouth.

"Well," I told them, sitting back in my armchair, "since I wasn't acting on my own directives I couldn't be accused of being manipulated, being desperate, being greedy, or sacrificial. I just took unbiased advice."

"Everyone has biases," muttered Matthew as he crunched on the Triscuits.

"But this person's biases didn't matter to me. She had no stake in my doing this or not doing it. It was pure, like tossing a coin."

I thought back to that night at the bar in April, the low light and candles, the strand of blonde hair trickling down Eugenia's forehead and over her eyes as she sang the praises of this arrangement.

"Think of what this will mean for the family. Maybe we'll all get a country house in the Berkshires or Cape May or something."

Tamara was beginning to follow my logic. She looked at Matt with a "maybe this isn't so bad" expression. But my brother was not on the page with us.

"You realize what you're doing? You're *selling* your body to Alessi and her hedge fund husband," he charged in a voice so upset that I didn't recognize it.

"Oh, come on, Matthew."

He got up from the sofa and began pacing around, like our father. But he wasn't as glue-lipped and pent up as Dad. I almost wished he was.

"Okay," he ceded, "maybe not selling your body. Renting. Like a prostitute, remitting the use of your body to people who are paying you—illegally, no less."

"You've been an attorney too long," I snapped. "Just listen to you."

"You've been writing ad copy too long. You can sell yourself on anything."

"Hey guys—this is getting out of hand," Tamara interrupted us. "Matt, this is her friend's personal crisis. You make everything sound cold and distant."

"You don't know these people," Matt shot back at his wife from across the room, where he stood by the window—that same window where Jordan and I had gazed down at Claudia in the alley searching for Buddha.

For all the instances in which I had defended my brother, I was now glad that Jordan had called him "a dork" and that Mom henpecked him for gaining weight.

Matthew was calling me a slut because I was helping Alessi have a child.

"I met Pete and Alessandra a couple of times," Tamara was saying to him. "They didn't seem horrible. She was kind of upbeat and witty."

"She comes from this oily Mafia family, and then she married old money."

"Not true." I stood up now myself. "You're parroting Mom."

"Mom's not wrong about everything."

"She's wrong here."

"Daddy manages how many trucking companies and contractors? And hubby was born with how many silver spoons in his mouth?"

From the couch Tamara glanced back and forth between us as if watching a swift ping-pong game.

"What did my friends ever do to you that you speak this way?"

Then my brother said nothing. I could tell by the way Tamara looked at him that she wondered whether he was being unfair.

"Crooks," he muttered. "All people in that line of work are crooks."

"And you don't have a 401K or an adviser—it's all in the mattress, Mattie?"

He didn't reply.

"Mattie Mattress," I mumbled. And then I reminded him, "A lot of people don't have the highest opinion of attorneys. Especially bankruptcy trustees like you."

"What they've asked of you is *wrong*. It's morally wrong," he insisted.

Just then my phone rang, and I answered it to get away from Matthew.

"Hey Molly, it's Bertie. You are one tough broad to reach."

"I can't talk now," I said, kicking myself for not screening the call. Talk about out of the frying pan and into the fire. "My brother and sister-in-law are here."

Tamara had walked over to Matt and spoke in hushed tones to him. She set her hand on his arm, and I watched him petulantly shake her off.

"When is a better time to reach you?" Bertie asked me.

"I don't want to discuss last week. I have nothing to say about it."

"Please let me explain—"

"Bertie, I said I don't want to talk about it. I've got enough on my mind, and my family's here now." Raised voices sifted over to me from Matt and Tamara. "Look," I told Bertie, "I'd better get off and be a hostess."

As I hung up I heard Tamara say, "So it would have been okay not to have Mira? Just as good to adopt a child?"

Matt stepped away from her, to the window. Outside, heavy rain slanted with the wind. "I would welcome and love any child. I don't need them to be *my* biological offspring."

He spoke at the downpour that pattered at my windowpane. I watched Tamara's face—Tamara, who was pregnant and already loving the infant in her body.

"Well, I disagree," she said.

He turned from the window to glance indignantly at her.

"I'm allowed, aren't I?" she continued. "Look, it's not like I wouldn't have loved an adopted baby as much as our own. But I do think family is kind of spiritual."

"That's exactly why genetics are beside the point. Look at me—chubby in a thin family, and I was born cross-eyed with a tendency to get carsick."

"Yeah, but it's endearing how you and Molly get the same expressions when you're thinking hard about something. I like that, I guess, feeling that my ancestors are living on somehow, that their genes are playing out in this world. So many of them got short shrift—in Hungary, in Russia..."

"There are plenty of biological family members who hate each other. You're talking about little mannerisms that are skin-deep. Family is who you care for every day—"

"Dahlia said she'd do it," Tamara interrupted him.

"What?"

"My sister said she'd be a surrogate, if we couldn't conceive."

"Thanks for telling me."

"Luckily we didn't need to go there. All I'm saying is that I don't think Molly's friend is wrong for wanting her own child and asking Molly to consider—"

"Asking Molly? You mean bribing Molly."

"Didn't you listen to her? She wasn't bribed—she tossed a coin."

"I don't believe that bartender story for one second. She was suckered into hedge fund greed, and Alessi knows that after Molly broke up with Thomas, she's become skeptical about having her own family. So now Alessi's just exploiting her—"

"I'm glad you're the expert on what I do and feel," I interrupted.

"You know, Mom really wants you to be married by the time you're forty." Matt pointed at me.

"Is this the marriage police? Will I be penalized if I'm not married by then?"

"Does Mom even know about this crazy scheme with Alessi?" he asked.

"No."

"Well good. Because when she finds out, she'll floor the pedal to their Mc-Mansion in Westchester—"

"Their 'McMansion' is a restored farmhouse from 1871, and it's in Putnam

County."

"Mom would rip out the steering wheel and throw it at Alessi. You know she'd do that, and you know why. Because Alessi is reducing your chances of having your own family by asking you to be her surrogate at this time in your life."

"Don't go telling Mom and Dad."

"I'm not touching this with them," said my brother, lifting both of his arms as though to avoid a blazing stove. "And pardon me, but I'm leaving. I want to get home. I've heard enough today."

"Well wait a minute," I protested. "Does this mean you don't want me to name you and your family as my heirs? You are, in the latest version of my will."

"Come on, Matt," Tamara begged him. "You're being so hard on her. I'm sure it wasn't easy for Molly to tell us all this."

"Are you coming with me?" he asked his wife gruffly.

I stomped over to him, charging, "You are more manipulative now than you accuse Alessi of being."

My brother looked at me with scathing pity, then turned to Tamara.

"Are you coming with me or will I see you later?"

"Matt," she said sadly. "Please. Let's work things out with Molly."

"It pains me to look at her now," he said. "My sister has *rented* her soul to the devil." Matthew then about-faced, opened my front door, and started down the staircase.

"Please don't feel obliged to stay with me," I told Tamara. "I understand."

She shook her head resolutely.

"He can't get away with this."

She perhaps had yet to learn how much disapproval and convenient silence my family did get away with.

"Don't forget your umbrella!" she screamed down at him, throwing his umbrella through the center of the spiraling banisters so that it reached the ground floor before he did.

Tamara remained with me for another teeming, thundering hour. But I could barely listen when she spoke about herbal teas to avoid during pregnancy, and offered to pass on her maternity clothes, her *schmatas*, and books. I had been clubbed over the head.

"Matt's never spoken to me like that," I kept saying. "He was hostile."

Tamara looked like she wanted to explain something but was deciding not to. She did mention, "He gets excited about certain topics, then he calms down. He'll probably apologize tomorrow. In fact, he'd better."

But her email the next day reported that Matthew was still distressed, needed to think things over, and had asked her not to speak with me until he decided whether he would be my heir.

I told Matt he's getting hokey about the photographs, Tamara added. He had apparently turned all their photographs with me to the wall—or removed them.

I don't want to make trouble between you two, I wrote back to her. *Especially now. This isn't like Matt. He's probably shocked and needs time to acclimate to my news.*

Let's give him a week to cool off, Tamara suggested.

I didn't want to believe that my relationship with him would change forever. But I certainly had learned that I could not tell my parents about this pregnancy. If Matt's response was any indication of my mother's, it behooved me to keep quiet for nine months. The big challenge would be not seeing them for Christmas, since we reserved that time of year for each other. I would have to craft a tactful way to exempt myself until Easter.

By then the baby would be a month old, and my mission would be complete. Meanwhile, I would be thirty-eight, a candidate to be married by forty if I wished, and if Fate behaved itself. Mom and Dad would never have to know anything about the pregnancy. Becoming Larry's partner would account for the time I spent away from them, and the infusion of cash into my life. This comforting plan convinced me I could cover all bases—do my bit for Pete and Alessi, progress professionally, and remain in good standing with my parents. If I wasn't breastfeeding, I might even visit Mom and Dad for Easter.

The only monkey wrench was that Alessi had not yet gotten her period. "Usually it comes like clockwork every twenty-eight days. Why is it teasing me now?" she wondered. If she didn't bleed in the next day or two, we would have to postpone IVF until July, or however long it would take to coordinate our cycles. That meant I might not be out of the woods by next Easter. If anyone had told me that the future of my family relationships would hinge on Alessandra's period, I would have laughed.

47

Speaking of unlikely soothsayers, when I hit my block after work the next day, I was surprised not to see Mama Cass. She usually sat outside on balmy afternoons, a tiara in her long, apricot-highlighted hair, a big T-shirt sliding down her shoulders, as she bellowed, "*Get* your readings! *Get* your tarot card readings!"

But when I glanced into the storefront, with its crouching sphinxes, thick candles, and crystal balls, I saw Bertie chatting away with her. Bertie noticed immediately—as though she had been waiting for me—and began waving her arms around. I shrugged angrily.

Bertie pulled bills from her pocket, handed them to Mama Cass, and marched out of the store. In rolled up jeans that revealed calves studded with pink mosquito bites, a loose undershirt, a man's vest, and plaid newsboy cap, she seemed like a vagrant from the underworld of Dickens' London.

"Hear me out, Molly. This has been weighing on me."

From behind the glass, Mama Cass and another Gypsy peered at us.

"Let's go to the park," I said quickly.

I didn't want to go upstairs with Bertie, lest we run into Claudia, or lest the peanut gallery in the storefront arrive at unwarranted conclusions. Besides, after yesterday's spectacle with Matthew between my walls, I craved a more public place to speak. It would keep everyone civil.

"Psychic my ass," Bertie muttered as we headed toward Union Square. "That Gypsy lady kept calling me 'sir.'"

"No comment."

Bertie lumbered up the street with long, bow-legged steps, the inevitable key chain dangling from her belt loop into her back pocket. I was sure that Jordan or Z walked with more grace than she did.

"Are you really mad at me, Molly?" she kept asking.

"I don't get why this is so important to you."

We crossed Union Square East, dodging aggressive beggars and kids on skateboards. In the park, we found a bench just across from the bronze-cast Abe Lincoln, his right hand over his heart. Behind us kids lay about on the lawn strumming tuneless guitars, talking, and reading paperbacks.

"Did Eugenia want you to speak to me?" I asked as we sat down. I suppose I'd been hoping so because when Bertie said no I felt a twinge.

"She wouldn't. Things are strange now."

"They are," I agreed.

Bertie lit her cigar, another reason I was glad not to be upstairs. I didn't mind the scent, but I didn't want my apartment to smell that way either.

"Sorry if I made everything worse."

"It wasn't you, Bertie. No guy has ever reduced me to such—indignity. Not that they haven't tried. But men come up with mousy women to throw in your face rather than beautiful ones. At least the men I've been with."

"She didn't set up that scene to hurt you," said Bertie, the cigar lodged between her fingers. "She didn't know you were there. You can't see the DJ stand from the bar."

"But I came in earlier and she *did* see me."

"Then you left. I'm sure she didn't see you when you returned. It was mobbed."

"She probably didn't."

I was not happy to comb through these details. I never had been one to obsess with others over my romantic plights with men and had less desire to start in about a woman. I felt Bertie's words weren't describing anything that pertained to me, even though those moments at The Bunny Hop had grown into bone spurs on my heart.

"She didn't see you talking with me. She didn't know this Brazilian girl was coming by. If I hadn't gone bonkers trying to hide everything from you, if I had let you see the kid trying to jump her bones, you would have had a better sense of it."

"What I saw spoke for itself," I said. "And she didn't manage it well."

"She has to humor people. It's part of her job."

"She was having a great time with that girl riding her."

"She was putting on a show for three hundred people that killed her back later. Anyway, the Brazilians took off five minutes after you did. It's not like they stuck around makin' her night. What really happened was around two, a couple of leather fags almost killed each other in a fistfight, and one of them got sick all over himself and the floor. Eugenia had to clean it up and then deal with the cops in the middle of her backache."

"Why?"

"Who else was gonna do it? I gotta say, though, the ordeal brought her back to earth."

"No more juggled beer bottles dropping?"

"Yeah, she's her old 'got a grip' self again, but something's funny. She doesn't meet my eye, we don't kid around at the bar anymore." Bertie inhaled her cigar as though she were taking a small bite of it. "I even worried about her, you know, walking home at dawn in her little cutoffs—I told her, 'Blondie, take a cab!' and she was like, 'I hope I do get beaten up. Won't have to come back here for a while.'

"Of course she was in the next day like the cat with nine lives. Haven't seen the Brazilian girl since and wanted you to know that."

"Look, Bertie, I appreciate that you're trying to help me feel better. And it's sweet that you describe that luscious Latina as a 'kid.' But how would you like watching someone you adore being kissed by a hybrid of Sophia Loren and Salma Hayek in Spandex?"

"It wasn't really a kiss. It was just a peck on the lips. Couldn't you imagine that if you ran into your sax player guy you might kiss on the lips like that?"

Of course, Jordan and I had done much more. But in my emotional economy of scale, Eugenia's winking at someone counted more than my fucking twelve people.

"Okay, I know," Bertie ceded as I remained glumly silent. "It more than sucks. It vacuums. When that shit happened to me in college, I jumped off a two-story building, landed in a parking lot, and broke a bunch of bones."

"Okay, so—suppose you were twenty years older and you'd never felt that way about a woman before? Or suppose it happened to you now, with a man?"

Bertie drew upon her cigar and held the smoke in her chest before exhaling ghostly donuts into the twilight.

"Not gonna happen with no man, Molly," she assured me.

"I never thought I would care for a woman."

I didn't want to elaborate how never I meant. It would offend her. "You say to yourself, this person isn't even my sexual preference so why should I get torn up over her? Anyway, she's so popular that loving her is one big cliché. Everyone wants her—women, men, cats, dogs, gerbils, houseplants, Martians. Anything special I felt for her has been pirated—or is in the public domain."

A scrawny woman barely balancing on high heels came up to Bertie, asking for a light. Bertie lit her cigarette graciously, and the woman tottered away as if on stilts.

"Molly, that night was the puss on a scab on a boil on a butt. Don't let it get to you. I've known Eugenia a while now and—trust me—she likes you."

"She probably likes the next in line now."

"Eugenia flirts her ass off and does what any gorgeous bartender has to do for tips. But that doesn't mean she's not lonely as hell. A ton of wrong people can be worse than no one."

"Somehow I fail to feel sorry for her."

Bertie slouched on the bench and drew again on her cigar. This time, smoke sailed from her nostrils. I noticed a couple of young guys walk by and look back at her as if trying to figure out if she was a man or a woman. No one ever had been confused about my gender, and no one would be.

"Besides," I said aloud, "let's just say something worked out between Eugenia and me, and was incredible—what would I tell my prude Irish Scottish family?"

"Just what I told my prude Irish German family. And I hear you—I told the

German side first."

But everyone in Bertie's family had probably guessed that she was gay by the time she was twelve. Regardless of my sincere, if not reckless, passion for Eugenia, I knew nothing about being homosexual in this society and wasn't a promising candidate.

"She said you were brilliant and generous and unpredictable, that it was the best time she'd had on a date in years," Bertie went on.

"That's true for me too, and I'm so glad she felt it. But what she liked was a hologram."

As Bertie faced me I involuntarily inhaled an apple-y waft of her cigar smoke.

"Why don't you just talk to her, Molly? It's not too late. And one day it will be."

"I tried!" I stammered, coughing a little. "I went to the bar twice. I left a note for her with Laurie. What am I supposed to do, prostrate myself before the beer taps?"

"Just talk to her," Bertie repeated.

"This won't be mended by 'just talking.' It's too intricate. She'll never forgive me, anyway. We had a precious chance and it's gone."

"Not gone. I see it in your eyes and hear it in your voice."

"But it has nowhere to go."

And that dull ache replaced the nerve we cut into when we sliced the green pepper together. Each of us had jumped back to safer terrain, like her bar flirtations, or my overtime with Larry, my debauchery with Jordan.

"Molly, you don't want to lose this." Bertie was pleading with me. "It's too hard to find."

"So are blue diamonds, and I can't afford them. I can't afford to know her."

But now I actually could afford blue diamonds.

"So are you just going to drop out of sight and not talk to her again?"

"That sounds harsh," I admitted. "But I had a blow-out fight with my brother yesterday, when you called. A lot of shit is hitting a lot of fans—I have to walk with an umbrella in every direction. One day I will seek her out."

"Even just to be friendly and not break the human connection..."

Beneath the brim on her newsie cap, Bertie's dark brown eyes sought mine.

"You broke your human connection with Claudia," I reminded her.

"Claudia's bat-shit crazy. There was never a human connection."

"She's seeing a guy now. A younger guy."

"Why am I not shocked?"

We sat quietly as Bertie pinched out her cigar with her thumb and forefinger and put it back into the little box that she carried in her vest pocket.

"Dominican?" I noted.

"I don't want Cuban anything after Claudia," she declared. "You know, that little whack job had only two other girlfriends before me. She's not this big lesbian. She's an identity chameleon. She'll go through ten more phases—including tap dancer, FBI informant, and Cuban communist—before she finds her Caribbean roots and takes up Santeria and black magic at the age of fifty. Mark my words…"

I managed a grin because it seemed all too likely.

"Why should I follow her example?"

"Oh come on, Molly—you actually feel something. I know it's not a game or a phase with you because I see your struggle."

"Well, maybe I don't want to drag Eugenia through my struggle."

Bertie leaned over, reached into her back pocket, and crammed a folded sheet of paper into my hand.

"I got her home phone number for you—no easy task. Gail didn't even give it out. I went through another source. I won't stay on your case about calling her, but I want you to have the option. I know it's not easy for you to see her at the bar after all that, and I know things are weird."

"Thanks."

I stuffed the paper into my purse with the idea that I might rip it up when I got home. Or maybe I would just carry it in my wallet for a while.

48

Upstairs two phone messages awaited me. The first, from an unknown number, began in an unknown voice: "You go, girl!" The unknown voice became Enrico's: "I got the message from Larry about my job. You work fast, don't you? I may have another deal, but let's talk."

He gave a number, but I didn't plan to call. Who else had a quarter-inch ponytail and earrings that glinted across a room? There was little question that I had seen him at The Bunny Hop that night.

The next message was Alessandra. While Bertie and I had been sitting in Union Square Park, it appeared that "the fertility goddess smeared raspberry jam on my panties in its divine scrumptiousness. Start packing, we're off to see the wizard."

I called back, imploring Alessandra to spare me her menstrual details.

"We'll all need strong stomachs," she advised. "Might as well get used to blood. You'll be giving birth."

And on the topic of "Stomach Boot Camp," was I interested in one more session with Dr. Betsy before we went out West? Pete was advocating that we tie up loose ends and leave on a good note. That kind of formality was important to him, like ending dinner with a digestive or a mint.

I told Alessi that I didn't care one way or another.

"What happened with you and Betsy?" I asked her.

"She just wouldn't drop this boob tube business. She even went so far as to suggest that Pete use the tubes to establish parental authority. Now I could see some Swedish hippie suckling his kid with that getup, but can you imagine my Wall Street husband doing that?"

"No."

"She was actually screaming at me, 'I'm right about this! Studies have been done about breastfeeding and parental rapport.' I think she's actually afraid that you and the baby are going to bond and disappear into the wild blue yonder..."

"Hardly."

"She was encouraging me not to use you—hinting that you were not up to the task emotionally since you don't have a partner. I told her that didn't matter to me at all, that I'd rather have you without a husband than any other woman with one. It's not her business to judge my choice of surrogate anyway. Can't wait to get this bitch out of our hair."

So we set up our finale for the following Tuesday. I showed up five minutes late, hoping not to be alone with Betsy, and furious with the empty chairs where Pete and Alessandra should have been sitting.

"How are you?" Betsy asked, as I sank into the armchair in which I had melted down last time.

"Perfect," I told her, glancing blatantly at my watch, tapping my leg, hoping the doorbell would ring. I folded my elbow on the armrest, hiding my lips behind my fingers.

"Did you talk to Eugenia?"

"Didn't need to," I muttered from behind my hand. "It's over."

Betsy looked surprised.

"What happened?"

"Less than nothing."

"I don't believe you."

I slipped my head into my palm, sliding two fingers up my cheek. She didn't press me but squinted as though trying to figure out what "less than nothing" meant, sitting there in her sleeveless white shirt with braided gold earrings, like little pieces of fried calamari on her earlobes.

"Okay," I ventured, raising my head, wanting to give credit where it was due. "You called it correctly. I fell for Eugenia, and Jordan caught me. He played music for me that morning."

If she could imagine me siphoning Alessi's child away on the wiles of breast-feeding, she could imagine what happened with Eugenia.

"I think we both agree that my life needs to be simplified," I said. "Still, I didn't appreciate the betrayal."

"Betrayal?"

"You know what I'm talking about."

"I really don't," she said with an uneasy laugh. "I didn't reveal anything."

As the doorbell rang, Betsy whispered, "Just please—get the emotional support you need during the pregnancy," as though she wanted to squeeze in her advice before Alessandra could fight it.

We heard Pete and Alessi grumbling at each other before they entered the office. Between them and my brother and sister-in-law, I had heard enough married couples bicker to be gratefully solo for the moment—if not forever.

Pete steered his wife through the door as if she was a defiant Rottweiler.

Betsy nodded and mouthed, "Alexandra," before saying hello to Pete. She never got the name right, and after this last session she wouldn't have to.

"It's happening!" were the first words out of Alessi's mouth. "We've finally stanched this cat-and-mouse fertility chase; it looks like my FSH levels are in fine fettle." She plopped into her chair and rooted through her womblike, leathery purse as we all watched. To my embarrassment, she produced a box of tampons.

Pete and I averted our eyes. Everyone in the room knew that I too was menstruating and that in two weeks he would masturbate into some Dixie cup and our high-tech tea party would be on.

"I wish you the best of luck," said Betsy. "I know how much all of you have undergone to make this possible."

"We'll have great luck," said Alessi, returning the box of tampons to her purse. I suddenly flashed on JackASS's ill-fated visit to my office when I had waved my tampons at him like an omen. Alessi continued in her sassy but reverent tone, "Everything works when Molly does it. Everything always has."

At one time in my life, perhaps when I'd forged my strongest impression upon Alessi, those words had been true. I'd made it my business to have anything Molly did succeed. But since then too much had slid quite out of my control; perhaps she hadn't noticed.

"That's why it sucked when you weren't on board with us."

"*A*, just cut it out, will you?" Pete snapped at her. I wondered if his annoyance was connected to the grumbling I heard when they'd walked in.

"Well," Alessi began explaining, "last time I was here alone, Betsy raised a question about Molly's fitness for this procedure, and I've been thinking all week…"

Pete threw his head back against his chair and squeezed his eyes shut with rage. I glared at Betsy, tightening my lips. Had she succeeded in discouraging Alessi from using me as her surrogate? Why would she do that? After calibrating my life to accommodate the big change, I felt cheated by the prospect of not having this baby—or the money. This plan was holding my life together, like a stitch in a suture. Without it I would be a woman nearing forty with only collapsed relationships to show for it.

"Knock it off right now!"

I had never seen Pete so livid with her.

"Oh spare me, Peter! It's not like you're going to be put through follicle stimulation and vaginal ultrasounds all next week."

"Sorry to disappoint you, honey. But hey, you think this is fun for me—or for Molly? It was *your* idea!"

I was glad he was yelling, glad his face was red. As for me, I kept glaring at Betsy.

"What did you think?" Pete went on. "Molly was going to drop her life for you on a dime?"

"I told you she wouldn't. And we offered more than a dime."

"She got her EKG and sonogram and everything when she needed to. She took time off from work, and she's been as cooperative as we could have hoped."

"Yeah, but—"

"Will you just let me finish? I know what you're going to say." Pete made a high-pitched voice to imitate her. "'I'm just so hurt that my oldest friend would listen to a stranger in a bar before she'd give me the time of day…'"

"Well, I am!" Alessandra roared.

"Well it's over!" Pete roared back. "It's a moot point. We've signed a contract with Molly, and we're moving forward."

"I know, but I still have feelings about this, and I want to deal with them here."

"You know, you fabricate *feelings* just to keep everyone on edge."

"Pete, for you all feelings are 'fabricated.'"

"You want attention and pity—like your dad!"

"Coming from your dynasty of stuffed shirts!"

I sat back and imagined a battalion of button-downs—blue, white, plaid—stuffed with cotton and galumphing around a room, colliding with each other.

"You know there is such a thing, *A*, as letting go and moving on..."

"Which I'll do. I promise. But I just don't want to keep anything inside and festering."

"I dare you to try, for once," he said under his breath.

I scowled at Betsy, wrinkling my nose very slightly. I might have been imagining her remorse.

"Let her say what she has to, Peter," the therapist suggested, "and then let's move on."

Reluctantly he yielded, lifting both arms and dropping them with a thud onto his armrests.

"Of course we're not retracting the agreement," Alessi assured me.

"You'd better not. I've even sacrificed my relationship with my brother."

"What's with Matthew?"

"He thinks you bribed me."

"Fat chance," she scoffed.

"I can vouch," said Pete, "for how hard it was to convince you to do this."

"We didn't even convince her. That's my point. We couldn't get through to you, Molly. It was so arbitrary—we had no respectful dialogue. Last time I saw Betsy, some of that frustration came up for me again." Then Alessi gestured with her hand, like a mad orchestra conductor. "If this stranger in a bar had not said yes, that she'd do it if she were in your shoes, then our lives would be totally different now. My child's life would never *be*."

"You don't *know* that," Pete interjected.

"Yes I *do* know it. You don't know how invested Molly gets in her little superstitions...Jeez, remember your crush on Dan Connelly in high school:

'Oh, if I wear this blue sweater on a Tuesday it means I'll pass him again after varsity practice...'"

"Alessi!" I groaned at her. "I was fifteen."

Pete caught my eye.

"Look, you've got a right to your process," he said. "There are no road signs for any decision. Clients ask Huang and me if they should sell a stock now. I can make a good guess, but it's not set in stone. Some guys trade commodities by tossing coins. Or they'll buy a stock because they see its symbol on a license plate that day. Sometimes Huang and I think it's as good a method as any."

"Bull*shit*. You and Huang spend hours comparing charts and reading news, making mathematical models of everything," charged Alessi.

"But it doesn't always work."

"It's working well enough."

Pete couldn't argue with his wife.

"There was an arcane mathematics to my decision," I asserted. I had subtracted my rational input and added Eugenia's instincts. Alessi nodded as though she understood. Betsy leaned in and squinted, trying to decipher, for the second time in ten minutes, what I was implying.

"What kind of mathematics?" she finally asked.

"The kind that leads to the right answer," Alessi replied. "And that's why I feel indebted to this woman who persuaded Molly to have our baby—whoever she is, I'd like to do something for her. You know, maybe a fat gift certificate to Saks or a cruise."

I could feel Betsy watch me squirm, just imagining Alessi in contact with Eugenia.

"Who is she again?" Alessi asked me.

"A bartender in a place downtown."

Pete shook his head angrily.

"Come on, *A*—I'm not one to tell strangers our private business. We've been through this."

"She's part of our destiny now."

"No. She was just Molly's device. We're our own destiny."

"What do you think, Molly?" Betsy asked me. "Does the woman who helped you decide to be their surrogate mother deserve anything from Alexandra?"

"Alessandra," I corrected her. As I gazed around the honeydew-green walls at the photos, macramé, and Betsy's diplomas, I noticed that her slate fountain was off. Maybe it was broken, abandoned in its corner, not driving us crazier than we already felt.

"I agree with Pete," I told them. "This is our private business. We should leave everyone else out of it."

He looked relieved. Alessi raised her hands and gave a little shrug.

"Just wanted to show some gratitude, but I guess I'm overruled."

"That's the nice thing about this setup," Pete remarked. "In marriage you never get a majority rule. But throw in a third person and hey, here's democracy."

"And I suppose," Alessi said, by way of yielding to us, "that in a dysfunctional world, you've got to love that Molly is actually normal."

"She is pretty normal," Pete agreed, smiling.

"Not to burst anyone's bubble," I began, "but if you're going by the statistical definition of normal, I leave much to be desired. I am so strikingly not a statistic these days that it's worrisome."

Alessi disagreed: "No! You're a successful, single professional."

"The type that never becomes a surrogate mother. I've been reading that most women who do this are struggling lower-class moms—army wives and the like."

"Exactly what we didn't want," Pete reflected. "No 'Baby M' dramas."

"Well, Sweet Betsy from Pike doesn't think I'm your best bet," I cut in. "So maybe Eugenia didn't do you such a favor."

"Sweet Betsy from Pike can learn when to shut her mouth," Alessi said aridly. "Or where to put it when it won't stay shut."

"Believe me," Betsy replied with emphasis, "Betsy has learned a thing or two."

But Alessi was murmuring: "Eugenia. What a great name. We should put it on our baby name list."

49

To pass the time as I waited for my sister-in-law, I tried guessing which shoes on the rack were hers. They were probably not among the New Balance sneakers, nor the Birkenstocks—but possibly the Aerosoles sandals with suede insoles and Greek-styled crossed leather straps. Clogs? I had never seen her wear those inelegant things. Beach shoes, flip-flops? Too casual, and Tamara came to this prenatal yoga class after work.

She had emailed me that Matthew seemed even more disturbed in the last few days. Then I received his letter. My finger absently traced the embossed black type on the envelope in my lap from Henderson, Fletcher, Kaplan and Royce—law partners always sound like a group of thugs.

On company letterhead he'd probably had his assistant type *Molly*—not *Dear Molly*, but just *Molly* with a comma—*After much thought and discussion with Tamara, I must ask you to change our status in your will. I do not want my wife, my children, or myself to appear as your beneficiaries under the circumstances you described.*

Tamara has helped me see that your gestures to our family were not meant as a slight to me. You acted with benevolence, even goodwill toward us. And while I am grateful, I cannot morally support your choice. I remain deeply wounded that you didn't discuss this important matter with me. Not wanting to be a hypocrite, I therefore must refuse any part of a prospective inheritance from you. Please honor my wishes.

Your brother,

And then he had scribbled his signature as though he were astride a galloping horse.

Yesterday I had sent him a card with one impeccably rendered word: *Fine.*

A trickle of fair creatures who drank water and carrot juice and barely looked pregnant issued from the opening doors of the yoga classroom, along with those hoisting more progressed bellies, like Tamara. One of her classmates could have been nearly sixty, with stiff gray hair. I smiled intentionally at her. On Manhattan, this island off the coast of America, so many of us defy statistics that by now we have become a bloc of our own.

Vivacious after class in her pine-green tunic with turquoise embroidery and sequins, Tamara smiled warmly at me. She took a plum-colored sweatshirt from a hook by the door and slipped on the Aerosoles that I'd guessed were hers.

"Did you have to lie in order to meet me?" I asked as we walked outside the yoga studio into a chalky-blue Monet afternoon.

"I didn't say anything to Matt."

It was ironically true to Matthew's point that Tamara, my non-blood relative, was behaving most like family now. But I felt sorry to initiate her into my secretive ways.

"I'm corrupting you."

"Molly, much as I adore you, I'm not here to gang up in some feminist coup against my husband. I'm here on behalf of..." And she pointed to her belly. "Are you aware that—how can I put this?"

We stopped for a moment on the street. Several of her sweetly smiling yoga comrades waved as they walked by us.

"Are you aware," Tamara went on, "and I say this with affection—that your brother is completely wigged out about money?"

"Wigged out in what way?"

"He's terrified of dealing with it."

"But his firm handles corporate and personal bankruptcy."

"He's squeamish about our finances because he identifies with his clients. So he's put me in charge of investments and budgeting."

I mused to myself that I should have guessed as much. Matthew had never trusted himself to manage money.

We started down the street, toward Broadway and the river. I wasn't even sure where we were walking to. Tamara had said something about frozen yogurt with sprinkles and sitting in Riverside Park. That, apparently, was her ritual. She left work around three in the afternoon, partook of the afternoon prenatal yoga class, then sat in the park and read.

Today I too had left work early to speak with her about my estate plans. While I didn't want to take excessive time away from the office before my big trip, Larry would grant me anything. After all, I was angling to become the partner who might save our company from our own bankruptcy.

"Some years ago," Tamara began, leading me around the corner when we reached Broadway, "before we were married, Matt had put aside thirteen grand. An investment banker he met through friends told him that he could make it into forty over three months, so Matt handed everything over to him—and, abracadabra, never heard from him again.

"Needless to say, this made him doubt his own judgment and completely mistrust bankers and traders. When you called him Mattie Mattress, you weren't off the mark."

"But he has a 401K, doesn't he?"

"I made him keep it. And we have assets that my dad and I manage—a few blue chips but mostly fixed securities. When you spoke about hedge funds, you hit your brother's phobic nerve. And he's always opposed in-vitro conceptions. He feels they'll lead to robotics and human cloning and that sort of thing."

"Well, with gestational surrogacy the womb that bears the child is…human! Perish the day that is no longer the case."

"A scary turning point," Tamara emphasized. "And if it came down to it, I'd rather see human IVF than robotic cloning."

"Same here. But it still seems I hit Matt's two ideological sore points."

"The jackpot. The very forces he predicts will ruin civilization. And you—his idol. Before I met you, he told me, 'My sister is basically right about everything.' That's how we younger siblings think."

"Right about everything" was a tall order. No wonder I had toppled.

We stopped at a frozen yogurt and ice cream counter on Broadway, where Tamara showed me her favorite flavors: Lemon Zinger, Vanilla Rose, and Chocolate Berry.

"If he doesn't want us to be your heirs, I'll make that sacrifice as Matt's wife—even though I don't agree with it," she confided as we strolled downhill toward Riverside Park with our cups of frozen yogurt. I had gone for Vanilla Rose with chocolate sprinkles.

"But I also told him that if you're moved, from the kindness of your heart, to give our child resources that can change her future, we shouldn't get in the way. That's between you and your niece. Who knows what might happen? When she's an adult, she may need a leg up."

This sounded rational and compassionate. But Tamara went on.

"Matt strongly disagreed. He said we shouldn't be setting a hypocritical example, and that it would confuse our kid—or, eventually, our *kids*—if their rights to your assets were different from ours. I told him that our kids would be your charges, but we're your peers. That's already a big difference. We fought so much that I slept in the guest room. For the first time."

"Lovely influence I am," I said, digging my plastic spoon into the mound of chocolate sprinkles as we got to West End Avenue.

"We made up the next night." She stopped walking, put her hand on my arm, and blushed when I looked at her.

I wondered about having sex during pregnancy, but it seemed in poor taste to drill for details.

"Matt and I have argued so seldom that we've gotten spoiled," she said, walking again. "It was actually helpful that this came up before Mira's birth."

We ate in silence as we approached Riverside Drive, where I noticed a row of townhouses with gabled roofs and dormer windows and realized that I could live somewhere like that one day. I followed Tamara across the street and down a set of stone steps into the park. We passed kids, just liberated from school, playing rowdy games of soccer on the grass, an older woman carefully setting up a tripod by a sturdy oak, joggers, and dog walkers. As we sat on the bench where Tamara often read after her yoga class, I watched a particularly diligent dog walker stoop with her Baggie. Now that was love—love or a strong stomach.

"I think you'll be comfortable with what my attorney and I are working out," I told my sister-in-law. "Of course, if I have my own kids I will amend the will. But as of now, half my estate will go to Mom and Dad. I'm sure they'd be generous with your family, once they'd get over the shock of my death and the extent of my assets. If my folks are no longer around, the power of attorney should revert to Matt and you—without my willing it directly."

"Let's hope we don't need to think about this anytime soon," said Tamara. "And look, even if Matthew can't thank you—please know, you're great. I don't like going behind his back. But Molly, when you're pregnant, you feel a sense of protection that outweighs anything."

I reached over and stroked Tamara's belly.

"She's not a choppy baby," Tamara commented. "Some of the women in my yoga class say their babies kick up a storm. Sometimes I feel this sweeping little hand or the faintest jolt."

"She heard our conversation," I said.

I was glad that Tamara had not thought to ask what I planned to do with the other half of my estate. I was still researching agencies that tried to save children from being trafficked, and I dared not share with her the horrid details I'd read.

Perhaps it was useful that my brother, Scrooge that he was, had refused his legacy from me. He had forced me to think of other ways I might give.

But I couldn't very well say this over frozen yogurt with sprinkles to my pregnant sister-in-law, and I was relieved that I didn't have to.

50

That evening I would go salsa dancing with Jordan, Dustin, and Claudia—one of the few prospects that put a smile on my face those days before the grand insemination. I didn't even dance so much as I stood around watching, swaying to the music. It loosened my thoughts and worries, now that I couldn't have a glass of wine; it helped me forget that my brother wasn't speaking to me and that I couldn't figure out how to ever speak again to Eugenia.

We all met at Claudia's, and I walked in halfway through Dustin's makeover. Shirt unbuttoned down his chest, he was leaning back over one of her kitchen chairs as she fastidiously applied cosmetics, insisting: "I am so attracted to men in lipstick and eye shadow." Dustin's lips glistened with blackberry gloss, his eyes were lined with cobalt and mascara, his brows had been tweezed, his hair bundled into two pigtails that really did bring to mind the stringy tails of farm-bred hogs.

"You look beauteeeful, dearie," Jordan crooned.

I'd decided that Jordan was like cayenne pepper—a dash of it was lively. Too much would dehydrate me.

There was no talk of our exchanging keys. In fact, he had not spent the night with me since the one where he'd played oldies on the sax until dawn.

Our sexual contact was skittish, almost like teenagers afraid of being caught; our fingers groping to unzip and unbutton each other's clothing; our sighs almost melancholic. We'd banished senses like sight and smell, only touching each other through at least one layer of clothes. And then we'd stop as though Mom and Dad were at the door.

I attributed my reserve to the progesterone shots I was getting now at the clinic. A week before *Inseminazione Tecnologico*—and I regarded the procedure as "technological," not "artificial," since we'd use real eggs, real sperm, and a real womb—these nasty boosters were administered to plump my uterine lining for implantation. The progesterone sat in an oil base that stung my hip as much as the ridiculously long needle. The ordeal put me into a tailspin, not the best mood for intimacy with someone I didn't especially trust.

Yet, in a fit of gratitude for Jordan's and Z's support on my Dark Night of the Soul at The Bunny Hop, I had offered to produce their first CD. Now Jordan whined to me about it, asking over and over when he'd get the cash. Of course I could spare it, but I hated the roles to which we were reverting.

Along with dunning me, he accused me of saving myself for other guys. "You're not seeing *anyone*?" he would persist. "Anyone, Chardonnay?"

Of course I couldn't deny, nor could I tell him, that the face I saw as I fell asleep each night was Eugenia's.

And then there was my standing in the world at large.

Mom left me a message saying that if I had indeed "moved on" from Thomas I should give myself "time to really find the right person." To that end she passed on the phone numbers of a radiologist and a research engineer so I'd have "some alternative dates to the Israeli." She added that Fritz might have made sense at our Easter brunch about my needing a "clever and successful man." But, she warned: "Not so smart that he'd want to commit suicide. Men in your generation tend to be fragile."

Apparently, Thomas fit into that desirable crevice of depressed enough-to-warrant-womanly-comfort, but not smart-enough-for-suicide.

The next day she called again to explain why she had given me these men's numbers rather than giving them mine: "You're *so* hard to get hold of, dear. I wouldn't want them to give up in frustration."

No, we wouldn't want superfluous suicides on our hands.

I called neither of them and had put off a second date with Ari as well.

As I sat on Claudia's sofa brooding about Mom's machinations, Claudia and Dustin laughed hysterically about Claudia's mother.

"I thought she was talking about pajamas," Dustin explained to us. "When she said 'my jammies...'"

"When I was in *Mi-jami*," Claudia imitated her mother's Cuban accent and shrieked with laughter. She seemed to have fun with Dustin. Their world was lighter than mine, like blown glass is lighter than crystal—even if it could shatter more easily at any second.

Still, this was Claudia's longest relationship without a litany of complaints.

Racked with giggles, Dustin now appeared like a pig roasting on a spit, being turned slowly over a fire, shiny with oil and nose rings and a necklace she had draped over his head.

"Mama thinks I should try dying my hair orange."

"No!" I cried to Claudia.

"Why not?"

"Because it's like pineapple toppings on pizza—just wrong."

From the other end of the sofa Jordan watched us and said nothing.

I lost myself at the dance club in swirling colored lights, sizzling percussion, and flashing bodies that knew how to spin and cradle each other, that sometimes moved in friezes, like erotic statuary. I watched a voluptuous blonde dance in the arms of another woman. A dark-haired man with exceptionally beautiful lips spread his hands over her butt and pressed himself against her. She reached her arms backward to him as the other woman held her, and they all drew closer, roiling and rippling with the drumbeat.

I turned to Claudia, who sat beside me in our wicker cabana. She was watching the same group, who were hard to miss.

"The revolution has begun."

I lifted my glass of Pellegrino water with lime.

Claudia sipped her piña colada, her eyes widening, dark curls tumbling over her bare shoulders.

We continued to watch the threesome whirl together on the dance floor, the woman in the middle crushed sweetly between her boyfriend's wiggling hips and her girlfriend's breasts.

"In an ideal world," I continued, "what woman wouldn't enjoy that?"

Claudia eventually replied: "Bertie. My mother. Your mother."

51

Ari Schwartzben either didn't hear or didn't mind that I was yammering on like my mother. This happened when I dated more-or-less normal guys who were more-or-less my age—by default I sounded brash and unpleasant, like my mother.

As he walked me home from our evening at a piano bar, I fumed to myself: *Just shut up already, Molly*—this was no polite "be quiet"; I was unbearable. And we were discussing the Messiah.

With a slightly pathetic man like Thomas, or a younger one like Jordan, my voice was understated and soft. I was the patient older sister who had shown her little brother the world. With Eugenia I had sounded like a friend speaking to another friend. I had even been shy. I might have sounded like Mom for a passing moment, no more than Eugenia might have sounded like her mother for a phrase or two.

But with Ari I was like a fire truck siren. I wanted to get home and be alone so the world would be relieved of me. I also wanted to get home because the progesterone oil was leaking through my dress with every step I took, and I was hiding that stain at my hip with a shawl.

Hand in hand we approached tranquil Gramercy Park, then Irving Place and a noisy, convivial tavern crowd edging onto the sidewalk.

Luckily Ari was not pouncing, since I was not ready to convert to Judaism. I had hinted about him to Ayelet, a conservative Jewish colleague. She seemed interested, and eventually I would find an appropriate way to introduce them. He was nice-looking, with shortly cropped dark hair to which a small yarmulke was bobby-pinned, and a long, sallow face with high cheekbones and delicate eyes. Though he was lean beneath pleated cotton pants and an argyle sweater, I felt no animal attraction to him.

"So I hope I have explained *Mashiakh*," he said as we crossed Third Avenue.

But he had not clarified as much as I'd hoped. Apparently I had raised a sensitive issue when I'd questioned the efficacy of any Messiah in the face of humanity's shortcomings.

Some rabbis, he now explained, believed that we could prepare ourselves for a better life by contemplating the Torah.

"Are women included in these lofty pursuits?" I checked. Presumably we were.

"But traditional rabbis hold that there is no way to push the speed of redemption. It will happen only through divine love and grace."

"Which implies that we are awfully passive."

"Maybe we are." Ari and I turned onto my street. "Maybe," he repeated. "No one in the religious or secular world cares to admit it, but we are awfully passive."

"Yet we grow, so we can't be that passive. Even biologically."

This was not a topic my mother would discuss, yet I sounded like her. I sounded like I was correcting Ari about some obscure metaphysical matter about which

I had no authority. I wished I could hawk her out of my larynx.

"You make such good points that it's a shame you're not Jewish," was all Ari said.

"Well," I replied, loosening my hand from his, "I'm home now. See that neon sign? That's my building."

"A fortune-teller." He turned to me and smiled. "Have you gotten your fortune?"

"No, but I'm barraged daily with an introductory rate offer. I don't think I've seen such an aggressive campaign in all my years of advertising."

"Let's do it sometime—just for fun. Let's see if we're meant to be married."

We crossed the street, still loosely holding hands. I was elated to be home. Tomorrow afternoon I was leaving town to get inseminated and hadn't even packed yet. I had so much to do.

But just as we approached my brownstone stoop, Jordan flew out of the Gypsy's door. He wore tight black jeans and a cotton T-shirt with holes in it. His usually thick, unruly hair was brushed back from his face. Although I had seen him the day before, when we met at the recording studio where I'd put down a deposit toward some sessions for his CD, I didn't even recognize him.

"Hello Chardonnay," he said coldly.

I dropped Ari's hand and stared at him.

"You know him?" Ari asked, after a befuddling silence.

"You know me, Molly?" Jordan repeated.

My jaw hung open like a broken steam shovel.

"Do you *know* me, Molly! Look at you, all dolled up, in heels and shit—you don't look like that when I hang out with you."

"Leave her alone," snapped Ari.

"Who the hell are *you* to tell me what to do with her?" Anger blazed in Ari's dark eyes, and he stepped toward Jordan, virtually frothing at the mouth.

"Why aren't you moonlighting behind your bar."

Ari looked to me and muttered, "Bar? Who is this chump?"

Jordan was raising his fists boxing-style as he scuttled backward, crying, "Fuck you, you coke-dealing, feel-coping scum bartender!"

Incensed, Ari tossed me his jacket. Jordan looked crushed when I caught it in a simple, wifely gesture. Meanwhile Ari advanced, throwing a swift punch that Jordan just ducked. But Ari was taller and broader, and he was going to swing again.

Now when I needed my mother's huffy voice I couldn't find it for the life of me.

"Please...come on..." I brayed meekly at them. I didn't want to even say either of their names, for fear it would offend the other.

I could see that Jordan had also assessed his physical limitations and was aiming to kick Ari in the balls. He raised his knee, the metal tip on his big black shoe reflecting pink from the Gypsy's neon sign. But Ari was no one's fool, and he turned his hip as Jordan's foot came at him.

I cringed, wailed, and covered my face with my hands.

Then Mama Cass threw open her door.

"Break it up, boys!" she hollered.

Slowly I lowered my hands from my eyes. She waddled out in a long, acid orange Disney World T-shirt and a tiara and planted herself between Ari and Jordan, grabbing both of their wrists. They were so stunned that they complied.

"Look, I can't have no trouble here on my sidewalk. The neighbors already complain that too many cars is honkin' for my husband after midnight."

"Lina?" a young man's voice called out from inside the store. "Everything okay?"

"Yah, we're fine!" Lina called back, as if they had this chat every night.

"You're okay, aren't ya?" Lina dropped my friends' wrists and turned to check with me.

"Uh, yeah. Uh—do you give tarot card readings at this hour?" I asked.

"Sure." She seemed gratified by my long overdue interest. "How wouldja like a Ten-Dollar Special?"

"I'll have one of those too," Ari decided, glaring at Jordan.

"Maybe we give the lady some privacy." Lina paused for them to consider.

Then she said very pleasantly to Ari, "But come back another time. Then we do yours."

"Okay," agreed Ari, catching my eye. "I'll be back for my Ten-Dollar Special. Another night soon." He blinked at me as though little bugs were in his face.

"Thanks so much for dinner," I managed to say, handing Ari his jacket. "It was a real treat."

Then Jordan bolted between us, his lower lip quivering.

"Z was fined for playing at Union Square without a permit. My parents just gave up their lease and say they don't want their own place. They're just gonna stay with other people."

"We'll talk," I said, mouthing "my mother," at him. Jordan looked doubtful; he knew that Ari would not rate with her any more than he would himself.

"Call me," I entreated him under my breath.

Then, before I could stop him, Jordan ran into the street, nearly colliding with a car that screeched to a halt.

"Let him go," said Ari softly as Jordan continued running to the corner.

After only two weeks of their lives upon it, the Gypsys' royal-blue carpet in the storefront had become embedded with cereal crumbs and broken parts of toys. Behind a black velvet curtain where Lina and her family lived, the TV buzzed and real people laughed along with canned laughter. I sat on a folding chair shuffling cards from a rather bent deck that Lina handed me while saint candles burned away on shelves around us.

As she laid out the cards, Lina's first words were: "You ain't pregnant, eh?"

"Why would you say that?"

"Not married, butchu pull boyfriends out of your hat. You gotta be careful, Fertile Myrtle."

"Am I fertile?" I tried to neither sound interested, nor to reveal the progesterone stain on my dress. "Could I have a child?"

"The cards say that you will, if you don't watch out."

"A healthy child?"

"You got nothing to worry 'bout, just you ain't married. See, every conception and birth card is right here. Motherhood very much on your mind."

Lina indicated a card with a pregnant woman surrounded by greenery set against a golden sky. This was startling. But, I supposed, this was news that Alessi would welcome.

Lina flipped out more cards, which didn't look so pleasant.

"And may I be frank witchu?" she asked.

"Please."

"What's your name?"

"Molly," I said.

"Okay, Molly—please don't be mad at me if I say your heart is broken." She pointed to a card with a tomato red heart pierced by three daggers. "And not by either of those two clowns out there. You was just havin' fun with them."

"Tell me more."

"Let's do a reading on him," she decided, briskly sweeping all the cards into her hand. "What's his name?"

"Gene."

"So shuffle the cards and think strongly of Gene."

"You know," I started, as I swished the cards around in my hands. "Do you ever think you see someone on the street, maybe riding a bike—but it's never them? It's just been so long that all sorts of people start looking like them."

"You and Gene don't speak no more?" she asked.

I shook my head no and set the cards upon her table. My heart was still pounding from the scene outside. I could see Jordan's trembling lip and hear their shouts and insults. Then I remembered my bags upstairs that I hadn't yet packed. And my butt ached on the folding chair from the progesterone shots.

When I finally looked up, I saw a little girl with long, wavy hair and a curly-headed boy peeking in at me from behind the black velvet curtain. They didn't understand the expression on my face, and quite possibly never would.

"Eddie!" Lina called into the back room. "Get these kids outta my face, I'm working—go on." She shooed them away with something in Romany that sounded like "*Jalpalal!*" They vanished like moths in September.

"It means: 'Get back there,'" Lina explained. "I'm sorry for the interruption, Molly. Keep shuffling and give me the cards when you're ready. "

It was good to have something simple to do just then. I handed Lina the deck of cards after a good shuffle. She asked me to cut it into several piles and put it back together. Then she slowly turned cards over and placed them one by one into a cross, then in a line.

"Oh, hmm," she said. "This one—your Gene—doesn't want to be known."

"What do you mean?"

"He doesn't like what I do. Uncomfortable with psychism and magic spells. Am I right? Where he comes from, they do this kind of stuff."

"How do you know?" I asked Lina, remembering that Louisiana, of any state, had a voodoo underside.

"The cards are trying to keep me out of his business—he's a private spirit, this Gene. That's why you like him. You're private too. Those boys—" Lina pointed to the street where Ari and Jordan had nearly mutilated each other. "No secrets. Cards are all out on the table, mind if I make a joke?"

She smiled awkwardly, and I suddenly realized that part of her face was paralyzed.

"Can you tell me why Gene doesn't like magic?" I asked.

"Because nobody pulls one over on him. Not anymore." Lina thumped out more cards from the pile and recounted rhythmically as she set them out: "This one's been double-crossed, in love and in business, more times than it's fair for one person. Slow to trust, his friends are few. But when he makes a friend he's more loyal than a dog. When he says something, he means it. Or he wouldn't bother."

"Are you sure?"

She nodded several times.

"Then how—?" I sighed. "How can anything change so quickly? Lina, this person seemed to care for me and then, all of a sudden, I didn't matter. Poof! More gone than Brigadoon." I looked into the bouncy candle flame before me. "Even fireworks fade slowly and leave a tint in the sky."

Lina picked up a card: a man on horseback carrying a wand.

"You know, all people gets self-absorbed. He didn't change his opinion of you. You misunderstood his mood. Happens all the time."

"Does Gene respect me?"

"He wonders where you are," Lina went on. "He's a little puzzled why you don't talk to him."

"Should I?"

Lina gave me the cards to shuffle again. She spread them on the table and blinked with surprise. Then she gathered the cards and gave them back to me.

"Shuffle again," she told me. "Give 'em a good shuffle."

"What does shuffling do?" I asked.

She leaned in, emitting an odor of bath oil.

"It puts *your* patterns into the cards."

As I ran them through my hands, Lina said she'd seen many ways to mix cards—the poker players who bent corners and turned the cards sideways, the people who "chugged 'em," the people who made little piles.

I returned them to her, and we both watched, amazed, as the same images came up again: a naked man and woman, a goblet overflowing with water, an archangel blowing a trumpet, a queen holding a staff, a blindfolded person surrounded by swords, and a corpse resting upon a coffin.

"The cards say that you and Gene could have the kind of love that all people want. But—I'm seeing that yous might never meet again." Puzzled, Lina looked at me. "What is that?"

I shut my eyes.

"Your paths never cross, and he won't come for you. He thinks you're playing hard to get, and he's just gonna wait it out."

"I've been weak with this person," I confessed.

"With all other mens, you're the strong one," Lina pointed a chubby finger at me. "It's in your stars. But only with Gene, you're soft."

"Yeah, well," I said, repositioning my sore butt on Lina's folding chair.

"If you see him again, it must be your choice. But the likelihood now is you won't do it." Her dark eyes seemed to grow as she looked at me. "I don't want to sound ugly or nothin', but it's like you're rolling over a baby bird with a car tire."

"You don't sound ugly. You're right."

And I wished we could give Eugenia the female pronouns she deserved.

"If you meet again, do it from strength. I'd say there's a very small chance you will. Like this much." She held her thumb and index finger close, though not quite touching. "There's a wall between yous." She pointed to the card with all the swords growing from the ground. "You got to go through that."

The black velvet curtain moved, and I thought it was one of the kids. But no little face peeked through. I glanced outside at the street, suddenly afraid that Jordan or Ari would be waiting for me when I left to go upstairs. I shifted forward on the chair, giving my butt a break.

"No one's there," Lina assured me. "It's the wind. Concentrate on the cards. They can't live our lives for us, but they can make things clear. People think if you meet 'the one' then everything's set. But the fun's just beginning, and nothing's easy. If you can find the power to grab it, by every grace of God, then you might have love that lifts your soul—and makes everyone around you jealous. But if you don't never find the power to grab it, then stay clear of Gene. Have your fun. Like I said, you pull boyfriends out of your sleeve. How many of 'em was waitin' around in my store this week? What did they do before I moved in here?"

Her laughter turned into a full, throaty cough. She balled her hand over her mouth to cover it.

"Will I see Gene again?"

"Draw three cards from the pile," said Lina, clearing her throat. The first one revealed a robed woman with a half-moon upon her head seated between two pillars.

"See," said Lina, pointing to the pillars, "one's black and one's white. Your future could go either way. It's not yet known whether you'll choose to see Gene. You need time to decide."

She didn't comment on the two other cards, which showed more goblets overflowing with water and rainbows.

"But look, you gonna hear from both those handsome boys." Lina waved her pudgy hand toward her window. "Men likes a challenge. And with you, my friend, there's no lack of that."

52

Symphonia de Inseminazione

Agitato

Usually I pack my bags a week before leaving town. But this time I crammed everything together just before the limo was scheduled to take me up to Alessi's.

I tossed in a welter of CDs from Brahms, Mozart, and Chopin to Billie Holiday, The Dead, Zeppelin, Metallica—music by which to gestate a friend's child. For luck I folded in the green-tea-colored tank top and sports bra from Eugenia. Sore and exhausted now, I remembered how incredibly well I had felt that day we played tennis and julienned a green pepper. I didn't want it to be "the past," or "an experience." I wanted it to be my life. But I agreed with Lina that there wasn't much chance of that. "Like this much." Lina had held her thumb and index finger almost close enough to touch. There was just that much open space.

A pile of bills lay on my desk, and I scrawled off some checks. Among them was one to Jordan, which I wrapped in an envelope for his roommate. *Dustin*, I wrote, *please make sure Jordan gets this payment for time at the recording studio.*

After last night, Jordan would probably just rip up any letter from me, as he'd ripped my note and left scraps like white rose petals on the doormat.

And what must Ari make of me? Did it matter?

As I stuffed more clothes into my suitcase and carry-on bag I fretted over how I would grow too massive to fit into these cute little panties or any of my slacks and jeans. For months. But I thought of Tamara and felt better; she was carrying gracefully. Maybe I could too. Then I thought of Matthew and felt worse as I shuffled papers around on my desk and shut off my air conditioner, not leaving my apartment in the usual tidy way I did before long trips.

Allegro Molto

An hour later my limo pulled into Pete and Alessi's long, pebbled driveway. A glaring sky seemed to suck life from the land and trees around us as the driver hauled my luggage inside. Now I would dress for a ridiculous fête to "thank and honor me" that would be held at Pete's parents' home in Hawthorne.

This promised to be an occasion where everyone felt put out but was equally convinced that someone else would appreciate it. Pete, Alessi, and I were all on antibiotics and restricted diets. We hardly wanted to watch everyone else devour tiramisu cake and slug Dom Perignon—but this was the kind of fuss Alessi's parents would make.

"I'm not going. It's sadistic," Alessi insisted at the last minute, planting herself on a bench outside their shingled farmhouse. Such outbursts were associated with things her father did.

After twenty minutes Pete managed to cajole her into the Jag. She sat in the back seat. They were always thoughtful about not stuffing me back there and casting me as more of a third wheel than I already was.

But when we braved a gravely stretch of back road, she shouted, "Dammit, Peter! Could you slow down?"

"What do you want me to do—five miles an hour?"

"You know I had my HSG shot today."

The big, nasty shot, worse than my progesterone boosters, put her eggs on notice that they must mature now in order to be retrieved.

"Molly's tush is sore too, remember?"

Indeed, what was left of it, whacked with each bump in the road for everyone I had upset in the last year: Thomas, Jordan, Matthew, even Ari, and for all I knew, Eugenia.

I sat beside Pete like an overgrown sandbag, taking it.

Dolce

Maddie and Dominic were just as they had always been to me, like an aunt and uncle. Both of them had dark hair when we were children, but now Dominic's was white and Maddie had frosted hers, so they appeared like bleached versions of the people I remembered as Alessi's parents.

But from my adult vantage point I now noticed Maddie's apologetic eyes and creased brows when she repeated, "You've made her so happy," cooing phrases to me in her dialect like a morning dove: *Che carina! Dolcissima!*

Dominic's open shirt revealed a huge golden cross on his hairy chest; he was perfectly typecast for *The Sopranos*. I briefly wondered whether Mom was onto something, though he seemed too jolly and sentimental to be a mobster. Altogether he and Maddie were more mismatched with Pete's parents than my folks were with the Szabós.

I watched Dominic by the tray of crudities, hoping he'd stick his finger into the dip and slurp it, wipe his mouth with his hand, drool on the celery, and double-dip it in front of all the stuffed shirts in Pete's clan.

But Alessi was making the racket, frantic from a week of follicle stimulation and enraged now with her father.

"Don't feed me sugar!" she was screaming at him.

Maddie fluttered around her chair while Dominic teased her.

"Nothing that makes you happy will kill you, or my grandkid."

Alessi threw a paper plate at him.

"It's all the drugs! They give her too many drugs," Maddie exclaimed, hovering between them while Alessi waved her off.

"Molly—get over here, beautiful!" Dominic called as he poured a glass of champagne.

"Dad, stop it," snapped Alessi. "She can't drink."

"Ease up on her, will you? How can I toast Molly if she's not drinking?"

"You'll find a way."

Pete's father, John Foley, took this in with a slightly cocked head, a beakish nose and an expression like a pigeon that was gently being choked. His wife, Constance, seemed an older female version of Pete, with sweet-potato-purée hair and more wrinkles. She too said nothing at all.

Alessi often griped about the "stuffed shirts," exasperated with their passive-aggressive social silences, commenting that "they're so filthy rich they pay people to change their light bulbs. Can you believe they pay sixty-five dollars a bulb? Then she's proud that they give to Catholic charities."

I could only think: John, Constance—constantly on the john.

John had shaken my hand awkwardly, and Constance had told me, "Nice to finally meet you," as though some great legend had preceded me.

Pete's analyst Huang and his young wife, Shenlei, watched all of this. I liked Shenlei, but since she barely spoke English we repeated essentially the same strained but well-intended conversation every time we saw each other.

The Foleys collected Hudson River School paintings, which proved the most interesting aspect of their otherwise drab, formal home. Shenlei and I admired a lavender *Highlands on the Mountain* painted by Homer Dodge Martin, and a misty, luminous Jervis McEntee *Twilight* from 1874. Then Shenlei startled me by asking, "Still single?"

I nodded. Wasn't this the point of the party? Perhaps she'd been spared some key details?

"Single good," she assured me. "No make meals."

Meanwhile, Alessi and Dominic shrieked at each other while Maddie flapped around them and Pete's family pretended nothing unusual was going on.

Affettuoso

I knew, from their earlier call to Pete's cell phone, that this household came in as *Private Number* on caller ID. I needed that blankness to call Eugenia. If I got a voice mail I wasn't going to ask her to call me back or worry about her doing so. I was too stressed already.

I wanted to contact her after Lina's tarot reading last night and the chat with Bertie. So I asked Constance if I could make a quick call to Manhattan. The upstairs bedroom to which she directed me looked less lived-in than I imagined the hotel room that awaited me in Oregon. But I welcomed the privacy.

Propped upon a stiff bedspread, I unwrinkled the paper with Eugenia's number on it from my wallet. I wouldn't say "It's Molly," or the more audacious "It's me"—I hadn't known her long enough for that. But what would I say? I jotted a couple of phrases beneath her phone number.

I got a recorded message, which was not her voice. It may have been Clay's. "Leave a message for us. Thanks," was all it said.

"I'm calling for Gene," I began, feeling far away from her in this bland bedroom the color of mushrooms, an amalgam of beige and taupe. "Hope you're well. Bertie gave me your number because it's been crowded and hard to speak with you at the bar.

"I wanted to let you know that I have to leave town for a couple of weeks. I'm going out West on that big job I mentioned. When everything's done I'll call you again or I'll come by the bar. I haven't forgotten the promise I made over that bottle of Pauillac. Gene, I don't forget my promises. Sorry it's been hard to talk lately."

As I hung up the phone I realized there was no backtracking now, no option of *Edit/Undo*. The act was complete, like a sun shower or a crack of thunder.

Bounding back downstairs, I ran into Dominic coming up.

"Heya, Molly! Come talk to me for a second."

I was glad for the distraction because I didn't want to think too much about this phone message and start regretting it.

Dominic led me into a corridor, where we stood by a window that looked out upon a wide, pastoral yard. Near a wooden trellis adorned with powder-pink roses, a few guests endured the afternoon torpor on a flagstone patio. Everyone else was inside relishing central air-conditioning.

Pete, Huang, and some other guy in a polo shirt were talking about the market, and Pete had that "trending up" look on his face. Weather had no effect on him when it came to this topic—he didn't look hot, tired, or apprehensive. It seemed, ironically, like an escape for him.

"You're a nice kid," Dominic was saying to me. "You know that? Goin' along with this razzmatazz…"

I wondered if he knew how much they were paying me for "this razzmatazz."

"I used to say to Maddelena—how'd this kid get so nice? You know, we always invited your parents to the house. We wanted to be friendly with them, since you and Allie were close at school. But they never seemed interested."

"I'm sorry," I said, still watching Pete and Huang. "My family can be snobby."

"Glad that came from your mouth, not mine. Gee, I remember your mother. Beautiful lady, so regal and refined. But I could tell she was never at ease with me."

She's convinced you're a Mafia don, I could have said.

"So how do they feel about what you're doing for Allie?"

"They don't know. I told them I'd be out of town on business."

"Always tryin' to pull one over on the old folks, eh? But we know more than we let on. Like I know about my son-in-law." He shook his head, frowning. "Rich fag. Can't get her pregnant himself, so he'll pay you the big bucks, right?"

I couldn't tell him about Alessi's scar tissue from the abortion and also didn't want to participate in this tasteless slur on Pete.

"Isn't it a matter of low motility?"

"They told you he doesn't have swimmers, huh?" Dominic laughed. His teeth were the color of cooked liver. "Hey," he whispered. "If that's the problem, why do they think it's going to work on you? What's the matter with my girl's equipment?"

"Slow sperm, lazy ovaries?"

He shook his head with a dismissive guffaw.

Legato

The plane dipped sideways to reveal grids of pinkish gray—festering wounds, the city I was leaving behind. I pressed my head against the window and stared down into those brick canyons.

I thought of Matthew, running from the subway to his office that sticky morning, hoping not to be late because he worried that his co-workers at Henderson, Fletcher, Kaplan, and Royce would notice. Twenty blocks uptown, near Rock Center, Tamara would be stuffed in a crowded elevator, maybe recalling chatter she had exchanged with Matt about where they'd left cash for the cleaning woman and when she would be home from prenatal yoga—the kind of thing married people say to each other on mornings like this.

At the southern tip of Manhattan, Eugenia Drury would be Rollerblading around Battery Park with strands of blonde hair poking out of her helmet. She'd savor the salty river air and the time away from other people's cigarettes and customers wanting to bite into her as though she were a juicy deli sandwich.

Of course Claudia Tesoro would be home, having a spat with "The Songbird" about who got to use the shower first. And Jordan Radfar would still be asleep on his uncomfortable mattress in Brooklyn.

Now the land beneath us turned hazy green where the Hudson River snaked through it. Back in the woodlands we were fast leaving behind my dad, who was taking his time getting to his clients' office in Waterbury, Connecticut. He had almost retired that year, but they had begged him to stay on, so he'd earned his kudos with them and could show up whenever it suited him. Mom would be sipping Irish breakfast tea with friends back in Torrington, grousing about "when will my husband finally retire so we can do the traveling we've talked about?" and "when will that fusspot daughter of mine get married?"

Then a cloud swallowed the land below, like steamed milk in cappuccino swallows a lump of sugar. Everything outside became white and sunny.

"How do you like business class?" Alessi asked me.

"I could get hooked."

I stretched out on the ample seat and Alessi smiled sheepishly, probably embarrassed by the melodrama yesterday with her father.

"How are you doing?" I asked.

"Bloated, cramped, worried but—did I ever tell you how 'the best' you are, Moll? I don't even care if it was you or Eugenia who made this choice." Now Eugenia had become part of her lingo, as if she were our imaginary playmate, or a symbol around whose meaning we danced. "Anyway, even if this doesn't work, at least I've enhanced your quality of life."

"Things work when I do them. Remember, A?"

I squeezed her arm.

Allegro Moderato

If the Intended Mother's disposition were calmer than Alessi's, we wouldn't be out West for more than egg retrieval and embryo transference. The sister clinic in New York where I'd gotten progesterone shots could have performed our sonogram. But Alessi didn't want to board that airplane home without knowing that the transference had worked.

I understood her sentiment; still, I dreaded feeling stuck for days on end at a hotel near the facility. But the taxi ride from the airport hypnotized me with its wavering vistas of Mount Hood and the Cascades, three time zones from everyone with a claim on me. We New Yorkers barely give Northwestern cities any credence—until we come here for some quirky reason and find ourselves bewitched by different mountains and clouds, imagining that we ourselves might take some new form.

Like most buildings on the outskirts of Portland, our hotel seemed like it was constructed ten minutes ago. I met Pete in the lobby, where a fountain hissed over a grand stonewall, a kind of throwback to the fountain in Dr. Betsy's office. Pete had arrived the day after we did and made his contribution to the collective effort that morning. I couldn't very well ask him, "Well, you flew across the country essentially to jerk off. How'd it go?"

During the five-minute drive to the fertility center, we chitchatted about how he was planning to sell short Dow futures—how he hated to profit by going against the market. But economists were predicting a decline next year, and when it came to protecting his investors he would do whatever it took. I listened, nodded, and looked out the car window wishing he didn't always talk about finance.

Once we checked in and took seats in a waiting room, Pete broached my prospective partnership with Larry.

"You've got to work out the equity stakes and the dispersal of retained earnings. My assistant can draft an operational agreement, if you like." He sat forward, his clean-shaven chin between his thumb and fist.

I knew he was trying to help me, but I couldn't concentrate. We were waiting for Alessi to come out of the OR, where she was undergoing "transvaginal oocyte retrieval." Dr. Masako Oshiro, our reproductive endocrinologist, was determining how many of her eggs would be viable. Meanwhile, Pete's sperm was being cleaned for the petrie dish rendezvous. By now Pete and Alessi were old hands at all this. But I, the virgin to assisted fertility, felt dazzled.

"I was telling Allie that if you go into partnership with Larry we might work out a different structure for your venture with her," Pete went on. "A private foundation might be best for taxes."

"A charitable foundation to flip houses in New York State? That seems kind of—I don't know—like a mixed metaphor."

"Well, since we proposed that house-buying idea things have changed. Back then, you thought Larry was going to ax you."

"That's right."

"For another thing, well—hmmm. How can I say this gracefully?" Pete scratched his head, digging hard with his fingers. "I don't want to get too involved with Dominic's business. You know, she wanted to work with his crews on renovating homes and what-not..."

"We'll deal with him. I can understand why you wouldn't want to."

"Realistically, Molly—between having this child and working with Larry, how much time will you have to facelift houses with Allie?"

"Probably not much."

"So it will largely fall into her lap?"

"I suppose."

"And you've seen how combustive things get with her and Dominic."

Pete was used to predicting trends; he had a knack for it.

"Also, Molly, you know she's been day-trading crude oil and gold this year. Finally I've taught her to put some profits aside before going into the next trade and losing it all. Now she's got a nice little cud."

"I remember she made a hundred grand back in May."

"It's more now, and time for a tax shelter. If we make a private foundation, you could be treasurer. That wouldn't take much time. You're doing so much for us already."

"Won't you have to donate some percentage of the holdings every year?"

"Never a problem for Allie," he said.

And suddenly there she was, plopping onto the sofa beside Pete with an exhausted sigh.

"How many eggs did she round up?" he asked.

"I don't know. Eighteen or something."

"And they looked okay?"

"I guess."

"*You* okay, Poogie?"

He leaned over and kissed her forehead.

Alessi sank into his arms. She was light-headed from the anesthesia, and she was upset. This process had failed them three times before. In several days, the embryos would be implanted in me. Dr. Oshiro had advised that we limit the implantation to three candidates—"the super-stars," she called them—to reduce the risk of multiple births.

I liked our calm but straight-talking practitioner, who was more suited to my style than Dr. Betsy. From her I learned what to anticipate during the next few days and was asked questions like, "when was the last time you had sexual intercourse?" and "did you use protection?" in ways that managed not to make me feel disgraced. I wished our social worker had shown half of Dr. O's tact.

During the days between egg retrieval and transfer Alessi took it easy, while Pete shuttled us around in a rented car. We drove over the river into Washington State and to the coast where we spontaneously booked rooms one night at a seaside inn. Back in Portland, I insisted that they spend at least a day alone together while I did ordinary things like ride streetcars and buy a shirt. In truth I wanted time to myself as much as I wanted to give them theirs.

Later that day we met up at the Chinese Garden with its pagodas and bridged lake. Pete took us to the teahouse before dinner downtown—an emperor with his wife and courtesan, I joked to myself. As he got up to find honey for our tea I watched his broad shoulders and strong arms with a kind of appreciative, feminine desire to venerate the body of the man whose sperm will live in hers.

Mezzo Staccato

When her husband left the next day for New York, Alessi came into my hotel room and sat on the overstuffed chair by my bedside. She seemed despondent, which I attributed to stress and hormonal zigzags. For a long time she said nothing, but gazed unhappily at the floor.

Finally she said: "You're intuitive. Do you think Pete is gay?"

I blinked at her.

"Where's *that* coming from?"

"You know how my father talks. Has your dad ever said that about your boyfriends?"

I'd never heard my father use the word *fag* at all.

"My father doesn't pay so much attention to my boyfriends. Dominic, on the other hand, is possessive of you—and he can't very well call Pete a lemon or a slacker, so he's found another grand-slam word."

Alessi pouted as though she didn't want to discuss it further.

But when we went downstairs for our specially cooked vegetable and protein dinner with mineral water, she told me, in the same breathless voice, "I noticed you looking at him the other day. In the Chinese Garden. "

"Should I ignore him or avert my eyes?"

"Don't you ever—I mean *ever*—get tired of cruising every guy who crosses your path?"

"You'd never guess how tired."

"Another time," she said, cutting into her tofu and Portobello mushrooms, "I walked into our gym"—she was referring to their lavish home gym with miles of nautilus equipment—"and he was lifting weights in nothing but his underwear, staring at himself in the mirror. Just staring, like he'd never seen anything so marvelous. I'm not even sure he saw me watching."

"That's how people are in gyms," I insisted. "Like Narcissus looking into the pool. I plead guilty."

She pointed to me, still chewing her food.

"Case in point: woman! It's how women and fags are."

"Please don't use that word. It's your father's, not yours."

"It's a nasty word," she agreed. "But don't you think my dad wants to protect me?"

"From what? You've been happily married for eight years."

"Nearly nine."

"This would have come to your attention," I pointed out. "You've raved about how compatible you are. Remember that trip to Tortola, where all you did was stay in the hotel day and night, tying each other's legs to the bedposts? I was actually annoyed—you didn't need to leave New York to do that. Do you think any gay guy would spend his time in Tortola like that?"

I could tell from her expression that Alessi felt silly.

"People's sexuality changes," she hazarded. "You hear stories of married men with kids suddenly claiming they're gay."

"It happens," I said steadily. "But it's not happening now with Pete. You wanted my intuitive sense. There, you have it."

I sliced my steamed vegetables and virtually sipped them from my fork.

"He's been very sweet to me. But we haven't had sex in a while," she confessed, barely above a whisper.

"You said *you* needed a sabbatical."

"I think all this forced performance has worn both of us down. It's almost like we're waiting with bated breath until you get pregnant. Then we'll make hay while the sun shines on us again."

Vivace

The night before the embryo transfer I dreamed of walking down a street in the kind of rain you can feel but not see. I wasn't in New York or anywhere I recognized. Suddenly Eugenia appeared with an umbrella and invited me to walk beside her. I saw the exact texture of her hair and remembered how clean her teeth looked when she smiled, that generally sweet brightness of her face.

"Where've you been?" she asked. "I keep hoping you'll come to the bar."

I awoke early, filled with yearning.

Inseminazione Tecnologico

It took lying around the transfer room in a hospital gown, my clothing shed and zipped away into a hanger bag, to actually relax me. And if I forgot who I was, I had a plastic bracelet slipped around my forearm with my name and Dr. Oshiro's on it.

The embryologist came in with her mask and indicated, on a large video screen, the three candidates that she and Dr. O had selected for implantation. That was my first glimpse of Andy; a quivering tiny creature, apparently known as a "blastocyst."

"How likely is it that I'll have triplets?" I asked Dr. O when she came in, ready to roll.

"We're not at high risk."

The unspoken hint was, let's hope that one makes it through—after thirty-five, a good embryo is hard to find, even if it would be implanted in Fertile Myrtle.

The embryologist went into a room behind ours. On the video screen, I watched her draw our little embryos into the catheter one by one.

"Please put your feet in the stirrups," Dr. O instructed.

Alessi had told me this "happens so fast you barely feel it." But I was startled by how little there was to feel—not even pain. After centuries of rice thrown at couples, May Queens and maypole dancing, ribbon pleating, egg hunting, and hawthorn gathering, mothers describing to their prepubescent daughters the "special sacrament of marriage" so obliquely that it sailed right over our heads—and now this nothing, this spawning in water like salmons.

I had performed more mammalian acts with Eugenia.

Andante Sostenuto

At Alessi's insistence I remained in the clinic for the next forty-eight hours, resting. When I wasn't listening to music I'd brought from home, she read me *War and Peace*. Maddie came out for a couple of days "to help," she had said, though I could hardly think of what she'd do.

As it happened she came in handy. Alessi had worried herself into a frenzy that her eggs had been fertilized with the wrong sperm, and her Italian mother took on the angst with requisite motherly devotion. They went and spoke with Dr. O and the embryologist, who backtracked their procedures and even produced files with Polaroid photos of blastocysts with Pete and Alessandra's names clearly noted along the borders.

Once that dust settled, Maddie sat with rosary beads in the room as Alessi read aloud to me. I was supposed to stay off my feet as much as possible and "only get up to eat or use the can," Alessi commanded. When Alessi and Maddie took off for their own meals I lost myself in Brahms, Chopin, and Mozart. Something of the cloudy slowness of these days, the coming and going of nurses and Dr. O, Alessi, and her mother were strangely soothing. I didn't even mind when Dr. O administered another progesterone shot "for the road."

On the second morning, as Alessi read aloud about the Countess Rostova, my cell phone rang. Alessi answered it as her mother sat beside her, whispering over rosary beads.

"No, this is Alessi. And you are—Gordon?" she looked questioningly at me.

Lina was right: "Men likes a challenge."

"Well, she can't talk now—sorry, Gordon. I don't know exactly when. I told you, she can't. No, I won't. I'm going to hang up."

Alessi shut my phone, commenting, "One of your million fans. Pushy beyond belief, isn't he?"

Allegro Assai

Maddie went back East, and I returned to the hotel. Alessi and I each had an executive suite to ourselves, with two king-sized beds—in case one was not enough for us fitful sleepers. Fluffy curtains with valences thick as pillows adorned the windows, and stacks of pillows were piled on every chair, sofa and bed. The room could have been a pillow theme park.

The second night we were there, Alessi knocked on my door after I indulged in an aromatherapy footbath. At first I was happy to see her in her robe and night-gown, as though we were having a protracted slumber party.

"You were right! You were right!" she sang merrily as she sat on my bed. "God, you're smart. God, I should always listen to you. Remind me to if I ever don't again."

"What are you talking about?"

"He's not gay, like you said. And now I have proof. I told you how the clinic gives guys porno to watch to get the juices flowing, right? Well, Pete just called—I don't know how we got on to this, but he told me they were out of hetero porn, so they gave him girls on girls. He said it was so hot that he nearly fell over—"

"Alessandra!" I actually shouted at her. "Stop!"

She looked shocked. It was more like her than like me to scream that way. But now I had her genes coursing through me. Of course I had the "stuffed shirt" genes too, but they didn't appear to be prevailing.

"That's not my business!" I continued, nearly hysterical.

"Wow. I hardly thought I'd offend you, with all your wild downtown friends and lifestyle—"

"That has nothing to do with keeping some boundaries with you and Pete."

"Yes, but we've confided in each other for years. I mean, you told me about wearing that nurse's outfit with Thomas…"

She put her hand to her lips to snicker.

I felt volcanic and must have been red in the face.

"You know," she suggested, "maybe the hormones are getting to you too."

"Just leave," I said, pointing to the door.

She looked despondent and bit her lip.

"I didn't mean to make you feel uncomfortable…"

I kept pointing.

When she walked out I slammed the door behind her.

53

The symphony of insemination ended fortissimo with bars of major chords and a spasm of percussion. I didn't need a sonogram to tell me I was pregnant.

My eyes popped open halfway through a night's sleep. From my extravaganza of pillows, I watched dawn draw leafy shapes from darkness out the window.

Welcome to Survival. Despite what anyone may say, this will be your bottom line once you have a body. So far as bottom lines go, remember that we are eighty-four percent water and bound by gravity. I wouldn't be too surprised if your first sensation might approximate a slushy vertigo. But you'll get used to it. You'll know you're acclimating when you start to feel hunger and craving. Welcome to that one too.

I'll do my best to feed you and to keep my own emotions in check so the watery aspect doesn't get out of hand. Right now, for example, I'm annoyed with your mother. That's not really fair to you, and actually I'm not upset with her as much as I'm upset with my own life.

But—you ask—am I not your mother? Your molecular assumption would be that this warmth, this sanctuary and nurturance, comes from Mother. Well, let's put it this way: I'm not far from your mother. I'm her close friend, like a sister. Maybe in a past life we were sisters or relatives of some sort. Do I believe in past lives? Frankly, it's hard enough to believe in my present life. So on that count, why not?

I nodded off to sleep again. When I awoke, the sky had assumed its confident morning blue, the brightest we had seen yet out here. I lay around, oddly melancholy, as concerns looped through my consciousness like suitcases at an airport baggage claim.

Shiny leather briefcase: should I become Larry's partner? Why had Pete been rattling on about equity stakes the other day?

Pink duffle bag: could I see myself walking around looking pregnant?

Then a scuffed knapsack rolled out: why had Jordan called yesterday?

A plaid suitcase with zipper tumbling onto the conveyor belt: "How are things in Glocca Mora" with Matt and Tamara?

A powder blue, round valise: "When will that fusspot daughter of mine get married?"

And then a vinyl yellow carry-on with the latest licensed cartoon character swooning on it: who is the child in my uterus?

A smart Liz Claiborne set with swiveling wheels: did Alessi really think Pete was gay, or was she just finding some distraction to fret over?

Finally, a soft amber carry-on slid out and fell on its side: could I ever tell Eugenia any of this?

The digital clock on the bedside table said it was 8:45 a.m., which meant that it was 11:45 in New York. I called home from the hotel phone that Alessi insisted I use, rather than "risking radiation exposure" from my cell phone. Barely any messages had accrued in my absence: pesky solicitations, my old college friend saying that she'd be in town this summer with her spoiled six-year-old daughter, and Enrico had asked again that I call him.

Maybe it was time for that call.

"I hear you're going to be Applebaum's partner," he said excitedly when I reached his cell phone.

"That's a strong possibility. Who told you?"

"I can't really talk now, Molly," he said, "I'm here, at this"—he lowered his voice—"very junior gig in a PR firm I got through a friend. It's less salary and more menial work than I did with you, but a clean slate. One of Bruno's friends told me, 'You don't want to go back to the bathwater where you left your dirt.'"

He giggled.

"Did you tell him it technically wasn't your dirt?"

"Oh, *she* knows the whole story. Molly, can I tell you? Women are much more simpatico about this kind of thing. Guys tell you to suck it in. They don't want to hear about problems they can't solve. But this girl—she's a bartender—kept serving me kiwi daiquiris with strawberry—like truth serum."

Just as I knew that I was pregnant, I knew that he was talking about Eugenia. Who else would serve kiwi daiquiris to someone down on his luck?

"So this friend thinks you shouldn't risk working with us again?" I asked.

"At first, yeah. She said don't go back to that dirty bathwater." Enrico lowered his voice even more. "But after I raved about your heroics—how you got rid of Jack, and how Larry apologized to me and offered my job back—she said it might be worth working for someone like you."

What understated, Shakespearian irony that Eugenia had spoken about me without even knowing it. I fluffed my mound of pillows and settled back on them.

"Just curious, Enrico. Did you happen to mention my name to this person?"

"Of course. Everyone in my life knows about Molly. You've been my superhero ever since you said let's go for a harassment suit."

"What does Bruno want you to do now?"

"Hold on a second—I'm walking away from my desk..." Now his voice grew lower again. "He wants me to earn as much as possible. As long as we're not pressing charges against Applebaum, he prefers that I go back and ask for a raise."

"Enrico? Your phone's breaking up. I heard what you said, though. Listen, we're out two designers. So if we hire you back and expand your duties, that might work for everyone."

"Yay!" he squealed, his phone still static.

"I'd love to have you on staff again. But why don't we wait to see how my partnership with Larry pans out, and then you can decide? You'll also have more time to evaluate your new position."

"Sounds good to me." Now his voice was clear. Maybe he had changed his position.

"By the way," —I couldn't resist—"this bartender friend who served your kiwi daiquiris—it's not Eugenia, is it?"

"Oh my God! You know Eugenia?" He pronounced her name in the Spanish way, with a soft *g* and short *e*. "I guess everyone knows Eugenia. Even straight people."

"My friend Bertie sometimes DJs at The Bunny Hop."

"I don't know her."

"Big girl who smokes cigars."

"That would describe a lot of 'em."

"Are you seeing Eugenia anytime soon?"

"Probably. She likes it when we come by. Gives her an excuse to get away from the groupies. Though I did introduce her to this Brazilian girl who stalked her for a while. I felt terrible about that."

"Stalked her? Really?"

I planted my ear next to the receiver so I could follow between the breaks of static from his phone.

"Jacinta is, like, twenty-two years old—Eugenia's in her mid-thirties and wasn't interested in more than a romp. She'd been honest with Jacinta, but you know how these things go. One person starts feeling more—hey, Bruno and I began as a fuck in a truck. So Jacinta was pretty devastated. She scribbled all sorts of horrible things in the girl's room there. Hell hath no fury like a lesbian scorned!"

The next chunk came in rather clearly:

"But now Jacinta has a girlfriend her own age. She's really happy, and they're

both going back to Belo Horizonte, where Jacinta is from. She introduced her girlfriend to Eugenia before they left New York, and it got pretty hairy. She was, like,
climbing all over Eugenia's back at the bar. Her girlfriend didn't care much for that.
Bruno and I went out with them later. Hello, Molly? Are you still there?"

"Uh—yeah. I was just thinking for a moment—"

Someone started knocking on my door, either Alessi or room service.

"Actually, someone's at my door. I'm at this hotel. Be right with you!" I called
to whoever it was.

I grabbed the receiver back, eager to hear anything more Enrico might say.

"When will you be back in New York?" he was asking me.

"Next week, after the Fourth. Hey…when you next see her…please tell Eugenia hello from me, from the West Coast."

"I certainly will. It's so madly weird that you know her."

When I opened the door, Alessi stood before me in jeans and a striped cashmere sweater with a little hood. I remember when she had bought it from a quaint
store in Litchfield that had charged something like four hundred dollars for it.

"Hey," she said, pouting cutely. "I apologize for being tacky last night."

"I apologize for flying off the handle."

"You were pretty insane."

"Come in," I said. "Sit down."

"Was it Gordon?" she asked as she stepped inside.

"Huh?"

Alessi lowered herself onto my pillow-smothered divan.

"Are you bummed about Gordon?" she repeated. "Do you miss him madly
and resent me for ripping you away from him?"

"His name is Jordan, and no, I'm not upset about him. He has more reason to
be upset with me."

"I thought he said *Gordon*—"

"Well he didn't."

"Let's not fight again."

"Let's have breakfast," I suggested, envisioning eggs Florentine and decaffein-ated tea. What I wouldn't give for a cup of real coffee.

"I appreciate your faith in my husband," said Alessi, looking up at me.

"We both know he's not gay," I said. "And so what if he is slightly vain or responsive to the male body? He's got one, after all. The point is, he can love you with it."

Alessi kept nodding, seeming to evaluate my statement privately.

"By and large, I'd have to say that men are more like light switches than we are," she began. "They're either on or off; in-the-mood, not-in-the-mood; gay or straight. We're like dimmers. We can be kind of—"

"Gradated," I said. "Coaxed. Or the reverse. Subdued."

"Exactly. But if everyone knew it was that simple, they'd lose profit on all these relationship self-help books and potency pills and gizmos."

I shifted my weight on the carpeted floor.

"But A, is it that simple?"

"I'd say that sex is. Emotions are not."

"Spoken like a true Italian."

"Like a true hedonist, at least. And speaking of which, everything you said about Dad being possessive of me is absolutely true. But some things are killers to own up to."

"Oh, I hear you. In fact, there's a thing or two I haven't told you yet."

And it was time.

54

Those famous Portland rains had flushed the Rhododendron Gardens several shades of green, from indigo to silvery emerald. Maybe people didn't like all the rain, but leaves did. I could practically feel their happiness as Alessi and I stood upon a wooden bridge, tossing crackers to ducks in the lake below us.

"You sure buried that headline," she finally said.

It was two in the afternoon. We'd been talking since breakfast at the hotel.

"Are you shocked?" I asked her.

"Nope."

I flicked my head at her as though to say, why not?

"Well, Thomas had already diagnosed you as 'oversexed.'"

I jostled her and she bumped back into me, like two children. We then continued walking across the bridge, saving crackers for the next ducks we would meet in this fairyland of ponds and waterfalls.

"So are you just saying you're not shocked because I'm carrying your child?"

I had spilled every bean, beginning with my guilt over the impulsive breakup with Thomas (of which Alessi heartily approved); my passion with Jordan and with Eugenia (of which Alessi also approved and wanted details); their respective bittersweet aftermaths; and my latest tussle with Matthew.

Alessi had listened steadily and sympathetically, barely reacting.

"It doesn't matter whether I, or anyone else, is shocked," she finally said. "But are you shocked? I mean, are you okay with everything?"

"*Je suis pleine,*" I replied. Alessi would remember our ninth-grade French teacher, Madame Michaud, explaining to us that in French, *pleine* could mean either *full* or *pregnant*, perhaps *swollen*.

I felt swollen with new life and feelings.

Alessi indicated a fork in our path, and we proceeded up a small hill dusted with crushed petals. I could hardly remember what day it was—Tuesday? Wednesday?—but barely anyone else was there. We passed families who spoke Slavic-sounding languages, a biker or two, and elderly couples who said "Hi," like nobody in New York City did anymore.

"What do you think Eugenia meant by 'imagine the difference good people could make with hedge fund money' when you surveyed her?" Alessi asked.

"I have no idea."

"Well, what do you think?"

"Probably that instead of redoing their twelfth kitchen for the seventh time, or buying a new wooden yacht, people with scads of money might contribute to the world at large." I spread my arms. "You know, gardens like this rarely come from proletariats."

"Contribution to just the sweet side of things, just the amazing side. I love that. You know, we should help her," Alessi said.

"Help her?" I shook my head. "She's not one to take a handout. I doubt you could pay her to take money."

"We'll help her open her Cajun place," Alessi persisted, as though this should have been obvious. "It sounds wonderful. The kind of thing I might have thought of and not been able to do if I hadn't met Peter."

Alessi suddenly stopped on our path, looking happy and sad.

"Remember those waitressing jobs I suffered through? Climbing stairs with trays of food that I usually spilled? And then I got into data entry, like it was some great shakes." She shook her head decisively. "Thank God I met Pete, and thank God we're compatible. I would have been screwed."

"You might have met another guy who'd support you."

"No one who'd know how to tolerate me. Shit, I would have wasted away. Ended up back home with Dominic and Maddie—that's where I was headed."

She continued walking up the incline and I followed, wondering if she really would have moved back in with her parents if she hadn't met Pete.

"This system of ours is based on raw luck, you know. People don't make money. Money makes money."

At one point I might have contested Alessi, being the competitive, pragmatic Yankee who was proud of my hard-won accomplishments. But after I nearly lost it all to the chicanery of JackASS, I could no longer vouch for the system's fairness— or any system's fairness.

"We should help someone like Eugenia. How else will she get started?"

"Listen," I said firmly. "Let's not get carried away. Eugenia told me that the whole topic brings back sad memories. That dream is 'dead in the water,' she said."

"Maybe it won't be so dead when I offer her the capital."

Part Four

55

I didn't see Matthew again until late July. Our aunt Blair and uncle Hamish were in town from Santa Fe—they tended to blow into Manhattan like a summer storm, see a couple of Broadway shows, shop, get tickets to David Letterman, ride the stinky, allegedly mistreated horses and buggies around Central Park, and do numerous other things that people who live here don't.

I knew only that their seeing Matthew and me for at least one evening of incessant drinking was mandatory.

Blair was actually not my aunt but my mother's cousin, daughter of late Aunt Eileen who had been known for driving into picket fences and getting her license revoked. Blair had replaced her mother as the family embarrassment. High-strung, skinny, and irritable, she probably could be diagnosed with something. I didn't know what, and I doubted even she was interested.

We found ourselves at a round table in a TGI Friday's near Times Square, Blair pointing at me with a trembling hand like a television evangelist.

"Now we know why Tamara isn't drinking, but what happened to you kids?"

My brother avoided looking at me. Tamara must have had told him I was pregnant. My reunion with Matt, after nearly two estranged months, had consisted of a tepid kiss on the cheek that brought to mind schoolchildren leaning into a water fountain to sip from the clammy spout.

"I'm a little off today. It may be the heat," I answered Blair.

"But it's freezing in here," she protested.

Indeed, the air-conditioning had brought sweaters to all of our shoulders, and Matt wore a denim jacket. Only Hamish remained in his hyacinth blue Lacoste polo shirt, happy to show off his barbecued forearms.

"Well, it will be hot again when we leave," I explained unconvincingly.

Tamara smiled at me, but Matthew didn't.

"C'mon, felluh." Hamish reached over and gave Matthew's shoulder a friendly shove. "You've got a kid on the way—have a beer at least. She won't be joining you anytime soon—nursing women tend not to drink, and since she's Jewish she absolutely won't."

"Excuse me?" said Matt.

When the waiter came by, Hamish ordered Matt a stein of ale. At one point in his life Hamish had been quite rugged and dashing, like the Marlboro Man. He had been cast in television shows and commercials, never as anyone too memorable. He'd been married twice before and had spawned a collection of offspring who roamed the world indefinitely. Blair too had been married before, but she never had children—so at least I wasn't our only family member who had fallen off that wagon.

"You owe my wife an apology," Matt continued to Hamish.

"For what? Saying that new mothers and Jewish girls aren't given to drink? That's the truth; why should I apologize?"

"Are you trying to be funny? You're not, especially."

Hamish made a long face and tried to catch my eye.

"He didn't mean to insult anyone," Blair assured us.

"In fact, if you wanna know, my own ex-wife was part Jewish. Pammy and Brian's mom. That's how I know they don't drink."

"Don't be oversensitive!" Blair commanded, pointing her quavering hand at Matt now. "It will get you nowhere. I used to be that way."

"Did I insult you?" Hamish asked Tamara.

Everyone looked at my sister-in-law with her large dark eyes like women on Greek Attic vases.

"I wouldn't say *insult*," Tamara replied, playing with straw paper in her fingers. "But I felt uncomfortable."

My brother put his arm around her chair.

"Well, I'm sorry if I made you feel uncomfortable," said Hamish with the polished charm of an actor. "I really didn't mean to."

"Would you have second-guessed her inclination to drink beer as a nursing mother if she were, say, African or Scandinavian?" asked Matt.

"Well, actually no," said Hamish. "Because then it wouldn't have been terribly flattering."

Cackling as though this was some brilliant punch line, Blair launched into a dull, gossipy story about how their neighbors in Santa Fe from Finland could drink even her around the block.

I thought sadly of my own neighbors. When I had returned from Oregon around July fourth, the Gypsy's storefront was vacated, a big blue ribbon of carpet ripped off the floor and folding chairs scattered around it. Someone said there had been a fire from their toaster, but Lauren the Songbird told me they'd moved in with relatives in New Jersey. Claudia insisted that their July rent check had bounced. Perhaps all the rumors were true. Every time I passed the storefront, which was often, I remembered Lina's half-paralyzed smile, and her index finger so close to her thumb: *a very small chance. This much.*

It felt like my time to leave the building too. I started looking at apartments with sunset views of the river in Chelsea and on the Upper West Side.

"So maybe you'll all live in the same neighborhood if Molly moves uptown," Blair was saying. "That will be convenient. And your mother likes her convenience."

The thought of Mom's convenience exhausted me. Upon my return to New York my mother had dug her nails deeper into my skin than either Larry or Jordan. Larry was mourning the loss of two accounts, one doubtlessly due to Jack-ASS' revenge, after he'd been unceremoniously sacked. Jordan had mouthed off about my imminent pregnancy to Claudia and Dustin in a fit of jealous rage over Ari. Then he received my check from Dustin and had tried penitently to apologize several times, his calls always intercepted by Alessi—"that Medusa of yours," he called her.

Despite this drama, I wasn't upset with Jordan or Larry. Only my mother's incursions into my privacy felt outrageous. I had to recover after our phone conversations by imagining that she was deathly ill and I might never see her again; that was the only way I could stand her.

She wanted to know where had I been and why had I not called those eligible, professional men whose numbers she had procured on my behalf? Why had I not told her that I was looking for an apartment—she presumed I might be asking her and Dad to help with a down payment. And speaking of Dad, why hadn't I called him on Father's Day? Did I realize how I'd insulted him?

And then Maddie called to ask me how I was feeling, to tell me that I was in Dominic's and her prayers, to invite me to their lakeside cottage.

"How nice for your child," Blair rambled to Matt and Tamara, "to have her auntie around. Not that my sisters wanted me nearby when they were raising their offspring."

"Pardon me for just a moment," I said, standing up and pushing my chair in as I felt the tinkles coming on.

I had few pregnancy symptoms other than a bladder always on the verge of bursting. When Alessi and I had driven around Oregon that week before my sonogram, we packed rolls of toilet paper for me to stop in the woods. I had learned to squat gracefully and not pee on my own leg, a womanly skill to acquire. I had also learned to use the men's room unabashedly if I needed it—and at TGI Friday's, I did.

Matthew met me in the corridor as I emerged from the men's room, and he was clearly surprised.

"The girl's room was occupied," I explained, noticing that his eyes were more gray and less green than my own.

"Look," he said, "do what you want."

"I don't understand why you're judging me for using the men's room."

"It's just gross."

"Why? There was no man in it."

My brother said nothing, but that carsick expression began to cross his face.

"Am I missing something?" I asked. "Do you and Tamara use different toilets in your apartment?"

"Hundreds of strangers don't trawl through our home."

"Well, I always wipe the seat first—and you know what? In many places, like my office, it's a unisex WC anyway."

"WC," he muttered. "It's a *bathroom*."

If this had been the good old days, I would have commended him for handling Hamish so well and we would have shared a stealthy little laugh.

But today I implored him, "What does our family have against thinking resourcefully? Where did we learn to be such homing pigeons?"

"You know, some of us got that chip off our shoulder in college."

I wanted to scream at him, "And some of us aren't thirty pounds overweight!" but didn't. I just lowered my eyes to his T-shirt that sloped toward me as we stood there, two affluent kids of parents who still hadn't fed us well, both our bellies growing now for different reasons.

"So you would bend over and ache if the men's room were occupied and not use an available ladies room?"

"It's a courtesy. Now if you'll excuse me…"

He walked passed me into the small tile room I had just vacated that reeked everlastingly of urine.

56

Set to meet with Jordan and Z about their CD, I figured that so long as Matthew was exiling me, Jordan could be fashioned into a kid brother. The idea was consoling enough to make his absence at our meeting a real blow.

At a place in the East Village, Z and I discussed over iced coffee how they'd include jazz standards and originals to demonstrate their range. Originals included Jordan's long, moaning ode to me. They were talking to a bass player, a pianist, and a trombonist. They wanted at least one chording instrument but no vocalists, Z emphasized. "Too crazy. Especially when they're good."

I would design the cover, and Z would send me a list of credits.

As we chatted he kept trying to call Jordan without getting an answer.

"Look, I'm here with Molly," he grumbled into his phone. "Did you happen to forget?" Of course he hadn't. He'd clearly come to the point that I had about

Eugenia—of preferring symbols and sentiments to an actual rapport.

Z slammed his phone on the table, shook his head, and muttered, "Seems you're doing a lot for someone who won't show his face."

"I've shown him two faces…Maybe this is what I deserve."

I swallowed something that stung my throat—a shard of ice cube or gob of dried honey. How could I blame Jordan for not wanting to see me after that scene with Ari when I couldn't face Eugenia after that Brazilian girl dry-humped her at the bar?

On my way home I bumped into Claudia and Dustin exiting the building. Dustin had become Claudia's disciple, business partner, lover, and roommate. The Songbird had flown out, and he'd moved in. I kept running into them as we all came and left our apartments.

In big sunglasses with rhinestone-spangled frames, Claudia wagged an index finger at me.

"Are you pregnant from some Orthodox Jewish guy or what?"

"No. Did Jordan say I was?"

"We can't make sense of what he says these days," said Dustin. "Like he thinks playing saxophone will feed him in this city? He's got another thing comin.'"

"He was sharper when I first met him," Claudia muttered.

They were clearly disappointed that Jordan had dropped out of their fray and was opting to pursue music as his livelihood.

"You're turning Jordan into a tax-paying citizen, but face it," she continued, rolling a bar of lipstick incriminatingly at me from its little golden tube, "he couldn't do that CD without you."

"He and Z would be nowhere," Dustin affirmed. "Playing bullshit at subway stations." His orange T-shirt said, *Take Me Drunk, I'm Home*. Claudia wore a skimpy, flowered shirt cut to her midriff, sunglasses, and the cherry-red lipstick that she colored over and over again on her lips like a kid with a crayon.

"Why are you wearing sunglasses to go out in the evening?" I asked her. "You know, the sun is setting, summer's gone…"

"My eyes get sensitive at this time of year. Remember?"

I didn't "remember." She probably needed to be incognito. God only knew where her latest schemes were taking her. I did know that she and Dustin were heading to Paris for a week in September with a jamboree of sex toys stuffed with weed.

"It's not really fair to Jordan," she continued, as we lingered on the stoop together. "You won't always be around to pad him. And his parents can't do a thing. Losers. Even my lunatic mother bailed me out a couple of times."

"You're the one he listens to," chorused Dustin as Claudia continued insistently to color her lips. "Not us or his family. He thinks we're all full of shit, but he'd do anything you tell him."

"*Me*? He was supposed to meet me with Z just now and never showed up."

"That's how important you are," said Dustin. "Hey. How do you have the bread to help them record anyway?" He raised the eyebrows that Claudia had tweezed.

"She has a salary," Claudia answered, looking at Dustin through her large dark sunglasses.

"Actually it's my Christmas bonus," I told them.

"So you must still dig him?" probed Dustin.

"I care about him."

"I saw someone else you care about today," said Claudia, as she finally rolled her cherry lipstick back into its tube.

"Oh yeah?" I asked her. "At The Bunny Hop?"

Claudia wrinkled her nose dismissively and said, "I don't go there anymore."

No, she'd been in Battery Park after meeting a "French connection." Apparently Eugenia had recognized Claudia and was Rollerblading around and around her.

"That girl's got legs to her arm pits. She goes on for days, doesn't she? I felt like the biggest midget..."

"Did you speak to her?"

"At first I didn't even recognize her, 'cause she was wearing a helmet. But then she stopped and took it off, and I was like—*Eugenia*. So check this out, first thing she asked me was not 'How are you,' or anything to do with me. Just 'Is

Molly still your neighbor?'

"So I go, 'Yeah, but I think she's moving to a bigger place.' Then I started to say, 'Have you heard the news?' because Jordan had convinced me you were pregnant with some *Yeshiva bocher's* kid, but I stopped myself when she said, 'What news?' Figured you might not want her to know. I tried to push my product for her establishment. Not a conversation she warmed up to. She put her helmet back on and just said, 'If you see Molly around, tell her hello from me.'"

"Really?"

"Guess you haven't seen her lately?"

"Not 'cause I don't want to," I said.

Climbing upstairs, I pondered Claudia's halcyon life of crime and romance. She was doing the American dream her way: launching a prototype, tasting success, then traveling internationally for business. And she'd captured the devotion of a younger man.

I couldn't imagine anything better for her.

57

Eugenia knew that I wanted to bare my soul, and that I'd come by the bar a couple of times. She'd probably gotten my phone message about going out West, and then Enrico had relayed my greeting. If she wanted to believe nothing was wrong, she might get away with that. She had even reciprocated this greeting to me through Claudia.

We seemed skilled with such random and remote diplomacies, but Alessi tightened the thumbscrews about ending the Mexican standoff. "You said you'd call. You really should. It's tacky not to." I knew she was right, but Eugenia had ascended to some aurora borealis that I didn't want to ruin with anything so vulgar as interaction.

"It's just a dumb crush," I told Alessi. "Like I used to have on guys before they started balding and ogling teenagers."

"You're one to talk. Your last guy *was* a teenager."

Alessi finally drove me to the bar by the scruff of my collar; we wafted in at seven on an August weeknight, thinking it wouldn't be too crowded. It wasn't, except for a cluster of girls playing pool and chug-a-lugging beer on tap. An unfamiliar bartender with just enough hair to be dyed platinum, as though someone had sprinkled Ajax on her head, was serving them.

After the buildup, of course Eugenia wasn't there.

Alessi described the place as "serious" and "ghetto." I explained that on some nights the women were indistinguishable from any you'd see at Club Med or Bloomingdales, that the bearing of this population varied like prevailing winds. We sat in a booth and a gal with spiked black hair and droopy eyelids approached us. She wore a white button-down shirt and a vintage tie. Clearly sweet on Alessi, she introduced herself as Vicky and offered to buy us drinks.

"We're pregnant," Alessi told her.

Vicky gazed from one of us to the other, probably noticing Alessi's diamond ring.

"Wow," she said. "Congratulations."

"Well, she's *physically* pregnant," Alessi clarified. "I'm *biologically* pregnant. So I can drink, but she can't."

"And the difference between physically and biologically is…?" Vicky pointed at each of us in turn.

"Use your brain, Jane." Alessi stood up, took her wallet from her purse, and handed Vicky a twenty. "Vodka gimlet for me, Shirley Temple for Molly, and you get whatever you want."

"First round's on me." Vicky declined Alessi firmly, pushing back her bill.

"Whatever," Alessi muttered when Vicky ran off to the bar.

"So where's Eugenia?" I asked when she returned, cradling our three libations perilously against her shirt. "She's usually here on Thursdays."

"Fire Island for her birthday," she said, distributing our drinks. "She couldn't wait to cut outa here—no bones about that."

"When will she be back?" asked Alessi.

"Next week I think. She seemed overworked, really needed a rest. But she's the best bartender here, and they lose half their business when she takes off. Gorgeous lady, and very nice."

"So I hear," said Alessi.

"You don't know her?"

"Molly tells me she can juggle beer bottles like no one's business and she's hotter than lava."

I kicked Alessi under the table.

"Just a sec…"

Our gallant hostess arose and went to the bar again, returning with a stack of photographs. Long strips of tape dangled at their edges.

They were mostly group portraits of Eugenia at the bar with women I didn't recognize—some gawky and buzz-cut, one or two frighteningly adorable. Relieved that the Brazilian was not among them, I leafed through a Polaroid of Eugenia dancing on the bar in cutoffs and high leather boots, and a wonderful shot of her juggling beer bottles. I grabbed it because I could see her navel ring and abs, her hammy expression. Though stunning, she offered the camera a lot more than beauty.

Alessi sighed. "Talk about drop-dead gorgeous…why isn't she famous?"

"I don't think she wants to be," said Vicky.

I uncovered the next photo.

"Who's that—her dad?" asked Alessi.

"Oh no, that's Arbie with her," Vicky said. "This older straight guy that sometimes hangs out here."

"Looks like Bruce Willis," Alessi commented. "Twenty years later."

"He's an expert on trees," Vicky went on. "He can tell you every genus that's native to Manhattan, and every tree imported from Europe or Asia. Hey, did you guys know that New York City has more male tress than female?"

"Really?" said Alessi. "And what makes a tree male—are his balls worse than his bark?"

Vicky burst into exaggerated laughter that grated on me.

"No, but female trees have their periods; they drop fruit that messes up the street, Arbie told us. No good for a city…or so some urban planners thought. Back in the thirties, when elms died off, they replanted a lot of male trees—maples, I think—that now have no one to pollinate with."

"Sounds like China's one-child policy," said Alessi, "which produced millions of more men than women over there. What were they thinking?"

"Oh, trees will outlast us…Arbie says most are hermaphrodites. They have male and female flowers that pollinate themselves."

"How efficient," commented Alessi. "Though probably less fun than human style. Not that I've had much fun with human reproduction."

Vicky looked confused. "I dated a hermaphrodite once. But she couldn't impregnate herself."

Changing the subject, Alessi asked, "So this guy Arbie, does he teach or write?"

"No, he makes his living from SSI and gambling. He and Eugenia buy lotto tickets together. He's devised some mathematical formula or something."

"And it's worked?" asked Alessi.

"Not significantly."

"I know about mathematical formulas and automated trades. My husband manages a hedge fund. There's something to that, but most of it boils down to luck."

"You don't think the market's fixed?" Vicky asked, narrowing her eyes, not yet over the word *husband*.

"Fixed by what? Space aliens? Not that big funds and insiders don't have an edge—but there are variables no one can predict. I'm sorry. Everyone gets eaten up in a trade sometimes. Still, it's a better deal than lotto for serious gamblers."

"Arbie's more serious than Eugenia. He won big on a horse a while back. Paid off debts, and now he's looking to build a retirement fund. If he wins millions he'll start an arboretum and help Eugenia open her own place."

"Oh, so that's what she wants to do?" asked Alessi, now kicking my leg under the table.

"Sure," said Vicky. "If she could."

"Wish I could swipe just one of these photos," I mused as I sifted through them again. I longed for a keepsake, some proof of Eugenia beyond my memory.

"We really can't," Vicky chastened me. "They belong to her."

"Suppose I buy one?" Alessi whipped out her wallet again, and stunned Vicky by producing a hundred-dollar bill.

"Well," the girl admitted sheepishly, "Eugenia will appreciate that, after being away from tips for so long."

And so Alessi grabbed a scrap of paper from her purse and scrawled, *Dear Eugenia, Welcome back from the beach. Hope you don't mind that I purchased a photo from your collection for your biggest fan. We'll be around again, Alessandra Piraino-Foley.*

58

When I got home, I picked up the telephone and blanked on my parents' number—pregnant brain fog, cured by an ice cream sandwich. Then I was shocked that neither Mom nor the machine answered.

"Dad?"

"Molly?"

My father sounded surprised too.

"Uh, your mother isn't here," he said after a typically awkward pause. "She's shopping with Addie at the mill outlet."

"I wanted to talk with you, actually."

"Oh yes? Is everything okay?"

"I'm sorry I didn't call you on Father's Day. Mom brought it up last week, and you've been on my mind."

More silence. This was, after all, my father, not known for his ready repartee. "Your mother tends to overstate," Dad finally said, clearing his throat or chuckling mildly. "Please don't forget that you sent me a dashing tie for my birthday—two weeks before Father's Day. It's just our luck that her birthday is three weeks before

Mother's Day. So we don't expect you kids to go all out."

"I'm still sorry."

"You know," he said, "I can't recall ever wishing my dad a Happy Father's day. Your grandma bought a card that we all signed. Something like that."

Suddenly I heard the croaky old-mannishness of his voice. It was fitting for a "grandpa," but I didn't know when that had happened. Despite his maddening reticence, my father was not someone who deserved a daughter pregnant with her friend's child, and—if that wasn't sufficiently scandalous—falling in love with a woman. Yet there I was, craving ice cream sandwiches in my first trimester and taping that photo of Eugenia to the wall behind my desktop.

"Mom and I will be in town next Thursday," he continued. "At the Carlyle."

It would be their first visit during my pregnancy, and not the time to tell them about it. Maybe it never would be.

"Good," I said, already feeling stressed and disoriented. "I'll look forward to seeing you."

"Sounds like your niece is ready to burst onto the scene any second. Mom thinks it will happen tomorrow. She says she feels it in her left knee."

Of course her left knee had also told her that Thomas was the husband for me. But this time, her left knee was right. Mira was born the next day.

59

August 2000 in New York was a pleasant time and place to be born. The summer had been more balmy than most, with only an occasional scorcher. Even the sunflowers in window boxes and ivy along brick walls seemed exuberant. But when I saw Pete, every other word out of his worried mouth was "Greenspan."

On my street, honey locust trees were in full bloom. Morning light gilded my bedroom walls with diamond-shaped echoes of window as I awoke each day. All over town couples were kissing as if that would keep the sweet season with us forever. As I passed them rolling together on blankets in the park or squeezing against lampposts, I mourned my own lack of kisses the day my niece was born.

For Tamara, the Lamaze and prenatal yoga had paid off. She stayed in the hospital only two days after giving birth. Matthew was by her side, so I didn't show up—not that I was invited. My parents wondered where I was, but I understood that no explanation was given.

Once Tamara had settled in at home, she invited me to visit the baby. Her sister Dahlia was in town from Chicago, and Tamara thought it would be opportune for me to come by when Dahlia was there and Matt was at work.

"I just have to warn you," Tamara had said on the phone, "photos of you are back on the wall. But only ones with Thomas, like from our wedding."

Well, thanks Matthew, I thought. What a fine way to reassert the notion of Thomas into Mom's craw.

My parents would have shown up too, but Dad had a luncheon with colleagues at which Mom was expected. So perhaps that afternoon I would be spared any big comeuppance from her about why Matt had a child and I didn't.

In the morning I had a checkup with my OB-GYN and sat in the waiting room at her hospital. I grabbed a magazine from the table beside my chair, thinking it was silly that medical doctors bothered to schedule appointments. They were often more delayed than air flights. My appointment was for eleven forty-five and it was half passed noon now. I'd told Tamara I would be over around two, so I would probably be late since I was going to have an exam and a sonogram.

I opened the magazine to some heady discourse on American ideals at the beginning of a new millennium when I heard someone call, "Molly!"

Startled, I looked up. But I didn't see a soul I recognized. Maybe it was more of my pregnant brain fog, or maybe they'd shouted "Golly!"

I continued reading and the voice called out again: "Molly! Over here!"

Now I saw the thin woman with short brown hair waddling across the reception area in a turquoise hospital gown. She clutched an IV pole, with dangling transparent bags, that was being wheeled by an aide.

"Terry! My goodness."

Dropping the magazine on my chair, I dashed over to where Terry stood swaying from side to side. The pretty face with sweetly gaping lips that I'd first seen at The Bunny Hop was now framed by shorter, choppier hair.

"What are you doing here?" I asked.

"My fibroids were removed Tuesday. I'm really sore, and I can't walk without help yet. Just practicing, with Lahvonne here."

She turned and acknowledged the nurse's aide who was over six feet tall, looked Caribbean, and smiled with formality. "Never guessed how much I depended on my abs to get around. Even to just sit up in bed.

"So we're waiting for my cousin. Thought we'd walk me out to see if she was here yet. Hey—" Terry's drawn face brightened. "Eugenia's coming tomorrow— she said she'd help me practice walking." Her smile seemed to wan. "What happened with you and Eugenia?" she asked.

Then it slammed me. The person who was going to visit Terry and help her walk, who had been to Fire Island for her birthday, had eluded me. Whatever was on her mind today or tomorrow, I didn't know. I'd been pacing my little room of obsession, loving her as ineptly and narcissistically as I'd ever complained men had loved me. Now I burned with embarrassment about leaving a hundred-dollar bill at the bar when I'd pilfered the photograph of her.

Terry's voice seemed unnaturally slow, perhaps from medication.

"Rick and I went to see her before the operation, you know, to tell her I was finally doing it. I hadn't seen her for a while because I was up in this treatment center for a couple of months."

"Treatment center?"

"A loony bin in New Hampshire that specializes in eating disorders. I told you about that, didn't I?" I nodded. She hadn't, until just then. "Of course we asked after you. Eugenia got kind of touchy and said, 'I don't know what happened to her, and let's not talk about it.'"

I ran over those words and the way Eugenia might have said them like a tide over sharp pebbles.

"Did you guys, like, fight or something?" Terry pried. "I can't imagine that. You're both such nice people, and you seemed to really hit it off. I remember thinking that it was a shame you weren't gay because you'd be hot together."

Now she gripped the pole with both her hands and started to sway more pre-cipitously. Lahvonne reached out to steady her. Terry looked at me like she wanted me to say something.

"I like her a lot," I said. "Back in the spring we played a little tennis."

Still ginger on her feet, Terry nodded with a preemptive smile.

"So you played for the other team?"

"You know, Terry—there are no teams. You play or you don't."

"Was it great?" she asked me, tossing her head with vague envy.

"Unimaginably great."

As I blushed, the receptionist called: "Molly Douglas! Dr. Spence will see you."

"You're a patient here?" Terry asked.

"Outpatient. I'm ten weeks pregnant."

Terry's mouth dropped open. Even Lahvonne lifted her brow.

"Who's the father?"

"My best friend's husband."

I left them gaping at each other, Terry bending over a bit, as I darted to my seat to pick up my bag.

"Would you have done it?" I swooped back and asked Terry, before surren-dering myself to Dr. Spence's table. "Would you have carried the child of a friend who couldn't do it herself, if she gave you a nice piece of change for it—enough to leave your job?"

"No way."

"Do you think I'm crazy?"

"Who am I to talk?"

"Please," I started. "Say hello to Eugenia for me when she visits you tomorrow."

I felt more nauseous in the cab up to Matthew's than I had in ten weeks of pregnancy. Maybe because the driver didn't know if he was braking or speeding and wouldn't stop shouting on his phone. Or maybe it was the grainy little sono-gram portraits of Andy in my purse.

At that moment, Andy was probably faring better than I. He was making good progress, according to the specialists. I sensed his independence from my vertigo as I rolled down the cab window, letting wind ease the gagging tension from my throat as we barreled through Central Park.

Matt and Tamara lived in a deco building with the kind of elevator you opened with a knob, like a door. There were also staircases with wrought iron railings that ran through the tiled corridors. Sometimes I would walk to the ninth floor, just for exercise. That day I took the elevator, trying to find my heartbeat and Andy's after the cab ride.

I was so accustomed to Tamara at their door that I thought Dahlia was she. But Dahlia was taller, and her hair longer and darker than Tamara's.

"Hey!" I greeted her. "Auntie!"

"Auntie," she said back to me. Tamara emerged behind her, whittled down to her natural size.

"Wow, look at you!" I teased.

"My waistline's making a comeback," Tamara answered with a tired laugh.

Their home had a new sweet smell of rubber and talcum powder. Dahlia's luggage was parked in the living room amid a greater chaos.

Though she was supposed to have joined Dad at his luncheon, Mom emerged, looking summery in a green cotton dress with bare legs and feet. She hugged me with unexpected tenderness. "Come, you must see Mira Jessica," she said excitedly.

"The baby's sleeping," Tamara explained, "but we can take a quiet peek."

We proceeded down the hall to the nursery they had prepared for her. I remembered helping them choose wallpaper from a book of samples months ago, when Matt still valued my input.

"The wallpaper looks terrific," I whispered to Tamara as we tiptoed through the door. Inside the crib and swathed in cotton blankets lay a tiny creature, pink as a medium-rare steak with fine black hairs on her head. Her tiny nose and lips replicated familiar features, like an ear that was shaped like Matthew's ears.

As though she could follow my thoughts, Mom said: "She looks so much like you did."

"I was that pink?"

"You certainly were."

"She's more like your baby pictures than like ours," said Tamara, and Dahlia added, "The mini-you."

"Like the world needs another," I murmured, reaching over her crib to graze her warm sleeve with my fingertip. Mira Jessica continued to sleep. I thought of Shakespeare's Jessica, who'd said: "Though I am a daughter to his blood, I am not to his manners."

I hoped this daughter would prove equally able to call her own shots.

"Now, listen," I whispered to her. "No Gatorade-colored hair and no rings or tattoos on your tongue. And you're going to speak in confident, declarative sentences. Everything's not a question. And everything's also not 'awesome.' Awe is special.

"When you get a cell phone, as you inevitably will, you are never to answer it like this: '*Helloooowww? Ooauw, hey-eyyyy!*'"

Mom, Dahlia, and Tamara giggled in the same hushed way I was speaking.

"Oh Molly," ribbed Mom.

"Kids are like that these days," I said. "The human race is mutating before our eyes."

"I know," agreed Dahlia, eyeing me like she had more to say about this.

"She's very mellow," Tamara told us. "Everyone warned me that I wouldn't get any sleep, but she's not much of a wailer. A cool, collected Virgo—what this family needs."

"Wait 'til she starts teething," Mom advised. "That's another story. Of course Molly was boisterous from the day she popped out into the world."

"Not at one week," I protested.

"Oh, we had to fix Daddy up with a set of ear plugs so he could sleep and get to work the next day."

As Tamara and her sister laughed, I realized that my mother's approach to being a grandmother was to acquire a comical edge. She would not be the kindly old lady with a warty nose so much as Granny Mame, the inimitable aging beauty.

"Let's get a picture of all of you with Mira," suggested Dahlia. "This is a special moment."

She held up a digital camera.

"No, Daya! The flash will wake her up," Tamara parried her sister.

"Just one picture," urged Mom. "She wasn't disturbed by our talking."

Tamara seemed more than weary of being overridden. But she stood beside me dutifully at the edge of the crib, and Mom stood behind us, an arm over each of our shoulders.

I hoped that Matthew would see this photograph.

Mira slept peacefully through a succession of baby paparazzi flashes. This would be the lay of her land for a while, with aunts and grandparents descending upon her from all directions with digital or disposable cameras in tow.

Still, Tamara insisted that we retire to the living room and let Mira be until she naturally awakened. I observed with interest that she was on a feeding schedule.

"Fritz and Zipporah fly in tomorrow," Mom said. "Daddy and I are throwing a little party in the hotel suite Friday evening. You must be there, Molly."

"Sure."

"Come here for a moment."

Mom sequestered me into the corridor as though she were putting me on detention.

"We're aware that Larry keeps you exceptionally busy," she began, her pale eyes beaming into mine. "But there are other parts of life, you know."

Yes, another part of life was growing in me.

"I frankly think your brother and sister-in-law would appreciate your being a little more in evidence. Babies are a handful."

"I'll be at the party," I promised.

"I should think you'd want to be—that it's not something we're forcing you to do."

I looked back at Mom as pleasantly as I could.

"I wouldn't miss a party for the mini-me. After all, someone's got to teach her the ropes."

Mom blinked at me with sudden embarrassment, as if somehow she understood, or at least had some sense, that she hadn't stopped pushing me since the day I'd come out of her.

60

The foundation would fund one new business a year through a non-profit organization that I'd manage. Our stated mission was to advance the cause of women in business. "It will be the best of socialism, capitalism, and coincidence," Alessi put it. We wouldn't accept proposals or applications but would function serendipitously, finding candidates through word of mouth and chance encounter.

Before I set out for The Bunny Hop, with photos of the girls from Nepal I'd sponsored and a letter to Eugenia, our first candidate for funding, Alessi emphasized: "Make sure Eugenia knows that my offer holds, regardless of what happens between the two of you."

"It probably won't get to that," I said. "I'll be relieved if she's cordial."

In late August the madding crowd was still away and the street felt serene, if not abandoned. No holiday lights or decorations adorned the bar. I stood at the tinted glass door for a moment, my hand shaking like I had malaria. I shouldn't do this. My time to make good with Eugenia had passed. I opened the door.

Barely anyone was there, and Eugenia stood behind the bar at the chopping board. Though she couldn't see me walk in, she seemed to know it. She wore a white tank top and faded cutoffs, a striped jersey tied around her waist, her arms and legs tanned from a season outdoors. As I got closer I saw that she was slicing fruit for drinks, her hands in plastic gloves. She looked even more perfect than I remembered, and I'd done some remembering.

A couple of girls knocked balls around on the pool table. Three others, in navy blue Yankees caps, were huddled at one end of the bar. At the other end Arbie sat alone, and I nervously took a seat beside him.

With a New York accent as thick as Claudia's, he asked no one in particular,

"So what do you win in the Million Dollar Polish Lottery?" And then he answered, "A dollar a year for a million years."

I alone chuckled.

"I can get away with that one," he commented. "Told you I'm part Polack, right? Right, Gene?" He then turned to me and said, "She doesn't give a damn."

"I've heard your jokes for a million years," she replied, chopping away at her oranges, lemons, and limes.

"She's been grumpy," he explained to me, "since she got back from Fire Island and quit smoking."

"No," she corrected him, still performing her task and not looking at us, "I'm grumpy 'cause I'm sick of this place." With that, she laid down her knife, scooped up the colorful fruit slices and deposited them in their tin, removed her plastic gloves and darted off, stage left.

Arbie remarked to me with a grin, "Haven't seen you around for a while."

I nodded bashfully and introduced myself, since we'd never spoken—though he seemed uncannily informed about me.

"Arbie," he said, pronouncing his name *Awhbie*.

I shook a large, calloused hand.

"Is it R.B. like roast beef, or Arbie like arbor?"

"Let's put it this way: I changed my confirmation name from Aloysius to Arboreous when I was sixteen and developed a passion for botany."

"So it's Arbie then. *Arbre*."

"It can be what you want it to be."

"But it's your name, and it should be what you want. Arboreous," I repeated. "I wonder if that's the same Latin root—pardon the pun—as arbitrary or arbiter."

"I've done it all plenty," he assured me. "And Molly, well, I loved that name since my lucky mare turned a twenty-dollar exotic at Belmont into my life."

Eugenia returned to the bar with a couple of beer cases.

"Hey Gene," he called out. "I ever tell you about Impossible Molly?"

She shoved one case on the shelf behind her and broke the other open with both hands.

"The perfect long shot at Belmont two years back. No one putting money on her, no rider to speak of, fifty to one odds—what did I know that no one else did?" He looked like he'd posed a rhetorical question. "She placed fourth—right where I needed her for my Super-fecta. I scooped up seventy-eight grand. My pals rushed me to the IRS teller's window; I was too busy genuflecting."

Gene produced bottles from the open case and stacked them on the shelf. Just as I concluded that she was telegraphing inordinate disdain in an effort to spurn me, she wandered over.

"Heard about the horse too," she told Arbie. "Couple of million times. But you never taught me how to win like that." She turned to me wistfully. "Hey. Whatcha having?"

"Cranberry juice and soda."

She made a darling face, leaned with her double-jointed arms on the bar.

"Why're you drinking soda when I'll serve you champagne, lovely?"

"Because I'm pregnant," I heard myself say. "Surrogate mother for an old friend who was having fertility trouble."

"We had a private party last night with Veuve Clicquot splits." A blonde hair dangled over her eye as she cocked her head. "I'll pop one for you."

"Can't drink." I sounded stiff and defensive.

"Was that a promise?"

"Look, I know you think I'm nuts…"

"One sandwich short of a picnic," she affirmed, looking over at Arbie as though he understood. "Three fries short of a happy meal. But there's a detail that trips me up."

"Which is…?" I asked.

"Why would Terry say she saw you on the maternity ward last week?"

"Because she did." And I repeated, "I'm pregnant."

"How many months?"

"Two."

"June," she said. "Big assignment?"

"That's right."

"When's pay day?"

"Every day."

"Well, let's toast that. We'll split the split with Arbie. You hear?" she checked with him. "Unsinkable Molly Brown rounds the bend."

"That would be Impossible Molly," he corrected her. As I was about to decline the champagne Arbie held up his own froth-streaked stein, saying, "Shouldn't mix my poisons."

Eugenia waved him off. "You're not driving anywhere. And a three-way split won't spoil your plans either," she assured me.

Then she knelt below the bar and emerged with the champagne and three fluted goblets. After she popped the cork, pale gold servings flowered into them. The bubbles settled, she held her glass to the ceiling, and, astonishingly toasted: "Every time I see you it's love at first sight."

"Good one, Gene," said Arbie. "That's a good one."

"Plagiarized," she said, bringing her glass down to clink lightly against mine.

"Should I read your horoscope from the *Daily News*?" he asked, and Eugenia shook her head. We all swallowed some champagne, which tasted pretty damn wonderful after three months of abstinence.

"Could we speak for a moment?" I asked her, meaning to say, speak privately. "I have something for you—could you possibly come around to this side of the bar?"

"Why can't you give it to me right here?"

"I don't want you to receive it in captivity."

She checked the clientele. They seemed okay, so she came around to sit beside me at the bar, crossing one long, rosy brown leg over the other. Instead of her leather boots, she wore black high-top sneakers.

"I'm sorry I've been…" I gestured, timidly thrilled.

Her gaze fell on the friendly side of opaque, her emotion impossible to guess.

"I'm glad to see you," she said, as though she owed me a statement.

"You don't—seem to be."

"Remember, I told you not to take my moods here personally," she reprimanded, as if she'd said that recently. Then she surveyed me and commented—apparently impressed—"Hell. You went through with it."

"I did."

"How're you feeling?"

"Okay."

"No morning sickness?"

"Not really. And I've almost scaled the first trimester. You stopped smoking."

"My buddies got me into hypnotherapy for my birthday. Now I'm on gum and lozenges."

"You must feel better."

"When I feel at all."

As if on cue, we both sipped a little more Veuve Clicquot. Arbie sat beside us, his head in the newspaper, perusing horoscopes and horses. "Chanson Bleu, Dimeadozen and Distant Star in the running…damned if I shouldn't have put cash on them this morning," he muttered.

I handed Eugenia the envelope with photos of the girls I'd sponsored in our names. She looked them over, nodding sweetly at me. Then we both cracked up. She wasn't angry. It was kind of a miracle, but she wasn't.

Heartened, I wanted to make her day as she'd made mine. I wanted her to know that she wasn't trapped in this dark bar.

But I should have saved Alessi's letter for another time.

"I know this name," she said. "Hey, you didn't leave me a hundred bucks, did you?"

"Well…I'm not in the habit of stealing people's photos."

With a peeved smile she shook her head and began reading.

Dear Eugenia,

You don't know me, but you changed my life. You heard my prayer when some-body had to. I am an old friend of Molly's. I have known her since third grade. I can tell you that she would never do something so radical unless…

Eugenia scanned the rest of Alessi's note, still as a statue, before she let it glide from her hand straight onto the floor. I couldn't understand what had happened.

"Do you think—do you possibly think—that you've played with my head enough?" she asked softly.

"I," I began, shocked. "I didn't write this—didn't ask her to—"

"Are you putting me on? 'Cause it's putting me off." She asked herself aloud, "What's with people in New York?"

When I realized I was losing her, after having found her again, I wanted to cry.

"Aw whatchu grumblin' over now, Genie?"

Arbie peeked at us from the *Daily News*.

"Stay out of it," she ordered.

"What did you drop there—your ticket to Shangri-La?"

He bent to pick up the letter, but Eugenia grabbed it from him, looking sternly into his face. I felt grateful that she was upset with someone other than me.

"My friend Alessandra wants to help her open her own place," I explained meekly. Eugenia whipped around with eyes like fiery blue medallions.

"Fabulous," said Arbie. Then he asked Eugenia, "So what's your problem?"

"I don't know this person," she snapped, placing Alessi's letter on the bar.

"Better yet," he said.

"But one thing I do know is a sucker's goldmine—like these vouchers you get in the mail...*Eugenia Drury, you are eligible to win the million-dollar sweepstake prize if you have the matching number*. Polish Lottery, Arbie—they make sure you never have the matching number."

She pushed the letter toward me and coldly said, "Sorry."

"Wait a minute. Why don't you look into it?" Arbie persisted. "It may be right for you—it may be wrong. But you won't know unless you look into it."

Standing up as if to leave, she muttered, "I'd give my life story for a cigarette now."

"And if you stick around here it's only a matter of time before you do shove a butt back between your lips and start ruining your skin and lungs."

"What do you know, Arbie?"

"Not much, but I've got two decades on you."

Then one of the girls down the bar in a blue Yankees cap held up an empty beer bottle and called, "Gene!"

Clearly glad to get away from us, Eugenia ducked behind the bar again. "Two decades," Arbie continued to rail at her as she procured an Amstel Light, "where it goes one of three ways: you keep serving beer and splits to Gail's customers, you train a staff to serve your customers while you toodle off to Maui, or you sit at a bar collecting SSI and pissing the hell out of every Archie Bunker knock-off you meet."

"Until you win big at Belmont one day…" she retorted, grabbing a fresh napkin for her customer.

"And only begin to pay your debts," he finished the sentence.

Eugenia hurried down the bar to deliver beer to her Yankees fan, to ask if the others needed a refill. When she came back our way reluctantly for a glass on tap, Arbie suggested: "Oh, for heaven's sake, just kiss and make up. Two beautiful women, and here's this old geezer rattlin' your cage."

"Jesus, Arbie!"

She glared at him as beer frothed over the glass rim and onto her hand before she closed the tap.

"Maybe I should get going," I said frantically.

"Yeah, maybe."

She said it through her teeth, but I heard. Not removing Alessi's note from where it lay on the bar, I stood up and made my way, for the last time, across The Bunny Hop.

I pushed the glass door open, stepped into the evening with its mild, muggy air like so many sighs. Almost nauseous, I began imagining how to tell Alessi that I'd made a mockery of her kind offer. I wasn't even sure how I'd managed to blow everything we'd planned in ten short minutes.

That tomato-red heart pierced by three daggers in Lina's deck of cards flashed before me as I headed up the sidewalk. What had she said? "If you can find the power to grab it, by every grace of God, then you might have love that lifts your soul…But if you don't never find the power to grab it, then stay clear of Gene."

"Molly," a man's voice called. I turned and saw Arbie at The Bunny Hop door, gesturing for me. I shook my head. He pointed to the doorstep. I turned away from him, continuing to the corner. When I glanced back, I saw Arbie running as fast as he could with a limp, so I waited for him.

"The essence of gambling," he cautioned, "is walking away only when you win big, or lose big. At any other point, stay in the game if it kills you."

"I was asked to leave," I reminded him. "You heard."

"She didn't mean it."

"Oh, she did."

"I can tell you the paint's still wet here. That's why it got messy."

"Because I'm a klutz," I said.

"Well, when you tip your hand like that she's not the type to say, 'Oh no. Please stay.' Even if it's what she felt."

The suggestion that I "should get going" had indeed come from me.

"I love her like a dad," he claimed, wiping his hairless head and catching his breath. "She's had her share of hard knocks and hell, I want to see her happy. While she's got the beans and jollies to enjoy it. Now I confess, when I first met Gene I was not exactly overcome with altruistic paternal affection. It took me a while to accept that for every reason, I'm not her cup of tea. But you, my dear, are."

"A cup of tea that just spilled in her lap."

"I've got a daughter," Arbie continued. "One daughter. Just a hair younger than you two. We haven't spoken in seventeen years because her mother turned her against me—I don't even know what she looks like now. Don't have a photograph—nothing."

"Sorry," I said, and started to cry.

"Gene, Gene," he said under his breath. "She always says, 'Never make a woman weep because God counts the tears.'"

"Sorry," I repeated, not even sure what I was apologizing about.

"Gene hasn't seen her old man in a while, though she was Daddy's angel once upon a time. So when business at the bar is dead and we've done our daily numbers, we shoot the breeze like a dad and his girl. I know what happened, Molly. She expected you to call her. She gave it 'til her birthday."

"So I'm a week late."

I wiped my eyes, willing myself not to cry more.

"Almost two weeks. I know why you didn't hurry back—I was there that night and tried to explain it to her."

"What night?" Of course I knew perfectly well.

"To the chagrin of Lola and the trannies, I was sitting at the bar when Bertie played 'The Bunny Hop' and you tore out of there like a bat on a bender. Even through my thick skin, I could feel your heart breaking."

"Mature of me, wasn't it?"

He hummed a few bars of "*Brazil…we stood beneath an amber moon,*" and I looked away, wiping my eyes again.

"You're not accustomed to women."

"I *am* a woman."

"In The Bunny Hop sense."

I pretty much melted into the pavement.

"That much she figured out, but not the pregnancy."

"Figured out?" I asked him.

"Enrico said this about you, Claudia said that. 'It was right under my nose,' she told me. 'But I liked her too much to see it.'"

"You're saying *liked*, in the past tense…"

"She didn't know if she frightened you off."

Between my nausea, tears, and embarrassment, I was most frightening to myself. For all her intuition, Eugenia had missed that.

"Molly." Arbie spoke tenderly. "She had her head in her hands. I asked her if I should go get you. She didn't budge. One of the Yankees fans shot me a 'fuck off' kind of look and asked Gene if she was okay. She shook her head no. That's when I said, 'I'll go out and find her.'"

"Is this supposed to be cold comfort?"

"Have I said anything phony to you in the last hour?"

Whether or not it was a coincidence, his eyes were that indescribable gray-brown of tree bark. I wondered what had brought him to betting on horses or playing lotto in a girl's bar. It would not be until years later—at Eugenia's Cajun, over the best crawfish soup in the Northeast—that we would learn our friend's story.

"Gene is flinty but never a bully," he continued to reassure me. "Her anger is short as a sun shower. She doesn't bear grudges. What she does have though—in great measure, if I must say—is pride. Pride will be the rope that girl hangs from."

He glanced apprehensively at the bar.

"I should get home," I said, feeling tired and pregnant.

"We know ants are drawn to sugar," he mused. "But is sugar drawn to sugar?"

The glass door opened, and Eugenia stepped out. First she looked the other way down the street, and then back to Arbie and me.

"Genie—get over here!" he called in a fatherly way.

"Can't. Y'all come back inside," she called back.

"Us all?" Arbie pointed from me to him. She nodded.

"How 'bout you meet us halfway?" he suggested.

Gene looked back into the bar and closed the door. She began sauntering over to us with her long summer-browned legs, the striped jersey tied around her waist.

Arbie laid an encouraging hand on my shoulder, and we started walking toward her.

Acknowledgements

As this story took form, pointers from talented peers breathed life into it. Thanks to Sonia Pilcer and her bimonthly writing group in New York City and to Elizabeth Ayres's group years earlier. I was also able to productively workshop parts of this novel with Richard Bausch at the Aspen Writers' Foundation.

I thank everyone at Heliotrope Books for your willingness to promote fiction that does not conform to the flavor of the day; thanks to Goodfoot Editorial, Moon PR, and to Judy Tipton-Katzman who lent a brilliant hand to the cover image.

Last but not least, I acknowledge the many muses, inspirations, passing conversations, crushes, and passions that found their way into these pages, and the dear, ongoing support of my family.

About the Author

A freelancer in marketing and communications, Dara Lebrun was a medical ghostwriter and technical writer for fifteen years. *The Bunny Hop* is her debut novel, the first in a series called *Children Who Aren't Ours*. Other novels in this series will be released in 2015 and 2016. A native and longtime New Yorker, Dara now makes her home in Kauai, Hawaii.

www.ingramcontent.com/pod-product-compliance
Lightning Source LLC
Chambersburg PA
CBHW031100260626
47172CB00001B/142